Nov

FLYING

Please

Jerry Maguire

Remembering Jim
- his story is on
page 201.

THE 1993 IAN ST JAMES AWARDS

Judges

CLARE COLVIN
Writer, journalist and book reviewer ·

DANIEL EASTERMAN
Novelist

CORINNE GOTCH
Marketing Executive, Booksellers Association

ELIZABETH HARRIS
Novelist

MARK ILLIS
Novelist

IAN ST JAMES
Novelist

NICK SAYERS
Publisher

CAROLINE SHELDON
Literary Agent

FLYING HIGH

The winners of
the 1993 Ian St James Awards

HarperCollins*Publishers*

HarperCollins*Publishers*
77–85 Fulham Palace Road,
Hammersmith, London W6 8JB

A Paperback Original 1993
1 3 5 7 9 8 6 4 2

A catalogue record for this book
is available from the British Library

ISBN 0 00 647654 6

All royalties from the sale of this book will be paid to The New Writers'
Club and used for the furtherance and expansion of the Ian St James
Awards

Set in Linotron Sabon

Printed in Great Britain by
HarperCollinsManufacturing Glasgow

Foreword

The sixteen stories that you are about to read emerged from over three and a half thousand entries for this year's Ian St James Awards.

There have been several new developments in the last twelve months: the introduction of a shorter category of fiction under five thousand words alongside the established category of up to ten thousand words; for the first time this year, we opened our doors to writers in the English language from outside these shores and this volume contains stories by writers from New Zealand and the United States; the launch of *Acclaim*, a bi-monthly magazine featuring stories by shortlisted writers in these Awards. *Acclaim* will publish sixty-four stories in six issues and include writers from Namibia and South Africa. All the activities associated with these Awards are co-ordinated at The New Writers' Club. In the summer, the Club organized its first Short Story Workshop as part of the 9th Birmingham Readers and Writers Festival. There will be more to come.

Every writer who enters the Ian St James Awards – and they have to be over eighteen without a published work of full-length fiction to their name – receives an appraisal of their work. The success of this operation can be measured by the receipt at The New Writers' Club of only eight letters consigning (a few of) our readers to the darkest depths. Not a bad ratio from such a large entry. The critiques are by no means definitive. In the time and space available, they can't be, but they are intended to highlight a story's strengths and weaknesses and are, hopefully, of great value to writers who find feedback so hard to come by. In addition, the Club also now appraises stories by member-writers outside the entry dates for the annual Awards and these more detailed reports are proving to be very popular.

To all the readers who have helped us arrive at this book, many thanks. Similarly, our thanks go to this year's panel of judges who gave freely of their time to decide on the stories that would be published in these pages. I am sure that the stories that have been selected – and there is as always a real cross-section of styles and subject matter – will entertain.

To all the writers who sent us stories this year and missed out, thank you for entering, good luck with your writing and there's always next year. This is the fifth Ian St James Awards book to be published in as many years by HarperCollins. Our thanks go to the many people at the publishers who helped with the production of this book and to all our supporters in the book trade. Finally, many congratulations to this year's sixteen Award-winning writers who are now, without doubt, 'Flying High'.

Merric Davidson
Director, The New Writers' Club

(You can write for further information on The Ian St James Awards and *Acclaim* to The New Writers' Club at PO Box 101, Tunbridge Wells, Kent TN4 8YD, or telephone 0892 511322. The closing date for the 1994 Ian St James Awards is 31 January 1994.

Contents

FIGURE OF EIGHT

Min Dinning

Min Dinning spent more than twenty years teaching English worldwide, travelling in Europe, South America, China, Papua New Guinea and Australia. She began writing fiction at the age of seven but lapsed for more than thirty years, only to begin again two years ago, inspired by a creative writing class. Until then she had written letters, diaries and academic papers and published some non-fiction. These days she teaches Business EFL and is trying to come to terms with domestic bliss in rural Cambridgeshire. She still has secret yearnings to run away to exotic lands.

FIGURE OF EIGHT

He tasted of sour pickle and rice porridge and stale tobacco. I had wanted this kiss for months and now I had it. Desire was injected uncomfortably into my bloodstream. His skin was hard and chapped as he pressed it into my face. I was shocked. It was not as I had expected. I was still unsure of why I wanted him. It may have been sex, but it wasn't straightforward; he wasn't attractive in a conventional way, like Martin. It may have been need and gratitude.

He kissed as if he didn't know what a kiss was. Or maybe he wasn't kissing at all. It was me who was doing it. His mouth was stiff and immobile but betrayed a repressed emotion that I couldn't define. It briefly occurred to me that it might be anger. I had caught him unawares, walked up to him from behind. But was it unawares? We both knew.

He was wearing his best jacket, tailored too large in stiff blue cotton in what used to be an imitation of Mao, and smelling of mothballs as most Chinese clothes do when they are seldom worn. Why did I focus on that? It detracted from the moment. Smells and tastes tried to deflect me away from the strange reality of it.

For a moment we remained in an awkward clinch, he with his eyes closed, me searching for reaction, wanting response. He took no initiative and then withdrew as I placed my tongue on his teeth.

'No, no,' he moaned.

'But we must, we've been waiting so long. We can't waste more time just thinking about it and doing nothing.'

'Somebody will find out. We'll be criticized.'

'We'll be discreet. Nobody will know. Anyway we haven't done anything wrong.'

'You don't understand. We're not in your country. In China this is impossible. I could go to gaol.'

'Don't be daft. Of course you couldn't,' I said, not sure. People certainly seemed to get into trouble for things that go unnoticed or are laughed off in the West.

Anyway – what were we doing? Was this adultery? Infidelity? It certainly wasn't fornication, nor was it likely to be.

Before the momentum was lost I drew his wiry body towards me again. I sensed tension, reluctance.

'If someone sees, it will be wrong.'

'But if no one sees it will be right?'

He relaxed a little and laughed.

'Chinese logic!' I said. The idea that a sin must be witnessed to be a sin struck me as peculiar but practical.

'Honestly, Alison. You know what I'm saying.'

Sometimes he sounded like a middle-class Englishman. These phrases, learned from World Service plays, tripped off the tongue like the rehearsed script of a thirties drama. He seemed more foreign at moments like that and a twinge of uncertainty unnerved me. Was I dealing with an inhabitant of another world? Were we as close as I thought or had I invented it out of want?

He gently removed my arms and buttoned the top button of his jacket. He did up the hook and eye on the collar and took a step backwards.

'I must go now.' He looked out of the blurred curtainless window at the bleakness of the early spring campus beyond. Grey concrete blocks, brightened by the occasional piece of vivid underwear hung on a bamboo pole out of a window to dry in the dusty air.

'Don't come down,' he said.

'Shall I come to the studio tomorrow?' I asked, suddenly unable to cope with the prospect of being alone in this chilly, dingy flat, not wanting him to leave.

To my relief, he smiled. 'Yes, come for your lesson as usual. The other guys will be there. We'll paint together.'

I heard his footsteps retreating down the concrete stairs fainter and fainter, then the click of his bicycle lock. I watched him as he pedalled silently down the path. I kept watching until he disappeared into the heavy stream of traffic on the main road beyond the gates of the campus.

Yes, I thought, I've done it. I've changed things between us at last.

I was trying to remember how it had been at the beginning. I cast my mind back to the day when I announced I was going to China.

'You'll never survive,' Martin taunted me. 'You'll be back in two weeks.'

I tried not to believe that he might be right. It had certainly been a rash decision for me, but he had this way of making me feel inadequate and I had to show him I could cope.

'Of course I'll survive. Anyway it's only nine months. I'll be back in the summer. You won't even have time to miss me.'

The thought of leaving Martin for so many months made me uneasy, but I told myself I had nothing to fear. He would be there when I got back and whatever happened in between would soon be over. He still hadn't been keen. He had wanted us to get married but I wanted to get my urgent need to travel out of my system. I thought I'd stay about a year, then go home and settle down for ever. I didn't think Martin had the right to tell me not to go, so I made up my mind to do it, to stick it out whatever it was like, just to prove to him that I had a mind of my own. I felt I needed another dimension to myself. Martin was not enough. He was reliable, kind and rather good looking but I wanted to deny to myself that I cared for him as I didn't relish the prospect of missing him. It would spoil my adventure. Besides, I was not interesting enough as I was. A tall, pale Englishwoman, over thirty, a virgin. A real spinster schoolmarm, in fact. I'd never worked abroad before and mistrusted foreigners on the whole. But something about China drew me. I needed to go there and see it. I wanted to be able to tell people I'd been to the Great Wall, the Ming Tombs and the Forbidden City. It would change me. The very thought was exciting, and my heart raced as I had fantasies of people in silk robes, gliding across the semicircular bridges and reading poetry in bamboo groves.

I'd got the job at the university through a friend who knew someone at the embassy. It didn't seem to bother anyone that I had no experience of teaching university students. They seemed pleased to get a real English teacher and in the first few weeks I was treated like a VIP. When the novelty wore off and winter began to set in I felt less excited and less keyed up to learn new things. What had at first been amusing curiosities and fascinating ways eventually became tedious routine. I got fed up with the way the cleaners bobbed around with their stinking mops, the way the cook, sweating even in the ice of November, hawked and spat on the kitchen floor, and the chore of shopping at the market where my fair hair and my height set me apart as a freak or a visiting Martian. If Martin had been there it would have been all right. I wouldn't have felt so self conscious.

6

He was even bigger than me. It annoyed me that I wasn't managing well on my own. 'You'll never survive' – his words echoed in my head as I contemplated my inability to stride out and enjoy myself.

I bought local clothes – an army jacket and some quilted shoes – in an attempt to melt in a little. The shoes were men's: no woman in China wore a size seven. But it made me more of a freak as the girls were by then starting to wear what they thought were Western clothes – hideous shapeless Crimplene jackets with twinkly thread and plastic high-heeled shoes. The daring ones wore lipstick. I knew I'd got it wrong, but I also knew I could never get it right. Not here.

My ideas about the country had been gleaned from *National Geographic* and the paperback book of the travels of Marco Polo. Reality was a rudely different shock. Nothing had prepared me for the drabness and alienation which seemed to make people physically ill in the winter, the strange food and the smells. Everywhere there hung in the air an almost palpable veil of smells. They were always stale and sickening. From the overpowering stench of lavatories which supplied fertilizer for the vegetables we ate to the acrid smoke of the miserable little market food stalls and the sweetish sickly aroma of hand-rolled cigars smoked by old ladies.

I became aware that I would have to learn the language or I would continue to feel autistic, sealed off into a bubble, in this world but not of it, as if I was watching it on television. There were no other foreigners in my unit, so I was obliged to seek out the company of Chinese English speakers, and this was how I met Liang.

'I wonder if you could arrange painting lessons for me?' I asked, standing at Dr Chen's desk in the Wai Ban, the office that was in charge of me as a foreigner.

I had always wanted to do Chinese watercolours,

though I was not artistic. It looked simple, so I thought I'd be able to produce something that I could hang, framed, over the mantelpiece at home.

'Please sit down. Can I offer you some tea?' came his high-pitched voice from behind a newspaper.

'I'd like to learn painting.' I remained standing. Once I sat down it would take all day.

There was a silence while Dr Chen finished reading the article he was absorbed in. On the shelf behind him there was a photograph of his son looking like an all-American boy at the University of Southern Illinois, and next to it a bottle of Mao Tai and two glasses.

'Of course, Miss Alison. We'll send you a teacher whenever you like.' This was the predictable response. The answer was always yes, but I was doubtful whether it would actually happen.

'I'd like to learn on Wednesdays.'

'I see. You have nothing to do on Wednesdays.' He laughed, coughed on his cigarette and peered over his newspaper.

They always seemed to think we were without inner resources. There was talk of getting a television to entertain me, as they thought I'd wither away without one. But of course there was no sign of it yet.

I wanted to snatch the newspaper away and yell 'Get on with it, then!' but I would have been wasting my time.

'Well, thank you, Dr Chen. Could you let me know how much the lessons will cost?'

'No charge,' he said. 'The painting unit will send someone.'

I forgot my request for a week or two, not expecting anything to happen quickly.

One afternoon I was idly staring across the microcosm of the campus, watching people going about their business. Students strode around in army coats, their numb fingers clutching texts to be learned by heart, mumbling to themselves, grannies wheeled babies dressed in jewel colours in bamboo prams, old men tended plants in pots or spoke to their geese, and cadres cycled by, puffing on their rancid little cigarettes as their bikes clanked along. I was the only one doing nothing. I was getting together the courage to go out and shop but it was always an ordeal to venture forth, head and shoulders above the nimble locals, stared at and laughed at and, I suspected, cheated by the peasants with their crooked teeth and filthy hands. I must have seemed like a millionaire, and without a word of Chinese still I couldn't do anything about rudeness or cheating except shout in English.

There was a tap at the door of the flat. I thought it would be the Wai Ban checking up on me again, coming on some pretext or other to see what I was getting up to. But when I opened the door I saw a small wiry man with a broad grin. His hair was longer than usual for a Chinese man, and he was wearing the height of fashion, a polo-neck sweater.

'How do you do, Miss Hutchings. I'm Liang, your painting teacher.'

He was at least six inches shorter than me and peered up like a confident child hoping to please a teacher. I almost expected him to hand me an apple.

'Hello, Mr Liang. Come in. Would you like some tea?'

'No thanks, no thanks,' he protested, waving a hand.

He sat on the hard plastic sofa. His shoes were covered in mud and I noticed with dismay that he'd left a trail across my mats that I would have to sponge off.

'The Wai Ban told me to come and teach you painting,' he announced.

'Well, Mr Liang, I just mentioned it. I thought it

would be nice to have something to do on Political Study afternoon.' I was free on Wednesday afternoons as foreigners weren't invited to Political Study, though it seemed they were often the subject of discussion. Sometimes we were in favour, sometimes we weren't. You could tell by the way they kept at a polite distance, courteous but not friendly. They usually tried to provide things we asked for and didn't want complaints or any kind of controversy.

Liang's real job, he explained, was to churn out numerous identical 'works of art' for 'dignitaries' and foreigners. He made me laugh. On Wednesdays he was to show me the fundamentals of Chinese watercolour painting.

'We'll go to the artists' store to get your paper and brushes and paints next week.' He paused and lit up a Phoenix, settling into the uncomfortable sofa. He slurped his flower tea and I wondered whether to offer him a piece of Cadbury's chocolate, but decided I didn't know him well enough yet.

So that was how it began. He used to pedal across town to my flat, where I would set up a table with newspaper, jars of water and my selection of paints, ink stick and stone and a row of brushes he had chosen for me, from the one like a feather duster to the wispy tiger-hair one. Sometimes he would talk about his studio and I hoped to be invited there one day. I imagined it. It would be romantic, arty. There would be paintings in various stages of completion and sunlight flooding in at a large window. He would be there working quietly with a few chosen friends. The little clique would have higher things on their minds than the price of oil and how to get something for nothing. It would be a haven from the turmoil of daily life.

'Liang, what's your studio like?' I asked.

10

'Just a big room. We all sit and get on with our work.'

'Do you talk to each other? Do you discuss art?'

'No. Not really. We chat about this and that, but it isn't really necessary for us to talk about what we're doing.'

The lessons were a bit of a disappointment as they consisted of copying various masters from a book of samplers. I spent hours trying to flick the brush into a bamboo leaf, whirl it into a rock, dab colour into peonies and lightly tease out hairs on the head of a dancer. He was a patient teacher – either that or he didn't care that I wasn't talented. He was just doing his job.

At last he said, 'Next week you must come to the studio to watch.'

I was so looking forward to being introduced to the charmed circle of artists. I hoped perhaps these people would become my friends. Here was an opportunity to get to know people. The language barrier wouldn't matter once we started painting pictures together. I felt quite privileged.

I cycled over an hour in the rain to get to the studio on the other side of the city. It was a large grey building with dirty cracked windows, and inside the main room, in light I would have thought inadequate for painting, there were rows of artists producing delicate watercolours for tourists and diplomats. Liang welcomed me with a large smile and looked straight into my eyes, which he had never done before. He was larger than life on his own territory. Complicity with foreigners was not on, so what was he trying to say? Then I realized he was beginning to treat me as a friend. I was glad I'd made the effort to come. With the weather being so foul and the prospect of cold wet clinging clothes all afternoon I'd nearly stayed in the flat, but indoors and

11

outdoors were equally cold and dank, so what did it matter? Anyway I was curious to see him on his own ground, I wanted to know what made him tick and I wanted to meet his friends.

'Mr Wu paints tigers. One of his pictures was presented to an African diplomat last month. We are all very proud of him.'

I smiled, slightly embarrassed. The idea of an art factory seemed so Chinese. Several artists beamed up at me as if I was visiting royalty. I still hadn't made enough progress with my Chinese to say more than hello.

One man was painting carp from life. I was disturbed to see the fish darting around an enamel bowl, confused, their scales reflecting light from the neon strip lights above, their silly eyes staring as if in fright and their mouths mouthing a silent message. They swam aimlessly round and round, sometimes in a figure of eight. The artist had captured their movement and their fearful staring. They would be trapped in the enamel bowl until the picture was finished, then, their aesthetic purpose over, disposed of in a practical manner.

'What will you do with them?' I asked.

'Eat them,' said Liang, a mock serious look on his face.

'But they're pets, aren't they?'

'We don't have pets here. Only rich people have pets. We like our animals best in the cooking pot.'

I was beginning to understand that my fatuous comment about a carp being a pet was very Western. The idea that eating carp was cruel suddenly struck me as silly in this context — it made more sense to eat them than to have these slithery cold creatures as pets. I had no choice but to start perceiving life around me in a more practical way. I started to see how much I was

12

spoiled, prejudiced and set in my ways. I had recently started to dismiss the voice of Martin that often echoed around in my head pointing out various wickednesses and cruelties. He had started to irritate me. Who was he to impose his pampered views on people?

The visit to the studio was the first time I'd been interested in the real China as opposed to the fairytale version that lingered as a fantasy. I had enjoyed it in an unexpected way. It wasn't how I'd imagined it at all, but better. It was as if the experience had taught me something, refreshed me. It was Liang who had gradually wrought the beginnings of change in me. I was at last starting to absorb those new experiences I so badly wanted and the catalyst was Liang. It was Liang who made it possible for me to open up. He too was beginning to change. No longer the distant and polite teacher. He began to be aware of me as a person. I was no longer just an awkward and large foreigner, but a source of information about outside, a companion and possibly even a woman. I reluctantly admitted to myself that I was beginning to feel a little excited in his presence. I found myself looking at the back of his neck, noticing his neat ears and his remarkable long eyelashes. I couldn't stop myself looking at him, partly out of fascination and curiosity at his differentness and partly in the way one looks affectionately on an intelligent pet. He seemed so young. He was about the same age as me, but his cheeks looked boyishly smooth. I wondered if he shaved. His hair had the gloss of a child's hair, which was a wonder considering the nasty sticky shampoo they used.

'You know, Miss Alison,' he said one day, 'I'm really interested in seeing your country. I often listen to the BBC and VOA. I feel I know the West already. It's different from here, isn't it? You've got so much

13

freedom. You can choose your job, your politicians, your friends . . .'

'But Liang, you can choose your friends too, can't you?' It occurred to me that my self-appointed role of 'friend' to him was perhaps not exactly his choice.

'Not really. We don't have many friends here, not in the sense you mean it. People suspect one another, and besides you've probably noticed that we often say "classmates" when we're referring to people we know. That's because they're people we studied with. What chance do we have to meet anyone else? You can see what it's like in my unit. Apart from them you're the only person I see. You're the only outsider in my life.' The idea that I was now 'in his life' sent a small shudder through me.

'What about your family?'

'Relatives,' he said with a grimace.

'What's wrong with relatives?' I asked, knowing what he was going to say.

'Obligation,' he said. 'My wife was given to me by my uncle. She's the daughter of some remote member of his wife's family. When I got to twenty-seven and I wasn't married, they said, "Liang, it's time you had a child." They're peasants, you see. Within six months I was married to Wang and a year later my son was born.'

'Couldn't you have chosen your own wife? Why did you let them do this to you?' I was beginning to feel resentment towards these primitive people who were his family. Didn't they realize that he had the right to make his own choices in life? How could they foist some stranger on him like that? It was absurd.

'It must have been awful for you.' I realized this sounded feeble, like a schoolgirl commiserating over an embarrassing parent.

'Not awful. I just did my duty to my family. They

14

were right. I needed to get married and I hadn't met anyone suitable. A man of twenty-seven can't stay single.'

I'd been in China long enough to know he was right. He would have been regarded as a freak or people would have suspected his reasons for avoiding women.

I wanted to ask him if he loved her. I needed to know. But I was certain he didn't. He was obviously trapped for eternity in an enforced relationship which was meaningless and gave him no joy. But he always seemed joyful enough as if it was never on his mind. He never mentioned the child.

We were seeing each other more and more. He was obviously growing fonder of me, wanting my company. And I wanted him too. I thought about him a lot. I often found myself daydreaming about him as I stood before my forty undergraduates, crammed into filthy Classroom Number Three where I attempted to teach the rudiments of English Literature. The uncomprehending faces stared back, obedient but totally unabsorbed. I must have looked as uninterested as they did. My mind was elsewhere too.

One day a group of runners training for a sports meeting ran past the open window. My adrenalin suddenly whirled as I saw Liang among them. But no, it was just someone who looked like him. It couldn't have been him. He was wearing blue cotton running shorts and a white singlet with a figure of eight on the back and grey plimsolls without socks. His thin legs were spattered with mud and his shoulders were hunched in the cold. So unlike Martin's rugby player's physique. I watched him as he ran, unaware of me, intent on his task of forging ahead of the others. I thought of Liang's slight body, unclothed – his knees and elbows, his small buttocks – and felt a blush spreading over my neck. I was

15

jolted back to my yawning class who had noticed nothing. They sat impassively picking their noses, scratching their armpits and staring blankly through me as before.

How Liang managed to get away from his unit I never discovered. The painting lessons continued, sometimes at my flat and sometimes at his studio and I eventually managed to produce a passable, rather sentimental picture of kittens and peonies which I had mounted on a scroll. We both began to be aware that painting was no longer the only interest we had in common. I positively looked forward to his visits. We would both invent reasons for him to come.

'I'd better have a look at your bike,' he'd say, knowing full well that the University Bicycle Workshop checked it regularly for me.

Or he'd say, 'Have you taken your winter ginseng? I'll get you some at the medicine store.'

And I would cut out articles about life in the West for him and save him my *Guardian Weekly*. Without a telephone, we had no choice but to meet often.

He helped me with many of the small things I found so taxing in my first months in China.

It was him who showed me how to eat properly. I had been trying to survive on boiled eggs and boiled vegetables which was all I could manage to cook on the pathetic gas ring provided in my kitchen. The oil smelt so vile I couldn't fry anything. When I tried, the wok sent up clouds of smoke and the food tasted as if it had been cooked in engine oil. Liang primed my wok for me and expertly showed me how to heat the oil to the right point. He flicked vegetables and fatty scraps of pork around and made feasts.

I gave up going to the market by myself. I waited for him to come and we would set out on an adventure.

16

What used to be a painful experience became fun. We tried out anything new that came into season and rushed back to the flat to cook it. I ate everything: eels, their tiny heads nailed to a board while their long bodies were split with a sharp knife, rabbits bought live and their fragile necks cracked, their white fur peeled off like peeling an orange, tiny salty dried shrimp, sweet creamy yoghourt in chunky pottery jars, and delicate translucent hundred-year-old eggs with their glinting green and orange hues. Food became a fascination to me and I even discarded the fork and spoon I'd carried everywhere and learned awkwardly to wield chopsticks. I still couldn't bring myself to use the bamboo ones in restaurants which you had to clean up with a bit of exercise book kept in the pocket for the purpose.

We started meeting on Sundays. Usually he'd come in the afternoon. I didn't ask what he did in the morning. I was vaguely aware he might have family commitments but kept the idea at the very back of my mind. When the weather was still cold in March I lay one Sunday morning beneath my quilt, comfortable, with the sounds of the campus outside. I'd been reading one of Martin's letters and thinking of home. He wanted me to meet him at the end of the term and have a holiday. He would come out on a package tour and I could join him in Peking. Somehow I didn't feel elated enough about the prospect of seeing him. I wouldn't say my heart sank exactly, but it almost did. While I was trying to sift through my thoughts on the subject, there was a tap at the door and I knew it was Liang, very early.

'Hang on – I'll put my dressing-gown on.'

I rushed eagerly to open the door and there he was, clutching a small parcel in pink wrapping paper tied with a piece of string.

'This is a little gift for you.'

17

'Can I open it?'

'Go on.' His eyes were wide with anticipation. More than ever he seemed childlike. I recalled the runners and had to look away.

It was a set of silk hand-embroidered handkerchiefs, totally impractical but pretty in a fussy Chinese sort of way. It was the sort of gift a man gives to a woman.

'But it isn't my birthday, Liang.' This was silly. Birthdays didn't mean much here.

'No, I thought you'd like them. My cousin works at the embroidery factory,' he said by way of justification. Suddenly I felt a rush of sentiment, of joy and of something I had never felt in the presence of Martin. I wanted to fling my arms round him and dance.

I can't think how I restrained myself, but I felt as if I was saving it for a later I knew would come. I increasingly enjoyed the thought of it. We went out on our cycle ride, him pedalling protectively on the traffic side of the cycle lane, telling me when to stop, when to turn, giving disapproving glances when other cyclists jostled me. He was still somewhat astonished that I could ride a bike as he was certain all Westerners drove around in large cars.

We sat together in a tea house in those low bamboo chairs. An ancient man in a grubby apron poured water from a steaming black kettle as we clattered the lids of our tea dishes. I looked at Liang and wanted urgently to know more about him. He was deliberately uncommunicative about his personal life, as if his life in my presence was the only life he had.

'Liang, why don't you bring your wife along?' I ventured, uncertain of his response. I couldn't even remember her name.

'She's busy,' he said evasively, looking at the violinist squeakily performing at the far end of the tea house.

18

'But you never talk about her.' Then I dared to ask, 'Don't you get on?'

'What d'you mean?'

'Well, aren't you and your wife good friends?'

'She's my wife,' he said as if this explained everything.

'And your baby? Isn't it wonderful being a father?'

'Yes, I'm proud of him.'

'But Liang, when do you spend time with him? You're always with me!' As I said this I realized it was true. I hadn't been aware until I said it that he was spending time with me that he probably should have been spending with his family.

'I see him once a week.'

It was then that I discovered that Liang and his wife didn't actually live in the same place and that Liang was effectively a bachelor, married in name only. Shocked but overjoyed, I sensed a tremor of anticipation. Hadn't it always been him and me, never a triangle?

'She's with her mother. She can't live with me. There isn't room with the baby. I only have one room. Anyway she prefers it.'

Liang's life must have been bleak until I turned up. I provided him with an excuse to go out and enjoy himself. Wasn't it his duty to see that the foreigner was kept content? It concerned me for a moment that maybe our friendship wasn't what I thought it was after all – then I remembered the little silk hankies. No, he wasn't pretending. The desire to kiss him welled up again, and I wanted to tell him how sweet he was and how much he meant to me and how he had freed me. I couldn't in the tea house, so I left it until he came the following week.

It was a Tuesday evening. He was going to call in and see me before a meeting. Although I was on the other side of town he never seemed to object to the long ride.

19

He would call in for a chat and a cup of tea. The note he had sent said he had some news.

His jacket made him look small as he stood at the door.

'Come in. A man came round the campus with some tinned lychees today. I got you some.'

He enthused about my discovery, but urgently wanted to tell me his own news.

'I may get a chance to go abroad,' he said, phrasing it carefully, not allowing himself too much certainty. Going abroad was like going to Heaven. Everyone wanted it and feared it and thought they'd never be good enough.

'You could come to England,' I said without thinking. Then it immediately struck me that this was not a good idea. It was a potentially dangerous displacement for us both.

'Maybe,' he said. 'Because I'm married it makes it easier. The authorities know I've got a son to come back for.'

Little did the authorities know the irony of this. From what I could tell, Liang's son did not have a father who would pine for him while suffering in a foreign land.

Liang was looking out of the window as he spoke, with his back to me. And it was then that I chose to kiss him.

The kiss did change our lives. The relationship did take on a sexual dimension but was dominated more by intimacy than sex. We both seemed to have difficulty in expressing ourselves sexually – we didn't easily fall into each other's arms, we were embarrassed about kissing and bed was never mentioned. Whether he thought of it I don't really know. It seemed out of reach, impossible and I'm not sure I wanted it. We substituted a physical manifestation of our closeness with looks into the eyes, standing close, touching fingers when we thought nobody would see. Of course, he always pretended it wasn't happening. It was not tantalizingly erotic as neither of us understood eroticism and wouldn't have known how to bring it about. I was certain this was more like love than the insipidness I had with Martin, who was, I suppose, a kind of fiancé. I was happy. I allowed myself the luxury of what I thought was illicit love. The fact that it might not have seemed like passion in other people's eyes didn't mean it was unexciting for me. Quite the reverse. I hummed with it. I had a permanent grin on my face, but in a country where grinning reflected embarrassment, a feeling appropriate to a tall foreigner, my secret was safe.

As the spring opened up into flowers and warmth in April, Liang and I began to be seen around together more. I used to get little gifts for him at the Friendship Store. He wasn't allowed in so he would wait with the bikes outside and I'd go in and spend my foreigner's money.

'What can I get you, Liang? Just say what you want. It's easy. I've got hard currency. Look!' and I'd wave my notes at him.

I couldn't fail to notice how his eyes lit up at the thought of goodies normally out of reach to all but party officials.

'No, really. I don't want anything, Alison.'

I'd go in and get him a bottle of Johnnie Walker Red Label and some Marlboros. He'd have to keep them at my flat. It wouldn't have done for him to be seen with these gifts. He'd have been criticized; that is, hauled up in front of some bossy committee to explain himself. I'd started smoking Phoenixes. I kept the Marlboros for him. I even bought him a silk tie of the kind favoured by visiting Americans, but of course he couldn't wear it. I wondered if I was overdoing it, making a bit of a fool of myself. I just wanted to please him and give him things he could have only from me.

As the chilly weather suddenly stopped I shed my army jacket and began to wear a skirt. People noticed and I thought they were making snide comments. I hoped I was beginning to look a bit less foreign. My hair had grown and I'd put it in bunches like the local girls. Actually, I didn't dare risk the pudding-basin barber. We must have made a comic pair, I suppose, me six inches taller than him. But it didn't matter.

At least so I thought until one day when he came along looking very agitated.

'The Wai Ban says I mustn't spend so much time with you.'

'What do you mean? Do they suspect? What did they say?'

I felt panic-stricken. This could mean trouble for both of us. It could mean him losing his job or worse. It could mean me losing him.

'They're worried about me being influenced by you. And they've told Wang about you.'

For a second I couldn't remember who Wang was. Then I remembered she was his wife.

'What did she say?'

'Not much.'

'What d'you mean "not much"?'

'Well, she has her own life. She's never met a foreigner. She doesn't know what to think.'

'Isn't she upset?'

'Why?'

'Well, you're seeing another woman.'

'She's Chinese.'

'But she's still your wife.'

'Yes. But she doesn't see it like you do.'

22

'You're close enough to have had a child together, and you're telling me she isn't jealous?'

'Anyone can have a child. It's easy.'

He was talking about the thing most Westerners thought they wanted out of their relationships and dismissing it as if it was the easy bit. Getting someone into bed made people forgo understanding and kindness, as if sex would replace friendship or be an improvement on it. But from what I could see Liang and Wang didn't seem to have much apart from the evidence of a fleeting sexual encounter. They appeared to have an easy-going or even apathetic tolerance of each other, and maybe some woolly notion of duty.

'Well, what does it mean? Are they saying we've got to stop seeing each other?' I couldn't bear to think about it.

'They want an explanation. They're trying to be reasonable. And Wang has offered to divorce me.' He added this last bombshell as a sort of afterthought.

I added up in seconds what it would mean if he was divorced. Would he then expect me to marry him? The thought ricocheted around in my brain. What about Martin? What about Mummy and Daddy? What about my friends? The thought of being married to a five-foot, two-inch Chinaman appalled me suddenly. He must have seen my expression of anguish and read it completely wrongly. All was confusion. Did I love him or had it suddenly stopped like a watch stops when it is overwound and the spring snaps?

'Don't you see?' he said. 'It would be wonderful.'

Wonderful for whom? I saw all the advantages for him and none for me. He would unload an unwanted wife and child and acquire the much coveted passport out of China – a foreign spouse. I would be married to a foreigner who would never fit in at home and who

23

would make me a laughing stock. The thought was impossible. Could I see him at the Point to Point or the Hunt Ball, or meeting the vicar or Uncle Basil? They would all be horrified. I began to see the value of Martin. He was of my world, my sort. I had stepped into an alien place and been befriended by an alien. Liang *was* China and was inseparable from it. I could not blend the two worlds – the only piece of this world that I could take home was my picture of peonies and kittens.

Since I was lost for words and Liang was evidently hoping for a positive response, he said, 'You could come with me to America. We could travel together and get out of this dump. We could be free together.' What did he mean 'free'? I was already free.

I looked into his eyes, then looked away to his frayed grubby collar and the tide-mark on his neck.

'But you can't just leave your family like that – they haven't done anything wrong.'

'I can. Lots of people do. I've been applying for scholarships for months and now at last one has come through. I'm going to Ohio in July.'

'You never said anything to me,' I said, hurt and beginning to be angry that I had not been part of this plan.

'I wasn't sure until yesterday.' He started to fidget irritatingly with a loose button on his jacket. He couldn't bring himself to look me in the eye.

So my part in the grand plan had been to help him prepare himself for the peculiarities of the West in order to make the escape less painful.

'Do you really want to marry me, then?'

'Of course. It would make things much easier. As the husband of an Englishwoman, I would be able to . . .'

I stopped listening. I was right. He was after a passport. How had I failed to see it from the very first?

Why had I thought he cared for me? An icy trickle of disappointment pierced me with startling pain. Facing reality was like discovering I hadn't won the jackpot after all. After months of the luxury of fantasy I now had to return to mundane reality. I couldn't let the ice sear an irreparable wound. I shut it out.

There had been a point in both our lives where he needed to turn away from China and I needed to turn away from England. We had met in the centre of a figure of eight, travelling in opposite directions. We generated a small spark, a misunderstood spark as it turned out, as we passed, and now our only route was away from each other.

'Take your wife,' I said. 'I'm leaving here and going back to England.'

He looked up at me. I had intruded on a dream. He remained lost in reflection for a moment, then seemed to emerge gradually like a creature coming out of hibernation.

'Yes.' He said it with an air of relief.

'I'm sorry if you misunderstood my behaviour. We Westerners are not like you Chinese. We're a bit impulsive, you know. It doesn't mean anything.'

'No.'

He made his excuses and left. I didn't have any more painting lessons and we did not communicate any more after that meeting.

Much as I wanted to weep and feel wretched, I couldn't. The moment had passed and I had evaded that peak. I was frustrated and even guilty that I couldn't summon up any real misery. I felt numb and blank. It wasn't the numbness of shock. It was the numbness of a bemused vacuum.

Eventually at the end of the summer term it was time for me to leave. Martin's trip was fixed and I was to meet him in Peking. While I was packing I discovered a pair of Liang's gloves. He had left them behind on the day we first kissed and I'd kept them hidden in my underwear drawer. I took them out and felt a slight pang. I sniffed them and they smelt of sourness and cheap plastic. They were too small for me to wear. They were useless and ugly. I threw them in the bin.

As always I had trouble at the airport, with nobody to help with my bags, being sent in different directions by different officials, and was glad to be leaving this irritating mayhem. I wasn't all that keen on the grand tour of China, but at least we'd be insulated from the chaos inside an air-conditioned bus.

I got on to the plane at last after much pushing and shoving, but of course someone was sitting in my seat. They never seemed to manage these things efficiently, and having got up at the crack of dawn to be chauffeured to the airport in the university limousine, I was pretty tired and irritable already. A woman with a baby had dumped her things across three seats – there were endless gaping bags of blankets, fruit, enamel cups and Heaven knows what else.

'Excuse me,' I said in English, hoping she'd get the message. She stared up at me. She was a tiny delicate woman, maybe from one of the Minorities. She was like a pretty doll with perfect almond eyes, peach cheeks and a long black plait, and wearing a pink silk jacket, old-fashioned among the Crimplene glitter creations worn by other girls. The baby was bundled into several layers of shawls in spite of the heat and was wearing those disgusting crotchless trousers so that his little raw bottom protruded. He laughed as she swung him on to her shoulder and kicked his tiny feet in his little red cotton shoes. I felt large and ungainly, gawky and imperfect. I shifted my bulky body into the aisle to let her pass as she gave up her seat without a murmur. She shuffled with her belongings towards the smoking section of the plane at the back.

I flopped into the saggy loose-covered seat and clipped on my belt. I was leaving. I'd said my goodbyes, had my banquets, drunk my toasts to mutual friendship and was now free to be a tourist with the rest of them. We soared into the sky, and the city, still grey in summer brightness with patches of dusty green where there were parks, receded.

I didn't look back.

Martin would be waiting in Peking and after a lot of hanging about waiting for bags to appear, I spotted him beyond the barrier and waved. I was more glad to see him than I thought I would be. I felt a bit like a soldier coming home after an arduous campaign. I had survived. I was comforted by his familiar brown tweed jacket and looked forward to his tobacco smell.

Emerging from behind him was a man that looked exactly like Liang. He had much shorter hair and was wearing a rather baggy Western-style suit. It *was* Liang – I recognized the tie I had bought him at the Friendship Store. Why was he here? How could he have known I would be on this plane? I was too noticeable to hide myself. I would have to brazen it out.

'Hello,' I said, smiling.

'Hello, darling,' Martin said, leaning forward to peck my cheek. 'It's lovely to see you.'

I looked away from him to see what had happened to Liang. He was standing there next to Martin, the same grin on his face as when we had first met so many months before.

'How are you, Miss Alison? It's a pleasure to see you.'

He was like a stranger.

27

'Mr Liang, my painting teacher. Mr Roberts, a friend from England.'

They greeted each other formally, Martin towering like a bear a foot over Liang and leaning slightly to reach his outstretched hand. I noticed Liang's dirty fingernails. Then Liang's grin changed focus and became a distant stare, his eyes seeking someone in the crowd.

'Excuse me, I'm meeting my wife. We're being briefed for our trip to the States.'

And Liang wandered off into the throng. A few minutes later he emerged carrying suitcases, baskets, nylon holdalls and string bags, followed by the doll in the pink silk jacket. She was exquisite: three inches shorter than Liang, carrying the beaming child.

He did not bring her over to be introduced, but as they walked away he looked smugly over his shoulder at me, as if he was carrying away the spoils of the campaign.

THE SPIRIT OF
THE TIMES

Jude Jones

Jude Jones is a native of Hampshire and studied singing at the Guildhall School of Music. An assortment of careers followed, including opera, music-theatre, archaeology, stage-management, acting, busking, script-writing and an unsuccessful attempt at shop assisting. In the eighties, she was artistic director, actress and writer for a small-scale touring theatre company based in the East Midlands. Now equipped with two small sons, she is back in Hampshire where she started out and is completing her third unpublished novel.

THE SPIRIT OF THE TIMES

My mum never knows when I skive now since I met the old girl up at Hob's Lane. Makes me laugh the things I get to do these days and mostly everyone leaves me be which is dead ace. I'd say bugger them all but I ain't allowed to. The old girl stop me from swearing, see? Though I does when she ain't around.

You have to go past the old mill to get to Hob's Lane. It ain't a proper road though. It's a kind of track with this stream by it and you get the cars go along it every now and then but only if they're coming up to the cottages there. It's a 'No Through Road' and it don't even go where it was supposed to go now they built the big motorway past it. No Through is right. There's this high fence at the end and then you turns and has to go back so the folks what walk their dogs there goes mainly round by the woods now and leave the Hob to me.

The old girl told me her name once but it was funny. I mean it weren't the kind of old-fashioned name your mum might have or your gran even. So I lets it go. I calls her Missis and she calls me Nipper and that's OK. We don't like fuss, me and her.

We does chatting mostly. She knows how to gab, she does. Not that she's particular lonesome for all she lives in the water. She got her mates same as me. I know most of them. There's Foreman, he's a slippery old sod. Pretends he's a fish. And Longman, he's the big oak. Then there's Ringman and I tell you about him in a bit.

The old girl says he's shy. I ain't seen Littleman yet. Littleman's whatsit — invisible.

My mum used to bawl me out when I went up the Hob but she's quieter now because we done the change. When I first seen the Missis I thought it was some bored old wrinkly what topped herself in the stream. I went close to look because I ain't never seen no corpse. Then she sits up, like she was finishing off a sunbathe and I wet me knickers. 'Course she ain't real old. Not underneath. Not like my mum.

'What them chaps doing over there?'

'They're building the new motorway, Missis.'

'A road? They're building a bloody road near my stream?'

'Yeah. Why you lying in the water?'

'A bloody road! If that don't beat all!'

'I thought you was dead.'

'Well, I ain't. A bleeding road! You know how noisy them things are?'

'Yeah. You'll get rheumatics, sitting in there. My gran has rheumatics every time she goes out in the rain.'

'Your gran's a wanker, Nipper, and no mistake. Why'd they build here? Why can't they go and mess up some other place?'

'My mum says it'll make getting over to Langley real quick.'

'Your mum's a wanker. Why'd she want to go to Langley to start off with? Bloody awful town.'

'Everyone's a wanker to you, Missis. I reckons as you're a wanker yourself.'

'You hold your tongue, smart arse. And don't swear. 'S'not becoming in a young girl.'

'You swear. You're swearing like buggery.'

'I'm allowed. You're not. You hear me?'

32

'Why?'

''Cause I says so.'

'I'm fourteen. I'm big enough to swear now. And smoke. My mum don't mind.'

'Your mum ain't brought you up right. What's your dad say?'

''E don't say bloody nothing, do he? I ain't got no dad.'

'Don't bleeding swear, girl. I told you once and I won't tell you again.'

'What'll you do if I does?'

'This.'

'. . . Oh! . . . Christ almighty, Missis, how'd you do that?'

'With practice, Nipper. I had lots of practice.'

'Could you show me how to do it?'

'Might. Depends.'

I got ordinary mates too, like I said. Not as many as when I was a kid but that's sort of how things go, ain't it? I got this bloke, Ian. He's leaving school soon but he ain't training for anything except thieving. No jobs round here, see?

I let him do it to me once when we was out down the Rec. I makes him get a thing, you know, a condom thing, because of the HIVs and he didn't know how to put it on. So I done it for him.

It was quite nice but it hurt a bit.

My best mate is Marie. I took her down Hob's a couple of times but the old girl didn't show up. Marie said I was a nutter and I got cross. Then the silly bitch told her mum about what I said about the old girl. Marie didn't say what her mum said back. I was real narked so I stole her trainers and slashed them with my Stanley. She keep her mouth shut now.

I didn't tell Ian about the Hob. Ian thinks he's tough. He'd think I was soft and I ain't. I told Dixey though. Dix is my mum's mate when they ain't slagging each other off. She lives two doors down with her brats. Dix is all right. She just nods and says, 'What, the old cow's still up Hob's Lane?' and carries on frying chips. She don't know nothing about Foreman and Longman though, so I scored there.

My mum give me some grief. Shit, she was a pain. Always going on about what time I come home at night just because some silly little prat has got herself done in over on the Park estate. She wanted me to be a nurse! A nurse, I ask you! And tight. God, tight as a duck's arse. Mind you, I don't have to bother with that lot nowadays. The old girl saw to it. She's got some sense, I'll give her that.

Mind you, the Missis come over mean when I tell her I seen Foreman down in the square drinking with the alkies. She tells me to hold my tongue and gives me a shiv when I cheeks her. I don't mind though. I'm going to learn how to do it back. Stands to reason, don't it? Like we was saying in Community Studies last term, it's everybody for theirselves, ain't it? Because there ain't nothing else to do. Nobody else cares about you but you. That's what the old boss, that Thatcher woman said and I agrees. The Missis calls it survival of the fittest which is what she said she'd done. Yeah, well, I'm pretty fit. And I don't take no crap.

Anyway here's how I first went up the Ridge.

The old girl says one day she's off on her travels, yeah? Could have knocked me over – I was gobsmacked. I never seen her walk about much, see? Most of the time she sits around in her stream like it was a chair in front of the telly. Every now and again she'll come and squat down besides me on the bank and wave at the cars when

34

they goes past. But I never seen her walk about before.
So I says, 'Where you going then?'

'Why? You want to come along, Nipper?' she says.

I caught the old bus and got off at Yalderton. Stupid
bloody place – not even a shop. Mainly farmhouses and
snotty kids riding horses. I walked up the big hill
like she said and threshed around in the wood at the
top for a bit. Full of sodding stingers it was. And wet
and muddy in spite of it being late June and dry everywhere else.

She was halfway down the other side under this great
yew tree sitting in a kind of pond thing like it was her
own personal swimming pool. I suppose there must've
been a spring coming out up above somewhere. Mind
you, I wasn't going to mess my tights up finding out.
Too many spiky trees around. Too many bloody bushes.
I was cut to pieces, you can believe it. When I comes
down to her I sees the old tree she's underneath is all
hung up with bits of rag and scraps of cloth like it's
some kind of mad washing line. Dead weird it looked.

She was making a kind of singing, droning noise too
when I comes down. It had words to it. They goes:

> 'Dance, Ringman, dance,
> Dance, my good men, every one,
> For Ringman, he can dance alone,
> Ringman, he can dance alone.'

Out of her barrel, I thinks. Always was loopy but
gone and ripped her hairnet now.

'You been doing your washing, Missis?'
  'What? Quiet, kiddo, or I'll smash you good.'
  'You finished singing yet?'
  'Yeah, I finished now.'

35

'What you doing up here?'

'Visiting.'

'Who you visiting? I don't see no one.'

'See that stone there?'

'What, the big one?'

'That's Ringman.'

'That's Ringman? Where is he then?'

'Told you before, girl. He's shy.'

'He won't come out like Longman does, you mean?'

'Might do.'

'Them blokes, Longman and Foreman. They ghosts?'

'Ghosts? Nah, Nipper. They're real. Same as you and me. They ain't dead, you know.'

'What's Ringman doing in that stone?'

'Waiting.'

'What's he waiting for?'

'Tonight.'

'What's happening tonight?'

'Depends.'

'Oh, come off it, Missis. Tell us. I ain't come all this way in that stupid bus just to fuck about.'

'You watch your language, girl. Or . . .'

'Or what, then?'

'Or Ringman might decide he don't like you, after all.'

'What d'you mean?'

'He's good looking, Ringman is. A sight better look-ing'n that wanker Ian you mess with.'

'So what?'

'If you was to play your cards right Ringman might make you his girl.'

'What if I don't want to be his girl?'

'I reckon you will. Oh yes, Nipper, there ain't much doubt about that.'

'What's he like?'

'Oh, he's nice, Ringman is. And he's good. Very, very good.'

My mum made one hell of a stink when I didn't come back that night. There were pigs out all over the place looking for me. God, the fuss they made. Where was I? Who did I talk to. Did I get raped?

Raped! Took most of my cool, but I kept a straight face. I mean, who'd tell the fuzz about the old girl and the bloke? Bloody fascists, the lot of them. And my mum, she raved so much I reckoned it was funny-farm time for her. Tried to ground me, she did. Locks me up in my room. But I got to go to the bathroom now and then, ain't I? And when I goes, it ain't my fault if the window's just above the extension roof. And it sure ain't my fault if I just tests it to see if I can climb down. Which I done nice and quick. Then I borrows old Dixey's bike and cycled the six mile up to Yalderton Ridge for another visit with the bloke.

It was all them social bloody workers what made me do it. If she'd have left them out I might have let her be. But she always had to be in charge, did my mum. I suppose I didn't mind when I was a kid but now I tells her I'm a grown woman she just laughs at me. And I won't have that.

I thought maybe the old girl could do something about it. And I thought right. Mind you, the old girl give me one hell of a time joshing me but I sticks to my guns.

'How'd you like it,' I says, 'if you had some prying old cow asking you questions night and day about everything you does and getting a pack of half-arsed women coming around too? Bloody nosy bl— idiots. Would I like to change school? Am I happy? Happy? 'Course I'm ruddy happy long as they leave me alone.'

37

The old girl had a little brood and she says she'll fix it for me. Which she done.

I got to roar each time I think about it. She got made up as one of them social workers, see? She come visiting my mum. They shuts theirselves in the kitchen and I hears Mum making her a brew and later they comes out and the old girl goes off. Didn't even look at me, she didn't, but she grab my hand niftyish and squeezes it and I knows she's pulled a stunt.

Mum went all pale after that like she'd had the spunk taken out of her and she stop fussing and telling me off and trying to keep me home. It was as easy as peasy. It was wicked. Excellent.

Dixey come round next day. 'What's the matter with Lynda?' she asks me. 'Why's she gone so quiet?'

'Dunno. Got a cold, probably,' I says.

Dix give me a nasty look and I gives her one back. And that worked too. She goes off like a little white mouse and don't even give me no grief for cheeking her while she's going.

It was more or less the same the rest of term. What's more I got bloody good at cycling.

In August Mum says Uncle Mick's given her some dosh and she wants to go to Majorca with Dix and her brats. I says that's well OK by me just as long as I don't have to go. And that was OK with them. So I nicked Dix's tent and went up to the Ridge. I was there all August with the bloke and he weren't shy at all.

In September he goes back to sleep so I comes down again and gets back in harness. I don't mind school too much, see? They learnt to treat me right now. In fact, I got school taped.

'What you done to all them creeps, Missis?'
'What creeps?'

38

'All them folks at school and my Mum and Dixey. All them people.'

'I ain't done nothing to them.'

'You must've. They don't mind what I do. They don't even mind me thieving and smashing things.'

'I ain't done nothing to them. I done something to you.'

'What you done, then?'

'That'd be telling, Nipper. You just be grateful I done it.'

'It ain't wrong, is it, what you done?'

'You slimy little squirt! I never heard such hypocrisy in all my born. You really take the cake, you do! You beat the rest of them hands down.'

'What you mean? What rest of them?'

'You think you're the only little tart I've ever talked to?'

'Yeah, I did . . . You ever talked to Dixey Foster?'

'Might have. Yeah, I remember. Snotty so and so she was. She weren't no good.'

'No good for what?'

'No good for nothing.'

'What about me, then? I'm good, am I?'

'Ringman says you are.'

'How long's Ringman going to kip for?'

'You missing it? I could get you some more, you know.'

'He woken up then?'

'Not Ringman. Someone else.'

'Who?'

'Longman's good at it. He's even better than Ringman.'

'I don't fancy Longman though.'

'Oh, you will, love, you will.'

*

39

In October I missed my third period and I got dead worried. I went to see the old girl and she thought it was a right joke, she did. I goes on about an abortion but she really let rip. I'd got to have the kid according to her. Abortions wasn't right. I told her it was all right for her to say that. She wasn't in the club.

She took me to see Longman. He was down by the copse over near the motorway works. He wanted to touch me but I told him to bugger off. He weren't nothing like as smashing as Ringman. I wasn't having him but the old girl said he knew how to fix it so it wouldn't show until it was time to get the bloody thing out and if I did it with him she might look after the brat herself when it come. So I let him and after that I didn't mind what he looked like just so's he didn't stop.

The old girl was a soft touch then so I got her to show me how to do the shiv.

I practised on everybody. My mum, Dix, the brats at school, creeps in the street. I got the Head. I even got Ian's dudes one time when they was feeling the mean Fridays and was all tanked up. I got them real good and nowadays they don't call me those names no more.

When it was Christmas I asked my mum for everything I could think of. Make-up, clothes, Nike trainers, a Walkman, a music centre with a CD player, you name it I wanted it and she come up sweet. Don't know where she found the juice to pay for all them things because you don't get big money working at the Co-op but I wasn't going to argue. Dixey give me lots too. Best Christmas I ever had and I made Mum let Longman stay nights with me. Up to then we'd been doing it outside but I never did enjoy getting my arse frozen off, though he didn't seem to mind the frigging frost. She didn't say much about Longman being there, except on Christmas Day when she bawled a bit when we stayed in bed. But then, she was getting proper grey round the gills. I reckoned she weren't long for this world, see?

I stopped going down the Hob when the weather turned nasty. I ain't good in the rain and after Christmas Longman just stayed in with us, fiddling with my CD and screwing me and that was like all I wanted. Besides the old girl had shown me how to do the shiv so sod her, I thought.

Past the New Year though, that bugger Longman ups and leaves. One minute he was listening to some old Motown crap of Mum's on the music centre – the next he's halfway down the garden path. I went after him yelling but he just gets over the fence into the field next door and disappears. I swears fit to bust. Who cares about the odd swear? The old girl ain't there.

Sneaky bastard, that Longman. After all I done for him!

I waits for him to come back that night but he didn't and I got mad. So I went round town doing the shiv to any creep what asked for it. Then I met some geyser coming out a pub and I let him do it to me round the back. He weren't much cop but he give me a tenner and that paid for a few drinks.

Up at the Ridge there weren't no sign of Ringman neither and I laddered my best tights climbing about round them bastard bushes looking for him.

'There ain't nothing for it,' I says to myself, 'I'll have to go and see the old girl.'

But you wouldn't credit it, when I goes up Hob's she taken a bloody powder too.

I got right moody that January, see?

'Missis! Where you been?'
   'Around, girl. Where you been?'
   'Looking for you.'

'You're a bare-faced liar, Nipper. I hope you passed a merry Christmas.'

'Yeah, it was great. Look, where the hell's Longman?'

'He had to go.'

'Where? When's he coming back?'

'Stone me, I never seen a girl so desperate for sex as you, love. Proper little nymphomaniac, you is.'

'Oh shut it, Missis. Just tell me where Longman's hiding out.'

'Don't you tell me to shut it, Nipper. You try and remember I don't take no cheek.'

'I ain't frightened of you, Missis. I knows what I knows. I can hurt you too now.'

'Oh no, dear. No, no, no. You can't pull no tricks on me. I ain't made quite the same as other folks and you never knows what I might do next if you was to try it, hey? It don't make sense to make me mad, do it?'

'Nah, well, all right. Just as long as you tell me where Longman is.'

'Ah yes, Longman. Well, Nipper, Longman's having his kip.'

'Like Ringman?'

'Yeah, just like Ringman. But don't you fret. They'll wake up in time.'

'In time for what?'

'For the baby, sweetheart. For the birth. And afterwards.'

'But what about . . . ?'

'I can arrange that too, girl. I arranged the rest, didn't I? Look at you! No unsightly lump. No morning sickness. No backaches. No funny cravings. A fifteen-year-old sylph, you is. And so pretty. It'd make Foreman's heart melt to look at you.'

'Foreman! I ain't going with Foreman!'

'Foreman's better even than Longman.'

'Oh, come on, Missis. Foreman's a nasty old sod. I seen him down the square, evenings. He's dirty and he smells. The lads throw their cans at him when he's pissed. I seen him throw up all over the bus shelter. He's well out of order.'

'Never judge by the outside, Nipper. If I'd have judged by your outside you would never have got where you is now.'

'What d'you mean?'

'You ever look in the mirror? You look incredible clean, girl, like some kid's Barbie Doll. You're so pretty, you're boring. But I thinks hard when I sees you and I waits till I sees your insides. Then I knows.'

'What? What you know?'

'You're the spirit of the age, see? The times. What you are is what this place is. You're what they calls an epitome. See, I likes to take what I can and I likes to get it right. I likes an accurate reflection and I likes to enter into the spirit of the thing, you get me?'

'What you mean, Missis? Can't you talk straight?'

'Oh sure, little Gemma. I can talk straight. Yeah, I can do that. So. You want a man, right?'

'I want Longman.'

'Ah no, ducks, you want Foreman. I can get you Foreman. Come on, now. Let's have a little sing. Join in. You know this one . . .

> 'Dance, Foreman, dance.
> Dance, my good men, every one.
> For Foreman, he can dance alone.
> Foreman, he can dance alone . . .'

'No, Missis, not him.'

'Ah, here he is, sweetheart. You just take a look in his trousers. Go on, don't be shy. Go on, take a peek.'

43

'No, Missis . . .'
'Where's the harm?'

All February Mum was like a zombie from Outer Space.
She didn't seem to notice me and Foreman rabbiting
about in the house at all. In the morning she went down
the Co-op and then she come back home at tea-time
knackered and quiet and sat in front of the telly till it
was time for bed.

Dix come in some nights with her kids and they all
sits down by the telly and just watches and watches.
It don't matter what. They watches whatever. One
night I gets up out of bed and I goes down to the front
room and watches *them*. I get the flipper switch and
fiddles around all over the shop. I give them a bit of
Channel Four film in Frog where you has to read the
words and they don't seem to mind that and then
we goes over to *Newsnight* with a couple of geysers
droning on about the economy and they don't turn a
hair. I messes round till one. The silly buggers was lap-
ping it all up. I finishes with this programme with some
arty doctor chap blathering on about the meaning of
life to a load of short-haired hippies and it was so boring
I wanted to shiv the lot. But did my zombies bat an
eyelid?

When I turns the set off they all got up, still being the
Living Bloody Dead and Dix and her brood goes back
home and Mum goes upstairs.

I says to Foreman about it when I went back. But he
grabs me and starts to do it again and I forgets about
them being crazy because you can't think about nothing
else when Foreman's doing it.

He goes out every now and again does Foreman to
get rat-arsed and he don't let me tag along. So I goes
over to Langley when he does and I tarts about down

44

round the town centre. He don't care. He knows I'll bring him some cans back anyway.

I got a bank account now.

End of March Mum got pinched. She'd been thieving from the till and the fuzz arrive and haul her off down the nick for a couple of days. My Uncle Mick come over from Fosshampton and bailed her out. He said he thought she'd get off with a fine because she ain't got no record and what the hell was the matter with her? I says I reckons she's sick but she won't see a doctor. He wanted to know who Foreman was and when I says he's my bloke he cut up nasty. Starts bad-mouthing him. I give Mick a well-lethal shiv and he shut his mouth and pissed off sharpish. Good riddance to bad rubbish I told Foreman but he just grunted and rolled over.

I near on gived up school. Who needs it? Sometimes I goes in for Community Studies now and again so's I can sound off and listen to them all agreeing with me like a load of sheep. It's a bit of a giggle and I just does it for fun, see? I might go in for politics perhaps. I'd be good at that.

When April come I got this bad turn. It wouldn't have happened if Foreman had stayed home like he was supposed to. But no, the bastard's got a big thirst and he's off down town. So I done my eyes over and nips across to Langley on the train. I done a few tricks and I thought I'd swank around the Town Hall bars and pick up some more trade but halfway along up the High I gets ill. Real ill. And while I'm trying to spew up and wondering what the hell it was I ate I hears this ripping sound and me best bloody dress starts splitting away at the seams. I got the sodding biggest bun in the oven you ever see. All at once. One minute a size twelve – the next I'm practically ten months gone! With my dress hanging around like I been in a hurricane. And Christ, did it sting! I starts bawling out and screaming and it being Saturday I gets a decent crowd. Some old classy bint comes out from one of the posh side streets and starts bossing my audience about. They get me an ambulance and about time too I says when I gets in because I'm wet all down my legs. Waters broken says one of the ambulance creeps and so I gets rushed into St Cath's with all the deedoos going.

Didn't take long to push the nipper out but it really bloody hurt. I ain't going through that, never again. I looks down at my belly after and I got these bastard scars just above my hips. Stretch marks says the nurse. And my breasts are all hard and big and they're leaking for God's sake! They wants me to breast feed but I ain't having none of that. Sodding disgusting. The kid'll make do with powdered milk, I tells the sister and I gives her the mean eye. Stopped her mid-lecture, that did.

Mum come in to see me the next day and she just sits there beside the bed staring at the kiddie as though it was something amazing. When the bell goes, end of visiting, she gets up and stomps off without a word to me like 'How are you?' or 'What can I get you?' Charming.

Next day I gets up and nicks some clothes out of a side ward while the woman's in the bog and I gets dressed and takes the babe and discharges myself. I'm going straight off to give the old girl a piece of my mind. What did she think she was doing playing a trick on me like that, hey?

'Ah, you had the kiddie, did you, Nipper? Let's have a look at her.'

'Yeah, no thanks to you. I thought you was going to take care of me?'

'Well, I did, didn't I? Best to have the baby in a nice

46

clean hospital with lots of doctors and nurses to keep
an eye on you.'

'I thought you was going to do it for me?'

'What, you mean you thought it'd be nice having the
kiddie out here by my insanitary little stream? I ain't
no midwife, sweetie, I never said I was. Or did you
think I was going to have it for you? I ain't no bloody
conjuror neither.'

'Ain't you?'

'Not so's you'd notice. A harmless eccentric, that's
me.'

'Where's Foreman then? I stopped off home and he's
gone.'

'Ah, yes. Well, Foreman got tired.'

'What you mean, Foreman got tired?'

'They all have to have their sleep, dear. You're a
demanding girl, see? You exhaust them after a while.'

'But what am I going to do now? What about
me?'

'Oh, I got a treat lined up for you, sweetheart, but
you has to wait.'

'What treat? Why do I have to wait for it?'

'You heard me talk about Littleman, ain't you?'

'Yeah. But Littleman's invisible, you says.'

'True. But on a certain night in the year he ain't. He's
good solid flesh just the same as the rest of us.'

'So what?'

'He wants you. He wants you bad. He wants you so
bad that he thinks he might spend the whole of his one
night with you.'

'Listen, Missis, why the shit should I get worked up
about that?'

'Language. Because, Nipper, Littleman's better than
Ringman and Longman and Foreman all rolled into one.
He's the best there is. The tops. And the things he can

47

teach you. The power he can give you. Makes me feel faint just to think about it.'

'What sort of power?'

'Ooh, real power. The power to get what you want just like that. You can have money, clothes, servants, fast cars, villas in the South of France, men, anything you bleeding like.'

'But I got that now.'

'No, love, what you got now's just a shadow of what you could have if you let Littleman spend the night with you.'

'If it's so good why don't you go with him instead of me?'

'It's you he wants, sweetie. He only wants you, see? And as for me I get my thrills by seeing you enjoy yourself. I like your appetite, Gemma. It feeds me.'

'What d'you mean?'

'Forget it. Just you nip up to Yalderton Ridge the last day of the month and I promise, you'll have the night of your life.'

'I don't know. I'll think about it.'

'Don't think about it, girl, do it. I ever let you down before?'

'No. Well, I dunno. I might. OK? I might. 'Bye. See you.'

'Aren't you forgetting something?'

'What?'

'Your baby, Nipper. Your little baby what you're going to give me to look after like you said you would.'

'What you want her for, Missis?'

'I got a kind heart, see? I reckons you might neglect the little one once you got your hands on Littleman. Give us the baby, sweetheart, and I'll see she wants for nothing a mother can give her.'

'I don't know . . .'

48

'Come off it, Nipper. You truly want a baby hanging round your neck once you're gallivanting round the world with your men friends?'

'Suppose not. All right. But I'll check up on her, see?'

'Good girl. You'd be unnatural if you didn't want to see her now and then. You just come and ask and I'll show her to you. OK?'

'Yeah, suppose so.'

'And don't forget. Be up the Ridge on the thirtieth. You won't regret it.'

'Might.'

It was hard waiting. Even though it was only a couple of weeks I was close to busting. Most nights I went down town trolling but it was stupid. After Foreman it didn't seem as if any guy I could find to screw knew how to do it. I started to dream about bloody Littleman and woke up howling. Mum took no notice. Once I'd got rid of the brat she'd lost interest. She was on the Social now because the Co-op wouldn't take her back. Hardly surprising, silly bitch! Fancy thinking she could get away with lifting money out the till! Still, she was quiet enough and give me no cheek when I got iffy which I do regular when I has to go without it.

Christ, them days went slow. Sometimes I'd plan out what I was going to do once I'd got this extra zip the old girl had said I'd get. I'd buy myself a Rolls or better still, a Chevvy, and I'd get a hunk to be my chauffeur and I'd go on the biggest spending spree anybody ever went on. Other times I'd think up faces for Littleman – Nick Nolte or Kevin Costner – and then I'd think about what the rest of him'd look like and groan. Yeah, it was a shitty time for me. Had to go round with crossed legs most days.

When the day come I was in the bath all afternoon. I shaved my pits, my legs, near on everywhere. I done myself up real careful and got my black dress out so's to look dead seductive. Not what you might call suitable for messing around in the woods up on the Ridge but the weather was fine and I'd got a spare pair of stockings ready.

In the bus going up there I was so fidgety I had to keep on changing seats. The bus creep tells me to sit down but I don't shiv him because we can do without a sodding crash. Jesus, I was impatient. I kept thinking when I was the boss round here I'd get the buses to stop only two or three times. This bloody bus stopped all over the shop. It even bloody stopped when there wasn't anybody wanting to get on. So I started to think about how I'd zap creeps when I come into my power. How I could even zap the old girl. Teach her a few lessons. A little respect. And then I goes back to thinking about Littleman. My hands is sweating and that's a sure sign I'm ready for it. Christ, was I ready!

It was near dark when I gets off but I knows my way up the Ridge backwards since last summer and I belted up and tore through the wood heading for Ringman's stone. There weren't no sign of Littleman so I sat down to catch my breath. After a while I hears the old girl singing bloody Top of the Pops. I can do without this, I thinks, but I knows better than to interrupt. Somewhere away in the woods she's droning on as usual:

> 'Dance, Littleman, dance,
> Dance, my good men, every one,
> For Littleman, he can't dance alone,
> Littleman, he can't dance alone.'

Oh, so Littleman can't dance alone, hey? He needs a girl to make him dance. I'm bloody trembling now at the thought.

It were getting real dark but I knew Ringman when he steps out from behind his stone and I knew Longman and Foreman who come with him. I know them by their smells, specially Foreman. They comes up and touches me sort of gentle and exciting and in a little I begins to pant. They carries me into the wood and we comes to a clearing place and they puts me down very careful, still stroking away. Then I sees the old girl sitting on a log, smiling at me like I was her true nipper and she lifts her hand and points over to a dark corner and crouching there is Littleman. I wants him straight away. He's big and blond and he looks at me like he ain't ate for a year. Well, he can eat me all right.

'Gemma,' says the Missis, 'let me introduce you to your dad.'

I begins to laugh and then I sees she ain't joking. For a minute I wonder whether I should run off but my legs is all weak. I licks my lips and goes hot.

I says, 'What the hell? I'll try anything once.'

I takes off my clothes and lays down inviting in the middle of the clearing.

Headline story, *Langley Evening Argus*,
15 May 1992:
MURDER VICTIM USED IN SATANIC RITES?

The body of a young girl, found yesterday in wood-land below Yalderton Ridge, was today identified as that of fifteen-year-old Gemma Hearnesley of 14, Coebrook Grove, Grigbourne. Her badly mutilated and partially eaten remains were discovered by a farmer's dog in a remote spot below the Ridge.

51

Chief Inspector David Marsh of the County Constabulary, *who is in charge of the case*, stated categorically today that the police are treating Gemma's death as murder. *Police from all over the county were out in force this afternoon combing the area for clues to Gemma's assailant.*

Chief Inspector Marsh went on to say that although the body was naked and had remained concealed for about a fortnight, forensic reports showed that there was no sign of a sexual assault made on the victim. However there were certain indications at the scene of the crime which suggested that she might have been subjected to some form of black magic ritual, though the evidence as yet is far from conclusive. Her other injuries have been ascribed to scavenging animals.

Two men, Neil Hogarth (31) and Dougal Smith (23) were arrested in the early hours of the morning after tip-offs from local people. Both men are members of a group of New Age Travellers encamped on common land near Yalderton Heath and have been described as Satanists. Later they were released after questioning.

Mrs Lynda Hearnesley, the mother of the victim, was unavailable for comment. However, all day, letters of support and comfort have been arriving at her Grigbourne home from relatives and friends. This afternoon some of Gemma's classmates delivered flowers and messages of sympathy to her door, shocked and stunned by the news of her death. Mrs Hearnesley's neighbour, Mrs Dixey Foster, said that Gemma's mother was too distressed to comment. She added, 'Gemma was a lovely girl, popular with us all. Nothing was ever too much for her. When her mother was ill earlier *on this year Gemma nursed her devotedly through it. We are all horrified to hear of her death and the sooner the police catch the madman who did this the better.'*

Another neighbour expressed his opinion that the reintroduction of capital punishment would act as a deterrent for this type of crime.

DRAWING FROM THE FIGURE

Cynthia Chapman

Since she gave up teaching, Cynthia Chapman's occupations have included market stallholder, pub pianist and running a fancy-dress hire business from her home in Kent. She has been writing for about five years and has had over thirty stories published in magazines. At present she is trying to find a publisher for her first novel while working on her second.

DRAWING FROM THE FIGURE

At twelve-thirty Mrs Oliphant removed her gardening gloves and laid them in the trug with the secateurs and bass. She straightened up from her task of staking delphiniums, conscious of a familiar twinge in the small of her back. Naturally one ignored this evidence of the advancing years; nothing was more boring than one's own minor ailments. The way to keep young was to follow the excellent advice of all those newspaper columnists; get out and about and take up new hobbies and interests so that one simply didn't have time to feel sorry for oneself.

However, she did feel a little sorry for herself when, just as she had arranged a lightly boiled egg and thin fingers of brown bread and butter on a tray, the telephone rang. She had to watch the egg growing cold as her friend Marjorie prattled on about nothing. As soon as she could she cut the conversation short.

'You must forgive me, my dear – I'm due at my art class at half past one. That's right, we're going to tackle drawing from the figure this term. Yes indeed – one only hopes it won't be *too* illuminating!'

After eating her spoilt lunch Mrs Oliphant hurried upstairs to change out of her pale-green cotton trousers and loose-fitting shirt. One did not of course *dress up* for an Adult Education class but on the other hand one did try to look fresh and summery. She selected a dress in a light, silky fabric patterned in soft shades of blue –

reminiscent of the delphiniums that one loved so much – and white shoes with a sensible medium heel. Her fair hair was worn in a short, casual style that needed little attention, but she carefully reapplied the rose-pink lipstick that these days seemed more flattering than stronger colours. After spraying a little lily of the valley toilet water behind her ears she was ready.

Since her husband had died Mrs Oliphant had been to classes in Embroidery, Flower Arranging, Yoga (for which one had been obliged to wear a track suit) and French Conversation. This year's choice – 'Discovering Drawing' – had made her feel quite adventurous, for although one had of course always adored Art it was amazing to find that one could actually produce quite recognizable pictures of assorted flowerpots, a bunch of bananas, or a jumble of kitchen utensils on a checked tablecloth.

This term the members of the class were ready to progress to 'Drawing from the Figure' and had been asked to pay an extra two pounds towards the services of the models. Their tutor Mr Redfern had stressed that the important thing about figure drawing was not to feel inhibited or discouraged by one's early efforts but just to have a go. He was a likeable, friendly man and they had now got over their initial reluctance to call him 'Teddy' as requested. He was in fact rather like a teddy bear, stockily built, with fluffy golden hair balding at the crown, a cheerful, ruddy face, and eyes the colour of brandy. After two terms with him they all felt like old friends.

Teddy Redfern was in his early forties and had a liking for alcohol and young women; a combination which had cost him both his previous teaching job at a sixth-form college and his marriage. These days he still drank a little more than he should, but his weakness for young

58

women was not catered for in his Adult Education classes, for the majority of his pupils were ladies of indeterminate age with more enthusiasm than artistic talent. Like Mrs Oliphant, they were charming, cultured and conventional, and if they ever detected whisky fumes on his breath they were much too well-bred to give any sign of it.

Now they were all busily engaged in drawing the young West Indian in jeans and T-shirt who leant against a table, his chin cupped in one hand, as if deep in thought. Teddy Redfern withdrew to the side of the room and surreptitiously lit a cigarette, tapping his ash out of the open window. Idly he listened to the snatches of conversation interspersed with ripples of ladylike laughter.

'My dear, I was quite expecting a *nude*!'

'Oh, we're not nearly ready for that yet, are we?'

'One does rather hope that one wouldn't have to cope with a *male* nude to start with!'

'But artists have to cultivate a detached viewpoint – just like doctors and nurses. The human body's simply a machine, isn't it?'

'Yes, of course. It's too silly to be apprehensive about drawing the nude figure – most of us are married women, after all.'

Teddy Redfern threw his cigarette-end out of the window and began to drift round the room, making bluff, hearty comments about the work as he went. No good being too discouraging, he thought, or he'd find himself without a class next year. Mrs Oliphant's attempt seemed to him slightly more competent than those of the other ladies.

'I say, Anthea – I do believe you're improving all the time! That head's really very good.'

'Oh, do you think so? I felt I was making a *frightful* botch of it.'

59

'Nonsense! Just have a bash at it and don't worry too much over the results. That's what life's all about, isn't it?'

As he moved on, a faint frown crossed Mrs Oliphant's face, for she found this simple philosophy quite alien to her nature. One could hardly 'have a bash' at *everything* in life; either one felt that one could be moderately successful at something, or one didn't.

It would be no use, for instance, having a bash at changing the flat tyre of one's car, she thought some forty-five minutes later, standing in the car park feeling particularly helpless. One would just have to go back into the centre and telephone one's garage.

As she walked up the steps Teddy Redfern swung out of the glass doors, talking away so busily to the West Indian boy that he nearly bumped into her. '. . . like a couple of balloons in a binliner. Ah – forgotten something, Anthea? I'd better come back with you. I've just locked up.'

'Oh, no, no –' she faltered. 'It's my wretched car; a flat tyre, and I'm afraid I'm a perfect *fool* when it comes to dealing with anything mechanical . . .'

'Is that all? I'll have it done in a jiffy. Can't have you messing about with oily tools, can we? Don't wait for me, Mick – I can get the bus.'

The young man rode off on a motor bike and Teddy Redfern accompanied her back to her silver-grey Golf.

'Is your own car out of action?' enquired Mrs Oliphant, watching him roll up his sleeves and set to work.

'Yes, temporarily. Bit of a nuisance, but I think there's a bus I can get in about twenty minutes.'

'Oh, but I insist that you let me run you home. It's the very least I can do after your kindness. I believe you live quite close to me,' she went on, as he gratefully slid into the passenger seat. She had seen him one day in a ramshackle Citroën Dyane coming out of the drive of a rather nasty-looking little bungalow.

'And you live . . . ?'

'Vine Cottage; I don't know whether you know it?'

'Ah yes, I think I've passed it in the car. Is there actually a vine?'

'Yes, quite an old one at the back of the house. Are you at all interested in gardening?'

'Love it,' said Teddy Redfern, who occasionally, in a wild spurt of energy, would go out to his garden and attack the lawn for ten minutes or so before collapsing into a deckchair with his heart pounding. 'I'm afraid mine's a bit neglected at the moment but I've got great plans for it. You must come round one day and advise me.'

'Oh, I *adore* telling other people what to do with their gardens,' she said effusively. 'But isn't your wife fond of gardening?'

'I live on my own. Was married for a time but it didn't work out; just one of those things, I suppose. My fault. I'm not an easy man to live with – put it down to the artistic temperament!'

He went on to tell her about his days at the Slade in the 1960s when he had been 'a bit of a terror' then gave her an account of his teaching career. He was naturally obliged to leave out all the most interesting bits but made up for this by enlarging on his reasons for 'opting out'.

'. . . had enough of the rat-race. I made up my mind I was going to devote myself to my own work, sink or swim. I'm simply not cut out for a regular nine-to-four-thirty job. Nowadays I can stay in bed till noon then work all night if I feel like it.'

How Bohemian he was! thought Mrs Oliphant, remembering her own husband setting off at the same

61

hour each morning with briefcase and bowler hat. One could see how the artistic temperament *would* be difficult to live with but at the same time quite fascinating.

'Perhaps you'd like to pop in and have a cup of tea with me as it's on the way,' she said, as they neared Vine Cottage. 'Unless of course you're in a frightful hurry?'

But Teddy Redfern was in no particular hurry and thought it would be interesting to see the cottage. As he followed Mrs Oliphant through the front door he was instantly struck by the unnatural tidiness of the place, then by the elegance and quiet good taste evident in the drawing room. His feet sank into a soft, pale carpet; the chairs were covered in blue-and-white flowered chintz; a few good pieces of porcelain were displayed here and there. On a low table with the colour and sheen of a new horse-chestnut stood an elaborate flower arrangement of mauve and white lilac, fat white peonies and purple irises. He felt large and ill at ease, fearful of bumping into some valuable piece of furniture or marking the carpet with his shoes.

Mrs Oliphant led him out to the neat little kitchen so that he could wash the traces of oil from his hands.

'I think it might be pleasant to have our tea outside, don't you? It's such a beautiful afternoon. Why don't you go out to my little courtyard and relax, and I'll bring the tray in a minute.'

The courtyard was delightful with its tubs of double petunias and trailing lobelia. Behind him the vine climbed almost to the roof of the cottage, its leaves a tender pale green against the faded coral of the brickwork. He sat down on a white wrought-iron chair and gazed down Mrs Oliphant's garden.

'You don't do all this yourself, do you?' he asked, as she set the tray down on the table.

'No, I must confess I have a man in to do the heavy work. But I think beautiful, peaceful surroundings are so important for one's well-being, don't you?'

This was an idea that had never occurred to Teddy Redfern. It was odd, he thought, that no yellow or orange or scarlet flowers seemed to grow in Mrs Oliphant's garden, and he remarked on the fact.

'But how frightfully clever of you to notice! To tell you the truth, I find those colours strike a jarring note – I love blues and mauves, and white of course, and all those heavenly things with silvery leaves. One tries to keep the effect muted.'

'And do you get many grapes from the vine?'

'Yes, certainly. More than I know what to do with. You must have some in the autumn.'

'Maybe if you decide to come to my class again we could use them for some still-life work.'

'Yes, what a splendid idea! I'm sure I *shall* want to carry on with the class – one feels one still has such a great deal to learn. I'm finding drawing from the figure a tremendous challenge. I think we were all a little apprehensive before today; one half-expected to be confronted by a nude!' She gave a musical laugh.

'Oh, we shall get to the nudes,' said Teddy Redfern with confidence. 'Oh, yes – the nudes are all lined up. Or nude, I should say; only one of the models will be doing it. We have to pay them more, you see.'

'Yes, I suppose one *would* have to . . . It won't be the young man who posed for us today, then?'

'Mick? Oh, no. The female figure – that's the usual drill. I shan't be inflicting any naked male bodies on you, ha, ha!'

That was rather a relief, thought Mrs Oliphant, after she had driven Teddy Redfern home. It wasn't that one would be shocked or embarrassed; more that one might

63

feel obscurely uncomfortable, possibly on behalf of the unclothed male model, so heavily outnumbered.

The next week Mick posed for them again. He sat on a hard wooden chair with his arms and legs crossed, and his body seemed to be all planes and angles, difficult to reproduce on the paper.

After the class she saw Teddy Redfern getting into his little red Citroën and felt slightly disappointed that there was no longer any need to offer him a lift.

The following week a new model appeared. To Mrs Oliphant and her contemporaries she seemed hardly more than a child, though one realized of course that she must have been in her early twenties. Her dark hair was cropped short like a boy's and her skin was as firm and shiny as a nectarine. In spite of the plumpness of her figure she was wearing black cycling shorts and an orange T-shirt that was really no more than a vest. Her black canvas shoes were dusty and her nail polish chipped.

How unattractive girls nowadays made themselves look! thought Mrs Oliphant, narrowing her eyes a little as she started to sketch the ripe curves that only too clearly needed the support of a good brassière. And how very unflattering those tight shorts were, made from some slightly shiny synthetic material ... Teddy Redfern had introduced her as 'Lynne', and at half-time sat on the edge of his table chatting to her and laughing a lot.

On the afternoon that Lynne came into the art room wearing a gaudily patterned short kimono a *frisson* of excitement ran through the class, for obviously they were about to tackle The Nude.

She really looked very little better without her clothes, thought Mrs Oliphant as, after discarding the kimono, the girl settled herself on an old *chaise longue*. She lay in such a position as to make it clear that she was not in the least self-conscious about the size of her hips. Today Teddy Redfern fetched her a cup of tea in the break, and though she shrugged herself back into the lurid kimono she did not bother to tie its belt. He sat beside her on the *chaise longue* and once again did a lot of laughing.

No doubt he was as detached as any doctor or nurse, the ladies reminded themselves, for after all the human body was merely a piece of machinery. Nevertheless, one did feel that it might have been more suitable *not* to have given the model that jolly slap on the behind just as she was about to start disrobing, or to have whispered whatever it was that made her giggle so uncontrollably.

After the class Mrs Oliphant walked to her car with Mrs Prentice, a nice woman of her own age, and they discussed Teddy Redfern's behaviour in hushed voices.

'Of course, one never knows with divorced men,' said Mrs Prentice sensibly. 'One shouldn't be surprised if they go off the rails.'

'Off the rails?' repeated Mrs Oliphant in a high, alarmed tone. 'Oh, but surely, my dear, there couldn't be anything like *that*! Goodness knows, one isn't a prude, but the girl *is* young enough to be his daughter. No, I think he was just being a little bit foolish in the way that middle-aged men so often are . . .'

Certainly Teddy Redfern was not foolish on any subsequent occasion that Lynne posed in the nude; indeed his manner towards her seemed offhand and almost brusque. Twice he complimented Mrs Oliphant on her work. A new model came and sat for them; an elderly man with a face full of unusual lumps and bumps like a potato. Teddy Redfern pinned Mrs Oliphant's drawing of the potato-like head on the art room wall.

At their final class Mick posed for them again. The

ladies had brought strawberries and cream to eat at half-time; Teddy Redfern had provided a couple of bottles of wine; a party atmosphere prevailed. Under the influence of this Mick became quite chatty and got out photographs of his girlfriend and baby daughter. At the end of the afternoon Mrs Oliphant walked out to the car park with Teddy Redfern.

'Will you be coming to the class again next term?' he asked.

'Well, naturally one would *love* to if it can be arranged. But I'm not quite sure what my commitments will be; I've promised an old friend that I'll go to Italian classes with her.'

'Oh, do come, Anthea,' he said, looking at her with his warm, brandy-coloured eyes. 'I can't manage without my star pupil. We'll be doing still life in the autumn; I seem to remember you were rather good at that.'

'Still life . . .' she echoed, seeing in her mind's eye a bunch of dark purple grapes lying in a pottery dish, perhaps beside a slim green wine bottle. 'Yes, I do feel that's very much *me*.'

'Jolly good!' he said, like an enthusiastic schoolboy. 'I'll expect to see you in September. You will come, now won't you?'

Yes, thought Mrs Oliphant, she *would* go, even if it clashed with the Italian class and she had to disappoint Marjorie. There were times when one had to be a little selfish, otherwise people would take advantage of one's good nature. Almost gaily she waved, as Teddy Redfern drove away from the centre still calling out, 'Don't let me down!' from his car window.

Mrs Oliphant spent the month of August visiting her married daughter in Canada. They did a great deal of touring about and the weather was very hot and, although of course one absolutely adored one's grand-

66

children, there was no getting away from the fact that toddlers were most frightfully exhausting.

It was delightful to be back in the peace of one's own charming little cottage, to rediscover the joys of solitude and the sheer bliss of pottering around one's garden. It was not until she had been home for a week that she chanced to pick up the new Adult Education Prospectus from the library.

Yes, there it was: *Discovering Drawing: Edward Redfern. For beginners or the more advanced. Drawing can simply record information, but it can also express dynamic emotion. Students will be encouraged to develop their skills in a free and original way, using a variety of techniques.* It really did sound quite exciting put like that, and she began to look forward to the new term.

One day in the second week of September she discovered that the grapes were ripe enough to eat. She could not remember having picked them as early as this in previous years; it had been an exceptional summer. She toyed with the idea of taking a bunch along to her first drawing class, then the happy thought struck her that there was really no need to wait for this. She knew where Teddy Redfern lived and could perfectly well call round with the grapes she had promised him. Perhaps she could advise him on his garden at the same time.

Mrs Oliphant arranged several of the ripe bunches artistically in a shoe box lined with crumpled pale-green paper napkins – almost as if one were taking them to church for a Harvest Thanksgiving service, she told herself mockingly. But one did like things to look elegant; even a simple gift should reflect one's personality. For similar reasons she dressed with care in a lilac cotton skirt and top that she had bought in Canada. It was still warm enough not to need a cardigan.

Teddy Redfern's bungalow, seen close to, was even nastier than she had imagined and the poor man's garden certainly *was* neglected! The hedges had simply been allowed to run riot and the last of the privet blossom gave out a warm, sickly scent; a lawnmower stood abandoned on the half-cut patch of grass; the flowerbeds were dry and choked with weeds. A large, untidy clump of red-hot pokers almost blocked the path that led to the front door.

Stepping delicately past these red-hot pokers, Mrs Oliphant rang the doorbell, then stood listening with her head on one side. She became aware of music playing somewhere inside – the sort of music with a heavy, pounding bass that somehow she would not have expected a man of Teddy Redfern's age to have liked. She rang the bell again but this time without much confidence.

His little red car was standing on the drive so he must be at home. Perhaps he was working in the back garden. She made her way round the side of the house, hardly noticing that the music had stopped. As she came to an open window she found herself looking into an incredibly disordered living room and was about to hurry past when she was arrested by the sound of voices. They seemed to come from a sofa covered in hideous mustard-yellow velveteen which stood with its back to the window.

'Have a heart, sweetie – I'm not a superman.'

'That's not what you told me half an hour ago . . .'

It was at this point that Mrs Oliphant caught sight of the black cycling shorts and orange vest which lay next to a whisky bottle on the carpet. She lifted her eyes and saw a plump but shapely leg rise into the air, the toes curling and uncurling. There was the sound of a slap then a giggle, followed by Teddy Redfern's unmistakable laugh.

'OK,' he said. 'Just let me change the tape first.'

The next moment Mrs Oliphant stepped back in horror as he got up from the sofa and crossed the room, revealing more of the naked male body than she ever wished to encounter again. It was clear that he had not been 'drawing from the figure', though he could have been expressing dynamic emotion in a free and original way, using a variety of techniques.

Her heart thudding, she tiptoed swiftly back to the front of the bungalow. Would it be best to take the grapes home with her? But then, looking at their firm, shiny plumpness, she felt a sudden distaste for them. Quietly she laid the box on the front doorstep and hurried out of the gate.

It wasn't that one was *shocked*, she told herself, standing in her cool, gracious drawing room a little later. If one had thought about it, one would naturally have assumed that he must have some sort of 'love life', to use the rather ridiculous modern expression. It was simply that one didn't expect *that* kind of thing to be going on in the middle of the afternoon, in broad daylight, and not even in his bedroom.

Absently she rearranged a spray of Michaelmas daisies in the vase that stood on the low table. With sprigs of purple hebe and a few creamy-white roses the effect was exquisite.

It was strange that she had not noticed the reddish tinge in Mr Redfern's hair before today; she had never cared for ginger men – just one of those little irrational foibles. Of course, one had always realized that he was not *quite* a gentleman . . .

She gazed out of the window at her charming garden, a restful, soothing vista of greens and blues and silver and white. It might be agreeable to take a tray of tea out to the courtyard, she thought.

69

Sitting there, sipping Earl Grey tea from a fragile, bone china cup, she turned once more to the Adult Education Prospectus. *Watercolour Flower Painting*; how delightful that sounded! The tutor was a Bridget Coombe-Stevens, and students were encouraged to bring their own plant and flower material.

There was nothing more ageing than to get into a rut and one really had a duty to oneself to ensure that this did not happen. And of course *this* class had the added advantage of not clashing with Italian, and so one would be able to keep one's promise to poor Marjorie . . .

BERLIN STORY

Philip Sealey

Philip Sealey currently teaches English at the European School in Munich. He has travelled widely and written two novels and the libretto for an opera. At present he is working on a third book set, like this short story, in Berlin after the Wall.

BERLIN STORY

Es war einmal – once upon a time.

The wood was dark and the thin ribbon of sky above their heads was already speckled with the first stars.

She was four and he was six and every few paces she had to break into a run in order to keep up with him. Her basket, filled with the berries they had been gathering, hung heavily in her small hand and she longed to abandon it somewhere. Her brother Hans had nothing to carry.

'Why do you always go so fast?' she called crossly after him.

'It's getting dark!' he shouted back over his shoulder.

'But we'll be home soon, won't we? You promised we'd only be gone an hour.'

In the middle of the path, he stopped and turned to face her. She looked at his wide, frightened eyes and, in her mind, saw the forest stretching away endlessly behind him.

'I don't know the way any more,' he said.

When Greta Maier opened her eyes, the sunlight was already filtering through the gaps in the half-drawn blinds. She lay still, listening to the faint voices she could hear from downstairs. Children's voices. How strange that, on this of all days, the old dream – or was it a memory? – should return to haunt her. But not only the

73

dream. The three words also that, like an incantation, seemed to float in the air around her, as though she had spoken them aloud in her sleep.

Es war einmal.

But perhaps, she thought suddenly, the words contained a message for her. For when she looked back over her long life, it seemed that everything she could remember, the century's swirling tides that she had been forced to sail upon, had now no more substance than a dream. And this city – in which so much of it had come to pass, in which more than eighty years had slipped like fine sand through her fingers – was not its history, especially its most recent past, as unreal as the events of a fairytale? And for each character, in every fairytale she had ever read, whether the ending was happy or sad, there was always a final page and one last, conclusive full stop.

There was a knock at the door. Too abrupt, too authoritative by far, for children.

'Mother.'

But, of course, it was only Hannah.

'Yes?' How faint her own voice sounded.

Her daughter knocked again. 'Mother, are you awake yet?'

Frau Maier raised her head from the pillow and cleared her throat. She must be still half-asleep.

'I'm just about to get up.'

'Can I come in?'

'Of course.'

The door opened and Hannah came into the room. She was wearing an apron over the new dress the old lady knew she had bought especially for today. She was smiling, though her face looked strained. She bent down beside the bed and kissed her mother on the forehead.

'Happy birthday, Mother. I wish you all the health

and happiness you could desire for another year.'

'Thank you, dear.'

Frau Maier reached out and hugged her daughter. 'Are the children being difficult downstairs?'

'You should know what it's like. There's so much to do and the little ones always seem to be under your feet. Lukas and Maria have baked you some currant bread. It tastes delicious. They insisted on using the old bread oven though, which meant having to light a fire. Miroslav had to chop up that old chair in the cellar for wood. You don't mind, do you?'

Her mother shook her head. 'I doubt if it was much good for anything else.' She hoped it wasn't the one she thought it was, but then was there any longer a point in hoarding these things from her past? The house was full of everything it had been possible to save from two world wars and their aftermaths. Each small ornament, photograph, or piece of furniture meant something to her, but perhaps the time had come to stop clinging on to all this debris. Maybe the oven, that had remained so long unlit, was the best place for many other things that seemed, on this morning of her ninetieth birthday, to have suddenly lost their meaning.

Hannah went back downstairs, closing the door behind her, and Frau Maier began to get up. She poured some water into the china bowl on the stand beside her bed and washed. The modern bathroom, that had been fitted at Hannah's insistence when she moved back to live with her mother after her husband's death, held no attractions for her. She washed, and lived, as she had always done. She took out a simple, dark-coloured dress, that she seemed to remember wearing for her eightieth birthday, and stood in front of the wardrobe mirror. Did she look any different from the last time she had worn it? The material seemed to hang more loosely from the shoulders, perhaps, her hair looked a little thinner, but other than that the only real difference she thought she could detect was a certain transparency of the skin, as if it might be possible soon to see the pale bones, like underwater coral, that had lain concealed for all these years beneath the surface.

She fastened a single strand of pearls around her neck and continued to stare at the reflection. A shadow crossed the glass and she realized that someone else had entered the room and was now standing behind her. He was dressed in uniform and his fair hair had been combed so meticulously it might have been parted with a razor.

'You look so young tonight,' he said, beginning to stroke the dark waves of hair that fell to her shoulders. She watched him in the mirror as he gently twisted her hair around one hand.

'How long have we known each other?' he asked suddenly.

She smiled, recalling that afternoon in the café on the Ku'damm when she had spilt coffee over him; the incident had lost her the job as a waitress, but gained her a husband.

'Almost four years,' she said.

'And yet you're still a mystery to me.' He pulled her hair a little harder so that she was forced to bend her neck back towards him. 'Look at your face, Greta,' he said. 'You're not a peasant girl from the Tannenberg forest at all, are you? Your ancestors weren't Prussian!'

Greta looked into his eyes, unsure as to whether he was being serious or simply teasing her. Still holding her hair, he pulled her head back against his chest, whilst his free hand began to caress her throat.

'Your hair's too dark, my love; your cheekbones

76

too high. Some of my friends have commented on it.'

Suddenly growing frightened, she tried to break away from him, but he held her too tightly. He contained her struggles and bent his head so that he could kiss her neck. She felt his lips brush the skin below her ear. He was pressing her whole body back against him and she relaxed, as he released her hair. She tried to turn her head so that she could kiss him, but he wouldn't let her. He held his mouth away from hers and moved his hands so that they rested over her small breasts. He squeezed her, forcing her body back against him so that she could feel the hardness of his uniform's buttons through the thin material of her dress.

'You scared me,' she said very softly.

'I didn't mean to,' he answered, still kissing her neck. 'It was just that when I came into the room and saw you there, you looked almost like someone I didn't know. Perhaps as your mother might once have looked.' He paused. 'I'm so sorry I never met her.'

She nodded dumbly, recalling the terrible months after they had first arrived in the city more than fifteen years before, when her mother, like so many others, had died from influenza.

'And your father? I have just begun to realize how strange it is to have married a girl whose parents one knows nothing about.' He paused and she felt his eyes piercing into her. 'I bet they were gypsies! That's why you've always been so secretive about them.'

'They weren't gypsies!' Greta cried indignantly. 'How can you say such things! My father was a Prussian farmer, who was killed in the war fighting the Russians. I was six years old and I saw him die. That's no secret! You've known that from the very beginning. You've seen a photograph of him.'

'Of course. How stupid of me to forget. I remember

77

thinking now how much he reminded me of your brother.'

'And Hans looks every bit a Prussian.'

She saw her husband nod slowly. 'He does indeed,' he said. 'But then you look nothing like him. You take after your mother – whose photograph I've never ever seen.'

'That's because I don't have one,' Greta answered quietly. 'You know what it was like then. Most of what we had was left behind in the East. Almost all the family records were lost.' She tried to turn round to face him, but found he was still holding her too tightly. 'You know the problems you had getting a marriage licence because I had no documents and they could find no records in the East.'

He nodded slowly. 'I remember.'

She hesitated nervously. 'Why are you asking me these things, Wolfgang?'

'Curiosity. Only curiosity.' He smiled suddenly and she saw his hands travel down across her body and begin to lift the hem of her dress. 'I'm sorry if I upset you.'

She stared, horrified, at their reflection, as though she were watching him with another woman. He pushed the fabric up around her waist and then began to caress her bare thighs. Closing her eyes, she leaned limply back against him, and then shivered as she felt his hands slide beneath the waistband of her underwear. He was whispering in her ear.

'You must make me a father, Greta. Tonight, when we come home. I want a son who will look just as German as I do.'

The fierce words dissolved into the sunlight and silence that filled the room but the shadow on the glass, though it seemed to fade, did not disappear entirely. Feeling weak and rather frail, Frau Maier turned away towards the window. She pulled up the blinds and pushed the curtain aside so that she could look out. She resented the way the past she had tried to forget, hers and this city's, still found it so easy to intrude upon the present. In the last ten years since they had pulled the Wall down she seemed, in the most unlikely places, at the most unexpected of times, to be at the mercy of these memories that, unchecked, surged up to overwhelm her. Once she had been able to control them, to limit their excesses and shut out those that she found too painful to bear, but recently, as if out of contempt for her age, faces that she had long forgotten had risen up to either greet or mock her. It was as if the Wall's demolition had released a host of captive memories that for the twenty-eight years of its existence she had kept locked within her.

She gazed at the building site across the road where the houses had recently been demolished to make way for a new apartment block. She hoped she would not live long enough to see the bulldozers at work on her side of the street. Beyond the rubble, the city stretched away beneath the cold, blue sky. She could hear the bells of the Maria-Magdalen Kirche pealing from a few blocks away and, above them, the noise of a jet engine as a plane took off from Tegel Airport. From her third-floor room, the skyline was dominated by the monstrous glass and concrete television tower that rose like a cyclops from the heart of Alexanderplatz. But if she turned her head slightly, she had a good view towards Schönholz which still, to her, lay in the eastern half of the city. Beyond, over the zigzagging line where the Wall had once stood, and where now a new road vibrated with the hum of traffic through the crisp winter air, was Wedding and the West. Only that these days, so the politicians said, East and West no longer existed. Berlin had been one great city again for the last ten years and this evening, the evening of her own ninetieth birthday, in the first year of the new millennium, that reunion was going to be celebrated in one more symbolic way. She sighed. Within her own lifetime, the city had been witness to so many false hopes and dreams, who was to say that this modern version would be any more enduring than its predecessors?

A movement in the street below caught her eye and she stared down into the Lutherstrasse, where she had been at home, in evil times and in good, for all but the first eight years of her life. A horse-drawn cart, piled high with household goods and old-fashioned furniture, had stopped outside the door. In it sat a woman with two children – a girl and a boy. As she watched, the little girl jumped down and darted across the pavement. A moment later, the bell jangled faintly downstairs.

The girl stared up at the imposing front door with its brass knocker. She listened to the footsteps on the other side and felt suddenly nervous as to what she should say to her aunt or uncle, when she had never met them before and they would not recognize her. She turned back to the cart in the road behind her and found that both her mother and brother were watching her.

'What shall I say?' she called out to them.

'Tell them who you are, Greta – you silly girl,' her mother replied. 'They've been expecting us for over a week. You're not going to surprise them.'

The girl nodded and looked at the place next to her mother where her father should have been. Even though he had been dead for three years now, more than a third of her life, she was still aware of him as an absence that had not been filled yet. Whenever the three of them sat down to eat, whenever they rode in the cart or she looked up suddenly from a book she had been reading, she saw an empty space that her father once occupied. And every time a door opened before her or she stepped into a strange room, she lived in the expectation of finding him, whole once more, before her.

She heard the bolts being drawn behind her, but she did not turn round. Instead, she gazed back along the narrow street and along all the other roads they had travelled since the start of their journey. She saw the surging, unpredictable crowds that had greeted them on their arrival in the capital city; she saw the flags, the banners with their strange slogans that she did not really understand; she heard the names they chanted and the frightening crack of rifle fire as the police charged into them. And before that, before they had ever entered this bewildering maze of brick and stone, where everyone spoke so differently, there were the great plains they had crossed, through towns and villages whose names she never knew; there were the haylofts they had slept in, above horses and cattle who softly munched the straw the whole dark night long; before that, at the place where all the roads started, there was just Tannenberg with its silent forests and icy lakes that were like windows on to the sky, and their small farm, the only home she had ever known.

And at the very beginning, before her mother had been forced to write to their relatives in Berlin, asking if they could stay with them for a while, there was the winter's morning when she had opened the kitchen door to discover how much snow had fallen in the night and seen, at the bottom of the vegetable garden, two strangers. They seemed thin and pale and their tattered coats did not look much good at keeping out the cold. One of them wore a bloodstained bandage around his head. She was just about to say something to her father who was sitting inside finishing his breakfast, when the man with the bandage saw her and put his finger to his lips. But her father was already speaking to her, telling her to close the door if she was going out. But she didn't want to go out, not with two strangers standing at the end of the garden. She hesitated and it was then she saw the two men had rifles slung over their shoulders. Only they didn't look like German soldiers.

She called out: 'Papa, come quickly!' The words were so familiar to her, she might have spoken them yesterday. But before she could warn him further, he was standing beside her and one of the men was pointing his rifle towards them. She saw the flash of fire and the curl of smoke that drifted up into the freezing air, she heard the beating of wings as some crows took off from the nearby trees, and she saw her father falling to the ground. He lay on his back staring up at her, whilst she was dimly aware of the soldiers running off. His mouth kept moving but no words would come out of it. She began to cry as she saw the blood spreading from the hole in his shirt, before it trickled down his side and into the snow he had so recently cleared from the path.

Greta heard the front door open behind her and she quickly turned round again. She gasped and was just about to cry out with joy when she realized her mistake. Though the tall, imposing man who stood before her looked a lot like her father, he was older than her father would ever be. He seemed to be looking down at her rather sternly. Greta stared at the buttons of his waistcoat which were level with her eyes.

'Excuse me, sir. My name is Greta Sesemann and that's my mother and brother.' She turned her head to point them out. 'We've come from our home in Tannenberg to stay with you.'

Frau Maier shook her head to try and drive out the troublesome memories, but though the image of her father vanished at once, she had the feeling that, when she went downstairs to breakfast, she would find her mother and uncle sitting at the table along with the other members of her family. She moved away from the window and was shocked to see a pale shadow beside her bed, as though Wolfgang too were waiting for her. What did they all want from her? Was she unwell? With a long sigh, she crossed the room and stepped out on to the landing, closing the door firmly behind her.

The rich smells of cinnamon and yeast filled her nostrils as she went down the stairs, and she remembered the currant loaf Hannah said the children had baked for her. But when she went into the dining room, she was thankful to find only Miroslav and his wife – her granddaughter, Dagmar – still seated at the table. Miroslav helped her to her usual place and apologized for the absence of the rest of the family who, it appeared, had either gone to church or were otherwise engaged in arrangements for the remainder of the day. Frau Maier smiled at him as he went to fetch her some fresh coffee; she had always liked the rather formal courtesy with which he treated her, and which seemed to be so lacking in most of her relatives, even though he was a Pole and had chopped up one of the two remaining Tannenberg farmhouse chairs without her permission. He returned from the kitchen with Lukas and Maria, two of his three children, who were proudly bearing the golden currant loaf. They were followed by Hannah who placed an envelope in front of her.

'This came for you yesterday, Mother, but I kept it till this morning as it was obviously a birthday card.'

The old lady stared for a moment at the foreign stamp and postmark and then recognized her brother's writing.

Hannah watched her. 'He never forgets, does he? It's more than fifty years since he went, but he still remembers his sister's birthday.'

83

Her mother slit the envelope with her knife and took out the card. As she expected, it wasn't a birthday greeting card, but a postcard of New York, the city in which Hans and his wife had chosen to make their home. She wondered if her brother realized that he always sent her the same view of the Manhattan skyline, or whether, after all these years, he was still trying to impress her with the spectacular sight, still trying to convince himself and her that he had got a bargain when he exchanged bombed and ruined Berlin for these glittering towers so far from his homeland.

His careful handwriting covered the back of the card. '*Herzlichen Glückwunsch, Schwesterchen*', he had written in the old-fashioned, formal German script that he still retained, uncorrupted by current usage. She could not resist smiling, as she always did, at his use of the diminutive – *little sister* – when he and his wife were in an old people's home and she was now ninety.

My heartfelt wishes on this your Ninetieth Birthday. It would be nice to meet once more, but I fear we have left it too late for either of us to make such a long journey. You have your family, of course. I shall be watching on television this summer to see the great moment for Berlin and our country, though I find it hard now to think of anywhere other than America as being my home. A few weeks ago, I found a very old photograph of the farm in Tannenberg, and I thought of that time we got lost in the forest and had to spend the night in the old woman's cottage. That was an adventure! Do you remember it too? I hope we will both be well this time next year, so that I can greet you again.

Your brother, Hans

84

Frau Maier put the card down on the table. 'I think he is sad he has no family over there,' she said quietly.

'He has his wife and he must have many friends,' Hannah said.

'But they have no children or grandchildren. Nor any great-grandchildren,' her mother said with a little smile, as she caught the eyes of Lukas and Maria, still waiting for her to try the currant loaf. She cut herself a slice and buttered it, whilst Hannah picked up the card to read.

'What a strange thing to remember after all this time,' she said, turning the card over and looking at the picture. 'Do you still remember getting lost in the forest, Mother?'

'Oh yes,' Frau Maier replied. 'Things like that one never forgets.'

She finished her breakfast, after complimenting the children on their baking, and then sat back in her chair whilst Hannah cleared the table. Miroslav excused himself and Lukas and Maria disappeared to play somewhere so, for a few minutes at least, she was left to her own thoughts. She looked around the room where, though bright sunlight streamed through the large windows, the corners looked unusually dark and dusty, as if her daughter had decided not to clean the house any more and to permit the spiders and beetles to live where they chose. She shivered and realized that she was also unable to rid herself of the feeling that today was going to be a family reunion not only for the living members of her family, but for the dead as well. And, if that was the case, what would she say to her mother who had been dead for eighty-one years? Had she lived her life as a dutiful daughter should?

'Are you all right, *Oma*?'

The voice seemed to come from under the table, but she chose to ignore it. Instead, she stared at the remains of the currant loaf that had not been cleared away and thought of the oven in which it had been baked. And she thought of the chair that had been chopped up to make the fire, and the place where the chair had been waiting in the dark for just such a morning as this. She had not been down to the cellar for a long time. The stairs were steep and difficult for her now and Hannah always went whenever it was necessary to fetch something, but maybe today, when the others had gone out, she should brave the gloom and the cobwebs to discover what secrets still remained in that room. Perhaps it was time for her to rediscover whatever details from her past she had tried to shut away down there.

Frau Maier pushed her chair back from the table and stood up. For a moment, she felt faint and put out a hand to steady herself.

'Are you all right, *Oma*?'

It was the same voice again. There was a sudden movement and a small figure wriggled out from under the table and ran into the living room. For a moment the old lady tried to put a name to the head of dark curls that had just vanished, but she knew she could not. There were so many of them now, her grand- and great-grandchildren, all with their smiling, well-fed faces, and their unfamiliar names which she had such difficulty in remembering. And they all called her *Oma*, which irritated her as the word implied no particular recognition of her age. The title made no distinction between herself and Hannah, who was also, of course, a grandmother. Most of the children spoke in different languages as well. Barely one of them talked naturally to her in German and, on the occasions when the family was all together, which admittedly did not happen very often, if she was allowed to sit back in her chair with her eyes closed, all she could hear around her was a babble of strange-sounding words and foreign accents. She found it impossible to understand how any of the eight or nine younger children managed to communicate with each other at all.

As a distraction from the other thoughts that kept filling her head today, she decided to sit down again and struggle with the great list of names her family had now become. Like the genealogies in the Old Testament her mother had once made her learn, she needed to recite them by heart from time to time, just to make sure she could still do it. She stared at the half-eaten loaf of currant bread. She must concentrate now. And, with a shock, she realized that the names of her dead friends and relatives had become easier for her to recall than those of the living. She closed her eyes.

In the beginning there had been her father and mother, Wilhelm and Sarah Sesemann, and they had lived in East Prussia and, later, in Berlin. Their first child was called Hans and she, Greta, was their second child. And after she had married Wolfgang and her name become Maier, she gave birth to Adolf and then Hannah. And her grandchildren from Hannah's marriage were Pieter, Dagmar, Matthias and Lena. And these grandchildren had followed the example of their great-uncle, Hans, and scattered themselves to all the corners of Europe. Pieter had married Anne-Marie and gone to live in Lyon and the great-grandchildren they had given her were called Juliette and Gabrielle. Dagmar had married Miroslav and their three children were Lukas, Maria and Mikhail, and they lived in Frankfurt. Matthias had married Lotte and now worked in Amsterdam and their children were called Stefan and Anders. Lena had married David, a Jewish boy from London, whom Frau Maier had only met once. And they had a baby called Martin and now lived in England.

She knew the names, but she was not sure she could match a face to each of them. Those she rarely saw caused her particular anxiety when she was expected to recognize them. One thing was certain, though – none of the men present today would be called David.

She recalled his face, thin and rather hawkish, with thick black eyebrows. 'Frau Maier,' he had said in his faultless German – why had he insisted on calling her that, as though refusing to admit he was now part of her family? – 'I have something rather embarrassing to ask you.' It was after the wedding reception, here in Berlin, no more than three or four years ago. And foolishly, though a little uncertain as to what to expect, she had smiled politely at him and invited him to go on. 'You lived in Berlin before the war, didn't you?' She admitted she had. 'I have always wanted to know,' he continued, with the over-deliberate emphasis of someone who has already drunk too much, 'when you got back from watching the parades and listening to the speeches, when you got home to find your neighbours had been taken away, when you closed your own front door and turned the key and made sure that you were quite, quite alone, when it was clear that no one and nothing could possibly eavesdrop on you, then, in the privacy of your own heart, how did you explain your silence to yourself?' And she had gazed back at him, shaken to her soul. Some other guests had become aware of the scene he was making and had manoeuvred him away from her. Later, sober, he had apologized to her but not before she had been forced to weep, not only for her inability to find the words which she felt did not exist in any language, but also in memory of her own suffering that she had, somehow, God alone knew how, survived; and beyond that, had she not wept too for the fact that, despite the length of her country's history, those twelve years of darkness – so few amongst so many – should still count for so much.

'Are you all right, Mother?'

The old lady opened her eyes with a start and saw Hannah standing beside her.

'I must have fallen asleep.'

'I thought you called out,' her daughter said.

'I'm sure I didn't. Maybe it was one of the children.'

Hannah nodded slowly, pausing before she continued. 'Mother, you don't mind that we're all going to this candlelit demonstration on your birthday, do you? As soon as it's finished we'll come straight home so that we can all eat together.'

'I don't mind, dear. Whatever's easiest for you.'

'You're sure?'

Her mother nodded. 'Of course.'

Hannah returned to the kitchen and the old lady left the table to go and stand before the French windows that led out into the garden. She gazed through the glass at the neatly ordered flowerbeds, the bare fruit trees, and the narrow strips of lawn, and she thought how lucky she had been, in the heart of this city, to have had her flowers and the few vegetables they had always grown. She opened the window and stepped out on to the small paved area behind the house, where there was a table and some garden furniture.

At the bottom of the garden, five tall fir trees rose against the winter sky. Brought as tiny seedlings from the Tannenberg forests, they also had survived in their new surroundings. And around their roots, still, would lie the scattered crumbs of dark earth that she, Greta, had taken from the farm. That distant kitchen garden with its alien figures appeared before her once more, only now the two soldiers were half hidden by the trees, whose shadows seemed to be reaching out towards her

89

in some disquieting fashion. She heard a movement and turned, half expecting to discover her father coming to take his place beside her, as he had on that terrible morning. But it was only Lukas and Maria.

'*Oma?*'

For a moment, Frau Maier could only see the two children as though she were watching them through the wrong end of a telescope, so far away did they seem to have become.

'*Oma?*' Lukas repeated, a slightly puzzled look upon his face.

'Yes, my child?' she answered at last.

'Would you like to go for a ride on the train with us?'

'The train?' The old lady felt confused. Where would they go?

'Papa says if you want to go, he can take us to the *S-Bahn* station and then meet us again later.'

'It would only be a little ride,' Maria added.

Frau Maier thought for a while and then nodded her head slowly. 'All right,' she said, with a smile. 'But only if you promise to behave yourselves and not to run about in the carriage.'

The children promised and shortly they were all sitting in Miroslav's car as he threaded his way through the traffic towards the station at Schönholz. At first, Hannah had tried to dissuade her mother from going. Even such a simple journey would be too strenuous for her, she had argued, especially as she did not seem to be quite herself this morning. But the old lady had insisted she was fine. And, in a sense, she was. It was only the feeling of tiredness that seemed to hang upon her shoulders like a heavy coat, that bothered her slightly, and of this she said nothing. Besides, she felt it would do her good to get out of the house that, on this morning of her ninetieth birthday, had become rather oppressive with its ghosts, its memories and its only half-forgotten secrets.

Having arranged for Miroslav to meet them in about an hour and a half, they boarded the train and sat down in the almost deserted carriage. The polished wooden seats gleamed as they always did these days and Greta recalled the years before the war when the *S-Bahn* had first been opened. Although completely refurbished, the trains and carriages were the same ones that had first seen service then and Frau Maier found the thought reassuring. She had always enjoyed travelling by train. Even when Berlin had been divided and the Wall had separated her from Hannah, the knowledge that the old-fashioned trains continued to link both halves of the city – despite the fact that she was not permitted to cross from East to West at will – had somehow comforted her, and she had prayed to that God she still dared to believe in that the iron rails might bind together what history had tried so hard to split apart.

The train pulled out of the station and, like her excited great-grandchildren opposite, she gazed out of the window at the peaceful streets, the shops that were closed because it was Sunday, the people out walking their dogs, the children playing in a park. She had not made the journey for a long time and was unable to rid herself of the sensation that she would not make it again; how unimaginably strange it was to consider that all these things would continue to take place, that life in this city whose history she felt was also her own would go on, exactly as it always had, when she was no longer there to witness it. Wollankstrasse, Bornholmerstrasse, Gesundbrunnen, Humboldthain – the names of the stations fled before her and, beneath her breath, she whispered goodbye to them all.

As they approached the Nordbahnhof she saw with

a shock, sprayed in livid letters across some old hoardings, the hooked cross and the words *Ausländer Raus!* And as the daylight passed away and the city vanished, a familiar anxiety began to steal over her; she clutched the leather bag in her lap more tightly as she found it impossible to escape the sensation that, like a woman drowning, she was sinking back into the past.

The echoing darkness of the tunnels was interspersed with the neon glare of the underground stations, the original Gothic script of their names – which she remembered so clearly – now replaced with neat, featureless capitals. But the presence of what had been lingered strongly down here in the unlit spaces between stations. They had already passed beneath the line of the Wall once, in a few minutes they would travel under it again. But though the concrete slabs had gone, leaving behind only the scar, as if from an old wound, the memory of the pain still remained. It was the same with the city centre that now lay directly above their heads. Modern apartments and office blocks could not erase the memory of the rubble out of which they arose. She saw the vast mountains of brick and mortar, which she herself, with her bare hands, had helped to clear, rising up from the broken ground and becoming whole once more. And she realized that whichever way she viewed these memories – like a film that could be watched both forwards and backwards – the effect was still the same: buildings became rubble became buildings again. The past could not be erased or forgotten: the layers of sediment upon the banks of the Havel and the Spree piled up forever.

And as they left the Anhalter Bahnhof behind them and plunged into the darkness once more, Frau Maier remembered the West German television pictures she had watched the November night the crowds surged through the Wall. She had stared at the disbelieving, tearful faces of fellow East Berliners, blinking in the sudden glare of the floodlights, as if emerging from thirty years spent underground. And she had seen, as a camera tried desperately to capture all that was happening at the walled and boarded end of Unter den Linden, the four horsemen, who had once been the proud symbols of Prussian power, perched upon the summit of the Brandenburg Gate; beside them, fluttered the red, black and gold East German flag with its hammer and dividers; to the left, she could see a building site where, she knew well enough, the Chancellery and its bunker had once stood and, to the right, though still for that moment on the other side of the Wall, was the Reichstag with the unadorned West German flag flying from the roof. It was not necessary to be a historian, all that was required was for one to have lived in the vicinity, to understand how much of her country's past, and her own, was contained that night within such a small space of ground.

There was a sudden jolt and the train came to a standstill. Beneath the floorboards, the electric motor whined, whilst the lights flickered and then expired. A baby started to cry. Someone coughed.

'Why have the lights gone out?' Maria asked – and Frau Maier knew she was back underground the day she lost Adolf, her son.

It was the last summer of the war and the three of them, mother, eleven-year-old son and eight-year-old daughter – for there was no father now – had taken the tram as far as they could go into the centre of the already ruined city. Greta was hoping to buy some food, either legally, or on the black market. In her bag she carried some items of clothing – silk stockings and underwear – which

it might be possible to exchange for more useful com-
modities. But close by Friedrichstrasse, in the middle of
the afternoon, they had been surprised by the air-raid
sirens wailing out over the city. And almost immediately
afterwards, as people began to run for cover, Greta had
heard the sullen drone of the bombers. She had pulled
the children down the steps into the underground
station, but in the sudden crush she had felt one hand
become detached from hers. In vain she had tried to
turn round and retrieve those clutching fingers, but the
surge of people, like a wedge, had come between her
and her son. So, unable to move, she and Hannah had
been forced to sit and wait, whilst the lights wavered
and then failed altogether, and the bombs detonated
over their heads, shaking the ground like the footfalls
of a giant.

Afterwards, amongst the smoking debris, over the
shards of glass that crunched like sugar beneath their
feet, she and Hannah had searched for Adolf. They had
shouted his name till their throats ached and their voices
were hoarse, and people had stared at them as though
they were calling out for the Führer himself to save them.
But in that awful stillness that always followed the
bombing raids, a silence punctuated only by the hiss
and crackle of the flames and the cries of others like
themselves, they could find no trace of him; so that, at
last, as the light began to fade from a red and sullen
sky, they had made their way home.

Greta had opened the front door of the house on
Lutherstrasse and then, speechless, the two of them had
stood in the hallway. Greta, her blackened face already
streaked with tears, had begun to cry again; great,
uncontrollable sobs that shook her entire body,
as a new, terrible reality collided with this familiar
world.

'Mama.'

She had barely heard Hannah's voice above the sounds of her grief.

'I can hear someone calling.'

She had held her breath then, her ears strained to catch some final whisper of hope.

'Mama?'

From under their feet, the small voice called up to them.

Greta flung open the door at the top of the steps leading down to the cellar and pressed the light switch. But, of course, there was no power. In the darkness, she could see nothing.

'Who's down there?' she called out, her voice unnaturally loud in her ears.

'It's me, Mama. Adolf.'

Then she and Hannah had heard his light footsteps mounting the steps, until eventually his pale and grimy face appeared before them. And of his miraculous journey home, alone, through the blazing debris and the falling buildings, ever afterwards, she was able to offer no rational explanation, though one of her neighbours did suggest that it was the name, which her husband alone had chosen for him, that had enabled him to come through the fire unscathed.

The motor whined again, the carriage jolted and, still in darkness, the train moved forward. Frau Maier could feel the ground rising beneath them and then, suddenly, they were out in daylight once more.

'*Oma*, why are you crying?' she heard Maria ask.

She looked at the children opposite her, but saw only Adolf and Hannah as they had once been. She stared out of the window and saw flames spouting from the broken spire of the Kaiser Wilhelm Memorial Church, as though from the devil's own chimney; she saw wild animals, freed from the zoo by the bombs, roaming Bismarck Strasse in terror; she smelt the stink of scorched stone and she recalled the last days of madness as they had waited for the Russians to arrive. She remembered Adolf's face as he had left her to go and dig trenches for the last time. He had set off with three or four older boys from further down the street, his shovel in one hand, the piece of bread she had given him for the day in the other and, in the shabby coat that he had outgrown, despite his thinness, and with his cheeks as white as flour, he no longer resembled the son she had once known. He had stopped at the corner to turn round and wave to her and she had raised her arm in reply, as if he had been setting off for school. But he did not come home that night and, though she had stood on that same corner on uncounted occasions in the fifty-five years since that day, she never once saw him, either in life or death, again.

The old lady took a handkerchief from her coat pocket and wiped the corner of one eye.

'I was remembering something that happened a long time ago,' she said slowly, as the train came to a halt at Yorckstrasse Station and they rose to their feet to get off.

The old house was still. Everyone had got into their cars and driven off towards the centre of the city. And each one had kissed her as she stood at the door to see them off. They were sorry to leave her alone on this afternoon of all afternoons, but there would be the celebrations this evening, the special meal that Hannah and Dagmar had been preparing since breakfast. Besides, she would be able to have a rest with the children out of the way. And, as each pair of lips had brushed her cheek, in her heart where no one could hear, Frau Maier had said her own farewells.

It was time to go down to the cellar. The moment to settle all outstanding debts had finally arrived. The old lady opened a drawer in the chest that stood in her bedroom and took out a thin gold chain that had been wrapped in a scrap of silk. Hanging from it was a small key. She went downstairs and opened the door at the top of the stone steps that led down into the darkness. For a few seconds she hesitated, disturbed by the draught of cool air that was exhaled in her face. Ever since she had been a child, this cellar had frightened her: the steepness of the steps, its unusual depth below the ground; and, while her uncle had still been alive, it had always been her job to fetch him a bottle of beer from the crates that were kept stacked against the far wall. How she had hated the approach of the evening meal with its inevitable summons. There had been no electric light in the cellar then and she had been forced to endure the nameless shapes that crowded around the wavering pool of light thrown by her feeble candle flame.

For a moment longer she stood still, listening for any unexpected sound, and she suddenly realized that, though the house might be quiet, it was not empty. As if sleepers were present in some of the rooms, she could hear the regular breathing of those who had already arrived to keep her company. With a shiver, she wondered who might be waiting to greet her at the bottom of the dark stairs.

Frau Maier switched on the light and slowly descended. At the bottom there was a short passage containing two doors. The first, and smaller, room had always been used for storing jars of homemade preserves, beer and wine. Everything else that a family can accumulate in a lifetime was crammed into the second

97

room. The door was ajar and she pushed it open, whilst fumbling for another light switch. Immediately she pressed it, the cellar sprang back out of her memory to confront her once more. She remembered the number-less nights, and days, she, Hannah and Adolf had crouched down here, wondering what new arrangement of their world might await them when the bombs finally finished bursting above their heads.

On the floor she saw splinters of wood, evidence, presumably, of Miroslav's chopping in the morning, but she was not concerned with that now. She was looking for the pinewood box her father had made and given to her on an earlier, long-ago birthday in Tannenberg. Only it was no longer in the place she expected it to be. In fact, it seemed that someone had rearranged all the furniture. The shapes and shadows with which she had once been so familiar were all changed. Tentatively, she groped about in some of the corners, but she found only boxes and containers she did not recognize. What if Hannah had thrown it away with some of the other old things which no longer seemed to be present? Frau Maier felt weak and sat down on the kitchen chair that had escaped Miroslav's axe. She rested for a few minutes and thought how absurd it would be if the few bits of debris she had saved from her life, the documents and photographs she had clung on to for all those years, despite the dangers and her sense of shame, should have been consigned to the rubbish tip by chance.

'Greta.'

The voice was soft, barely audible, and, for a second, Frau Maier thought that she herself had spoken aloud. But then she heard it again.

'What are you looking for?'

The old lady stared uneasily around the cellar, search-ing for the owner of the familiar voice, but saw instead, partially covered by an old rug, the box. She stood up and carried it back to her chair; then she fitted the key into the lock, so fragile that a child could have forced it, and opened the lid. She took out the picture of the mother who, after her marriage to Wolfgang, she had denied for so long, just as, in the years before the war, she had denied some of her oldest friends who, one by one, had simply faded from view as if they had become over-exposed to the light. She opened her father's family book – that she had always claimed was lost – with its details of all his relatives; and there, despite the passage of years, unchanged and inviolable, she read once more her mother's maiden name.

Was this it then, her secret? Was this all it amounted to? She thought of Hannah and Adolf as they had been in that terrible time and she wondered what mother would have acted differently. She thought of the father, still sitting upstairs on her bed perhaps, who had abandoned them. Abandoned them all because, despite his name, their son's face contained nothing of her husband's ancestry. He had waited until shortly after Hannah's birth, hoping, presumably, that the second child might give him what the first had so miserably failed to provide, but when she too possessed her mother's dark eyes and delicate features, as if disowning the father's blood, he had left them. But he had not denounced them; despite her fears, the Gestapo had never come calling for them in the early hours of the morning. Once, a long time after the end of the war, she thought she had caught a glimpse of him in a Frankfurt street, but she had never been certain, and his presence in the house today testified to the fact that he was no longer amongst the living.

And as she sat in the chair from the Tannenberg farmhouse kitchen, in the presence, she knew, of her mother, she supposed it might now be possible to answer the question her granddaughter Lena's husband had asked her. For despite the evasions and the little self-deceits, she knew she had always known the truth. But she had known it in different ways and with different intensities. And she had known it most vividly here in this cellar on the night that Adolf had failed to return from his trench-digging. As she had sat with Hannah, listening to the noise of the last battles in the nearby streets, waiting for the sound of boots and Russian voices on the stairs, had she not been forced to admit finally that they had been living in the witch's kitchen all along, that the oven had been prepared not simply for the Jews, the Communists, and the gypsies, but for all of them?

Still holding on to the small box, she rose from her chair and, having switched out the light, she climbed the steps to the hall. She went into the living room and, without really thinking what she was doing, she switched on the television. One of the children must have interfered with it, however, for the picture was only in black and white. Still adrift in the world the cellar had returned her to, she stretched out her hand towards the controls that she had never properly understood, when with a start of horror she realized she recognized the scenes on the screen. She saw the banners, the athletes marching round the vast Olympic stadium, the three figures on the tribune built high up in the stand. What had happened? Had these too come back from the dead to haunt her?

But then, without warning, the colour, like life itself, returned and Frau Maier realized they must have been showing an old newsreel about the first Berlin Olympic Games in 1936 when she herself had been a spectator. The screen was now filled with pictures of the new, virtually finished stadium that had been built to stage the twenty-seventh Games that coming summer. And as a helicopter whirred in the background and she saw live film of the evening's candlelit demonstration against anti-Semitism and intolerance of foreigners, to which almost all her family had gone, she heard, as though in a dream, the announcer saying that in these first days of the new millennium, in the Olympic year when the eyes of the world would be turned towards Germany in general and Berlin in particular –

The voice faded. Frau Maier was suddenly tired. The day that was not yet half over had already been too much for her. Abandoning the television to an invisible audience, she put on her coat and hat, and went into the dining room to open the French windows once again. Then, she stepped out into the cold, moonlit garden. She stared at the silver shadows of the fir trees that now, strangely, no longer seemed to implicate her in anything for which she felt any guilt. She sat down on a garden bench and, with a barely perceptible sigh, she closed her eyes.

She and Hans were in the forest again. It was morning and sunlight filtered through the branches over their heads and sparkled on the cottage's small, round windows. The little house looked pretty once more, as it had the first night they had seen it, when the lamplight and the smiling old woman had welcomed them in out of the darkness. Smoke rose from the chimney.

'Aren't you afraid?' she whispered.

'Of what?' Hans asked.

'That she might one day escape and come and find us again.'

'She won't come back.' Her brother laughed. 'She's in the oven now and even a witch as wicked as she was can't return from the dead.'

101

He held out his hand to her and they began to follow the path through the trees once more. After a while they came to a track that bisected the way they were going.

'I know where we are,' he said with a smile. 'We must have passed this track in the darkness. We'll be home in no time at all.'

He paused and sniffed the air for a moment and, when she did the same, Greta found that the smell of smoke from the oven had followed them. She looked at her brother questioningly, as if expecting him to say something, but instead he let go her hand and the two of them began to run over the thick carpet of pine needles towards the distant, but clearly visible, fringe of light that marked the end of the forest.

The ghosts of number eleven Lutherstrasse stood at her back. Frau Maier could sense their fingertips upon her shoulders, she could hear their soft voices murmuring in the shade behind her. She did not need to look round to discover who had come to visit her on her ninetieth birthday: her father, from faraway Tannenberg that now lay deep inside the heart of Poland, was present; so was her mother, who had climbed the cellar steps behind her and whose photograph now rested in the box in her lap; Wolfgang, who in life had abandoned her, was there, and so was Adolf, who had been buried somewhere beneath the city's ruins. The old lady tried to turn her head to catch a glimpse of her lost son, but it was not possible, she could only gaze ahead now towards the approaching shadows and be content with the whispers she could not quite decipher from those gathered at her back.

She sighed again and her breath, containing the molecules of all she had ever been, rose up into the chill, early evening air to mingle with the other gases, both natural and man-made, that enveloped the great city. Like the finest ash from an incinerator tower, her last exhalation hovered over Berlin, high above the urban plain with its illuminated houses and factories, its isolated, invisible lakes and woods, its roads and railways that now stretched unbroken both East and West, its millions of people.

Nor simply the breath of Greta Maier (née Sesemann, mother's maiden name Rosenberg) but, in this final moment, she felt herself borne up above the city she had loved and hated for eighty years. And though in the ice-cold darkness it was not possible to see the churches and places of government that had risen, burned, and risen again beneath her, she could hear, rising above the static and the rushing solar wind that threatened to tear her away from this brief anchorage, the sounds and voices of all that she had known: the shouts for Liebknecht and Luxembourg; the laughter of her mother; the chants for Goebbels, Goering and Hitler; her son's small voice; the crack of breaking glass; the cheers for the breaching of the Wall.

Looking down, she saw the long streams of candle-light from the demonstration weaving their way throughout the Berlin streets, crossing and recrossing the scar of the old Wall, binding, binding the old wounds together. And as she thought of her daughter, grandchildren and great-grandchildren holding up their small, flickering candles to the darkness, in defiance of those who had marched by torchlight beneath black and scarlet flags sixty years before, she was forced to notice the scent of wax, the inevitable smell of burning that, it seemed, like the past itself, like the thin trail of smoke from the witch's chimney that had followed Hans and herself from the depths of the forest, all the way home, could never be wholly extinguished.

103

Her last thought, though, before the great wind flung her out towards the distant stars, was of how her whole, extraordinary life had been spent trying to cling on to things, places and people that were forever slipping out of reach. And her last prayer was for the city beneath her, her great and forever growing family, that they might have the chance she had somehow been denied: to live happily ever after – *glücklich zu leben, bis an ihr seliges Ende*.

KARMIC MOTHERS – FACT OR FICTION?

Kate Atkinson

Kate Atkinson was born in York and has two daughters. After graduating from Dundee University and doing research she did all kinds of jobs, from being a home-help to teaching with the Community Education Service. In 1989, she won a short story competition in a women's magazine and has been writing stories for magazines on and off since. Recently she made the decision to give up the day-job and turn to writing full-time, hoping to surprise everybody by actually finishing her novel, *Behind the Scenes at the Museum*.

KARMIC MOTHERS – FACT
OR FICTION?

The choice of reading matter on the suicide ward was eclectic – Volume Four of the *Encyclopaedia Britannica* ('Delusion to Frenssen'), a copy of *Jackie*, a book called *Fact or Fiction?*, the Penguin edition of Chekhov's plays and a Hare Krishna book about reincarnation. Agnes dipped into them all at random.

She was particularly engaged by 'Liza's Dilemma' in the *Jackie* – would Liza realize that Matt Greene was just a chancer, despite his surfboard looks? Or would she recognize the good qualities of Robbie Davidson who was nice to his little sister and spent his Saturday afternoons playing football? Agnes suspected she would, but had no way of knowing as the *Jackie* was two years old. The book on reincarnation was considerably less confusing.

The ceiling of the suicide ward was a long way off when you lay flat on your back on the bed. It was just a room really, painted in apple-green gloss and ivory – Agnes liked the names of colours. The floor was covered in a speckled linoleum made from minced-up mushrooms and magnolia blossoms.

With an effort, Agnes lifted her head. Her chins concertina'd uncomfortably. She waved the book on reincarnation in the air. 'Did you know,' she said to Jeannie, lying on the bed opposite, 'that according to the Swami Prabhupada, you get the body of your choice?'

Jeannie snorted dismissively. 'I widnae have chosen mine.' (Agnes had to agree it did seem an unlikely theory.) Jeannie was the first Glaswegian that Agnes had ever met and she liked the way her voice was laced attractively with nicotine – it made everything Jeannie said sound emotional. Jeannie put the Chekhov down on her bedspread with a sigh (she'd run out of romances). 'I don't know about this Chekhov guy,' she said, shaking her head. 'They're an awfy miserable bunch of folk. I mean, I like a happy ending – you know? What kind of an ending is that – "If only we knew."?'

'It's the mysterious nature of the meaning of existence,' Agnes said, transferring a wad of gum from one side of her mouth to the other.

'That'll be right,' Jeannie said glumly. 'De youz wanna cuppa tea?' She swung herself off the bed and put her feet into a pair of powder-puff-blue, fluffy mules. In another life, Jeannie would have been a dancer – she had a dancer's legs, all muscle and tight, spare flesh, their shape distinct beneath her black nylon night-dress.

Agnes was Jeannie's counterbalance – plump like satin cushions, with rosy cherub skin and flesh like ripe apricots – Agnes weighed fourteen stone, one for every year of her life.

'No, ta – I've got juice,' Agnes replied, letting her head fall back down on the pillow with relief.

Agnes had been on the suicide ward for nearly two weeks now. There were two things that could be said in its favour – 1) It was better than school, and 2) It was better than home. It was nothing like the hospital afterlife she'd expected. She had imagined waking to the soft faces of concerned nurses and the terse, urgent conversations of doctors as they engaged in the dramatic struggle to bring her back to life. (There had actually been quite a lot of drama in the Accident and Emergency ward when Agnes was brought in, but she'd missed most of it because she was unconscious.) Nor was there any sign of the experienced, kindly psychiatrist she'd anticipated, an understanding man who would unravel the tangle of her life and give it back to her as a clean skein, free of snags. Or better still, explain that a terrible mistake had been made and she'd accidentally been given the life of Agnes Ballinger for the last fourteen years, when in fact she was really . . .

There were twenty-six and a half polystyrene tiles on the ceiling one way, eighteen the other, all painted – in bold defiance of Health and Safety regulations – in the apple-green gloss paint that, if there was a fire, would fall in great flaming, melting lumps on to Jeannie and Agnes, lying below on their salmon-pink cotton bedspreads and lily-white sheets. Agnes heaved herself up on to one elbow and searched in her locker. It smelled of old plywood and other people's things. With some difficulty she trawled a half-empty bag of liquorice allsorts from it.

The red-haired nurse flew in, looking for Jeannie. 'She's not away to the toilet, is she?' she asked, a wild look in her eye.

'The hair and nails continue to grow after death – fact or fiction?' Agnes quizzed her.

The red-haired nurse stopped to consider for a moment. 'Fact,' she said decisively.

'Fiction!' Agnes said triumphantly.

She offered the bag of liquorice allsorts to the red-haired nurse who chose one of the ones that are covered in little blue dots, the colour of heaven, before rushing out again. Mostly the red-haired nurse bustled – she was born bustling. Agnes imagined her bustling from the womb, tiny arms and legs angling furiously.

109

Jeannie and Agnes were the only patients on the suicide ward. This was due not to a shortage of suicides, but the relocation of the old suicide ward to the new hospital. Jeannie and Agnes remained, leftover suicides, in an old side ward of the maternity wing (the maternity department wasn't due to move for another month yet, although the occasional baby got sent on ahead by mistake). Agnes couldn't work out whether she and Jeannie had been left due to an administrative oversight or because they weren't regarded as true suicides. The suicide staff had, naturally, moved to the new hospital along with the suicides, so Agnes and Jeannie were looked after by midwives.

Agnes parked her gum on the side of her bedside locker and ate the rest of the liquorice allsorts quickly.

Jeannie came back carrying two thick, white mugs of tea. 'I brought youz wan anyway.' Agnes put the mug on the glass top of her locker, placing it carefully so that it would overlap the previous circle stain. She was building a pattern, like a slow Spirograph, of milk, orange squash, tea, Ribena, hot chocolate. No one even bothered to clean any more in their neglected little ward. 'I understand now how Gregor Samsa felt,' Agnes said to Jeannie.

'Who was he?'

'A giant insect.'

'Oh, aye – I've got a cousin like that.'

Jeannie thought it was jammy on the suicide ward for one reason – 1) It was better than prison. Jeannie was doing time in the local open prison for fraud. ('Life is an open prison,' Agnes said, comfortingly.) Jeannie didn't admit to being a suicide, she claimed that she'd been in the sewing room of the prison, pinning up a hem, when she'd laughed so much that she'd accidentally swallowed the pins and needles she was holding in her mouth. Now

110

the nurses were waiting for the pins and needles to 'pass' as they politely put it (hence the red-haired nurse's interest in Jeannie's toilet activities). Jeannie herself seemed blithely unconcerned about the whereabouts of so many sharp objects in the vulnerable interior of her body. Agnes was reminded of the martyrs of the early church, she thought of Jeannie as a kind of inside-out St Sebastian. It would account for the expression of dreadful anguish that convulsed her haggard good looks occasionally.

Agnes tried to re-enact the prison sewing room scenario, using the contents of a box of matches, but couldn't get it to work. They were allowed anything – matches, razors, nooses – further proof that no one took their suicides seriously.

Jeannie delicately peeled away the cellophane on a packet of Player's Number Six. They were allowed to smoke. They were allowed to lie on their beds all day, smoke, eat chocolate – do anything they wanted in fact. Nobody seemed to care. 'Regular holiday in here,' Jeannie said with a sigh of satisfaction and dragged so hard on her cigarette that her lips retracted, showing pointed yellow teeth, a shade somewhere between crocus and mustard on Agnes's private paint chart. Jeannie was forty but her teeth were older.

'Catgut is made from the guts of cats – fact or fiction?'

Thoughtfully, Jeannie removed a flake of tobacco from her lower lip. 'So,' she said, coming over and sitting on Agnes's bed and picking up the book on reincarnation, 'I could come back as a cat?'

'Correct. What about the catgut?'

'Fiction.'

'Correct.'

'That widnae be so bad, eh? Cats have an OK life. What would you come back as, wee Agnes?'

Agnes shrugged her shoulders. 'Anybody but me, really,' she said after some thought.

Jeannie stubbed out her cigarette in a bedpan. 'Come on, let's go look at the weans.'

The babies, or the 'weans' as Jeannie insisted on calling them in her foreign language, were next door.

There were twenty-two babies and two suicides (or accidents, depending on how you looked at it), creating a temporary imbalance between birth and death.

'Typical of the marginalization of rites of passage in our society,' Duncan, Agnes's boyfriend said earnestly, looking round and sniffing the heady cocktail of baby urine, cooked vegetables and disinfectant. 'How are you?'

'Did you bring the crisps?' Agnes asked, allowing him to peck at her cheek.

Agnes didn't know why Duncan wanted to be her boyfriend, and presumed he must like fat, clever girls, which wasn't really the kind of boy she wanted. She wanted someone who'd just climbed off a surfboard, but she occasionally let him run his hands over her flesh just to see his pot-holed face assume that weird, tranced look that boys got at times like that. And at least having Duncan as a boyfriend meant she had a visitor, bringing relief supplies and schoolwork and news of the unreal, outside world. And nicer than her mother, which wasn't difficult.

Agnes's mother – Vera – didn't come every day to the hospital because she was busy in other places, she had a 'little part-time job' and (really frightening this) she was a hospice visitor. Agnes imagined the chill of fear that must descend on the terminally ill when her mother's icy wings wafted over them. 'Pull yourself together,' she could hear her whispering in their dying ears.

112

Agnes knew that was what her mother said to the dying because it was what she had said to her, the accidentally suicidal child, when she'd discovered her. Agnes was just entering the peaceful passing-out stage (ignorant that this was a temporary lull before entering the triple-Technicolor ride on the rollercoaster from hell), lying on the burnt umber and caramel of the autumn leaves living-room carpet, when she saw Vera's legs, like cartoon legs, moving across the carpet, crunching underfoot Agnes's leftover pills that looked like sweets spewed up by a rainbow ('Rowntrees Of York Give Best In Value'). Agnes wondered what Vera told them in Accident and Emergency, 'My daughter's accidentally swallowed the entire contents of the medicine cabinet'? Yeah, that sounded like Vera.

Jeannie had a lot of visitors – the prison chaplain, the governor, the wardens, even a couple of fellow prisoners. They brought her sweets, flowers, cigarettes, magazines. They pulled up their visitors' chairs eagerly and chatted and threw back their heads and laughed. Jeannie's visitors always made a point of including Agnes in their get-togethers and Agnes began to think that prison didn't look like such a bad place at all and she wouldn't mind ending up there, because, 'After all,' she said to Duncan, indicating the suicide ward, the hospital, the town, the country, the planet and slightly beyond, 'if this is freedom, I'm not impressed.'

Agnes followed Jeannie on her rounds of the babies. Jeannie's already hoarse voice got all chokey when she saw the babies. She claimed to have 'twa weans' of her own, although their whereabouts was mysterious. There were two wards of mothers and babies. The babies all looked remarkably similar; swaddled in their white cellular-cotton blankets they seemed, Agnes thought, like cocoons, all waiting to turn into something.

They must look at the ceiling too, she realized, storing up their first shadowy memories of glossed polystyrene tiles, seventy-two one way, thirty-six the other (their ward was bigger). Agnes wanted to paint them a different ceiling, a celestial view of azure skies and golden, fiery-edged clouds.

The mothers, beached on their beds, weren't very interesting– plump and smug in their cotton nighties with frills and ribbons. They spent a lot of time putting on their make-up and talking about how 'orful' they looked and how they longed for a curry or a visit to the hairdresser. They made Agnes feel sick when they went on like that.

One of the mothers reminded Agnes of Vera – like Vera she thought she knew everything. She was called Dolly, which Agnes thought was a stupid name for a grown woman, and had permed hair, dyed a cough-drop yellow with coal-black roots. Her baby girl had much nicer hair, it was like sooty kitten fur and Agnes would have liked to touch it. Dolly was always knitting, she was knitting her baby's future in the colours of sugared almonds.

There was only one mother that Agnes liked, a girl called Mary with big, soft doe-eyes who was in love with her baby in a way that made the rest of the mothers uneasy.

The babies were nearly all being bottle-fed because the mothers felt breast-feeding was 'disgusting'. Jeannie explained this was because breasts were sexual objects, so it didn't seem right to stuff them into babies' mouths. Agnes looked down at her own large wobbling bosom which seemed to give such pleasure to Duncan. What were they like? Turkish Delight – a thin layer of pale milk-chocolate skin covering a solid, rosy jelly?

The babies were learning about time because the

mothers liked to feed them by the clock, reasoning that if they got fed when they were hungry they would become spoilt and demanding. (The generally held belief was that the babies were in a conspiracy against the mothers.) So the babies were left to scream until they were exhausted. The ceremonial feeding ritual was then rigidly adhered to. First they were fed, then they were winded, then they were changed, then they were laid down like little parcels and ignored. Agnes wondered what would happen if they got mixed up by mistake – what if, say, all the little baby parcels were put in a big bran tub – would the mothers be able to pick out the right one?

Agnes herself had been taken home from the maternity hospital by the wrong mother. Of this, if nothing else, she was certain. The Hare Krishna book said that people were given the mother they needed for a particular incarnation, but Agnes couldn't even bring herself to *think* about why she might need Vera. Somewhere, in the parallel universe where things went right, roamed Agnes's real mother, ladling out milk the colour of Cornish cream. Her real mother was a fierce, hot-breathed lioness padding around the hospital grounds. Her real mother was the Queen of the Night, a huge galactic figure who trod the Milky Way in search of her lost child. Her real mother had been one of the ones who dropped garnet-red blood on to linen-white snow and picked up shiny jet-black raven feathers and wished her heart out for the perfect baby girl and –

The little blonde midwife with mature acne stood at the door of the ward and shouted to Agnes, 'Your mum's here!' and two startled babies woke up and started crying. 'Bloody hell,' the mother of one muttered under her breath.

Vera! 'Mum' she was not. Centuries ago she had been

115

'Mummy' – Agnes had the diary entries to prove this: 'Mummy met me from school and we went and got my hair cut.' 'Mums' were what other children had, Agnes had Vera, so unlabelled as a mother, so lacking a maternal noun (mum, mummy, mother, mam, ma mama, mom) that Agnes was never able to address her directly.

'You've lost weight,' Vera said, sitting down cautiously on an orange vinyl armchair in the maternity ward day-room.

Agnes looked down doubtfully. She couldn't actually *see* her feet.

'You're skin and bone,' Vera said.

It was Vera that was skin and bone. Vera's arteries were flat grey electric cables, binding the skin and bone together. She was so thin that when she turned sideways she disappeared. 'You can come home soon,' she said.

'But I haven't had any treatment,' Agnes protested.

'There's nothing wrong with you.'

'I tried to kill myself,' Agnes pointed out.

'Don't exaggerate,' Vera said dismissively. Out of a plastic carrier bag she produced lemon barley water, salted peanuts and banana sandwiches made with sliced white bread. ('Sandwiches were named after the Earl of Sandwich – fact or fiction?' The book was unusally dismissive on the subject of sandwiches, 'It seems unlikely that no one before 1762 had thought of wrapping a couple of slices of bread around a piece of meat.')

'I have to go,' Vera said, getting up, 'I'm needed somewhere else.'

Jeannie put her head round the door, 'Time for Baby Bath Demonstration!'

Agnes had seen it all before, but it was something to do, so she went through to the maternity ward anyway and observed politely. After all, it might come in useful

116

one day, if she survived long enough to have babies. A baby started crying and someone identified it as Dolly's. 'What does the little bugger want?' Dolly asked no one in particular, her head wobbling rather like a budgerigar's. 'She's been fed, she's been changed. She hasn't got wind,' her voice became threatening, 'but she will have if she goes on like that.' Agnes looked daggers at the back of Dolly's nodding skull, thin silver stilettos that went – Thunk! Thunk! Thunk!

Everyone murmured their sympathy for Dolly. Why babies cried was a mystery, there was no doubt about *that*. The blonde midwife looked up from the soapy-wet baby she was demonstrating on and glared at Dolly's baby. 'It's having a temper tantrum,' she declared.

'You're going home tomorrow,' the red-haired nurse said to Agnes when she wheeled in the supper trolley.

Jeannie jumped off her bed, screeching, 'Aaw – al miss yew, hen!' and pulled Agnes to her scrawny bosom.

'Who says?' Agnes asked, pulling herself free.

'The gynaecologist,' the red-haired nurse said.

'I want to see a psychiatrist,' Agnes said reasonably.

'Wouldn't we all?' the red-haired nurse laughed and bustled out of the ward.

Agnes tiptoed into the nursery where the babies were kept at night. They were taken away from the ward like flowers, perhaps in case they used up all the mothers' oxygen ('fiction'). The babies were all sound asleep, their little mouths half open, their top lips puckered. Sleep rose off them like the vapour of a milky drug. ('Cats suck the breath from sleeping babies – fact or fiction?' Fact.)

Very carefully, Agnes lifted Mary's baby, cradling its head in her hand like the midwife had shown them in Baby Bath Demonstration. The peaceful rhythm of its breathing didn't change as she carried it across to the other side of the room and placed it gently in a spare cot. Then she took Dolly's baby and placed it in Mary's baby's cot. Then she took Mary's baby out of the spare cot and put it in Dolly's baby's cot. *Voilà!*

The reasoning behind this sleight of hand was logical – Mary's baby had already been given a good start in life, whereas Dolly's baby hadn't a chance in hell.

Agnes's father came the next day to take her home. She'd only reached 'Doge' in the encyclopaedia. Liza was left suspended in her dilemma forever. She had a tearful farewell with Jeannie, who kissed her wetly on the cheek and told her she was like 'wan of her ain weans'. Agnes missed the drama later in the day when the prison social worker visited Jeannie and told her, regretfully, that her ain weans had been taken away from her for good.

Agnes walked through the front door of the mock-Tudor semi. At the end of the hallway she could see into the kitchen where her mother was sipping a 'tiny sherry'. Vera turned and said, 'You're back then.' Agnes wondered if this was the real world. Agnes herself didn't feel at all real. She floated along the hallway, the house smelt of roast chicken. 'I'm cooking you a chicken,' she heard Vera say. Beyond her, the back door stood open and Agnes could see the garden – the neatly clipped lawns, the carefully controlled beds of pansies, busy lizzies and nasturtiums. Behind them was the vegetable patch, then the fruit bushes.

But further away was a wood and then a whole forest of birch trees. Agnes floated towards this landscape, buoyant with hope. The vista went on forever rolling on towards steppes, foothills, mountains – wherever it was, it looked a lot like home to Agnes. In an azure sky, fat cherubs bounced on white, woolly clouds. Vera shut the back door quickly. 'And a rice pudding,' she said. 'You like that, don't you?'

They found Jeannie in the hospital grounds the next morning – not such a fraud at all, it turned out. They discovered her hanging from an apple-green tree, one fluffy mule had fallen off and lay on the ground, the other somehow dangled precariously from one toe. Her unslippered toe pointed gracefully towards the ground, you could almost have imagined her in a mid-air jeté as she jumped off into another life.

Mary gazed at her baby, sound asleep in her cot. She picked her up and held her to her breast. The baby purred and smiled the smile of a very lucky baby.

'Look – she's smiling,' Mary said to the blonde mid-wife who'd just come in.

'Wind,' she replied dismissively.

Mary's real baby began to scream in her cot, noisily protesting at her new life. The red-haired nurse bustled in and picked it up. 'Why do they do that?' she asked the blonde midwife, a look of exasperation on her face.

'If only we knew,' the blonde midwife said, shaking her head, mystified. 'If only we knew.'

THE HOUSE WITH THE HORSE AND THE BLUE CANOE

Cheryl Nyland-Littig

Cheryl Nyland-Littig grew up in rural Minnesota. She was born in 1968 in Pennsylvania and has lived in Ireland, Texas, New York City and Oregon. She studied English and Women's Studies at the University of Minnesota. Nyland-Littig is active in the feminist and progressive movement as an organizer, writer and editor. Her fiction has received several awards, though the story that appears here is her first published.

THE HOUSE WITH THE HORSE
AND THE BLUE CANOE

Dan liked to tell us about the rats. He promised, in a jolly and threatening kind of way, to get his hands on a pair of good binoculars and then he'd show us. This is when we lived in the trailer on a low ridge overlooking the town of Chaska, Minnesota. Below us there was a pickle factory, and alongside it an enormous field of vats full of cucumbers, vinegar and, Dan said, rats. He knew because he'd worked there twice.

We had the best trailer, one on the edge of a whole spiralling ring of trailers. There was a patio where Dan sat with us and tried to hush us up long enough so rabbits would come out to sit in the weeds where we could see them. He made us memorize the capital cities of all the states in the entire nation. He'd say, 'Kentucky.' We'd yell, 'Frankfort!' Dan would think a good while, then, trying to catch us. 'Maine.' 'Augusta!' He stood us up and tried to show us things from the patio. The Minnesota river where it curved out of Chaska, coursing bravely away from the Mississippi. The high steeple of the Catholic church and school where he was made to go to mass every morning and had nuns for teachers who rapped him on the hands with rulers. He pointed out the other factories beyond the pickle factory. The sugar factory, the egg plant, and the plastics factory where my mother worked until she made a mistake and got her pinky finger burned and broken. After that my mother had both her pinky fingers broken. She would hold them together to show us. They jutted and bumped away from one another like carrots planted in rocky soil. The other finger was broken by my real dad when he got mad at her for baking a birthday cake for the guy who lived next door to us. I was four, but I remember. He dragged her around the kitchen and she got away from him – all but her pinky finger. He twisted it until it snapped. It sounded clean and painless like when you crack a chicken wing apart at the joint.

Dan was not our father, or anybody's father, though we loved him as one.

He was eight years younger than our mother. He had thick glossy hair that went down to his waist when we met him. At Hallowee'en he dyed it green and let it slowly fade out by Thanksgiving. Later, a year or two after he'd married my mother, he fell off a roof and hurt himself. They shaved all his hair off in the hospital because they thought his head was cut, though it ended up being just blood from where he'd touched it with his bloody hand. A nurse gathered it all together in a white string and set it on the hospital dresser in front of the television as if it were a bouquet.

Dan was a carpenter. He'd started at a new company after giving up on making it on his own. They gave him all the work that nobody else wanted to do because he was the newest guy. Jobs like sheetrocking and scraping glue off a floor and roof work in the winter. He slipped on ice and fell off the roof of a mansion three storeys high. The woman who owned the house found him huddled under a bush in front, mumbling and moaning, sucking on a gash in his hand. He'd crawled there from the place where he hit the ground, searching for shelter by pure instinct like an animal.

At the hospital we could see him two at a time. My

mother went in to see him first, pulling Joshua along with her nervously. When they came out my sister Leah and I were shuffled in. He was wrapped in white gauze across his middle. He had a neck brace on and a complicated sling came down from the ceiling, suspending him from the bed in several places.

Dan had a hard time staying awake. He said, 'Hey! What's your name?'

Leah and I stood on opposite sides of the bed. 'You know,' I said, drawing my words out, teasing. I touched his hand then, the one on my side of the bed. I touched it barely, with one finger. Dan was a hard-working man. His hands were thick and rough as tree bark. At night he cut the calluses off with a jack knife. But then, in the hospital, his hands looked sore and swollen. I thought if I held one the way I wanted to he might cry. 'I'm Stephanie.' I rested my small hand on top of the mountain of his knuckles then, delicate as a spider's web.

'Oh, right, right, Jesus, how are you? How the hell are you?' He wagged his head around, not focusing on either of us. 'Can I get a cigarette off you?'

Leah twirled her hair the way she did when she was nervous or bored. Dan tried to lift his head from the pillow but couldn't. He said, 'Oh boy.' His glasses were on the table beside me. One lens was missing, the other had a thin crack straight across it. He clenched his eyes shut and trumpeted out a little tune between pursed lips.

Leah said, 'We're here to see you, Dan. To see how you are.'

He opened his eyes then and stared at the ceiling. He didn't make a sound. What he did was let one of my fingers fall from his knuckles down in between two of his own and held it there.

*

125

All of this happened before we lived in the trailer. When Dan fell off the roof we lived in a two-storey farmhouse on highway 41 out of Chaska. Apart from the highway we were fairly secluded. There were woods and fields all around and a hill behind the house that went down to a muddy abandoned lake named Grace. There were seven colours of paint on the outside of the house, though you could only see two at a time when you stood in one spot. There was a long porch on the back with a cement floor and old-fashioned pictures painted right on the wall. Pictures of roosters and young women with assertive behinds and breasts and plump forearms holding baskets of brown eggs.

By the time we lived here – it was the late 1970s – it hadn't been a real farm for years. We had cats and dogs and one horse named Lady Highland Stonewall Jackson who we called Nancy for short. She drank her water from a blue canoe that we'd smashed when we used it as a toboggan the first winter we lived in the house. The blue canoe sat on the edge of her pasture, in plain view of the highway. When people asked where we lived, all we had to say was the house with the horse and the blue canoe and everyone knew exactly where we meant.

It was the first house Leah, Josh and I had lived in. Before that it was apartments. And once, when we still lived in Pennsylvania with our real dad, we lived in a boxcar that was converted into a house of sorts. It was in a whole row of boxcars parked in a field by the coal mine where our father and grandfather were working. This was when the mining jobs were getting slim, when we had to go on the road after such jobs. There was a huge structure at the end where we all ate and took showers, in shifts. Later, after we were long gone from there, my mother liked to make a big deal of us having lived in such a way. She called Joshua 'Boxcar Willy'.

She imitated the sound of a train whistle for us when she talked about that time of our lives. The miners with families lived on one end and the single men on the other end. Those men, the ones without families, drank after work without showering. They sat on their steps with mangy hair and spit and drank and smoked. They howled at my mother when she walked by, or cheered when she hung clothes on the line wearing her bathing suit. My mom would laugh and wave them away or scold them kindly.

So apart from the boxcar, this house – the house with the horse and the blue canoe – was the first for Leah, Joshua and me. We had a good deal in the way of rent because the place was so run down. Paint was splattered on the wood floors and there were garish brown stains on the walls and ceiling. The floorboard heat didn't work well enough to keep the dog's water from freezing into a thin layer of ice on the top.

Dan unhooked the heat altogether and made a gigantic wood stove by welding two metal barrels together. He set it up in the middle of the kitchen in a wooden sandbox. My mother macraméd hangings full of feathers and beads to put on the walls to cover the stains. Together they painted a mural on the ceiling of the living room. Dan did the golden lions and parrots and a rainbow lizard and my mother followed behind him, painting in the vines that twisted among them, the roses and thorns that sprouted up near the waterfall, snakes and bugs and lily pads. When it was finished it covered half the ceiling, rounding out from two corners. The five of us took turns standing on a step ladder to press our palms, full of yellow paint, into the place on top they left bare. Each of our handprints touched the next, forming a sun.

*

That is how it was for a brief time in our lives, when I was ten eleven twelve.

My mom and Dan bought two canoes – new ones to replace the one we'd wrecked. On Saturdays we'd canoe the Minnesota river. We bolted them together so we wouldn't tip over. We floated down the river, slow and wide as a pontoon. Dan knew the river, he'd grown up on that river. He called the names of the towns out to us as we floated by: Carver, Jordan, Belle Plaine. When we went far enough, we came to a place where there was a herd of cattle with no fence on the river side. Dan would shut the motor off then, or if we were paddling he'd tell us to stop and sit quietly. We'd let the river carry us down, sideways, backwards. My mother would take her sunglasses off. We'd look at the cows, they'd look back at us. The cows would lift their heads and stop chewing the way rich people do in movies when someone says something startling at dinner: mouths open, forks in mid-air. Dan whispered that these cows belonged to a very wealthy man who owned that side of the river for miles. We weren't allowed to stop there. The cows would watch us float away from them, craning their necks lazily. Joshua wondered why the cows didn't jump in the river and escape and Dan would ask, 'From what?'

Dan told stories of the river in a way that made me associate him with Tom Sawyer, only Dan's stories seemed even more legendary. Crowded with hair-brained boondoggery and high adventure of brushes with near fatality and permanent injury. Dan knew the old men who sat in lawn chairs at the landing in Chaska. Scooper Reint, Vick Yodel and Tag Weinert. They smoked cigars and held cold cans of baked beans and dipped potato chips in them to eat. When they saw Dan they'd pound on their arm rests and yell at him, 'How's Eddie! How's your old pops?' Eddie was dying of Alzheimer's disease before anyone knew what Alzheimer's disease was. At that time it was just an increasing knowledge that something was gravely wrong. Eddie forgot the names of grandchildren. He wet his pants because he couldn't find the bathroom in his house. Scooper, Vick and Tag weren't surprised. People began to cough at young ages, they lost hands and lungs and eyes. They died and nobody complained. When Dan said, 'Not good. The old man ain't good,' they were already nodding their heads, expecting as much.

Tag Weinert liked to show me his tattoos. He told me what he thought I'd look like when I was eighteen. 'A looker. A knock-out. A heartbreaker.' I had an image in my head of a large blonde woman, gleaming in a white puffy dress with cleavage and perfectly coy and curling lips. A woman who was in no way connected to me, but a woman whom I would magically become. He said he'd like to get his hands on me then. He told Dan to get a big stick because he'd have to beat them away. He advised Dan of the headache I'd become. Tag was the second person I knew who had been in jail. I supposed that's where he got his tattoos. I imagined that they sat around in their cells, rolling up the sleeves of their black-and-white-striped jail outfits, giving tattoos and talking about their hard luck.

I'd heard Dan's mother, Joy, tell my mother about Tag one afternoon in Joy's kitchen. (This being the way I learned just about everything during those years. I was young enough to pass for a child too dumb to understand, and old enough to know perfectly well what they were talking about without offering my opinions and giving myself away.)

It was a big scandal, having to do, of course, with

129

love, betrayal and a pretty woman named Lucy (who, without having to be told, I was sure had red hair and chewed her gum aggressively). Lucy worked the counter at the bakery in town. She was engaged to be married to the baker, Hal Barnes, but she fell in love with Tag instead. Back in love. They'd been high school sweethearts. Tag had joined the army and was sent to Korea. In his absence, Lucy had become engaged to Hal. When Tag came home he brought her a blue silk robe with a dragon embroidered on the back and her name stitched in white on the front. He drank coffee at the bakery just to see her. He left extra quarters on the counter when he left; and once, brave, he kissed her without warning.

Joy stopped there, significantly, 'Well we know how the story goes.'

She fell back in love with Tag and out of love with Hal. (I had come already to know that is how love was: this swaggering, swerving emotion that could change and change back again, outside of anyone's control.) Lucy was afraid to tell Hal. Something about his terrible temper. Something about how he once broke the collarbone of a man who got fresh with Lucy at an oven and appliances auction in Minneapolis. Joy spoke hushed, 'He may even have hit her.'

So it went on. Each day it became more pressing that Lucy tell Hal that she wasn't going to marry him and intended to marry Tag after all. By then everyone in Chaska knew except Hal and a few of his best buddies, 'the guys who drank at the Hilltop – Bud Jenkins, Davie Stewart, Ot Grenwold and the like,' Joy said by way of explanation.

'He's there when he finds out.' Joy said this like it was the worst part. 'At the Hilltop. The way I know is Eddie told me. He seen it all happen because Wert's was

130

closed down, something wrong with the taps, so he and the guys went to Hilltop instead.'

Someone joked with Hal about it. Said some wise comment about Lucy working a double shift. 'A brick wall falls on his head.' Joy smacked her forehead with the heel of her hand to demonstrate. Hal put it all together. Tag hanging out at the bakery, the way Lucy had been acting. 'So what he does is starts slugging 'em down. Tells Billy to line 'em up and he slugs them down and the guys are yelling go go except for good old Ot who's trying to talk some sense into his head.' Joy leaned towards my mother and said, 'There ain't no doing that, talking sense to a jealous man.'

Joy's face was flushed and smiling like she was telling a good long joke. 'He gets so drunk that he can barely walk. Eddie always says the Lord only knows how he was able to drive his truck from that bar to Lucy's house, but he did, and he was a-pounding away on that door! Sure enough, there's Lucy inside, crying and yelling at him to go home, clutching on to Tag's arm so he won't go out and get killed by Hal.'

Tag shook her off and went out anyway. It was winter, bone cold, but he didn't put a coat on. Hal wasn't wearing one either. They stood in the walkway in T-shirts. Lucy watched them, on her tiptoes, peeking through the diamond-shaped window in the door. Hal swung a few punches at Tag, missed him for the most part. Tag hit Hal square in the face, then in the gut, and took his face and shoved it into the snow. Hal rolled over to look at Tag, but didn't get up. Tag walked back towards the house. Before going inside he turned and yelled, 'Go home!'

'But he doesn't go.' Joy pressed her hands to her face and stretched the loose wrinkles back from her eyes, making her look younger for a moment. 'He stays right

131

there. Lucy starts feeling bad and talks to him a bit through a window. He doesn't say a word. He stays and stays and stays until finally the cops come by and pick him up.'

It had been a while by then. A good while, maybe two hours, more. They took him straight to the hospital where they chopped off two of his fingers and all of the toes on one foot for frostbite. 'That's why Tag went to jail.' Joy pointed her finger and tapped it hard on the table. 'Assault or battery. Nineteen months.'

What happened to Lucy? She married Tag, quietly in a jail ceremony. She knitted him sweaters, baked him cookies, held hands with him across the table as the guard watched. 'Bad fortune looked upon that girl,' Joy pronounced. 'It wasn't a year that Tag was out before she died in a car wreck.' Joy paused for a moment, then brightened up. 'But now, Hal, he did fine. Married a real nice girl, Evie Polasky.' And that, to Joy, was the end of the story.

But jail. That's what I was most interested in. That's where Tag Weinert went. Jail for making a guy freeze his toes and fingers off. There was a time when I'd believed that in my whole life I'd never know anyone who went to jail. Criminals. But by then, by the age of eleven, I'd already met two. Tag and Dan's brother, Joe, who went in and out of jail for things I only caught whispers of. Stealing a garbage truck, selling marijuana, driving drunk.

They went to the Carver County jail. I knew what it looked like on the inside because in third grade my class had taken a trip there. The warden gave us a lecture first. He made us count off. Thirty-eight of us. He stood a few minutes, breathing in his tight brown uniform, doing the math. 'OK. If we're going to go by the statistics, oh about six of you will serve time in a correctional institution at some point in your lives.' He paused to look intently around the room. Hair rose on the back of my neck, terrified he might point me out as one of the future criminals. He stood with his legs wide apart, like a football coach, and his hands folded in front of him. He continued, 'Now that does not mean that you can't beat the statistics. It's your choice. Do you want to grow up to be worthy citizens?' We were silent, aghast, sweating. I had a fear of containment. Prison, or accidentally becoming a nun, an unfounded fear since I'd only attended church a few times in my entire short life.

'Ask yourself that question, boys and girls – girls too. Girls are a growing prison population, just a reality of the times.' He crossed his arms on his chest. 'Ask yourself if you want to be a good citizen. Let's go take a look at the alternative.' He led us down a narrow beige corridor, his club and gun wagging along against his hips. He told us to line up single file to walk through one of the cells. It was clean, unoccupied; with two thin bunk beds and a toilet perched white and long as a tulip in the corner. When I walked by the toilet I saw a single cigarette butt floating in the water and felt sure someone horrendous had smoked it. There was a window in each cell where the wall met the ceiling. It was thick as a block of ice and the only thing that could be seen through it were streams of colour and light: not really a window at all.

Dan never went to jail, though I feared he would. I saw him siphon gas from cars in parking lots. I knew that he stole a case of Polish sausages from a place where he used to work. Once he pulled our van up behind a closed gas station and grabbed two tyres off a pile and threw them in the back. He never got caught. My real father almost went to jail for strangling my mother nearly to death, but at the last moment she decided

133

not to press charges. When I brought it up, my mother scolded me. She scolded me in a kind of way that let me know that it was for my own good not to discuss such things. My mother liked to let bygones be bygones. Let lying dogs rest. Bury the hatchet.

My real father never hurt us, Leah, Joshua and me.

Except for once when Leah flunked first grade and he hit her in the chin with a wrench and she bled all over the carpet in our bedroom until our mother came home and took her to the emergency room for stitches. And a few other times, I suppose. Mostly when we got in the way of some fight between them, or later stepped on a piece of glass that had been broken during one of those fights.

My mother and Dan did not fight in that way, did not fight at all beyond an occasional argument. The first time I saw Dan he was holding Joshua upside down by his ankles, shaking him, as if Josh had some money in his pockets that he was after. He had come to have dinner, to meet us. We lived in a complex of apartments especially for single women and their children. The apartments were small. There was nowhere to put the kitchen table, so my mother cut the legs off and set it in the middle of the apartment. We had to sit on the carpet, our legs folded under us, to eat. This is how we ate, the five of us, on that first night together.

There were no pets allowed, but we had a bird anyway. His name was Canary and he got to fly free through the apartment. In the middle of dinner Canary landed on top of Dan's head and stayed there. We laughed so hard that we couldn't eat. Dan looked innocently at each of us. He asked, 'What? What's so funny?' as if he didn't know a yellow bird were perched on his head.

A few months later, again in our apartment, Dan

134

asked us if we wanted to find a house to live in with him. Our mother was not in the room. We loved Dan desperately. He said, 'Your mom said to ask you kids.' He reached for a magazine from the table. 'How about it?' He began to page through the magazine as if he were relaxed and distracted, as if our answer were nothing to him.

Dan was twenty-five. I thought of him as old. He had an enormous sharp German nose and bright blue eyes; eyes like our mother, only more muted. He was the best man I'd ever met. Joshua began to hop and sing a song. 'Yes, yes, yes.' Leah looked at me. She was three years older, but by then she had stopped being the one to speak for us. I said, 'That would be nice.'

Dan was holding that magazine. He looked up at me. 'Good. That's what we'll do then.' What I remember is that his hands were shaking.

So that is how we came to live in the house with the horse and the blue canoe. My mother and Dan married there, down the hill, under a willow tree beside the lake named Grace. Then my mother's pinky finger got burned and broken and Dan fell off a roof. Bad things happen in threes, that's what my mom always said, so when we were evicted from the house nobody was surprised.

The landlord came one day. His name was Lyle Sweet. Mr Sweet. He was the only person I'd called Mr anybody except for my teachers. He had thick dark hair with a wide chunk of grey in the front that made him look as if someone had swiped him by accident with a brush full of silver paint. When I was near him I was constantly on the verge of reaching out to touch it. He wore baggy polyester pants and a button-up shirt with a tie that he loosened the moment he was in our presence.

135

Dan said, 'It's not that you won't get your money. It's just that I got hurt.' Dan was sitting in a chair in the kitchen. He had spent the last few months sleeping in a special bed from the hospital that we rented and set up in the living room. He was wearing a white cloth brace around his middle on the outside of his T-shirt. We called it his corset. When his back wasn't hurting too much, he pulled it tight and posed for us like Scarlett O'Hara. He continued, 'I'll be back to work soon. I've got this money coming to me as soon as we get the suit settled.' He paused. There were troubles. The company wouldn't pay the worker's compensation. His voice took on a quieter, ashamed, more reasoning tone. 'We can give you . . .'

Mr Sweet wouldn't let him finish. 'Look, it's nothing personal. You tell me this story like it's personal.' He scratched behind his ear where he kept a green pen. 'I'm sorry. I know what you're going through.'

My mother was washing dishes. She turned to him and raised her voice, 'Oh you're real sorry, you're so . . .'

'Don't give me this crap! The point of it is it don't matter to me *why* you can't pay the God-damned rent.' His face turned redder as he spoke. 'It don't matter *when* you can pay it. It matters if you got the cash now. What I wanna know is are you gonna hand me seven hundred and fifty bucks across this table right now?'

My mother reached into her pocket and threw a wad of bills on the table in front of Dan. She reached in her other pocket and slammed some coins down. Dan gently counted the money. He held it, slowly arranging it into a neat stack. 'Two hundred and seventeen.'

'That's not going to answer my question now, is it, Mr and Mrs Echt? That's just not going to do it, is it?'

'I guess not,' Dan said. My mother stood next to him with a wooden spoon in her hand, ready.

Mr Sweet took a sip of the apple cider my mother had given him and set it down on the nearest counter. He looked at my mother and Dan. 'My hands are tied.' He pressed his wrists together and held them up. 'What do you expect me to do?'

Neither of them looked at him.

Now louder, gaining steam, more exasperated, he yelled, 'My hands are tied!' Pushing his wrists closer to Dan and my mother he asked again, 'What I wanna know is what you people expect me to do.'

My mother turned and went to the sink. She plunged her hands back into the cooling water and began to wash the remaining dishes. Dan stared at the table. Mr Sweet stood shaking his head for a moment. He grabbed the stack of bills sitting in front of Dan, counted it and put it in his pocket. He snapped his fingers. 'I'll take this against your balance due and send you a bill for the rest.'

Dan stood up slowly, using the table to help him. He looked about to say something, but didn't. Mr Sweet cleared his throat and said, "Bye, then. Luck to you.' He tightened his tie as he walked towards the door.

We moved into the trailer then. In the trailer perched over the town of Chaska. Over the Minnesota river way off in the distance, over the sugar factory, the egg plant and the plastics factory where my mother's pinky finger got burned and broken, over the pickle factory and the rows of vats full of vinegar and cucumbers and, Dan said, rats.

Dan couldn't work a job because of his broken back. While my mother was at work and we were at school he cleaned the trailer and cooked dinner. He sat on the patio and carved little wooden people out of scrap

137

wood. He made an entire tiny village – a man pulling a sled, a grandmother with her hands on her broad hips, a child bent to gather a snowball. We already had a miniature log cabin we put out each Christmas and, slowly, Dan filled it up. Each week the scene became more complex. There were teacups as small as tacks and warm yellow lanterns balanced on the mantel. He made an outhouse with a slice of the moon on the door and a man inside who sat permanently with his pants down and a bewildered expression on his face. He painted the figures too – the men had burly red and green flannel shirts and the women wore rich blue skirts with maybe a pattern of tiny white flowers on the hem.

That is how it was for a brief time in our lives, when I was ten eleven twelve.

We would sled on a hill a little ways from the trailer. We poured into the trailer, wet and cold and flushed. It was in December, near Christmas. Dan brought a tree in and we set up the tiny village and the log cabin beneath it. We gathered around cradling cups of hot cocoa and pretended we lived in the log cabin. My mother made us fantastic promises. She told us that we would live in an enormous house with a swimming pool in the middle and a horse for each of us to go around on. Dan's hair was still short from being shaved in the hospital, but growing. He told jokes, made faces, tickled us, kissed our mother.

It was dusk, but we let the house grow dark around us. My mother sang. She sang Christmas carols, right through her untrained voice. *Oh Tannenbaum.* Any song she could think of that had a tree in it. We decorated the tree with years of ornaments, hours of popcorn and cranberry strung the days before. Dan gave us each a gift: the last ornaments, made by him. There was one for each of us, wooden, with our names carved in the back. A Santa. A candle. Two angels and a reindeer. We each stepped forward, taking our time to hang that last one, then stepped back. We sat, spread out around the tree, hushed. My mother switched the strings of lights on and it was how it always is.

Magnificent.

Our faces glowed like gentle unformed stars. We believed then, at that moment, believed fully that things would only get better and better for the rest of our lives.

THE WEE MAN

Lorraine Lorimer

Lorraine Lorimer was born in Kilmarnock in 1962. A self-employed optician, she now lives in Northamptonshire with her husband and two young sons. She began writing last year, encouraged by her creative writing class tutor. This is the first work she has produced.

THE WEE MAN

Silver splinters of April rain peppered my face, stinging my cheeks until they felt raw and numb. I ran through it, up the hill to the top of the village, pressing my left side where the first stab of pain from exhaustion burrowed into my flesh. Sucking in the cold air, my lungs filled with the musky damp odour of my duffel coat.

At the top of the hill, through a streaky curtain of water, I could see Dr MacKay's three-storey surgery, with its pebble-dashed walls and entrance porch hung with ivy. It stood like a sentinel at the highest point of the village, pockets of light spilling from its numerous sash windows. I quickened my pace, the muscles in my legs tightening as they met the upward curve of pavement beneath them. Jumping the three steps to the surgery's porch in one leap, I half slid across its tiled floor and into a large entrance hall, with a partitioned reception bay to the left of the wide staircase. The wet day dripped from shoelace strands of my hair as I crossed the hall to the reception.

'I have to see Dr Mac,' I panted to a middle-aged lady who inspected me through a sliding glass window in the partition wall.

'The doctor is with a patient,' she said, opening an appointment book in front of her. 'If you take a seat in the waiting room I'll fit you in when I can.'

I swung round to the open double doors of the room

143

she had indicated. Every seat was occupied, other coughing bodies were stacked against the walls and children were huddled in a corner emptying a toy box.

'It's an emergency,' I said, turning back to her. I could feel myself perspiring as the warmth of the building suddenly hit me.

The receptionist's lopsided pink National Health Service spectacles hooked over the narrow bridge of her nose, rising above one eyebrow and dipping below the other. She jerked her head to peer at me again, then spoke, her shrill voice passing through narrow lips. 'It's an emergency for many of those people too.' She gestured to the waiting room, dismissing me. The bulging room wheezed and spilled part of its contents into the hall. My eyes travelled from the room to the stairs, at the top of which was Dr MacKay's consulting room. Giving the receptionist a parting glance, I darted to the stairs, scaling them two at a time.

'You can't go up there,' she yelped from behind me.

At the top of the stairs, I burst through a wooden panelled door into a square room with a black examination couch along a whitewashed wall, and a heavy oak desk under the window. Dr MacKay was listening to a baby's chest through his stethoscope and the baby obligingly gave a cough. He and the baby's mother turned towards me, annoyed by the intrusion.

'Inez!' scowled Dr MacKay. 'Never burst into this room uninvited.' Raising his short, portly body out of his chair, he stepped towards me.

'My mother sent me,' I puffed. At five feet, six inches tall I was the same height as Dr MacKay and was often mistaken for being older than my thirteen years. 'You've tae come right away. The wee man's bad.'

A sweet antiseptic odour filled my lungs, like a rush of opiate and, for a moment, as I inhaled it, the room

144

rounded like the view from a fish-eye and Dr MacKay's voice wound down like the slowing revolutions of a gramophone record. Exhaustion claimed my body and I reached for the side of the examination couch to steady my juddering legs.

'I've a surgery full of patients to see, Inez,' he growled, pointing a short, fat hand at the hallway.

The thud of heavy footsteps told me the receptionist had reached the top of the stairs, and she lumbered through the door behind me.

'I'm sorry, Doctor,' she said, taking hold of my arm with the grip of a mountaineer.

Defiance etched itself on to my face, tightening my lips and narrowing my eyes. 'I've not to leave here till you say you'll come.'

Dr MacKay pushed open his jacket and planted his hands on what must once have been his waist, his arms sticking out like the handles of a toby jug, his stethoscope curving over his rounded belly like a sleeping snake on a mound. 'What are his symptoms?' he sighed.

'We've all had the 'flu, but the wee man's taken it worse.'

Hooking his right thumb behind the braces that held his trousers over his stomach, he frowned, gave a quiet snort, then abruptly turned and sat down at his desk. He picked up a pen, scribbled hastily on a prescription pad, then tore off the sheet of paper and handed it to the woman who was still seated holding her baby. With a cursory glance at the three of us, she crumpled the prescription into her coat pocket, draped the baby over her arm, and strode out of the room.

'Go home,' said Dr MacKay, rounding into his swivel chair. 'Tell your mother to expect me.'

I nodded, shrugged my arm free from the receptionist's grip and left the room.

Outside the downpour had quelled to a drizzle. Night was spreading its shadow across the evening sky and I thought how like sparklers on bonfire night the car lights looked through the rain-washed windows of the entrance porch. Stepping into the Ayrshire wetness, I felt the muted tap of water droplets hitting my duffel coat hood as they slithered from the variegated ivy that wreathed the porch.

As I looked downward from the surgery, the village spread before me, bisected by a road leading westwards to the coastal town of Ayr, and eastwards to the industrial town of Kilmarnock. Slow-moving cars sliced through patches of puddles, throwing spray on to the legs of pedestrians who looked like moving mushrooms under the concealment of dull umbrellas. In the hollow at the centre of the village, surrounded by a bracelet of shops, the disused town house, belonging to the village forefathers, raised its stone body from a plinth of steps. The tall, angular building with its jut of steeple had, long ago, been used as a meeting place for the council members and as a jail. The jougs to which offenders had been shackled still hung on one of its plain stone walls. The building was known locally as 'the Jougs' and it was the only historic curiosity the village possessed. A mile away, beyond a cluster of houses, the kirk spire rose from amidst a sway of cedars.

We had lived in this part of Scotland for generations. My ancestors had worked at local fishing ports or surrounding farms and, more recently, in Kilmarnock – at the Johnnie Walker whisky-blending and bottling plant or Massey Ferguson's combine harvester plant. In 1970 my father was the village minister and my mother worked from home for a gent's tailor. There were six of us in our family. Two adults, four children. We lived

146

in the manse, to the right of the kirk, behind a thicket of beech.

Thrusting my hands deep into my coat pockets, I descended the hill to the village centre, skirting past the site entrance to the new housing development where dollops of mud deposited by yellow earth-movers were collapsing into sludge, like mounds of melting brown ice. The shops were already closed, the last of the pedestrians huddling under the Plexiglas roof of a bus shelter. As the footpath became level with the Jougs and curved towards it, a feeling of dread swept over me. Slouching against its gable-end were my classmates, Ross Curren and Jim Gallagher.

Ross was leaning against the wall with one leg bent at the knee, his foot flat against the stone and his shoulders raised level with his chin. He held a lighted cigarette between his thumb and middle finger, brought it to his mouth and dragged deeply on it, the smoke escaping in a pair of tubular clouds from his nostrils. He flicked the underside of the cigarette with his fourth finger, stabbed its smouldering end on to Jim's hand and crowed with laughter as Jim jerked his hand away.

Nearing them was an elderly lady in a clear plastic rainhat, wheeling a navy shopping trolley behind her. I heard the cackle of their laughter as she approached, the words they threw at her masked by the slush of the 18.10 bus to Ayr as it sliced the flood of water in the bus bay and stopped to collect its waiting passengers. The laughter died when Ross saw me. The foot that had been leaning against the wall moved to the pavement and he stepped forward, peering into the murky rain. I felt my stomach knot and hoped my face was obscured by my coat hood.

'They let you out of the asylum then, Inez?' shouted Ross as he flicked the cigarette butt into the gutter where it sailed towards the storm drain, circled once around the grate then plunged inside.

I pulled my coat hood further over my head and counted the lines of paving slabs ahead of me.

'You deaf or just too thick to understand?' He was moving, walking parallel with me on the opposite side of the road. I glanced around for a means of escape, my legs suddenly becoming heavy and the evening menacing as it reached the interval where day is over and night has yet to claim the sky.

Ross wrapped an arm around a lamppost and stopped walking. The rain shimmering through its light settled on his outline. 'When you gonna bring your loony brother out again?' he shouted.

The echo of their laughter followed me until the road swung a slow curve to the right, and the lights in the windows of the manse welcomed me home.

Dr MacKay's blue Ford Cortina was parked under the shelter of a lime tree, at the entrance gate to the manse. I walked to the side door of the Georgian-style house, stepping over a family of six-inch-long black slugs congregating on the wet paving slabs, and passed the terracotta plant pots stacked haphazardly against the wall. The warmth of the kitchen enveloped me and I was pleased to close the door on the wet night outside.

The smell of a ham bone simmering on the stove permeated the air, and on the oak table, in the centre of the room, a selection of root vegetables were grouped beside a Tupperware bowl of lentils soaking in water. I peeled off my duffel coat, took a towel from a drawer and entered the living room. Stretched out on the sofa with his head buried in a Superhero comic was my ten-year-old brother, Davy, his mop of blond hair visible above its cover. Laura, my seven-year-old sister, sat in front of a blazing fire threading a green ribbon through her long, sandy hair.

In the corner of the room, the sewing machine stood idle. On the floor beneath its table was a yellow basket containing a pile of men's tweed jacket sleeves. They hadn't been touched since my mother had placed them there that morning, and I knew we would hear the purr of the machine into the night as she ran a seam from the cuff to the underarm of each sleeve. The work was a distraction to her. It concentrated her mind on the banal and erected a barrier to contemplation of the insurmountable problem she had been given. To the left of the sewing machine was the ironing board, my father's black, ministerial robe draped, half pressed, over its rounded end.

I hung my coat on the back of a chair and placed it near the fire to dry, then listened to the sound of muffled voices filtering through the open door to the hallway.

'How long has Dr MacKay been here?' I asked Davy, as I rubbed my shoulder-length hair between the towel.

'About five minutes,' Laura answered. Davy didn't look up but turned the pages of his comic and scanned the drawings.

After placing the damp towel with my coat, I walked across the room, picked up the hot iron and finished pressing my father's robe. Touching the iron to a shirt, I continued the chore, listening for movement upstairs.

I was folding Laura's pinafore when my parents and Dr MacKay entered the room. Davy slid from the sofa to the floor and sat with his legs crossed, his open comic lining their crib-like shape. My mother sat on the edge of the sofa, her red hair piled loosely on top of her head with no attention to style. She wore a pair of washed-out jeans and my father's Fair Isle sweater that sagged over her narrow shoulders and gathered at her elbows where

149

she had pushed up the sleeves. Her bare feet were thrust into tan moccasins and she sat forward, her right elbow placed on her knee, her long, thin fingers spanning the side of her face, gently stroking her temple. The fingers of her other hand encircled her wrist and her eyes rested on Dr MacKay sitting opposite her in the only armchair in the room.

My father was dressed in black trousers, grey shirt and white dog-collar. He leant his six-foot, four-inch frame against the wall by the side of the fire. His dark eyes, set beneath thick, wiry black hair, jetted with grey, focused on my mother's face until he picked up the brass tongs that hung beside the grate and added a piece of coal to the fire.

Dr MacKay sat forward, his stomach sagging between his open legs. 'He's over the worst,' he said.

My mother nodded, her eyes blinking heavily. The sound of coughing drifted along the hall and she turned towards the door, listening, the palms of her hands resting on the sofa ready to push herself upright.

'I'll check him,' I said, placing the iron on its base and moving quickly out of the room.

'He's a dreadful worry to you . . .' said Dr MacKay as I crossed the narrow hall and climbed the stairs. If my mother answered I didn't hear her.

A light glowed dimly beside the wee man's bed, casting fuzzy shadows on to the rounded contours of his face. He felt the weight of my body sink into the mattress beside him, opened sleepy eyelids for a moment and faintly smiled. I watched him as he drifted in and out of sleep. His eyes – that could be vacant one moment and smiling the next – were closed, their movement perceptible through translucent lids. His lips – that often drooped open allowing a trickle of saliva to escape and dribble over his chin – parted slightly, allowing the exit

150

of rhythmic breath. Seeing him lying there, his head cupped in the pillow, no one would have known he wasn't a normal little boy – wee Craig, our wee man.

At five years old he was small for his age. He had the physical appearance of a three-year-old child and the mental ability of a six-month-old baby. When my mother began her daily work at the sewing machine she would sit Craig on the floor beside her, surrounded with toys. He had never reached for any of them. Instead, he would watch her, silently rocking himself back and forth. The rocking would stop when she momentarily left the room, his eyes fixing on the door that had taken her. When she returned, the rocking would begin again.

I traced a finger across his forehead, smoothing his hair into a tidy fringe, and wondered just how much he was aware of. Did he sense the heartache and the joy each minute achievement created? Did he look at other children and wonder 'Why me'? I straightened his bedclothes and lightly kissed his cheeks then turned towards the door and left the room.

No one had moved when I re-entered the living room. My mother looked frail, her body sinking deep into the sofa, her face a canvas for the dancing yellow light of the fire. She stared into its flames, unblinking. Her silence creating the discomforting quiet everyone wants to fill.

'There are places that will take him,' said Dr MacKay, as he opened his domiciliary bag and pulled out a prescription pad. 'He would be looked after by qualified people and . . .'

'Under no circumstances.' My mother had turned her face towards him. Her eyes, that had been bright in the fire's glow, were now hooded by a shadow that settled on her face.

'It isn't going to get any easier,' Dr MacKay

continued, pressing his hand against his jacket for the outline of a pen. 'You'll be dealing with the body of a young man.'

The fire gave a crackle and spat a hot ember on to the tile hearth. Little flares of embers were sucked upwards into the blackness of the chimney.

'If he's put somewhere now he'll think of it as his home, the people around him as his family,' said Dr MacKay.

My mother sat forward, lifted a cushion and hugged it to her body, picking unconsciously at its worn frill of lace.

'You need to accept it and get on with your life,' he said.

Suddenly she was standing, her tall slender body silhouetted by an enormous shadow that cast itself the full length of the wall and on to the ceiling. 'What would you know of it?' she said, each word sizzling from her tongue. 'You sit here making sympathetic noises, regurgitating advice you've read from a book. When you walk out of here you can forget the whole bothersome episode.'

'I was only trying to . . .'

'Well don't. You're not involved. You can't understand.'

'Fiona!' shouted my father.

'Don't say a word,' she snapped, raising her hand in emphasis. 'Dr MacKay, just go.' Her voice was barely audible. 'Thank you for coming.' She sat down on the sofa, her gaze returning to the fire that licked at the coal and smouldered the wood in shared cremation.

Dr MacKay drew on his overcoat and fastened its buttons. Snapping closed his domiciliary case, he picked it up, handed the scrawled prescription to my father and left the room. When a car coughed into life outside, I parted two slats of venetian blinds and watched the Cortina pull away from the kerb, into the falling rain.

Silence dominated the room. Davy's comic drooped from his hands, his round, blue eyes stared upwards at my mother. Laura twisted her green ribbon around the fingers of her dimpled hands and bit the corner of her mouth, as she often did when something upset her. My mother sat forward on the sofa, her arms crossed around her body, her eyes veiled in shadow.

'I have to go out,' said my father, in a voice that seemed too loud above the silence. 'I have a meeting with the church elders.' His dark eyebrows were drawn into a frown that formed a cleft between them. As his large hand reached for the door handle he paused and looked back towards my mother. 'Don't do anything foolish while I'm gone.'

My mother sighed, shaking her head in the barest of movements. Her arms fell limply to her sides then she stood, turned away from him and passed through the door to the kitchen. The front door clicked as my father closed it behind him and silence curled around the hearth again, punctuated by the occasional crackle of the fire and the rain, as it played its beat against the window-pane.

In the kitchen she was drenched in harsh fluorescent light that seeped into her skin. She stood at the oak table grating carrots into a large soup-pot, the orangy root leaving its colour in the creases of her fingers. Looking up, she smiled when I entered the room. I picked up the empty kettle and held it under the tap, the blast of water against metal masking the scrape of carrot against grater. Placing the kettle on the stove, I lit the gas, then turned towards my mother.

'Is Craig going to be all right?' I asked.

She nodded and pushed a strand of hair from her face

with the back of her hand. 'Dr MacKay has given him some antibiotics. He can't fight infection the way we can.'

With a clatter, the grater fell from her hand on to the tiled floor. She sucked a rush of air across clenched teeth and moved to the sink, clutching her finger in the palm of her other hand. Turning on the cold tap she placed her finger under the pencil of water. A mingle of blood and water trickled from her hand and swirled around the sink. The kettle whistled and spat a globule on to the stove. It sizzled and moved like a droplet of mercury. I switched off the gas, poured the steaming liquid into the teapot and placed it on the table with two cups. My mother wrapped her hand in a tea towel and sat in a chair beside me. Strands of hair fell around her bare neck, settling on her shoulders and her face relaxed into a smile.

'I do that every time,' she said, stirring a teaspoon of sugar into her cup, creating a whirlpool of rotating liquid. Abruptly, she changed the direction of the spoon and ended the flow.

'Would you ever send Craig away?' I asked, noticing the smile fade from her face, the blue-white skin around her eyes tighten and faint lines fan outwards. She unwound the tea towel from her freckled hand before answering, in her usual steady voice.

'All four of you are part of me, like the fingers of my hand. I could no more send Craig away than I could cut off my own finger.' She paused, turning the teaspoon in her hands. 'When Craig was born I thought I was the luckiest woman alive. I had more attention than with any of my previous babies.' The spoon rested in the saucer with a click. 'On the day we were leaving, the entire ward staff came to say goodbye. One midwife pressed my hand between hers and said, "Good luck."'

She held the brim of her cup to her mouth, letting the steam condense on her smooth cheeks. 'I realize now that they all knew. None of them had the heart to tell me. It was six weeks later when I questioned the doctor. Six weeks of spoon-feeding him milk because he couldn't suck. Six weeks in which I'd never heard him cry.'

Her voice was fragmented by a faint quiver and she sipped her tea, blowing into her cup before she did so. When she spoke again the quiver was gone. 'We saw all the top people. One specialist told me, "You don't understand what you've got. There's no operation, no cure. Your son is a cabbage. Do not have any more children."'

Standing up, she walked to the sink where she turned on the hot tap to fill the basin with water. From under the sink she selected several large potatoes and dropped them into the basin. Slowly the vapour rose, coating the window, blotting out her reflection in the blackened glass.

'You're completely on your own with a handicapped child,' she said. 'No one is really interested in helping you because they cannot appreciate the difficulties.'

I picked up the grater and the remains of the carrot that had been discarded when she cut herself and shredded it against the jagged metal. 'I want to help,' I said.

Stretching a hand towards me she touched my face. It felt wet and warm from the water. 'You do help, Inez,' she said. 'Sometimes I wonder how I'd cope without you.'

There were no more words that night. Each of us withdrew into the confines of our own thoughts. I wanted to take away her hurt, bargain with hell if Craig could be a normal little boy. Then everything would be as it was before he came – my father embracing my mother when we weren't supposed to see, gathering the hair from around her neck and brushing her skin with his lips. But that was when they used to touch, when they could simply look at one another and laugh.

The following day the sun and moon hung in the same clear blue sky looking down on the last veneer of winter frost that made the paths so treacherous and kept the elderly indoors. Laura and I walked around the pools of black ice paving our route from school, past the half-dozen ornamental cherries with their pink blossom tumbling like a mane to touch the lily of the valley that scattered, like pearls from a broken necklace, across a coverlet of green. Running towards us, her coat flung open and her socks in folds around her ankles, was one of my classmates. As she reached us, she dropped her hands on to her knees, bent forward and gasped for breath. Her words floated on fog as she spoke.

'Inez,' she panted. 'The doctor's been out to your mother.'

I felt a fist of panic punch my stomach and I reached for Laura's hand.

'Your Davy smashed a concrete slab over the head of another boy,' she continued. 'Your mum found the boy with blood down to his feet and took the screamin' abdabs. Davy ran off. No one's seen him since.'

I started to run. Shallow stabs of breath chafed against my dry throat and I felt as though I were running on marshmallows, each step laborious and slow.

'My mum says the doctor's given your mother somethin' tae knock her out.'

The words pounded after me, merging with the thud of my heartbeat and Laura's protestations for me to slow down. The thought of my mother lying tranquillized only hastened my speed. Tranquillized, she couldn't escape sleep's shackles, nor the montage of dreams that flowed to a dismal premonition of her future. Tranquillized, she couldn't get up to kiss the faces of her sleeping children or watch the ruby dawn rise over the Ayrshire hills.

Dr MacKay's blue Ford Cortina was parked at the gate to the manse. He and my father stood beneath the branches of the lime tree, its craggy outline casting dull shadows across my father's face. Laura ran to him and he lifted her into his arms. Dr MacKay's short, round body looked squat beside my father's height. He placed his domiciliary case on the front passenger seat of the car before turning to my father.

'She needs to rest, Iain,' he said. 'She thinks she's coping but she's suppressing everything . . . never given herself the chance to grieve . . . doing far too much . . . she'll make herself ill . . .'

The words seeped towards me like a toxic spill. As they oozed their way to my ear, my consciousness gathered them, arranging them in a semblance of order. My mother ill – I had misheard. Bolting past my father, I ran into the house and bounded up the stairs, composing myself before entering her room. The curtains were closed but for a tiny crack that let in the peeping sunlight. The narrow slit of light spread out as it settled on the bed and my mother's face. Pale skin highlighted her freckled cheeks and shoulders, their fine transparency threaded by faint blue veins that crossed her collar-bone. Her red hair tumbled over the white pillow settling in its natural wave. Slipping from her left hand was a leather-bound book of Robert Burns's poems. I took it from her and in the semi-darkness read in my father's hand, 'I hope the words inspire you the way they have me. With love, Iain.'

157

'Inez?' Her eyelids parted as she squinted to make out who was watching her.

'I'm here, Mum,' I whispered, sitting down on the bed beside her.

'Find Davy for me.'

I took her hand and squeezed it. It felt peculiarly heavy, almost lifeless.

'Look after the wee man.' She spoke through dry lips. 'Your father doesn't cope with him too well.'

I wanted to cry but the tears wouldn't come. Anger immersed my thoughts. Anger that this had to happen to us and at my childishness because I didn't know how to change things. As I watched her fight unconsciousness I noticed a line of silver tears running from the temporal corners of her eyes.

'I couldn't sleep last night,' she said. 'I went through and lay beside Craig. It hurts when you love someone so much but you know that they're destroying you.'

She closed her eyes, the mucous tears matting her fair strands of eyelashes. 'The hardest part is when the hope has gone,' she whispered.

I held her hand until the weight of it caused it to slip easily from me and rest on the bed. I watched the rise and fall of her breathing until, remembering her words, I left to look for my brother.

Davy was sitting in the concrete foundations of a house with his elbows planted on his knees and his head cradled in his hands. His anorak was spotted with blood and his face and trousers covered in cement dust. It was difficult to imagine his cherubic face exploding with enough anger to inflict such violence. He straightened as he saw me approach, slid his hands under his legs and rocked himself back and forth in the same way Craig did.

158

'Is Mum still angry?' he asked. His blond hair, which needed cutting, fell over his forehead and caught among his eyelashes as he blinked.

'She's asleep,' I said, sitting down beside him. 'The doctor gave her something.'

Davy tapped the toe of his right shoe softly against a brick and wrinkled the line of freckles that ran across his nose.

'What happened, Davy?'

'I just snapped,' he said, the anger and frustration appearing for an instant in his round, blue eyes before it vanished – compartmentalized somewhere in his mind. 'Don't you ever feel like lashing out when they start on about Craig?'

My mind scrambled for the words that might justify his actions. None came. Yet I understood his impulse more clearly than I liked to admit.

'Mum and Dad want me to take Craig to play football,' Davy continued. 'I just can't. It's too embarrassing, everyone staring at him.' He turned his eyes towards me searching for reassurance that it was all right to feel the way he did. Confusion at my confusion flitted through my head. I recognized his feelings, the guilt, the love, the anger, all mixed together so that after a while you didn't know which one you were reacting to any more.

'It isn't my fault he's the way he is,' said Davy. 'Maybe they'll think twice before calling him any more names.'

'Let's go home, Davy.'

We walked in silence, as though cocooned by our own individual thoughts – impressions of thoughts that remained unarticulated and redundant in our minds. It was as though the tranquillizer given to my mother had taken effect on my mind and I felt like a jigsaw piece that had been forced into the wrong puzzle. Everything

159

I valued was being eroded away and I didn't know how to stop it.

The kirk stood at the end of a single-track road, bounded on both sides by a sprawling hedge of hawthorn, and canopied by the overhanging branches of trees. Through the chestnut and oak tree yeomanry that lined either side of the road, I could see the angular protrusion of spire, obscured by fluttering leaves rising and falling with the gentle undulation of air. At the end of the road the gate to the kirk lay open and I passed through it, my feet scrunching into the gravel that covered the walkway to its stone steps.

The Ayrshire country rose in rolling green hills behind the kirk. Rectangular fields, bounded by hedges and freckled with cows, spread out in each direction. The estuary that cut through the valley floor was empty but for the flat-bottomed boats stranded in its bed and the gulls, flat-footing through the mud, picking at invertebrates deposited by the receding tide.

As I breathed the salty west coast air I wondered how, on the day that April greeted May, the clouds could part with such an under-blanket of powder blue, how the gulls could ride the wind so effortlessly, and how newborn lambs could frolic in the fields without care.

The great wooden kirk doors, studded with brass, were open and I walked through, passing the stacks of Bibles and hymn books and brass collection plates ready for Sunday service. I walked along the stone floor of the aisle and ran my hand over the sculptured font at its end, before climbing the wooden steps to the pulpit. Lines of wooden pews were bathed in light that rainbowed through the stained-glass windows, trapping dancing particles of dust in its beam. The sound of my father's shoes scuffing against the stone floor echoed through the shower of light and, as he stepped into it, it swathed him in its brightness.

'How's my best girl?' he asked, walking the length of the aisle, his black robe swaying gently as he moved.

'All right,' I answered, realizing what an ineffective reply this was.

My father sat in the front pew and I looked down on him from his pulpit. His hands were placed loosely in his lap, large toughened hands that didn't look in any way ministerial. His legs were stretched out in front of him, crossed at the ankles and his eyes were raised upwards, watching me.

'I don't believe in God any more,' I announced. He made no reply, but seemed to be waiting for me to deliver my sermon. 'If there was a God, Craig would be normal.'

My father nodded his head seriously, drew his legs towards the pew and sat upright.

'You teach us to search for the best in people, to turn the other cheek.' I looked into his patient eyes, then continued. 'Turning the other cheek doesn't work, Dad.'

As I descended the steps of the pulpit the kirk echoed with the clump of my shoes against their wood.

'Come with me,' he said, standing up. 'There's something I want to show you.'

I followed him into the sunshine, through the grave-yard of multi-shaped headstones, the newer ones with flowers placed neatly at their base, the older ones stained with bird droppings, their edges chewed by salty rain. As we reached the hedge of hawthorn that marked the periphery of the kirkyard my father raised his index finger to pursed lips and whispered, 'Shshsh.' In the twist of branches, hidden by leaves was an untidy nest of contorted twigs and holly and feathers. Filling its centre was a large nestling with a spattering of brown downy feathers. Balancing on the rim of the nest was a single egg and, beside it, a naked pink chick.

'The nest is a hedge sparrow's,' he whispered. 'The small chick and the egg have been pushed to the edge of the nest by the cuckoo. It hatched several days ago.'

'What about the baby sparrow?' The chick was on its stomach, its neck stretched piteously across razors of holly leaves.

'It's dying. The last egg won't hatch now.'

'Can't we do something?' The cuckoo raised its head, opening a red, fleshy mouth. 'What if we take the cuckoo out of the nest?'

'It'll die.'

'But it isn't the sparrow's chick. It killed her babies.'

'She thinks it's hers.'

'She must know that it's a freak. It must be twice the size of her.'

'It's nature,' he said, stepping back from the hedge. 'She recognizes it as her own and she'll exhaust herself trying to feed it.'

'If this was made by God then He's a cruel God,' I snapped.

We walked away from the nest, into the cavern of green that tunnelled the single-track road from the kirk.

'Have you ever read any of Robert Burns's poems?' he asked.

'Sometimes, at school, we're given one to memorize, but I always forget it after the test.'

'Ayrshire has two world-famous exports.' He folded his arms across his chest as we walked and I watched the moving shadows of leaves roll over his black robe. 'Johnnie Walker whisky and Robert Burns,' he continued. 'Johnnie Walker allows all men to be poets some of the time, but the master is Robert Burns.'

The trill of a wren drifted through the foliage. It was

unperturbed by our closeness; its music never wavered.

'Burns was an observer of man and nature, their harmony, cruelty and inconsistency,' he said. 'I believe his intuitiveness was God-given.' He had adopted the air of a sermon, transported in his desire to impart his enthusiasm to his audience. I listened to the melody of his voice and the rustle of the overhead leaves as a breath of wind passed through them, until we reached the gate to the manse where he stopped and turned towards me.

'You may find in Burns what you can't find in people,' he said. Opening the gate, he walked towards the house. The curtains in the windows were closed, as though there had been a death in the family.

Later that day, when the noon-day sun was suspended above the Jougs, its brilliance glinting from the chrome panelling of parked cars outside the circle of shops, Laura and I entered the village centre with Craig, asleep in his buggy. I carried a stretchy bag that looked like a string vest with handles, and clutched a list of essentials my father had sent us to buy. We visited the assortment of merchants who each enquired about my mother and gave us free quantities of groceries extra to those we had been sent for. When the string bag was stretched around tin cans, bread and meat, we walked towards the Jougs and the kirk spire beyond. I felt my eyebrows mat together and my face collapse into a frown when I saw Ross Curren and Jim Gallagher approaching from the direction in which we were heading.

Ross was trailing a stick along the kerb, rattling it against lampposts, fences and a post box that barred its way. Dropping my head, I hoped they wouldn't notice me.

'Well, if it isn't the loony and his cretin sisters,' said Ross, a smile curling about his mouth. His voice bore through me like a maggot. He lifted the point of the stick and jabbed it at the pram wheel, his gaze moving from the wheel to my face as he waited for a reaction. Laura's small, plump hand slid into mine and she twisted a button on her coat with the fingers of her other hand.

Touching the point of the stick to the sole of Craig's shoe, Ross watched me, then slowly he pushed the point into Craig's foot. Craig stirred and moved his foot away. Behind Ross, Jim was laughing nervously, his eyes wide with anticipation.

'Wake him up,' Ross ordered.

'Dad says we've to let him sleep,' said Laura, still twisting her coat button.

'I want him awake.' Ross looked at me as he delivered his command. Slowly I wrapped the handle of the string bag around my hand and wheeled the pram away from him.

'You don't get past till we see the spaz awake.' He held the stick horizontally in clenched fists, barring our way. As I studied his twisted smile his face became featureless, just the oval, smooth flesh of a bigot, frightened of what was different, of what he couldn't understand. I looked down at Craig asleep in his buggy, a trickle of saliva running from the corner of his open mouth, forming a wet patch on his anorak. He was a baby. When time changed his body from child to man he would still be a baby, but he would no longer be cute, and those unable to accept him as a child would loathe and fear him more as a man.

Ross raised the point of his stick to Craig's shoulder and pushed it into his anorak, indenting the quilted fabric. An explosion of anger coursed through my body, the string bag became unexpectedly light and I swung it towards Ross's head. Clutching his jaw, he fell to his knees, dazed, and held up his other hand to fend off any further attack. His stick lay useless at his feet and, as he tasted his own blood, his eyes widened in disbelief. Jim took several steps backwards, almost tripping on a broken paving slab. As I raised the bag towards him he turned and ran. Ross dabbed at his mouth with his sleeve as he attempted to stem the flow of blood salivating on to his jacket. Kneeling beside him, I took his face in my hands and skewered my fingers into his plump cheeks.

'Don't so much as look my way again,' I said, my voice spilling out resentment that had choked me for five years. 'Do you understand?'

Ross nodded. My fingers dug deeper into his fleshy cheeks.

'Do you understand?' I roared.

'Aye.'

Letting him go, I watched him scamper to his feet and run away from us. I turned to Craig, straightened his feet on the metal rest across the base of the buggy, then moved behind him and pushed the buggy towards home.

Pink geraniums had been planted in the terracotta pots and symmetrically arranged on either side of the front door to the manse, and the honeysuckle that clambered over the front of the house exhaled its spicy fragrance through a mass of tubular flowers.

The house was still. I climbed the stairs expecting to find my mother in bed, asleep. Instead, the room was empty, the bedclothes perfectly straight. The smell of freshly cut grass and the squawk of a seagull flying overhead were carried through the open window on a gentle breeze that lifted the lace curtain as it entered the room. Trapped between lace and glass was a yellow butterfly, its open wings fluttering towards the sunlight. For a moment the room seemed to exhale its gloomy air, the lace was sucked into the window-frame and the

165

butterfly's flimsy body thudded against the glass and dropped on to the sill.

I sat at my mother's dressing-table and picked up an ornate gilt picture frame, cupping its contoured sides in both hands. Craig smiled from beneath the glass. He was sitting cross-legged, hugging a football to his chest, and I was surprised by the rush of emotion I felt as I studied him. I traced the outline of his smile with my finger and made a silent vow to protect him, always. As I replaced the frame in the centre of the table I noticed the book of Robert Burns's poems lying open, a leather bookmark separating its pages. Four lines of a poem were underlined and I raised the book to read the words.

When Nature her great masterpiece design'd
And framed her last, best work, the human mind,
Her eyes intent on all the wondrous plan
She formed of various parts the various Man.

'It's my favourite piece.' My mother's voice startled me. She stood in the doorway, her body inclined against the frame, her head tilted to touch the wood. Her long hair was the colour of burnished copper and she wore a white calico shift dress that hovered above her knees.

She walked across the room, sat beside me and gathered my hair behind my neck. Taking the book from me, she closed its cover and laid it beside Craig's photograph. Her fingertips rested lightly against the frame and for a moment I thought she might pick it up. There was an intensity in her eyes that appeared only when she talked about her children.

'No one understands unconditional love until they have children,' she said. Her voice was almost as quiet as the flutter of the butterfly. 'For a long time, I blamed myself for Craig's handicap. It must have been something I'd done – or something I hadn't.' The sound of laughter came from the garden and she walked to the window, looked out and smiled. As the sun blazed down on her flame of hair, I thought she'd never looked more lovely.

I walked over and stood beside her. She placed her arm around my waist, still smiling, and we watched my father collapse under Davy, Laura and Craig who were all trying to piggy-back ride him at the same time. I knew then about inevitability. I knew that when you stopped wrestling with anger and praying for a miracle there was peaceful acceptance. My parents had made the transition, just as surely as the hedge sparrow had accepted her cuckoo nestling – but not without first wondering why it hadn't chosen her neighbour's nest.

I watched my mother's smile, listened to the laughter from the garden and felt an inner peace. The frustrated yellow butterfly fluttered nearer the open window. The room exhaled once more and it escaped on a breath that carried it to the rolling green hills behind the kirk with their rectangular fields bounded by hedges and freckled with cows.

THE BIRTHDAY TREAT

Linda Pitt

Linda Pitt grew up in Donegal and went to school in Sligo. After she graduated from Trinity College, Dublin, her first teaching post was in Switzerland. She is married and has two grown-up children. Linda lives in Derby and has recently taken early retirement from teaching. She has written for children but this is her first story for adults.

THE BIRTHDAY TREAT

Between husband and son, caught in the beam of their expectant smiles, Dorrie feels trapped.

'Come on, love.' Frank is growing impatient. 'Tom's come up from London to surprise you. He'll begin to think you're not keen on the idea.'

Somehow she must conceal her dismay, dredge up an appropriate response.

'It sounds lovely, Tom. It's very kind of you and Ruth.'

After all, it is well meant. She will be fifty in August. This holiday is her present from Tom and his wife, a very special birthday treat.

She listens to Tom's enthusiastic description of the converted farmhouse in the Dordogne. It belongs to Brian, his producer, is absolutely fabulous. She'll love it.

They are so alike, father and son – alike in their assumption that what pleases them will also please everyone around them. In looks, too, they are alike. Frank, at fifty-six, is an older, more faded version of his son. Once, her husband's grey hair had been just as dark and springy, his brown eyes equally alert.

And yet, strangely, he seems much more real than Tom. Now that her son appears so often on television, he seems to Dorrie not more familiar, but less. It is as if he is always at one remove, belonging to everyone and no one.

'Zoe wants to bring Charlotte, a friend from school. I hope you don't mind, Dorrie.'

Zoe is his stepdaughter. Ruth, a few years older than Tom, has been married before.

'Of course I don't mind. She'll need the company.'

Why does her son have to call her Dorrie? That started when he went to Cambridge. It never bothered Frank but to Dorrie it brought an immediate sense of loss, a disowning. Sometimes, even now, she longs for him to call her Mum. She never says so, of course, and he never will.

'Right!' Frank is beaming with satisfaction. 'That's that, then. You're a lucky girl, Dorrie.'

'Yes, I know.'

A map of France is produced. The men pore over it, planning routes. Dorrie, listening, feels a momentary surge of anger. She hates long drives, does not suit the heat.

But what can she do? What can she say?

She can't say that she hates the whole idea, that she never feels at ease with Tom's wife, that she wants to return to the little cottage in Cornwall that they rented when Tom was a boy. They can only leave the shop for a fortnight and she doesn't want to waste that precious time.

Of course she can't say any of these things. That would be selfish – selfish and mean.

And so, here she is, sweltering in the back of Tom's large estate car, on the last lap of the long drive south. Ruth also sits in the back, the two girls between them.

Zoe, at nine, has the self-possession of an adult. She is like her mother, dark-haired, slim and tanned. Charlotte, from the same expensive private school, is plumper and more childlike. But they seem to Dorrie to share an enviable self-confidence, to look at her from time to time with cool, appraising eyes.

'Are you all right, Dorrie?' Ruth is solicitous.

'Grandma's sweating,' Zoe observes. She and Charlotte giggle.

'Don't be rude,' Ruth says sharply. 'I'm not surprised you're feeling uncomfortable, Dorrie. I've never known it to be so hot.'

'I'm all right. I'll get used to it.'

Dorrie is miserably conscious of the wet stain spreading under her armpits. Her legs feel as if they're covered in grease. She is afraid that, when she stands up, the back of her skirt will be damp with sweat.

Even in Nottingham this has been the hottest summer for thirty years. In the shop, newspapers and magazines curled unpleasantly in the heat. At the end of each long day Dorrie's feet were swollen and her varicose vein throbbed. She can feel it now.

The rest of the journey passes in a haze of heat. It is dark when they reach the farmhouse, still unbearably hot. Dorrie feels as if a sledgehammer is beating at her head.

'You look done in, Dorrie.' Frank is concerned. 'You'd best go straight to bed, love. You'll feel better in the morning.'

She lies there, still sweating in her cotton nightdress. She thinks about Cornwall, the quiet cottage and the cool sea breeze. She thinks about herself.

On the thirteenth of August she will be fifty. It is not really old, not nowadays.

Lately, almost against her will, she has taken to studying herself in mirrors. It is as if, unbidden, a time for stocktaking has arrived. She is not reassured by what she sees. Once, she had a delicate, china-doll type of prettiness. She has scarcely noticed, over the years, as her trim figure has thickened, her face grown plump. Sometimes, she catches herself gazing at the mirror, mildly surprised by the middle-aged stranger who stares back. She notes that the cheek colour is too high, the hair, neither grey nor brown, badly in need of a rinse.

For weeks, months now, the magazines in the shop have been urging her to liven herself up; exercise, diet, plan a tan, an exciting summer wardrobe. She has done none of these things.

In the morning Dorrie feels more optimistic. It is pleasantly warm as they breakfast on the terrace. Tom has fetched croissants, crisp and delicious, fresh from the local bakery. Below them, fields of sunflowers and maize slope down to the Dordogne. It is a generous river, wide and slow.

'It's lovely, Tom. And perfect weather for sitting out here.'

'Not for long, Dorrie,' warns Ruth. 'Even the locals are finding the heat unbearable this year.'

'I'm sure I'll get used to it.' Dorrie doesn't want any more fuss. 'Can you show us around the farmhouse after breakfast, Tom?'

The farmhouse reminds Dorrie of pictures in the expensive, glossy magazines. In cool, white rooms objects are tastefully arranged, splashes of colour provided by plants, paintings, pottery, the odd rug. Outside, the rich, massed colours of geraniums and petunias spill from terracotta pots, placed with a careful casualness on the steps, around the courtyard.

Already, at mid-morning, it is much too hot for Dorrie. The relentlessly blue sky is becoming lower, more solid, closing in on her. She wants to push it away, to breathe.

In the swimming pool, Zoe and Charlotte are diving

174

and surfacing like a couple of performing seals. 'Come in the pool,' they chant. 'Come in the pool.'

'It's the only place,' Tom says ruefully, 'in this weather. No good for sightseeing. What about you, Dorrie?'

'You know I don't swim, Tom. I'll get my book and sit over there under the tree.'

'Can't you swim, Grandma?' Zoe has padded damply up behind them. 'I thought *everybody* could swim.'

'I never learnt,' Dorrie explains. 'We lived right out in the country, Zoe, on a farm in Derbyshire. There was no swimming pool near.'

'But Grandpa can swim. Daddy says you're a very good swimmer, Grandpa.'

Frank laughs, flattered. 'Not that good, Zoe. I was lucky, brought up in Nottingham. Went to the baths every week.'

Zoe shrugs. 'Well, hurry up, everyone. Charlotte and I are waiting.'

She returns to her friend. Dorrie, watching, sees the two heads huddle together, turn to look at her. The collapse into helpless giggles is covered up by jumping into the pool, splashing about. But Dorrie knows they are laughing at her. Little girls can be very silly, she tells herself. Very silly and very cruel. She mustn't let it upset her.

The phone rings. It's the Armstrongs, Ruth informs them – old friends, also in television, coming for lunch. The phone rings again – more old friends.

'Do many English people come to these parts?' asks Frank.

'Thousands,' Tom answers cheerfully, 'and we seem to know most of them. I sometimes think Ruth would like a holiday without another English person in sight. Wouldn't you, darling?'

'Yes,' says Ruth quietly, 'but you'd hate it, Tom.'

Dorrie glances at her quickly, imagining a slight note of resentment. But Ruth's face is impassive. You can never tell, with her.

The heat grows stronger. Ninety-eight in the shade, according to Frank. Sitting under the lime tree, Dorrie can believe it. She tries to read but even the open book seems to trap and exude heat. Words dance on the page.

The Armstrongs, blond and tanned, arrive with their three children. At lunch, the talk is of people Dorrie doesn't know, films she hasn't seen, books she hasn't read. In spite of lavish applications of sun cream, her skin is on fire. Her head aches.

The days pass. They follow the same pattern. The weather does not change. Dorrie enjoys the mornings, that brief, cool time before the remorseless heat sets in again.

Sometimes, in the afternoons, she retreats to her bedroom, shutters closed against the sun. Mostly she sits under the lime tree, painfully shedding and renewing her skin, pretending to read.

'There, love,' Frank says, 'you're having a good rest, aren't you? Just what you need.'

Dorrie agrees. But it is not what she needs. Not at all.

'Should be a grand birthday party on the thirteenth. They're really doing you proud, love.'

Dorrie agrees. Her heart sinks.

Friends, more and more of them, come and go. Figures loom momentarily over her, utter polite greetings, make for the pool. Dorrie marvels at their slimness, their smooth, brown skins. She has never been so conscious of her body, of its limitations. She should have listened to those magazines. She should have tried.

*

One afternoon, the pattern is broken. She drives with Ruth to a local farm to buy some peaches and plums.

Madame Borel, the farmer's wife, is a large woman in a flowered overall. She has a pleasant face and work-reddened hands. Dorrie takes to her at once.

While Ruth buys the fruit, Dorrie looks around. At the back of the farmhouse, under an enormous, wide-spreading willow tree, are some tables and chairs. Beyond the green fronds of the willow are fields and fields of sunflowers.

As they leave the farm, Dorrie points to a sign by the gate. 'What does that mean?'

'*Chambre d'Hôte?* It means they do bed and breakfast. I think Madame Borel does other meals as well sometimes.'

There are lights by the pool for Dorrie's party. Caterers come from the nearest town and the guests arrive. They kiss Dorrie. They laugh and swim and drink. As Dorrie watches them, a vague idea, a longing, hardens into a decision. In spite of the noise, the crowd, the persistent heat, she feels suddenly at peace. She smiles serenely as she cuts the cake and, arm around her shoulders, Tom makes an appropriate and touching little speech. He is the perfect host, the perfect son. Zoe, her grandchild, kisses her prettily. She does not like Zoe, she thinks calmly. She is not a likeable child.

As they all sing 'Happy Birthday', Frank's eyes are shining with pride and pleasure. She must not weaken. She must not give in.

She announces her decision next morning.

Frank is astounded. 'Bed and breakfast! Have you gone out of your mind, Dorrie?'

Tom is hurt. 'I don't understand, Dorrie. Aren't you

happy here with us? Didn't you enjoy your party?' He looks like a small boy whose toy has been suddenly snatched away.

'It was a lovely party, Tom. Of course I enjoyed it. This is just something I want to do – for myself.'

'But ... but ... this is all for you,' Frank protests. 'The holiday. The party. It's your birthday treat.'

To this there is no reply.

Ruth comes to her rescue. 'I think Dorrie must do what she wants,' she says firmly.

'Ruth!' Tom is cross. 'Are you trying to get rid of Dorrie? Has something happened between you two?'

'No,' says Ruth quietly, 'it's just that we understand each other. Come on, Dorrie. We'll phone Madame Borel. If she has a room for the weekend I'll take you at once.'

As they go into the house, they hear Frank muttering something about Dorrie's time of life. The women laugh.

'It's nothing to do with the menopause, is it?' asks Ruth.

'I don't know. But it'll make Frank more comfortable to think so. I don't want him to be upset.'

Ruth pats her arm. 'Don't worry, Dorrie. I'll sort them out.'

Dorrie nods gratefully. She can rely on Ruth. The thought surprises her.

On the way to the farm she notices for the first time that there are shadows under Ruth's eyes. She looks tired.

'You do understand, don't you, Ruth? It's not that I'm ungrateful to you and Tom.'

'I understand perfectly. I've often wanted to do the same.'

'Why don't you?'

'I haven't the courage,' Ruth says simply.

*

178

At the farm, Dorrie has a white-walled room looking out on to the willow tree and the fields of sunflowers. At the edge of the first field she can see what looks like a small, round swimming pool.

'*Piscine*,' says Madame Borel, making swimming movements with her hands. 'It hot.'

Her English matches Dorrie's French. They will get along.

'*Oui*,' says Dorrie, 'very hot.' She indicates that, regretfully, she has no swimming costume.

'Wait!' Madame Borel bustles out of the room and returns with a green, hideously floral costume. '*Pour vous*,' she beams.

'*Merci*,' Dorrie says weakly. She cannot refuse.

This morning there are no other guests. Dorrie lowers herself into the cool, soothing water. The pool is obviously used, not only for pleasure, but to store water for the farm. At no point is Dorrie out of her depth. At the side of the pool is a rubber ring. She slips it on. There is no Zoe to laugh at her now. She floats. She is free.

After her swim she gets dressed and sits reading under the willow tree. She has her lunch there too, bread and pâté and a glass of the local red wine. From time to time there is a small, warm breeze. Through the gently waving tresses of the willow, the yellow sunflowers seem to nod and smile their approval.

She is thinking only of herself. She is selfish. She does not feel guilty.

In the evening she eats her meal in the dim, shuttered dining room. A few other guests have arrived. They smile at Dorrie. They chat to each other and scold their children. They are ordinary people, like the people in her street, the customers in the shop.

For the first time, in bed, she feels strangely alone.

179

Except when she went into hospital to have Tom, she and Frank have never slept apart. She misses him.

Over the weekend, people come and go. Most leave straight after breakfast. Dorrie stays on.

She feels a sense of richness. These few days are hers, to spend as she pleases. Sometimes, in the heat of mid-day, she lies on her bed, the shutters closed. Vaguely, she is aware of Monsieur and Madame Borel talking in the farmyard below. She hears the tractor starting up, the clucking of hens. These are familiar sounds, the sounds of her childhood.

Ruth comes. It is time to leave.

Madame Borel says goodbye. 'You like here?' she asks. 'It is good?'

'*Oui*, Madame Borel,' says Dorrie, smiling. 'It is good.'

THE OLIVE TREE

Hilary Waters

Hilary Waters is an actress. She lives on a Thames Steel Lighter on the South Coast. After graduating in Italian and European Literature from Warwick University, she spent two years teaching English in Venice. She then returned to the UK to pursue an acting career. She has worked in film, television and theatre worldwide. Inspired by Daisy Ashford, she began writing at the age of eight, but only in the last two years has she applied herself seriously.

THE OLIVE TREE

At the back of the Da Vinci farmhouse are two paths, which, starting at the same point by the wine store, split almost immediately and wend their separate, meandering ways down the stony hill under the olive trees. Although they both wind and curve, the two paths always diverge and at the bottom of the hill the distance between them is just over one kilometre. The incline on the hill is so steep that it is impossible to descend without sliding on the scree, except by way of one of the two paths. To catch at the sparse vegetation to prevent a fall would also be undesirable, as the occasional clump of greenery is coarse and spiky.

Every day La Signora Trepuzzi walked down the left-hand path on her way to the village and every day returned home by way of the right-hand path. Her reasons for so doing were not of a practical nature (for the paths were no less easy or difficult in their descent or ascent, nor was one path nearer to the village than the other), but because she was superstitious.

She always carried her basket over her right arm, leaving her left arm free to touch the olive trees on that side. As she touched them, she counted them. Their gnarled trunks always felt the same; warm, dry and knotted.

At the bottom of the path, she turned right along a public bridle-way. At this juncture, she took a comb from her basket and combed her long, black hair. Half a kilometre along the bridle-path, she turned left down another track. Orchards of cherry trees, owned by her husband, undulated away to the right and left. She knew all the men in her husband's orchards and part of the routine was to see how many times she had to say '*buongiorno*'. She practised all kinds of facial contortions to go with the greeting. She'd start with a smile, then a straight face, a long face, a curl of her upper lip, a frown thoughtful between the eyes and a vacant stare. She knew they pitied her. She'd heard them talking.

'It's a damned shame she got hitched up with the likes of him.'

'He's too old for her. Just shouts at her.'

'She's got her father to thank for the match. Silly old fool; thought he'd get rich.'

At this point in her journey, La Signora had their words flying around in her head and as she thought a word, she'd throw it softly into the sultry air, walk four paces and emit the next one. She felt nothing though, but the pounding of her heart and the rhythm of her step.

Eugenio, at fifty, was thirty years her senior. They'd been married just twelve months. La Signora's father, who had worked for Eugenio until his retirement, had seen the bachelor and his two thousand acres of cherry orchards, olive groves and vineyards as a profitable investment.

A deal had been struck between the two men. However, before agreeing to marry the prettiest of his ex-employee's daughters, Eugenio had made it clear to La Signora's father that he would be marrying way beneath his social station. In return for this step down the social ladder, Eugenio would not financially benefit La Signora's immediate family, but bequeath his entire estate to his own first male offspring.

La Signora's father had been slow to realize the injustice of the deal. He had found Eugenio a wife, more beautiful, more gracious and more willing to work than any the bachelor might have met. For Eugenio seldom went out, never mixed socially and was very unattractive to the opposite sex. He had prominent eyes, a large forehead, receding hairline and was always very red in the face. If he wasn't perspiring droplets of sweat, globules of spittle would catch in his drooping moustache and produce the same effect.

But hands had been shaken and La Signora Trepuzzi's father was a man of his word.

The scales were tipped in Eugenio's favour. He acquired without effort a pretty wife to clean, cook and serve at table and he had no fears that his money would be inherited by a son, for Eugenio had a secret. He was sterile. However, with the suggestible innocence of his young wife, he was soon able to convince La Signora that she was the barren one.

The track between the cherry orchard and the vineyard was very straight, narrow and dusty. Every so often La Signora would step aside and let a farm truck pass. Any interruption of this kind had a penalty attached; she had to count to one hundred before continuing along her way. The dry dust would blow up in her face in the wake of the receding vehicle and she needed about the count of one hundred to cough up the dust from her throat. She spat.

The village began at the end of the track. Just as a large wave is suddenly created from a seemingly calm sea, so the village rose dramatically from the smooth land. The houses were built around a hill, but being so densely packed together, the hill itself was invisible; just a mass of pinkish-brown stone, broken here and there by steps linking, interlocking, climbing, falling.

La Signora climbed the steepest steps. There were eighty-seven in all and the thirty-second was so worn that it had almost disappeared. In summertime she would buy a watermelon from the crippled woman who sat on the bottom step shouting, '*Cocomeri*', her one leg outstretched in front of her. Then she would begin the steep ascent, counting all the steps and red doors.

Her rituals in the village were silent. She did the counting in her head and always did her shopping in the same order; bread, milk, meat, vegetables and the mini-supermarket for groceries. Her conversations with shopkeepers were brief; just salutations and affirmations of her own well-being. Eugenio did not like her to fraternize with the locals.

'You shop and you come home,' he would shout, pointing an accusatory finger at her. She obeyed, just as she had promised to do a year ago in the Catholic church of S. Maria della Pietà.

The wedding ceremony had been a pitiful affair. Eugenio did not invite anyone, purposefully emphasizing the disgrace that he wanted his new wife's family to assume he was feeling, and he limited the young girl's guests to six.

The priest had swung a great deal of incense to hide the tears of injustice in the eyes of La Signora's father and the incredulity on his own face that this young woman could be marrying such a tyrant. He had seen the bride through baptism and confirmation and now he had to watch her digging an early grave with Eugenio Trepuzzi.

Before leaving the village square, La Signora would slip into the Catholic church, genuflect to the beloved

Virgin and confess her state of barrenness to the patient priest. She didn't consider her one-sided ramblings as fraternization with the locals.

The young priest found these daily sessions with the young woman very frustrating. To assure her that infertility was no sin would be in direct opposition to the view of her husband, who blamed her inability to produce children on the inevitable sins of her peasant background. The priest had deemed it politic not to oppose her husband.

Father Ambrosio would sit, his head in his hands, listening. He was of Eastern European origin and had made a pilgrimage as a graduate to the holy Vatican City. The result of his trekking days was an ecclesiastical position in the tiny Tuscan hamlet. After six years, his Italian was perfect and his native accent a mere memory. For just as an actor changes costume and assumes a different character, so the young priest had adapted and integrated effortlessly. But he was fair-haired and blue-eyed and apart from the occasional itinerant Sicilian of Norman extraction, his colouring was unusual. This he could not alter.

The return journey was always slower, laden as she was with her basket now cutting the flesh on her right arm. After acknowledging the crippled woman at the bottom of the steps, she'd set off along the straight track. On this monotonous stretch of dust-covered road, she'd try to empty her mind of patterns and think about nothing, but always ended up thinking about the very task she had set herself.

The men in the cherry orchard were on mid-morning break by the time she passed by again, so her mental torture could continue unabated until she reached the bridle-way. Here she would turn left, but before doing so, would lower the heavy basket to the ground, undo the top button of her blouse and dab at the glistening sweat with a handkerchief.

The uphill struggle made her think of Christ carrying his heavy cross, the burden of her basket bruising her arms and the effort to reach out to the trees leaving her more exhausted with every step. Every so often, she'd bend over to counteract dizziness.

Then there was the stone, shaped like a tortoise. It lay in the shadow of a big boulder. She always stopped to caress her face with its smooth back.

'I love you,' she'd whisper and gently replace the petrified animal in its rocky niche.

Such was the pattern of La Signora's life.

One morning in August after a heat-induced thunderstorm the previous night, La Signora set off down the left-hand path. Immediately she saw that her way was impeded. One of the olive trees lay outstretched across the path. It looked clumsy and undignified with its branches pointing heavenward and its twisted trunk like a limb out of joint. Although the trunk of the olive tree was not too thick to step over, its deformed torso had fallen awkwardly, the branches and not the trunk covering most of the path. Nor could she find a way around it, for at this point the hill fell away sharply and she feared she might slip.

The other path also presented her with a dilemma. Should she follow her usual routine for that path, but in reverse, or apply the routine for the left-hand path to the right? For twelve months she had conformed to the same pattern, her superstitious nature resisting a change in the order. However, satisfying herself that a change of some sort was unavoidable, she decided against either. It would be more detrimental than to do nothing at all. So she just walked.

As she walked, she thought. She thought about Eugenio and his vice-like grip on her shoulders as he took his pleasure in the darkness, she thought about her family whom she hardly ever saw, and wondered whether her mother's hair had turned grey yet, about the dog with one eye that Eugenio kept on a chain in the back yard. She thought about her room, small and cramped, adjacent to the kitchen and wondered why rich men's wives had to live in such tiny spaces between washing-machines and fridges, when their husbands had big bedrooms with king-sized beds and sliding wardrobes. She thought about the stone tortoise and how she always said, 'I love you.' She never said that to her husband, but then he had never said it to her. She wondered whether he had something he loved like her tortoise. Then she felt guilt and blamed herself for his bad humour. 'He'd love a son,' she thought. Finally she thought about herself, but she couldn't think of anything, except that it was strangely liberating to have a brain full of unadulterated thoughts, rather than a brain full of numbers and sequences.

She was moving towards the end of the path now and, in a deliciously radical moment, decided not to comb her hair. As she was revelling in the rejection of her own rules, La Signora saw someone approaching. She fumbled for the comb in the bottom of her basket, but it had disappeared. A young fair-haired man in an elegant beige suit, striped shirt and tie, was advancing rapidly. As they passed each other, he smiled from the core of his pale-blue eyes and, in a voice as soft as the hue of his eyes, said, '*Buongiorno*.' Her own eyes as dark as black olives, ripe and shining, flitted shyly in his direction.

She continued on her way, but the memory of the stranger's smile flickered across her brain, distracting

189

her from the cherry-pickers. They greeted her as normal, but she hardly saw them as she hurried on. They watched her scurrying out of earshot and then all at once, like a flock of chatty starlings, put forward their opinions.

'Looked all fussed she did. He's probably been hitting her and she don't want us to see the bruises like.'

'Or he's told her not to talk to us – told her to keep her mouth shut.'

She was far down the track now, breathlessly approaching the village. She didn't stop for a watermelon or count the eighty-seven steps. She just strode on, trying to evict the smile from her mind and the voice from her ears. He'd looked at her, looked at her from within and she felt the pulse of happiness, the glow of enjoyment. But the growing sensation of delight felt wicked in the cramped world Eugenio had created for her, between the fridge and the washing-machine.

On the top step, La Signora very uncharacteristically sat down and gazed up at the Catholic church in all its majestic splendour. It loomed oppressively, casting a dark shadow over the square and she, like the tortoise under the boulder, was protected by the massive wall of stone and yet hidden from the light.

Instead of working her way around the shops, La Signora went into the church first. For a while she remained motionless, staring at the Madonna and child over the ornate altar.

The interior of the church was dressed up like a royal wedding cake in gold, red and white with icing-like whorls on pillars, in archways and round the altar. Great red hurricane lamps stood in alcoves in the semi-circular apse and occasionally the Madonna's face would flicker red, as the lights in the lamps wobbled in an imperceptible breeze.

190

La Signora genuflected to the Virgin and sidled into a back pew. For a long time she kept her eyes on the statue of mother and child. Then, with a rushing that began in her abdomen and caught in her throat, she wept more sorrowfully than ever before, the guilt of infertility in the pit of her stomach like a dead foetus.

For the best part of a year she had disguised her sorrow by blinding her mind with the penance of superstitious routines and covering her aching heart with the trivia of daily life. Now though, the latent trauma triggered by a fallen tree and a man with a smile, like a disease in her inner psyche, spread out its fingers touching the surface.

Amidst the sobs she prayed to the Virgin for a child.

Father Ambrosio was now standing at her side, holding the shaking shoulders. Unlike Eugenio's hold, his was soft and comforting. When the heaving and weeping had abated, he raised her gently from her knees and looked kindly into her swollen eyes.

'What's the matter, Signora?'

Her head still hung in supplication, she requested to go to confession. The priest parted the curtains and entered the booth. The purple curtains fluttered in anticipation, the hurricane lamps flickered in sympathy and the Virgin Mary reddened.

And she brought forth the imaginary demons, one by one, laying them out, turning them over, examining them.

'Today, Father, I have committed many sins.'

Father Ambrosio flinched, bracing himself for her innocent expurgation. He wished he were a psychiatrist, a counsellor, a friend, her mother, anyone other than the village priest, destined to listen to confessions.

'I always go down the left path and come back up the right. Today I went down the right path and I started to think about things.' La Signora was twisting her handkerchief around her little finger.

'I felt different. I was happy going down that path, thinking. Some things I thought about were sad, but I was glad to be thinking them. That can't be right, can it, Father?'

He shifted uneasily on his stool, the counsellor in him desperate to wrench apart the grille between them. Then, unable to contain himself further, leant down level with her and, in a voice that wafted and intoxicated like incense, he spoke.

'It's good for you to think, Signora. Let your thoughts flow freely. The Virgin will not chastise you for thinking, as long as you do not think ill of others.' He thought about Eugenio Trepuzzi and made a mental note to ask for forgiveness later.

La Signora continued, the burden lightening with every syllable.

'At the bottom of the path, Father, I met a stranger.' She coloured.

'Do not be afeard of strangers, Signora.' Father Ambrosio heard himself now, the confident counsellor moving deftly amongst the tangled web of somebody else's emotions.

'But, Father,' she continued, 'he smiled at me and I smiled back and I liked it.'

There was silence for a moment, the confessional now so full of guilt and pleasure that it seemed to strain at the hinges. Then softly came the voice of reason.

'Christ smiled at strangers. He smiled at strangers as well as friends and he –' he paused – 'he touched them.'

She flushed. He recoiled in horror, as he realized the implications of this remark and then very definitely fixed La Signora between the eyes, his own face, peeping

192

boldly into the forbidden secular world of men, women and unborn children.

Through the criss-cross of the trellis and the purple darkness, La Signora could only see the whites of his eyes.

'Take my advice, Signora. Be glad of any happiness that comes your way, embrace the comfort of strangers.' His voice was soothing and intimate and his eyes seemed to twinkle in the dim light.

'Do not blame yourself for your barrenness, Signora. God does not blame you for it. Rest assured that it is not the proof of a tainted past. Go now with a free spirit and keep praying to Our Lady. She hears us all.' He hastily performed the absolution as a matter of form and then emerged from behind the curtain. Momentarily he thought La Signora looked like the Madonna herself; deep, dark and beautiful. Hastily he crossed himself and just in case absolved them both.

It was a thoughtful Signora who emerged from the holy darkness into the intense morning light. Thoughtful, but lightened. She went about her business later than usual and in a random order, raising a few eyebrows amongst the village women.

The following morning La Signora went down the right-hand path again. The fallen olive still lay stripped of its dignity. She didn't like to mention it to Eugenio. He hardly ever used the paths, most of his day spent overseeing extensive vineyards at the front of the property. She felt it would annoy him, but also she felt something else; a magnetic pull towards the adventure of the day before. She went steadily down the path, thinking all the while, not about Eugenio and his anger, the dog in the yard or her ageing mother, but about the young man in the beige suit.

As she neared the end of the path, she took the

precaution of brushing her long hair. It hung like silk down her back, almost oriental in its blue-black glistening uniformity. She turned the corner expectantly. There he was, striding Adonis-like down the track.

'Embrace the comfort of strangers. Be glad of any happiness that comes your way.' The priest's words rang like many joyful bells in her head.

She greeted him first, her smile innocent and yet welcoming. The young man stopped and put his hand into his pocket.

'Your comb,' he said. 'I think you must have dropped it yesterday.'

He held out the comb to her. She noticed his large, strong hands, strong and yet refined, and on the little finger of his left hand he wore a white-gold ring with a single diamond embedded in its centre.

Very tentatively, she reached for the comb and, in the moment of taking it, their fingers touched. The diamond flashed. She drew away quickly. She thought about Christ touching his flock and wondered if he had blushed in the way that she was now; a burning, flooding the olive skin.

He smiled the same smile that seemed to come from the essence of his being.

'What's your name? Mine's Angelo.'

La Signora hung her head at his persistent use of the intimate second person. Perhaps he hadn't noticed the connubial band on her fourth finger.

'He would have used the polite form if he'd noticed,' she thought.

'Signora, Signora Trepuzzi,' she laid emphasis on the 'Signora', but he still continued in the informal.

'But what is your real name, your first name?' He was looking at her searchingly now, exploring her unashamedly with the second person.

At this moment the engine of a tractor could be heard rumbling in the distance. She very abruptly turned on her heels.

'*Arrivederci*,' she said faintly.

'Until the next time,' he called back.

She heard his cry in the wilderness and held it close to her heart.

The tree barred the way for a week. On the third day La Signora could hardly contain her excitement and was ready with the shopping basket well before the usual hour. She waited, watching the clock.

On that day he wore a dark-blue linen suit and straw hat. His elegance was unmatched in these parts. Eugenio, despite his noble background, always wore ill-fitting trousers, which provided a shelf for his middle-aged paunch, and his shirts were so tight that you could see the pools of sweat in his armpits, spreading dark like an ink-stain on blotting paper.

Angelo was carrying a bunch of flowers wrapped in paper. He cradled the flowers in his arms, as if suckling them.

'I have a gift for you,' he said sweetly as they met. 'Red roses to match your red lips.' Her whole face shone as red as the roses in the paper. She accepted them graciously and laid them in her basket, wrapped like a new-born in its swaddling clothes.

She desperately wanted to break away from him. He made her feel uncomfortably physical. So, thanking him for the roses, she took her leave and turned towards the village. Occasionally she would peep at the flowers, still in bud and barely showing above their paper blanket.

She greeted the cherry-pickers hastily, her red lips tightening self-consciously.

'I must get used to my lips,' she muttered as she hurried on.

By the time she returned home, La Signora's lips were sore with biting and the roses crushed by the weight of provisions. Behind the wine store she hastily extracted them from the basket and hid them by a vat. Later that same afternoon, as Eugenio lay sleeping, she crept out with vase and water to resuscitate the beleaguered blooms. She hid them by the stone tortoise, made a little cross from two sticks and wedged this between the tortoise and the vase.

'Just in case anyone's passing,' she thought, 'they'll think it's a grave.'

There she left her most precious gift to revive.

Because the olive tree still prevented access down the left-hand path, La Signora could justify her new freedom.

'It won't be for long,' she reassured herself, but in truth she was delighted to find the tree still there.

For the following two days they met. He talked, she would listen and respond in monosyllables, enjoying the honeyed tones of his softly spoken words or the searching, all-encompassing look in the pale-blue eyes. She noticed these things and he noticed the blue-black gleam in her hair, the frightened black quality in her eyes and the red of the scarred lips.

'You mustn't worry your lips,' he had said, laughing. She had laughed too, her teeth flashing white against the dusky brown of her skin, her face almost thrown back, so that he could see the shape of her neck; swan-like, unwrinkled.

The spring in her step became more emphasized and as the week wore on, one could say that her whole being had lightened, that she had grown two or three inches taller and that she looked fuller and fresher.

On the fifth night she had a dream. She dreamed that she was lying in an open coffin in her wedding gown.

The coffin and the gown shone, incandescent. A translucent white light glimmered around her body. The gleaming coffin floated high up in the rafters of a big room and an angel, equally white and shining, stood by her side. The angel smiled down at her, waiting to greet her. She opened her eyes and smiled up at the angel.

The dream stayed with her all morning. She floated about her business and with very little effort prepared to go out. Instead of one of her usual black skirts and second-hand blouses, she wore her white confirmation dress, which still fitted around the tiny waist and, although tighter in the bodice, suited her better now than before.

Eugenio did not see her leave. He was already in the vineyard. She glanced down the left-hand path, which seemed almost foreign to her now. The tree still lay in supplication. She daintily zigzagged down the right-hand path, stopping by the roses. They were beginning to open in the early morning sun. She took one from the vase and inhaled the almost intangible new perfume. Then she laid it in her basket and, almost flying now, descended airily to the end of the path.

He too was dressed in white. White linen. His shoes were of white canvas and even his straw hat looked whiter than before.

They acknowledged each other's whiteness, admiring and smiling all the while. She gave him the red rose. Her first gift to him. She felt vulnerable, but the feeling only lasted in the brief moment of giving, for his face broke into a multitude of creases and his eyes lit up with gratitude.

'It's open,' he cried enthusiastically and, just as she had done moments earlier, raised the rose to breathe in the deliciously fresh scent.

As if prearranged, La Signora turned and accompanied

the stranger on his journey. They walked side by side, occasionally looking at each other and smiling. In this way they continued, until they were just two white blobs in the cracked landscape. If anyone had overheard their conversation, they would have recognized a new intimacy.

'Tell me your name,' Angelo insisted.

'Concezione,' she said and it sounded strange and naïve on her new red lips.

The next day being Sunday, Eugenio and his wife went to church. They always drove in his car, which meant taking a circuitous route around the hills. After the service, Concezione spent a long time at confession, so long that Eugenio left without her. Father Ambrosio emerged from his part of the confessional looking hypnotized. He crossed himself in front of the altar. The priest had just listened to a dream, a beautiful dream about a man in white, a dream that shimmered white like the candles on the altar and yet glowed red hot, like an iron in the fire. As each detail was explicitly unwrapped, he had listened, tortured and yet tantalized. He had crossed himself repeatedly, as from the young woman's new lips escaped the power and purity of a new passion. It was worthy of confession though and for the first time a delighted Father Ambrosio absolved her in good faith.

By the Monday morning the olive tree had been removed. Both ways now lay open, equally steep, equally winding and equally accessible, but to Concezione they were very different paths. The one on the left, like a stagnant pool, stultifyingly still, feeding off its own putrid waste. The one on the right, like a fast-flowing freshwater river, constantly invigorating. So into the river of life she plunged once more, her own body in harmony; moving in its lower depths, its fluids shifting and changing, re-forming, creating. But that day the stranger did not come, nor the next day, nor ever again.

Concezione grew. As her body blossomed, Eugenio's withered, his secret like a poisonous canker within.

Concezione gave thanks to the Virgin Mary, who between her blushes seemed to smile a knowing smile. And the confessional sat redundant, its purple curtains hanging sulkily.

At the end of the ninth month, a son was born to Concezione Trepuzzi. She called him Angelo in memory of a dream.

Twenty years on, Concezione's aged parents live with their daughter and grandson at the Da Vinci farmhouse. The house is a mass of colour and light floods in through every crack. There are red roses in every vase.

Eugenio Trepuzzi died shortly after the birth of his first son. The less knowing said that the sheer joy of fatherhood overcame him, but others said that he burst in a fit of temper. Whatever they said, his secret is still safe. That is, almost safe; there is a middle-aged priest who lives in early retirement in a monastery on a hill. He has renounced all worldly goods, save a white-gold ring with a single diamond embedded in its centre that he wears on the little finger of his left hand.

BLACK LIZZIE BLACK

James Maguire

James Maguire retired five years ago from a career in higher education both as a lecturer and administrator. His retirement allowed him to indulge his love of the written word and to develop his talent for fiction. He was born in Scotland in 1931 and many of his stories are based in the Glasgow of his youth. This year's Ian St James Awards was his first attempt at publication. Sadly, Jim died suddenly at his home in Durham in January. His family are very proud of his success.

BLACK LIZZIE BLACK

The eight lads playing five-a-side in Thistle Street weren't used to a good ball. Normally they made do with newspaper tied up with string. They were kicking diagonally across the street using the lampposts on opposite sides for goals, but they just could not keep the ball down. They kept skying it. If the tenements hadn't been three-storey high, they would have lost it by now. Once when it rattled a street-level window, the sash had been rammed up and an angry head had been thrust out.

'Sod off! If I get a hold o' that thing I'll put a knife to it. Mind I'm telling you!' But he was shouting at an empty street. The lads had vanished.

Neighbours apart, Thistle Street, off the Caly Road, was good for fitba'. There was no traffic except for the odd coal-cart or brewer's dray. Soon the kids were back. They were irrepressible. Heedless and energetic; careless of everything but their game, they kicked and called, cried in triumph, yelled for passes, dribbled, screamed and disputed decisions. Noisy and joyous as pups they yelped and exploded around their Thistle Street pitch.

'Keep it down, lads,' shouted Jacky Cosgrove, who had borrowed the ball without asking, and would be in trouble if it was lost or damaged. But within a minute an over-enthusiastic player had thwacked it into the air and they watched it arc up and go through an open second-storey window. They froze and fell quiet, for all of them had recognized that window. Exuberance gone, they glanced silently at each other, afraid and unwilling to look up again. They were fearful of what they might see; worse, they were scared to meet the eyes that might now be seeing them. They had not broken the window, but they had shattered a taboo and they feared the unknown consequences. Their dread was unreasoned. It was absorbed; felt, not understood, and was the more powerful for that reason.

'Oh Jeez! Black Lizzie's! Go and get it,' whispered Jacky, turning to the offender.

'I'm not going up there.' The reply was incredulous.

'You're scared.'

'Aye . . . so are you!'

'That ball's only a lend. I've got to get it back.'

'Get it yourself. Look what happened to Glaiket.'

'Oh don't be stupid,' said Jacky Cosgrove; but they all half believed it.

Glaiket was a not very bright lad. It was hard to say what age he was. He had a withered arm. The rumour among them was that one day he had raised his fist to Black Lizzie and his arm had shrivelled, and he had never been right in the head again.

There was other evidence of Black Lizzie's power and wrath around the Caly Road. Infrequently she was seen limping along the street. She wore a black shawl and a flannel blouse that looked like a pyjama jacket, her black cotton skirt trailed the ground. She carried a stick and when she hobbled past, you could see that she wore one sandshoe and one slipper with the toe-piece cut out. Her white hair was scraped back into a tight bun which had a huge spike through it. No concealed weapons for Black Lizzie. Yon thing could have skewered a horse. She hadn't been seen in the street for a bit, which was no great loss.

'Well somebody's got to fetch it,' said Jacky angrily.

The others laughed to hide their fear. They made gags, and skeltered off, hopping and running and calling back over their shoulders. They disappeared up different closes and around the corner, Jacky was left in the street looking up at that ominous window. Nothing stirred behind Black Lizzie's dirty lace curtain.

It was getting dark, a passing man stopped to light a Woodbine. A woman pulled her shawl closer as their paths crossed. A child was fishing for lucks down a grating a few yards away. He was using a half of a Cherry Blossom boot-polish tin, filled with mud. He was dropping it over the objects at the bottom of the dunny hoping something interesting would stick to it, so that he could fish it up on the string from which he dangled it.

A bit of wind disturbed Black Lizzie's curtains behind the sash. The night was chilling.

'I'll get the ball tomorrow,' Jacky decided. He was off home.

'Ma, is it true that Black Lizzie lost Mrs Angus her baby?' Jacky's question caused silence at the dinner table, which was usually a babble of scattered conversations. All seven of them fell quiet. His younger brothers and sisters looked speculatively at their mother. A few minutes earlier his father had come home from work and immediately sat down, still in his dungarees and jacket. Dinner had to be ready the minute he arrived. His mother, who was dishing out stovies from the pot, put it back on the range. She wiped her hands on the hips of her wrap-over apron and eyed her husband.

'That's enough o' that kind of talk,' said his father sharply.

'What about Glaiket?' Jacky risked his father's anger.

205

His mother made a dubious mouth and shook her head. 'She's an odd yin right enough,' she said.

'Katy, don't fill their heads wi' that kind o' badness.' His father's voice was impatient, but Jacky wouldn't be put off.

'Why do they call her Black Lizzie then?' he persisted.

His sister giggled nervously. His father took a mock swipe at him. 'Eat yer tea,' he said.

Jacky bided his time. His question was still in the air. The mealtime conversation remained stilted. The children could sense disagreement between their parents. They were unclear about its cause.

During an awkward pause Jacky asked again, 'Well why are folk afraid of her?'

His mother collected their plates, she eyed him meaningfully. 'Ask your granny,' she said from behind his father's back.

'Aye, ask yer Granny Cosgrove,' said his father. He meant ask *his* mother, not their other granny.

Jack's mother made a sound of annoyance, but she wouldn't challenge her husband, not in front of him anyway. His father scooped a handful of small change from his pocket and sorted through it. 'Here,' he said. 'Take the mennoge money round to her and you can ask her yourself. Kate, where's the card?'

'Let him finish his tea,' said his mother, but she leant over and opened the dresser drawer. She found a small green card and handed it to him. He picked it up along with the shilling and dashed out of the house, down the three flights of stone stairs and out of the close into the street. His granny lived four closes away. He covered the twenty yards in seconds and rapped on her window. She opened the sash.

'It's you, Jack,' she said. 'Come away ben.'

He made to clamber through the street-level window.

206

'Use the door,' she said. 'What do you think it's there for?'

Two men were standing at the close-mouth. He squeezed between them and went up the stone passage to his granny's door. When he went in she was spreading jam on a slice of buttered bread. 'Want a jeelly-piece?' she asked, folding it in two. 'I've just had my tea,' he said, but he accepted it. It was her traditional way of welcoming a grandchild.

'My Da sent the mennoge money.' He put down the bob on the coal-bunker by the door and came and sat down. Granny Cosgrove was tiny. She was less than five feet tall. He watched her stretch up to the mantelpiece and reach down a hard-covered book from behind the clock. She opened it, leafed through it, found his father's name and entered this week's shilling against it. His granny ran a money club. Her neighbours and family gave her small sums weekly. She put the cash in the Clydesdale Bank, and paid it out at Christmas and for the Fair holidays. Jack's mother said that she did it for the interest, but he could never see anything interesting in it. His father said she did it to help less careful folk.

'Granny, you know Black Lizzie.' It was an opening not a question. She put the book back behind the clock on tiptoe. The gas mantle was being erratic. The light was fluctuating. She adjusted the net mantle, it was brittle with heat, then she turned up the gas. The light was better.

'What about her?' she asked quietly. He loved his granny's voice. It was a soft Highland tone and always gentle, not like the Gorbals accents.

'Is it true she puts curses on people?' he asked.

She sat down looking suddenly weary. 'No, son. It's not.' She smiled at him. 'It's true she curses people sometimes, but that's a different thing.'

'How's that?' he asked. 'What do you mean?'

'When she is out of fettle, she swears at folk. Aye, and sometimes curses them. But you know that is not what folk mean. There is no real badness in Lizzie.'

'Why do they call her Black Lizzie then? Is it just 'cause she dresses all in black? Is that it?'

'No, no.' His granny was smiling ruefully and shaking her head. 'When she was young, before she married she was Lizzie Black. Then when she wed Geordie she was Mrs Robson. And that's what you should call her.'

'But they call her Black Lizzie,' he insisted.

'Aye. Well at one time there was no harm in it. When she was a lassie, she had the bonniest blackest hair you ever saw. She was very dark-skinned too, so with a name like Lizzie Black it's not surprising she got called Black Lizzie. Folk liked her in those days though. It was a compliment. She was Bonnie Black Lizzie.'

'Why are they frightened of her now?' he asked. 'What did she do?'

'Only weans and fools are frightened of her. Which are you?' she teased.

He explained about the football and how he had to get it back. 'But you are frightened of her? Frightened of her curse?' His granny wasn't being dismissive like his father, or complicitous like his mother. She understood. He could see she was thinking so he kept quiet.

She rose stiffly. 'Aye, well she has plenty to curse about, I suppose, but she will do you no harm. Here,' she said and fetched a half-used loaf from the press. 'Take this to her and tell her I sent you. Say I haven't seen her about, and that I wondered if she needed some bread.'

Jack had complete trust in his grandmother. To go with a gift from her, made it possible to approach Black Lizzie, but he was still apprehensive. 'She will not hurt you, Jack,' she reassured him. 'She has never really been right since her man died. That's all.'

'I don't remember Mr Robson,' said her grandson.

'No, you wouldn't. He died years since. He was gassed in 1916, he was left with a bad chest. When he got soaked through at the shipyards he caught pneumonia and died within the week.'

'And that left her . . . funny?' he asked.

'That and other things! It started with that.'

'Why do they hate her?'

'Oh . . .' she pondered '. . . for trying to help another unfortunate woman . . . like herself.' She looked at her grandson. 'There is a lot of badness in this world, Jack, and some awful people, but Lizzie, Mrs Robson, isn't one of them.' She paused. 'How old is your cousin Jean?' she asked.

'Twenty-four.' The boy was surprised by the question.

'I don't suppose you can picture Mrs Robson being that age?' She left the question to work on his imagination, whilst she busied herself looking for her crocheting.

'Lizzie was only twenty-two when her man died.' She studied the last row of her work, then looked up.

Jack thought of his cousin and her two children and Douglas her husband.

'She had no bairns. She was left on her own. She wasn't one of us either. She came from the Borders. Her folk were miles away. Geordie Robson hadn't been much for friends, so she'd few of them either, except maybe myself; both of us outsiders.'

The boy could not think of his grandmother as an outsider. It hurt. It undermined his sense of belonging.

'Me and your granddad arranged things for Lizzie. After the funeral service I brought her back here for a bit of tea. Your granddad and Peter went to the graveside.'

His grandmother was speaking slowly, intimately, to

209

an equal. She sighed heavily, remembering. 'After an hour or so with me here, Lizzie went back to her empty house.' Helen Cosgrove's calm left her. She put her crocheting in her lap, gripping it fiercely.

'Aye, empty. Empty indeed. Stripped bare. While she had been here, while her man was being buried, some bad souls had broken in and burgled her. They took all his things. His watch, his tools, his clothes, and the few pounds she had kept by her. It must have been neighbours to have known when to do it,' she said bitterly.

Jack had never heard harshness in her voice before. It shocked him. The word 'neighbours' had been said with vehemence, the tone carried with it her highlander's hatred of betrayal, a sense of outraged hospitality, which he could only guess at.

'Is that what made her ... like she is?' he asked quietly.

His grandmother regained her composure. She became aware that she was upsetting the boy. 'No, no, she coped with that not so badly. No, it was some more neighbourly help that did for her.'

Jack could see that her mind was not here with them in the kitchen. It was back there somewhere with Black Lizzie Black. He watched her silence.

'Jack, you are nearly twelve. You are surely not afraid of an old woman like Lizzie.' It was not a judgement. It was an appeal. 'Be a good boy, go and fetch your ball. Take her the bread. Come back and tell me how she is. I'm anxious about her. She has terrible feet.'

The boy reflected that bad feet and varicose veins seemed to be the common lot of old women, but it didn't make them scary.

'On you go,' said his granny encouragingly.

*

Outside the winter streets were bleak, everything was stone, and each stone was cold. Stone buildings, stone streets, stone pavements, stone closes, stone stairs. The thin strip of sky between the tenements was grey. The wind which canyoned through the narrow ways chafed the skin and sought out under-nourishment. The first thin skin of ice made the puddles fragile underfoot. The boy made his way back to Thistle Street in the dusk. On the corner he stood looking towards Black Lizzie's. It was not hard to see. Every window but hers glowed with light. Behind each was warmth and family. Black Lizzie's gaped like a dark mouth.

'My mother says she kills babies.' Jack turned, startled. It was the youngest member of the football squad.

'Rubbish,' said Jack. The nine-year-old did not merit serious conversation.

''Tis not!' protested the child. Jack ignored him. He left the corner and walked on.

'Ask anybody,' the boy called after him, shamed by the rebuff. 'I bet you won't go up anyway,' he cried out fiercely to Jack's retreating back, and scurried off as the older boy turned in annoyance.

Jack stood on the pavement opposite Black Lizzie's window, gazing up. He felt isolated. His grandmother was not here. Only he was here. Him and Black Lizzie and the dark. He felt himself shivering – with the cold. He could not take his eyes off that silent window. He hugged the loaf and wished he had been old enough for long trousers. In the gloom something reflected briefly, wraith-like behind the sash. Then it took shape, dim but solid now. His eyes focused. It was her. He could discern her shape; a head, a body, hands, strange hands, grotesquely malformed arthritic claws. She was leaning forward. Her waist-length hair was down. Her claws were

211

separating it, pulling it away from her face, revealing her open mouth. Petrified the boy watched her arm extend in his direction. She was gesturing towards him, beckoning him. Her mouth opened and closed; an evil fish, a predatory creature calling the boy to its lair. He pressed his back against the cold stone wall, pulling away from that reaching hand as though it were thirty inches and not thirty feet from him. She thrust out an arm at him, out of the black room it extended into the dark night. She was throwing something at him. The object fluttered like a moth. Halfway to the pavement it flapped open into a piece of ragged paper, blew away, gusted down the street before it came to ground. He watched it tumble in the air, saw it swirl and float till finally it disappeared in the gloom. When he looked back Black Lizzie's head was resting in her hands, her elbows on the sill, her hair streaming in the wind. She rose, levered herself up by painful inches until she was erect then slowly she disappeared from sight.

The boy stood for a minute, unable to move. He got to the corner crab-like, his back protected by the wall. He turned out of the street into Cumberland Road and hurried away homewards. He realized he was still carrying the loaf. He ought to go back to his Granny Cosgrove's but he did not want to return diminished. She wouldn't blame him. She would be gentle as always. But she would know. He was sure now that he would rather face Andy's anger over the lost ball than try to retrieve it.

'Never mind the bliddy thing, it's only a ball.' His mother was impatient.

'We'll get you another.' She did not understand.

'What do you think of your mother sending him up there?' She was accusing his father now. His Da said nothing.

212

'Unfortunate! She's not unfortunate. She's bad. A real messin. You keep away from Black Lizzie, d'you hear.'

The boy started to explain . . .

'Never mind that. I don't care what your granny said. She'd excuse anybody anything. Nobody ever did wrong according to her.'

The boy's father raised his head.

'Aye well,' said his mother more quietly. 'She'll die of goodness one of these days . . . your granny. That one nearly killed Jessie Boyd's lassie, your granny would not tell you that!'

The boy was hating this. His father rose. His look silenced his wife.

'Get you to bed,' he said to the boy. 'And take that loaf back to your granny tomorrow.'

It was unusual for the boy to pay an unwilling visit to his grandmother. But so it was today. He had not returned last night and she would have been expecting him. He knew she would be concerned. Besides he had, in a way, been on her errand, and he had let her down . . .

When he got there he went straight in. She was rinsing something in the sink. The kettle was boiling on the single gas ring on top of the range. The coals of the fire were bright. His grandmother turned to him wiping her wet hands on her apron.

She smiled then she noticed that he was carrying the half-loaf. She said nothing. Presently she came over. 'What happened to you last night?'

'I didn't see her.'

His granny looked puzzled. She turned back to the sink. 'Make a pot of tea,' she said after a minute. Jack went to the mantelpiece and fetched down the tea-caddy. He put two spoonfuls into the teapot which was warming on the range-top. The bars of the fire basket had soot flakes on them. He left the tea to brew and picked up the poker and started scraping the soot into the ash can below. He made a grating sound which he found comforting. His grandmother came over and took the poker from him and put it back beside the range. She sat down.

'Get the cups,' she said. 'There is milk in the press.' When they were both sitting down she said, 'What is it, Jack?'

'Mrs Angus's baby.'

'That was God's will,' she said softly. 'It is common enough, Lord knows.' She drank her tea. 'What happened about your ball?'

'Her light was out.'

'Maybe she was sleeping,' said his grandmother. She was unconvinced. They drank in silence. Only the sound of the fire and the chink of the cups disturbed the serenity of his Granny Cosgrove's room.

'Granny McGregor says Black Lizzie is evil.'

She reached out and brushed his hair back off his forehead with her fingertips and rested her warm palm on his head momentarily.

'You should pray for her, Jack . . . and you should pray for Mrs Angus. It is an awful thing to lose a child.' She looked concerned.

'Lizzie had nothing to do with that,' she protested. Then with growing comprehension, she asked, 'Have you heard them talking about Black Lizzie's bairn? Is that it?' She held his gaze, trying to read his confusion. She seemed to consider and then to make up her mind. She spoke to the boy slowly and deliberately. 'After Geordie died one of his mates came to see her, to comfort her. Thought she would be in need of male company. She wasn't. She was grieving, but that didn't

214

deter this Good Samaritan.' His grandmother paused allowing the boy time to react; watching him.

'She had a baby. Folk never forgave her.'

The boy shook his head not fully understanding.

'Jack, son, do you see, he forced himself on her.' Helen Cosgrove leant forward and took her grandson's hand. 'The bairn died when it was a few months old. It was a blessing maybe. But that is when Lizzie Black started cursing her neighbours.'

The grandson and the woman sat staring into the fire, then she said, almost to herself, 'The cheek of them. Blaming her for having a bairn after Geordie was dead. The pious hypocrites. Her priest would not comfort her. Half the street cut her dead. And when the wee thing died, there was some as made it clear they were pleased. Poor Black Lizzie Black.' She shook her head. 'And now folks are feared of her, frightened of her strangeness. It can be an awful world, Jack.'

She got up and took her shawl off the hook behind the door. 'Come away,' she said. 'We had best see if she is eating, and we will get your ball. I'd like her to meet you.'

'No. I'll go myself, Granny,' he said.

She smiled fondly at him, pleased. 'You are not frightened of her then?' she asked softly.

'No, Granny. I'm fine. It is not dark. Don't you come out in the cold.'

'Be sure to come back and tell me how she is.'

He is at Black Lizzie's close. There are three like it in Thistle Street and he hates them. He had delivered papers until he went to the academy, so he knows the area well. You never know what you will run into up these three closes. They are pitch black. There are no windows on the stairhead landings, and the gas lamps

215

never work. The place is seldom swept and it stinks of cats and leaking gas and worse.

He feels his way along the passage, and up the first flight of stone steps. The walls are damp. On the first landing something scutters under his feet and startles him, a stray cat probably or a rat more likely. He is halfway there, going back is just as worrying as going on. A door above slams. He hears a baby wailing briefly. Then it is quiet again. He carries on upwards to the next blind landing. He can feel that there are two doors. He knows Black Lizzie's is the one on the left. He knocks firmly and tries the handle. It gives a little. It is not locked. He pushes it gently and it opens. From the doorstep he can see the usual single-end. The room is semidark, lit only by the light from the street. The curtain at the window is flapping in the wind. There is a through draught now that he has opened the door. He can see only half of the room. The narrow entry created by the coal bunker on one side and the bed-recess on the other, obscures his view. In the light from the open window he can see Andy's ball by the sink.

'Mrs Robson?' he calls tentatively. There is no response. 'Are you in? . . . Mrs Robson?'

He takes two nervous steps inside. Now he can see the whole of the room. She is in an armchair by the ash-cold range, in the corner opposite him. One naked swollen foot is propped up on a stool. Her elbows are sharp through her shawl. She is grimacing sightlessly at him. She is motionless. She looks awful. She is even more frightening close up than he could have imagined. A broken cup lies in a puddle beside her chair.

Despite the numbing cold, the fire is dead. Who, in their right mind, would leave their door and window open and sit there in the freezing dusk? A rancid

216

milk bottle and some cheese are on the table. The breeze from the window cannot disguise the stench. The place is swarming with mice. He leaves the ball and runs.

GOOD NEIGHBOURS

Stephanie Egerton

Stephanie Egerton has been an avid reader since childhood. After a spell as an au pair in Switzerland and France she worked in London, first for a publisher then for eight years with the BBC.

She lives in East Anglia with her husband and two daughters, where she juggles with writing, family, garden and part-time editing work. Her special interests are music, natural history and vicarious travels around the East.

GOOD NEIGHBOURS

Sybil is on the bowling green. She wears a white jersey that shows off her breasts, still good and pointy, and a grey skirt that shows off her legs, still slim and shapely. A colour tint ensures that her hair remains deep brown and she wears a full panoply of make-up. She likes to hear people say: 'Sixty? You? *Never!*' She bowls with the fierce concentration of the very competitive, wasting no time on idle chat with her team-mates, Marjorie Frame, Father Hanlon's housekeeper, and Francis Mayhew, schoolteacher and bachelor. Her woods she bought in Kenya, for she travelled a lot while Bill was alive; their marks are like tribal marks, she thinks, and she cherishes them as another woman might cherish her jewellery or her houseplants.

But despite her concentration she cannot completely block two interlopers that niggle like threadworms in the back of her mind. She is waiting for that pea-brained Marjorie Frame to send a wood wide into the next lane, causing irritation to both teams, and for the too-early arrival of her daughter Jenny with her fidgety children, Hannah and Ben, products of a failed relationship.

As she stands amid the woods that cluster around her on the green like blackcurrants, she sees the family troop in; Jenny with her old beret on her glowing hair, the children self-important as acolytes at a religious ceremony. They sit down in the spectator area. Jenny will have no money to buy the children a drink and a chocolate bar, which might keep them quiet for a few minutes, and Sybil's own money is in a locker in the changing room.

Jenny never has any money on her: her mother manages the purse and gives her what she considers necessary when she considers it necessary. Francis, who knows more than Sybil realizes he does, passes a couple of pound coins up to her. Jenny smiles her gratitude and goes to the bar to buy two orange drinks for the children and a cup of coffee for herself.

As she sits back, sipping her coffee and watching the bowling, she is aware of a feeling of contentment. It's an almost totally alien sensation. Perhaps it's the warmth, perhaps relief at having safely negotiated the town traffic in her old mini. Maybe it's simply a rare feeling of being cherished, because Francis had bought her a drink. She even waves to Sybil, who grits her teeth at this further intrusion but has no other option, in a public place, than to wave back.

Jenny is strawberry blonde, pale, unmade-up, inward. She bears no resemblance to her robust mother; Marjorie Frame suspects she was adopted.

Father Hanlon says, 'Ah, she's a fine woman, Sybil Godbold. It would be like her to offer a home to a child in need.'

Marjorie is not so certain. Sybil is not beyond altruism, especially when it reflects well on herself, but to describe her as 'fine' shows, she thinks, a certain lack of perceptiveness.

Marjorie Frame is short and squat, with a sallow complexion and straight, dark hair, streaked with grey.

'At least no one is going to suspect Father Hanlon of any hanky-panky there,' Sybil once remarked, to the delight of the parish ladies.

Francis leaves as soon as the bowls tournament is

222

over. He is a grey man, Francis. Teaching at a local comprehensive school is a Via Dolorosa and at forty-eight retirement is uncomfortably far away.

He hasn't yet drawn back the curtains at home. The rooms are gloom-filled and smell musty. He opens a few windows, and hastily washes up his breakfast and lunch things and makes his bed. He shakes out the green baize cloth on his dining-table and turns on the gas fire. He is not cold, but in twenty minutes Hannah, Jenny's daughter, will be here for maths coaching, because Sybil is aiming at a grammar-school place for her grand-daughter.

Francis doesn't like Hannah. She is a watchful blonde weasel. She says little, but her slate-coloured eyes miss nothing. Francis often wonders how much gets back to Sybil. Francis's home is a lair, a refuge, imbued with his scent only, not for public sampling. The pale child is an interloper, unwelcome, admitted grudgingly because of the money, and because of Jenny. The image of Jenny's bright hair and withdrawn face hangs on the air like an icon during the teaching session. How much softer and more vulnerable is her white skin than that of her daugh-ter. There are veins just beneath the surface of Jenny's skin, waiting to be squeezed into haemorrhaging, trans-lucent violet shadows beneath the grey eyes. There are no spikes or corners on Jenny, all of her is malleable, even, he imagines, her bones. When he makes love to her it is like making love to a pliable white doll. Jenny poses no threat even to the least secure male; Francis suspects that her husband used to hit her.

'We must have a word about Hannah's progress,' he says, at six o'clock, when Jenny comes to collect her daughter. 'Can you manage a few minutes tomorrow evening?'

Jenny is always on auto-pilot after these 'consultations'.

223

It is a miracle to her that she ever gets back safely. Tonight, she manages to find a parking space only a few yards from her front door, nose to nose with Father Hanlon's Sierra. They live just half a block from the church. 'The noise of that blessed bell is enough to drive one to dementia,' says Sybil.

She lets herself quietly into the house. She is still vibrant with Francis's passion, which seems to throb through her body like arterial blood. She sits in the bedroom, waiting for the pulsing to stop and looks at herself in the mirror. Her image dances with black dots.

Then she hears her little boy, Ben, calling her. There's anxiety in his voice. As she comes down the stairs, he grips her round the legs. 'Mummy, I can't find Marmite.'

Sybil appears from the kitchen. 'I don't know how many times I've told you I'd have the wretched animal put down if it sprayed up my button-back sofa again.'

'Granny's teasing you,' Jenny reassures Ben. 'He'll turn up like he always does.'

'He'll have a job this time,' says Sybil.

Jenny stares. Behind her white mask unaccustomed heat and colour rush in. 'He was Ben's cat. You can't just take someone else's cat and have it put down.'

'It's my house,' returns Sybil equably. 'I don't need anyone's permission to have who and what I please in it.'

'It's *all* our house,' states Hannah.

'If by that you mean that the house belongs to us all, you're mistaken,' says Sybil. 'I've taken the three of you in out of charity, but I won't extend it to any smelly old tom off the streets. If you want another cat, get a kitten and train it properly.'

Ben doesn't understand. 'Where have you put Marmite?'

'She's taken him to the vet to be put to sleep,' Hannah informs him.

Ben's face is crumpled and tear-stained over supper; as she puts him to bed Jenny rocks him in her arms. She does her best to defend Sybil's high-handed action and assures him that one day they'll get their own house and as many cats as he pleases. But, with her chin on Ben's silky head, she weeps too, because she can see no way of fulfilling that promise. The only certainties are Sybil, poverty and Francis's probing hands and panting cries.

And they are not unconnected. Jenny is a *tabula rasa* ready to be defaced by anyone who wishes. She has been moulded for tyranny, violence and the sexual act, with her white skin, her anaemic mucous membranes, her curious, pinkish hair spilling over the pillow, or forwards across the sofa, for Nigel had liked his pleasures that way. Jenny was never married, just imprisoned; imprisoned by her own nature and anyone with a mind to take advantage of it. An adoption, two abortions, Hannah and Ben, sterilization, and all before her twenty-first birthday: that was Jenny.

'I've tried with you, God knows I've tried,' says Sybil, retracing a well-trodden path. 'I can't think whose genes you've got – not your father's, certainly not mine. Perhaps you're a mutant. All I ask while you're under my roof is that you keep your nose clean and behave as a decent Christian should. At least you can't saddle me with any more bastards, thank God. And while we're on the subject of Christianity, Father Hanlon is trying to ask me, as subtly as he can, which is not very, why you never take Communion. I told him you're a divorcee, understand?'

Jenny knows Father Hanlon's concern for her is not wholly spiritual. Jenny can recognize an undeclared sexual interest in the same way a doctor can diagnose

225

an as yet unmanifest disease. Any interest in Jenny is also, partly, social prurience; Jenny is a mystery. She has an appearance to make people turn and stare, even the most devout. Yet she never says anything, offers no one her friendship, does nothing for the parish beyond standing silently beside her mother on the produce stall at the annual fête. Sybil has let it be known that it is she who has to carry the household.

'Sybil's a tower of strength,' say the parish jackals, admiringly.

They speculate as they polish the church brass and poke chrysanthemums into vases. Maybe Jenny Martin is mentally defective. Terminally ill (God knows she looks it). A by-blow of Bill's. They reject that – he wouldn't have dared. It was well known he went in mortal fear of Sybil. Marjorie Frame thinks she has been adopted. It is the most plausible explanation, but the least interesting. Marjorie Frame has been playing bowls with Sybil for four years now, ever since the Godbold family moved into the parish, and knows as little about Sybil as she did then. She only knows that the bowls team now wins more often than it loses.

Ben has started wetting the bed again. First thing in the morning Sybil runs a bath and puts Ben and the bedding in it together.

'You're a dirty little boy, aren't you?' she says conversationally.

Ben has a theory that if he can cut his willy off he won't wet the bed any more. He examines the offending organ closely in the bath, and gives it an exploratory nip, which hurts. Ben's fear of pain battles with his fear of this shameful emission which comes uninvited when he is off his guard. He tries to think. 'Think, think,' says Mrs Dalton at school. 'Think what two and two are. Think what letter comes after F. Think what side of the paper to start writing on.' Ben can never think. The more he strains the more paralysed his mind becomes. Mrs Dalton goes to his church; he's seen her there on Sundays.

Mrs Dalton has her theories about the family, too. She thinks Ben ought to be seen by an educational psychologist but hesitates about how best to approach the matter since success is only possible with the co-operation of that awful grandmother.

She seeks the advice of Francis Mayhew. He is a teacher like herself. He coaches Hannah Martin; he also plays bowls with Sybil Godbold. Francis recommends giving Ben more time to settle down, and implies that any hasty action on her part might unleash a Pandora's box of problems.

Francis thinks of Jenny's bruisable, compliant white body. He would like to urge her to see a doctor, her blood count must be way below the safe minimum; but there's the question of that Pandora's box again. The guardian of that box is Sybil, unassailable Sybil who has the ear of the parish priest and the backing of the parish ladies, who are all afraid of her. (As is Francis himself.) Francis sometimes thinks of marrying Jenny, but he is not ready for a permanent mate in his lair. He's even less ready for surrogate fatherhood. He is getting on for fifty, undistinguished as a teacher, unimposing as a man, but the little boat of his life is precious to him and he doesn't want it rocked.

Jenny dreams of life in her own home, far from Sybil's hectoring and Father Hanlon's prying questions. She is reminded of her early teens, her very early teens, before her hopes of a brighter tomorrow were wrecked by her own treacherous hormones.

Jenny thinks of her first pregnancy, the one that went to term because, in terror, she could do nothing except

227

pretend it wasn't happening. She remembers, though she would rather not, the eventual confrontation with her mother: Sybil, hissing, lips drawn back over long canine teeth, clawed hands gripping Jenny by the shoulders and shaking her until her head rocked back and forth and her bladder emptied on to the bedroom carpet.

She thinks of the social worker who came with her to the antenatal clinic. ('There are things I draw the line at,' said Sybil.) She was relentlessly bright, and devoid of all compassion. I have seen too much *real* suffering, her attitude implied, to be particularly sympathetic towards *you*.

There are certain things she can think of, but whenever the baby comes to mind, the squirming red grub with the greasy black skull-cap of hair, which, after sixteen hours of turmoil, was squeezed so painfully out of her body's tubes, she flicks the thought away like a slug out of a lettuce.

'No point in going back to school,' Sybil had said briskly to the pale fifteen-year-old who stood in the kitchen, pressing her thumb into a bowl of bread dough, a child still, but for the sagging fold of her abdomen and the occasional ooze of milk from her breasts. 'Make yourself useful here, for a change. I'm sorry your poor father should see how low you've sunk.'

So Jenny, having remembered her past and dreamed of her future, now stands in Francis's living room. She has pulled her beret off, like a child arriving at school, tousling her peach-coloured hair. Like a child, too, she comes straight to the point.

'Can I come and live with you? Just for a week or two till I find something permanent?'

'What sort of a permanent place had you in mind?' says Francis cautiously. He knows she has no money.

'A council house, maybe.'

228

'Jenny, it'll be years before you'll get a council house. You're not a priority case.'

'I have two children,' she says stubbornly.

'Yes, but you're not on the streets. You have a home. You'd have to prove it was unsuitable. Or that your mother abused the children.' The question hanging in the air that Francis dares not ask.

'I'd keep the children out of your way. I could cook for you and clean the house.'

'But how will you live? You'd have to get a job. I don't suppose your mother would support you, and I certainly can't.'

'I wasn't asking for that. I want somewhere to go, that's all. I've promised Ben a home of his own. Francis, my mother went and had his cat put down! He's in a terrible state, poor little boy, wetting the bed again . . .' She pauses, realizing she has weakened her case. Francis is silent.

'You're the only person I can ask; you're the only real friend I've got,' Jenny says pitifully.

Francis feels compromised by this sad admission. But he continues to defend his sanctuary. He cannot, out of charity, explain to Jenny that it is simply out of the question to have two young children in his home, even for a fortnight, with their noise, toys, junk food and television programmes, not to mention the wet sheets. Now, if it were just Jenny . . .

'Have you asked any of the parish ladies? They may know of something to rent.'

'Don't be funny,' says Jenny bitterly.

Francis is torn between compassion and guilt. He tries to embrace her, but she ducks under his arms and picks up her beret from the table. She is close to tears.

'Forget it, Francis. I'm sorry I asked.'

Jenny goes and sits on a bench near the river. She has

229

with her a copy of the local newspaper, in the hopes that someone wants to sell an old caravan cheaply, but she is too dispirited to open it. A dull grey mist clogs the air, the wooden bench is damp and tacky. The brownish-grey river, swollen after heavy rain, swirls along turgidly. Through the trodden mud of the footpath tramps a man in wellington boots, with a dog. He looks at Jenny as he passes and she is aware of the rousing of the familiar old demon that she had thought dead.

She is still sitting on the bench when he comes back, her hair gone dark in the rain.

'Are you all right?' he calls.

'I'm fine, thank you.'

'I don't mean to be personal. I just wondered. You look very pale.' He hesitates slightly. 'You know, you want to be careful round here. There are a lot of people who'd take advantage of a woman on her own.'

The dog comes bustling up, and Jenny touches its wet head, lightly, like a blessing.

'I know,' she says.

It is not long till Christmas. The decorations are already up in the High Street, twinkling their message of tawdry commercialism. In the window of the town's big store a Santa Claus with a jolly dipsomaniac face rocks back and forth in an electronic sleigh waving his hand woodenly, while his reindeer turns its head from side to side. The reindeer's face is louche, even sinister. Ben is afraid of it. He drags back as they approach the window and won't look. Sybil and Hannah uncomprehendingly berate him – going to see Santa in his grotto is supposed to be a treat. But Ben knows that the reindeer will be there too, and the grotto will be dark, except for a spooky blue light and he bursts into unavailing tears as he is towed by the steel hawser of Sybil's arm down the stairs to the grotto entrance. There his tears become screams: Sybil remonstrates, Hannah gives him a furtive pinch. Finally, a kind lady takes Hannah into the grotto with her own child.

'You little moron,' Sybil hisses at Ben.

Jenny is preoccupied these days. She is often out, and when she comes in her hair is damp and her shoes covered with mud. She says she has gone for a walk.

Every evening, swiftly and furtively, she washes the mud off her shoes and the tool of her trade, a plastic mac. She raises her bruised and aching arms to comb out her hair. She camouflages the purple bite-marks on her neck with cosmetic cover-stick and a scarf. All over her arms and legs are swollen, scarlet slashes, mostly from the undergrowth. She should put antiseptic cream on them, but she has no heart and, it being winter, they can be hidden beneath long sleeves and trousers. At all times she carries in her nostrils the whiff of hot, damp body odours, the odours of her trade.

Even by her own unexacting standards she feels she is near bed-rock. Enough money for a deposit on a second-hand caravan is only the first hurdle in an obstacle course that must include severance from her mother, for Jenny feels like an unseparated Siamese twin; a maldeveloped embryonic growth welded on to a more robust sibling who possesses all the vital organs. She dare not contemplate her chances of individual survival. Never a conversationalist, even in the most minimal way, she now has a profound distaste for speaking at all.

Sybil ascribes this to sullenness, Hannah to a sore throat, which is partly true: Jenny is never well. Ben does not notice: he is the only one she talks to.

231

'One day we'll have a lovely snug caravan, and two cats,' she tells him.

'And no school?' Ben asks hopefully. Then: 'Why didn't you come to parents' night, Mummy? Mrs Dalton wanted to see you.'

(Three miles away, in her mock-Tudor home, Mrs Dalton has deferred worrying about Ben Martin till next term. School has broken up now, she has two weeks' and three days' freedom.)

Jenny's caravan fund has made a modest start. It goes into an account at another bank – not the one Sybil uses.

But Sybil's intelligence net is comprehensive.

'Pat Roscoe says she saw you in the Midland Bank yesterday. What on earth were you doing there?'

'Oh. Francis Mayhew asked me to pay in a cheque for him.'

'I didn't realize he'd changed his bank,' says Sybil, and produces, for Jenny's inspection, a cheque from Francis made out to the Bowls Club, which he has asked Sybil to deliver.

'Perhaps he has two banks,' says Jenny, making to go upstairs.

'Perhaps you are lying,' says Sybil.

Sybil has her eye on Jenny, mistrust of her daughter being a staple of the last twenty years. Her eye is all-seeing: it can spot grease marks, dusty ledges or wilting flowers in church as unerringly as a hawk's. She regards Jenny darkly: dark eyes, dark hair, dark-red lips applied with the firm hand of the very sure. Jenny feels that Sybil leeches out of her what little colour she has left, not to mention the last light of her virtue, the last of her health. For all she knows her being may now be host to an unmentionable virus, invading every corner of her system. She daren't kiss Ben. Can Sybil see the

232

virus? Is it visibly spreading through her like a dye through water? She would like to make her mother a present of the virus: she can think of no more appropriate punishment.

It is the Sunday before Christmas. Francis has not seen Jenny for weeks. The Jenny he sees today has lost her pellucid glow. She looks like old wax. He kneels in his pew and prays, without hope, for a solution to her problems; one that preferably doesn't involve him. He also prays that the tales he hears about her hanging about the towpath are unfounded. He knows the towpath. He walked it, once. It is a muddy trail between an unsavoury river and a wasteland of brambles. At one point it passes beneath a railway bridge, stinking of urine, littered with old paper and spent condoms. Female joggers avoid it.

He can see the family two rows up on the other side of the aisle. When they stand to sing the hymn he sees that Jenny's nose is bleeding; she clamps a stained handkerchief to it and holds Ben's sympathy at arm's length while Sybil irritably wipes red drops from the pew. Hannah turns and sees him looking at them. She regards him aloofly, till he drops his eyes back to the hymn book.

Hannah thinks she looks good today. She has on new white socks and a blue anorak that suits her colouring. Granny bought it for her at a jumble sale. 'Never been worn, by the look of it.' Hannah glances up at her. She is the tallest of them all and Hannah likes the richness of her dark hair and red lipstick. Granny knows about everything. There is security in Granny for Hannah, and a role model too. Granny never does things like have nose-bleeds in church. Hannah sometimes thinks her mother is fading away and one day she will suddenly

233

become muzzy and disappear altogether. Things would be better if she did. And as for Ben – 'Ben, Ben in his smelly little den' – she slaps her brother's hand away from the front of his shorts. Hannah is already over-aware of people who let the side down.

Father Hanlon has chosen as the text for his sermon the parable of the Good Samaritan.

'Picture this road,' he says, leaning intently from his pulpit. 'It's probably a short cut, perhaps an alleyway, the sort of place thieves and muggers love. And there, lying at the side, in a pool of blood, is this man. First a priest passes by, then a Levite. They cross on to the other side, with their noses in their newspapers, so to speak. If challenged, they plan to say, 'Wounded man? What wounded man?' People are always getting beaten up. It's a rough area. Best not to get involved. It may even have been domestic – we all know better than to interfere there, don't we?'

Obedient titters from the congregation.

'Then along comes this Samaritan. He stops. He isn't afraid of getting involved. He sees a man who needs help. He gets wine and oil from the saddlebag of his donkey, cleans up the wounds, bandages them with strips of linen, helps the poor victim on to the donkey and takes him to a nearby inn. Not only that, he pays the innkeeper to take care of him.

'And who can remember the point of this parable? It was *love thy neighbour as thyself*, wasn't it? Who is your neighbour? Children, can you tell me that?'

'Everyone,' chant the children in sing-song chorus.

'Everyone. Our neighbour does not have to live in the same street, go to the same church or have the same skin colour. It is our duty as Christians to care for anyone in need who crosses our path, no matter how much we dislike that person or how undeserving he – or she –

234

may appear to be. To extend a hand to someone in need profits those who give as much as those who receive; for it is by loving one another that we shall surely attain the Blessed Light. May God bless you all.'

The last hymn is sung; everyone leaves the church, spiritually uplifted and privileged to be in the position of helping those in trouble.

Francis waits by his pew till Jenny passes.

'I'd like a word about Hannah,' he says, watching to make sure Sybil and the children keep walking.

'What, now?'

'Could you come to my house this afternoon, about three?'

To Jenny's dissenting silence he mutters in desperate undertone, 'What is it, Jenny? Why don't you come and see me these days? Has your mother found out about us?'

It's the only explanation he can think of.

'I'll come and see you after Christmas,' Jenny promises vaguely; and he has to be content with that.

Father Hanlon stands by the door, portly in his cassock, receiving congratulations on his sermon. 'Goodbye, God bless,' he murmurs to his departing flock, occasionally varying the drone with: 'How's Tim, then, Mrs McEnery?' or, 'Good to see you about again, Hugh.'

He nods to the Godbold/Martin family as they file out; but he cannot meet their eyes. Disturbing rumours about Jenny Martin are spreading like nettle roots around the parish: every day they crop up in a different spot. The men of the parish are not more given to fornication than those anywhere else, and for all Father Hanlon's shortcomings the seal of the confessional is sacred to him, so it would be impossible to say how they started. The parish ladies whisper among themselves that Sybil is a saint, putting up with that dreadful girl. They know what *they'd* do. As they wash the stone floor and shake the church banners out in readiness for Christmas, the jackals dismember Jenny Martin's character.

As for Father Hanlon, he perplexedly squeezes his thick peasant's hands together, or rubs them up and down his clothes, for whenever he thinks of Jenny Martin they begin to sweat. He cannot decide from her demeanour whether Sybil has heard these rumours or not, but surely to goodness she'd have to be deaf not to have done. His heart goes out to her. Sooner or later the lamp of pastoral concern must be taken to that household. He decides to tackle Jenny first.

So when, on Christmas Eve, he sees Sybil stepping briskly past the presbytery on her way to the shops he seizes his chance, picks up the phone and summons Jenny to his presence.

Jenny brings with her the pudding Sybil has made for Father Hanlon, as everyone knows Marjorie Frame's Christmas puddings are credible substitutes for cannon-balls. Father Hanlon, feeling himself wrong-footed by the gesture, holds the pudding in both hands before him like an oblation and prefers to address it rather than the young woman standing before him.

'Jenny, you know your mother is very worried about you,' he begins. A downright lie, he has never discussed Jenny with her mother, but the interview is going to be a whole lake of thin ice, anyway. 'So I thought it was time we had a little chat. But it wasn't your mother's idea, so it might be better not to go mentioning it to her. Now, Jenny,' he clears his throat, looks round for somewhere to deposit the Christmas pudding. He never knows how to talk to Jenny – she has no personality, no warmth, no humour; only a body around which his

236

most shameful fantasies are centred, and a soul which it is his duty to save. Jenny waits, with all the patience of the meek.

'You know, you should marry again,' he achieves at last, 'an attractive young woman like you. Ah, I was forgetting. You're divorced, aren't you? That's tricky. Wasn't it a blessing your good mother was on hand to give you and your children a home, eh? Sit down, Jenny, we might as well make ourselves comfortable.' His rich, jolly laugh booms out; Jenny obediently takes a chair and sits looking at the clerical black knees spread opposite.

'Now: your mother and I both feel that something is troubling you, Jenny. Are we right? Is it your financial situation that's bothering you, or is it a relationship you need? Hmm? You can trust me, you know, Jenny.'

Jenny is encouraged by his kindly tone. With a brightening face she begins to tell him of Ben's problems, her difficulties with Sybil, her hopes for her own home, even if it's only a caravan. She hasn't spoken at length for so long that she finds communication difficult; she gropes for words to express her desperate need for independence while endeavouring to present fairly her mother's point of view. She explains about the baby, about Nigel's violence. She admits she is lonely and that she has a desperate need of money. And she looks up at him hopefully.

His face is hard as rock.

'I don't think that's the whole story, Jenny. I'm waiting to hear the rest.'

She looks at the floor. Father Hanlon reads obstinacy in her silence; his colour, and temper, mount.

'Don't think I haven't heard that you hang about the towpath with men. Is that how you mean to finance this scheme of yours? You'd bring shame on your good mother and your little children for the sake of a second-hand caravan? Pull yourself together, girl. It's gross selfishness, leaving aside the morality of it. Your mother is devoted to the children; she is also getting no younger, and she'll need your help more and more as time goes by. There are other ways of making money. Get some training then go and do something worthwhile. Nurse, or teach. If it's an outlet for your physical energy you're needing, there's a lot of voluntary work you could do in the parish. But don't let me ever hear you've been seen loitering on the towpath again. You've seen the types that go there – do you want to end up on a mortuary slab? And surely to God you've heard of the diseases you can get.'

Jenny, tricked into opening her heart, turns her head away so he will not see her tears. She gazes through a blur at the Christmas pudding made by her 'good' mother, and the cards wishing joy and peace propped on the sideboard behind it. Joy and peace are not for her: she has forfeited the right to them. But Ben has the right: Ben must be given joy and peace.

'Ben has the right to joy and peace,' she says, turning her wet face to the priest.

'Not at that price,' says Father Hanlon.

Jenny gets to her feet, weeping, and goes out, pulling the door shut behind her. It clicks to like a security barrier between herself and the priest. Her beret is lying on the floor. The sight of it enrages Father Hanlon, and he kicks it from one end of the room to the other. Then, ashamed, he picks it up. It smells of her hair.

He goes into the church. He lowers himself on to his knees before the altar, and tries to pray. Tries, because he cannot decide who has the priority claim, Jenny, or himself. He tries to vindicate his insensitive handling of the situation but his mind, like a runaway train, races defencelessly towards its habitual fantasy: Jenny, pinned beneath his bulk, her thighs parting to receive the benediction of his sex.

Sybil and the children are still out when Jenny gets back. She is cold and trembling. She puts on the gas fire and makes herself a cup of tea, but it nauseates her and her body expels it from her pale mouth, between the curtain of her hair, down the kitchen sink. She knows it is now only a matter of time before Sybil learns everything. She cannot imagine what form her punishment will take. Fear makes her feel physically ill. She bears no animosity towards Father Hanlon for his outburst, for she is too familiar with the ambivalence of human sexuality. But she feels all the mortal sadness of the outcast whose life is so grubby that not even a healer of souls wants to touch it.

Christmas night. The church sparkles with lights, glows with swathes of golden chrysanthemums. Carols swell their message of rejoicing up to the rafters and out into the street. The church is so packed that, arriving late, the family cannot sit together. Ben turns often to look at his mother, three pews behind on the other side. It occurs to him, with anxiety, that she no longer wants to be with them, she has forgotten her promise of their own home, and a cat. So he keeps twisting round to keep her in his sight and whenever he thinks he's caught her eye he gives her a big beaming smile, but she doesn't smile back. It's as though she can't see him. Mummy was sick just before they left for church. Perhaps that's why. He twists round so often that Sybil seizes his arm and drags him, legs tripping and trailing, to the other side of her. Now he can't see Mummy any more.

Jenny stands with her carol sheet in her hand. She cannot sing. She feels trapped in the suffocating piety of these ardent people. Sybil has intimated that they would have something to discuss later, whilst they filled the children's stockings. She cannot hope for mercy.

The congregation sings the final carol. Preceded by the processional cross and the altar-servers in red and white, Father Hanlon passes down the aisle and takes up his station by the door. If his normal bucolic cheer is somewhat lacking, his flock are too fired by the spirit of Christmas to notice.

As Sybil walks down the aisle, the children trotting beside her, people lower their eyes in deference to her regal courage. At the door, Father Hanlon takes her hands in his and presses them warmly, hoping to convey sympathy and support, but the eyes he meets are as flinty and fixed as a reptile's. They give him a shock; he begins to wonder whether he's ever really known Sybil God-bold at all.

And Jenny, where is Jenny? He has been watching for her, but like a pale fry among larger, brighter fish, she has slipped through the net unobserved and is already outside, somewhere among the surge of people spilling out into the street in a widening arc, chatting, laughing, wishing each other Happy Christmas. Francis is looking for her too, and Hannah and Ben dart in and out of the pools of light from the streetlamps like golden fish surfacing in a pond.

But Jenny stands silently in the dark shadow of the wall and marshals the last of her endurance while she waits for Sybil and for what is to come.

NOBODY WE KNOW

Carey Jane Hardy

Carey Jane Hardy trained as a nurse at the Queen Elizabeth Hospital in Birmingham and specialized in haematology. After eleven years she decided to take a break to study fulltime for a degree in English Literature. She enjoys amateur dramatics and wide Norfolk skies and is a great admirer of the Brontës, Daphne du Maurier, Gregory Peck and her husband, John.

NOBODY WE KNOW

When the old hotel was closed down it was not demolished. It was left to stand empty and forlorn at the edge of the cliffs. Its front windows gazed reproachfully towards the town that had discarded it, while its rear windows gazed wistfully out to the sea that would perhaps – another century from now – reclaim it. The water in the swimming pool was replaced by autumn leaves, and the echoes of guests who had once stayed there were left to play in the deserted rooms where nobody could hear them.

The hotel was a part of my childhood; not that I had ever stayed there myself. My mother could not afford the apparent luxury of the Hotel de la Mer. We stayed at Mrs Viney's guest house in one of the little back streets at the end of the town. We went summer after summer; an accepted routine that was never questioned – at least, not in those early years. If I had questioned it, I would probably have been told that it was a clean and respectable guest house. It was within our income, and besides, Mrs Viney liked children; an apparently rare commodity in a landlady. And it was true. She did like us. I suspect that my sister Jean was the favourite. Mrs Viney preferred girls to boys. She liked my mother too. She called her 'Dear Mrs Devon', or just 'Dear', for short, and with a child's acute ear for sincerity or falsehood, I sensed that her endearment expressed genuine affection.

The image of the young widow and the two fatherless children probably appealed to Mrs Viney. I knew, of course, that we had a father, and that therefore my mother must have a husband. But we never spoke of him. I harboured a natural curiosity about my father, and made up countless stories about him which I never disclosed to anyone. I may even have been secretly afraid that they were true.

We passed the hotel every day on our way to the beach. A path led from the road, around the hotel to the edge of the cliffs and down to the beach itself. It was a steep path, thrilling and dangerous to run down at top speed feeling the world spin away from beneath our feet until we fell, giddy and breathless, on the sand below. It was quite another matter to climb up after our excursions. It seemed an endless trudge, carrying our baskets and buckets and spades, already tired from our exposure in the sea air, and cross at the interruption to our games. Then we would gaze longingly at the hotel standing so proudly above us. If we were staying there, we would be nearly home, and have no need to walk the extra mile.

We saw afternoon tea being served in the lounge, and the vast dining room laid ready for the evening meal. As the path brought us round to the front of the hotel we peered into the entrance hall and saw what seemed to us a display of unthinkable wealth. Heavy chandeliers hung from the ceiling and blue carpet covered the floor and swept up the elegant staircase. In the centre of the hall there was a large circular sofa upholstered in blue velvet. It probably wasn't real velvet, but at our age of make believe we were prepared to be convinced.

'Isn't it beautiful?' murmured Jean.

'Splendid,' I said. For beautiful was not a word I used in public. I considered it to be soft.

244

'I wonder who stays there?' said Jean, gazing at the windows that rose secretly above us.

'Nobody we know,' said my mother, ushering us along. Her tone of voice almost implied that it was not quite nice to know anybody who stayed in such a place.

For years I played a game with myself. I would watch people; on the beach, in the town, even back at home in London. And I would look at their faces and wonder if they were the sort of people who would stay at the Hotel de la Mer. For surely such an event would have left its mark, indelibly and forever on the face of any human being. I knew that one day I would recognize it and be able to say categorically, 'That is the face of one who has stayed at the Hotel de la Mer.' And then one day, I saw it.

It was, as they say in books, my thirteenth summer. Years afterwards, I considered making it the title of a book I planned to write. I never wrote it, so it required no title. Somehow I could never turn the events into someone else's story. It also happened to be our last summer at Mrs Viney's guest house. Jean was ten years old that summer. She always had her birthday when we were on holiday. It was part of the ritual. It gave us a certainty that we would always return. 'Next year, on my birthday . . .' Jean would say. And we would know that as surely as her birthday arrived, year after year, so we would spend the summer in our accustomed place.

Mrs Viney met us warmly with her usual greeting of, 'Ah, there you are, my dears,' as if she had been waiting for us on the doorstep through all the intervening months. She showed us up to our usual rooms at the top of the passage, the two doors facing each other across the corridor. For the past seven years Jean and I had shared the larger of the two rooms while my mother occupied the smaller one. Our room took on a life of

245

its own despite the conventional furniture, and the dull guest-house colours: for there we played games during wet weather and my mother told us stories. There she tucked us up at night when it was still too light to go to sleep, and we begged her to stay and talk. There Jean and I slept during the hot windless nights of summer and listened to the sea weaving in and out of our dreams.

There was a change this year, however. It was small in itself and yet immense to me in all that it signified. My mother placed her suitcase on one of the beds in our room and bent to unlock it. Jean was talking to Mrs Viney in the passage and my mother said to me, 'Now that you are the man of the family, I thought you'd like to have a room of your own, and Jean and I will share this one.' She had her back to me as she spoke so I could not be certain of her expression. Her voice was quite matter of fact, with a hint of a suggestion that her proposal was to my advantage. Yet the whole idea was so unexpected that I reeled with the shock.

It had not occurred to me that the time might come when it would be inappropriate for me to share my sister's room. My mother obviously thought that now I was a teenager that time had come. She must have been thinking of my privacy rather than Jean's, for Jean was still a baby, with no sense of modesty or impropriety. I reddened slightly at the implications of my mother's words and was grateful at first that she did not turn to look at me. She seemed to take it for granted that I agreed and began to unpack her clothes and hang them in the wardrobe. Only then did I feel a tinge of jealousy. It was not that I harboured any great feelings for my small sister but she was, after all, my companion on these annual holidays. I imagined the confidences and chatter that she and my mother would now share without me and I felt shut out. My mother's words jarred too. Now that you are the man of the family. I experienced a sudden intense fear of growing up, of things changing, of time passing without my consent; and beneath it was another sensation that had recently begun to wind its way into my consciousness. I missed my father.

I had begun to realize this only in the last few months and it had been vague, hardly capable of being put into words. Yet now, walking across the passage to that other room with a great weight of leaving something behind me that I did not want to lose, the feeling flooded over me. It was as if the lack of my father was a new and raw bereavement, rather than a reality with which I had grown up. I went into the little room and walked across to the window. I rested my elbows on the sill and looked out into the small garden, to the terraced barricade of the houses that backed on to this one, and beyond them to the sea. I wished that I was not thirteen years old. I wished that I did not have to spend the next three weeks in this house of women; Mrs Viney, my mother and Jean. Though I never prayed, I prayed then to my father to take away this pain.

I was sullen for days. Even Mrs Viney noticed and passed comment that I had obviously reached the awkward age.

'He's always been awkward,' said Jean over the breakfast table. 'But he used to be fun. Now he won't do anything. He's so boring.'

'That will do, Jean,' said my mother. Jean shot me a withering look and slurped her milk.

'It's not fair,' she continued. 'Why does he get a room of his own anyway?'

'Because he's the oldest,' said my mother, in a voice that implied that the conversation was over. I knew it wasn't true. If Jean had been the oldest, I would still have had the small room. They would still go on talking about me as if I wasn't there.

Gradually though, I got used to this unwanted privilege. It seemed foolish to waste the holiday moping. So I consented to join in as usual. Yet something had changed. I could not be the carefree boy I had been before. I was dogged by strange moods that made me irritable. I condemned all women in my heart for being silly females who did not understand. Jean teased me, dancing round and chanting in her sing-song voice. My mother simply looked at me with kind and knowing eyes that made me still more angry, but with an anger that was no longer directed at her.

I had always been fiercely protective of my mother. If I had deigned to use the word 'beautiful' I would have used it to describe my mother for she was lovely. She was tall and graceful, and made me think of a beautiful swan, gliding on the river, her dark hair flowing out behind her. She was aloof and quietly spoken, uncomfortable with strangers. I, being more gregarious, learned to act as her spokesman even as a child. Sometimes I would tease her for her shyness, and she would laugh quietly and put her arm loosely around my shoulders, and we would understand our need of each other. The idea that anyone else – certainly any adult man – could love her did not occur to me. I presumed that once my father had loved her. I was old enough to know that two children did not appear in the world without a physical union between a man and a woman. But a boy does not associate these things with his mother. Her singleness, the only state in which I had known her, helped to establish this concept of chastity and separateness from the world.

Now, the intangible changes that had come made me

far more protective of myself than of her. Jean and Mrs Viney complained that I was quieter and too withdrawn. Yet within, I was teeming with words, unexpressed fears and doubts, and a need for male companionship. I went off for walks alone, sometimes leaving Jean behind in tears, to be comforted by her company of women. I climbed the cliffs which I had been forbidden to do because of the subsiding soil. I clambered over breakwaters and skimmed pebbles off the surface of the sea. I hung about the hotel, spying on the guests. One day I met Nathan Strong.

He was on the beach, leaning against the breakwater, looking out to sea through a pair of binoculars. I studied him for a while, and when he did not move, I also looked out to sea, wondering what had caught his attention. 'What are you looking at?' I said. He still did not move but let out a long slow whistle from between his teeth. 'I can't see anything,' I said.

'Look at that seagull,' he said at last. 'It's seen a fish.' Then, just as I had hoped he would, he passed the binoculars to me, though he never took his eyes from the spot he had been looking at. He simply pointed. 'There,' he said. 'Any second now, he'll dive.'

The scene rushed in through the lenses and I saw the white winged bird hovering above the waves, as if held there by an invisible cord. Then suddenly it dived, swiftly and mercilessly, and plucked something from the sea, gulping it greedily even as the wings bore it up again.

'Did you see it?' said the man, earnestly.

'Oh, yes,' I said. 'I'm sorry you missed it.'

'Oh, that's all right. I've been watching him for some time. He has a large appetite.'

He was a big man. Even sitting on the breakwater while I stood, his head was high above mine. I guessed

249

that he was in his forties. His eyes were creased against the sun and his head and chin were covered with fair hair, shot with red. He ought to have had a straw panama and a pipe and be sitting in the foreground of an Impressionist painting. We exchanged names but it seemed of secondary importance to what we had just shared.

'Do you live here?' I asked. But of course I knew before he spoke what the answer would be. I had seen it in his face.

'I'm staying at the Hotel de la Mer,' he said.

I wanted to plague him with questions. What was it like? What did he eat there? But I simply said, 'Oh yes, I know it. I pass it every day.' Then I examined the binoculars which I still held in my hands. 'Are you a bird-watcher?'

'Of a sort. Only for my own pleasure though. It passes the time.'

'Have you seen much today?'

'Yes, plenty, but nothing that would be considered very important by the professionals. I could sit for hours watching one bird. I find their behaviour quite fascinating.'

'Do you come here every day?'

'Most days. I usually come early before the beach gets too crowded.'

'This is the quieter end anyway,' I said.

'Yes, I've noticed that. Are you a regular?'

'Oh yes,' I said carelessly. 'We come here every summer. We're practically locals now.'

From then on I made it a rule to be on the beach early, slipping down immediately after breakfast. Most days I would find Nathan there ahead of me, and I ceased to act surprised. He seemed to accept that I would join him. Mother and Jean also came down to the beach and I was forced to introduce them. My mother seemed pleased that I had found a friend, albeit one so much older than myself. She addressed him as Mr Strong, although I claimed the privilege of calling him Nathan. He was very gracious to my mother, for which I respected him, and very kind to Jean, which I reluctantly condoned. She had, after all, been my first friend, and although she was childish, she usually meant well.

At the end of the first week, my mother invited Nathan to tea. I felt that this was an intrusion into our time together, and besides, tea was sissy, but Nathan seemed genuinely pleased. Mrs Viney made a great fuss of him, and served us a splendid tea. Jean eyed the salmon sandwiches and fruit cake and apple pie with amazement and said, 'We don't usually get tea like this. Mrs Viney must like you!' Nathan laughed and so Jean laughed too, loudly and long until my mother said, 'Hush, Jean.' Her head was bent towards Jean, but I noticed Nathan's eyes linger on my mother, and I blushed for her, without quite knowing why.

Then, as I hoped it would, the conversation turned to the Hotel de la Mer. 'What's it really like?' asked Jean, her eyes wide and excited.

'Well, it's very comfortable,' said Nathan. 'But of course, hotels are not always very homelike. Everyone seems to be on their best behaviour all the time.'

'Where is your room?' asked Jean. 'At the front or at the back?'

'At the back,' said Nathan. 'The rooms are smaller but I like it because of the view of the sea from my window.'

'It must be so beautiful,' said Jean. 'We've looked at it for years and years but we've never been in.'

'Well, you'll have to come and see it. I can show you

251

the downstairs rooms and the gardens. Perhaps to-morrow?'

'Tomorrow is my birthday,' said Jean. It might have taken me a while to forgive Jean for this outrageous comment, except for what followed.

'Well, if it's your birthday, you must all come to tea with me at the hotel.'

So, at the age of thirteen, I finally entered the Hotel de la Mer. Because of Nathan, we became regular callers at the hotel. He never took us up to his room, but we had tea in the lounge, and sometimes even dinner in the dining room as his guests; and often we would call for him and wait in the grand entrance hall, sitting on the circular sofa we had so admired. My mother showed a certain timidity at first at the frequency of these invitations. I supposed she accepted them for our sakes, because for us, they meant a dream come true.

I said before that I never prayed and this was true, but that summer Nathan Strong became my god. He seemed to enjoy my company and I gloried in his. We spent much of our time exploring the coast. He shared his knowledge of bird life and pointed out all that his sharp eyes saw. He taught me how to use a camera and make the most of every angle and trick of the light. I took picture after picture of the sea, trying to capture it in all its moods. We walked for miles, and in the evenings we would go fishing, casting our lines out into the sea. Sometimes we would just sit and talk, often about very unimportant things, but all things were important to me then. Once, and only once did we talk about my father. He asked me if my father was still alive.

'Oh yes, but we never see him. My parents separated when I was very small. I don't remember him at all.'

He was quiet for a while and then said, 'Would you like to meet him?'

'I don't know,' I said. 'I suppose so. I do miss him.'

'Yes,' said Nathan. 'I'm sure you do.' Then we went fishing and he never asked about my father again.

As the days passed I was painfully aware that summers do not last forever. I knew that soon we would return to London and I would have to say goodbye to Nathan. I had a sense of time slipping away too quickly, and wanted to make the most of every moment. Although he was my particular friend, he seemed to have been taken into the shelter of the whole family. All our plans included him, and his included us. At first I had been jealous of other people's claim upon him, but it meant that I also enjoyed more of his company, and it pleased me to know that he liked my family. Even my mother had begun to drop the formality of 'Mr Strong' and called him Nathan. Jean, much to my chagrin, called him Uncle Nathan. I considered this twee but as Nathan made no objection, neither could I.

There were only a few days of our holiday left when Jean burst into my room one morning before breakfast, and jumped on to my bed. I was already dressed and anxious to be out. I would have left at daybreak some days, but my mother always insisted that I had breakfast, and as Mrs Viney served breakfast at half past eight and not a moment sooner, there were certain restrictions on my time. It was now 8.20, and I was sitting on my bed reading. Jean was still in her pyjamas and snuggled up to me, trying to get my attention off my book and on to her. She obviously wanted to play. I pushed her away. 'Stop messing, Jean. Why aren't you dressed yet? It's nearly breakfast time.'

'We can't have breakfast till Mummy gets back,' she said.

'Back from where?' I asked.

'Back from the beach. She's gone to see the sunrise with Uncle Nathan.'

I pushed her away again, more roughly than I meant to. 'Don't be silly, Jean!'

She set up a tearless cry because I had hurt her arm. 'She has, she has. She told me. She's gone to see the sunrise with Uncle Nathan.'

'Don't call him that,' I said sharply. 'He isn't your uncle. He's no relation at all.'

'I'll call him Uncle if I want to,' she said. Real tears had sprung to her eyes and she began to punch me with her small fists. I sat up and caught hold of her wrists.

'Jean, what time did she go out to see the sunrise?' She quietened down at the softer tone in my voice.

'I don't know, but it must have been ever so early 'cos when I woke up she'd already gone.'

'Then how do you know where she went?'

'She told me last night and said that I wasn't to worry if I woke up and that she'd be back for breakfast.'

I felt strangely numb but I turned a bright smile on my little sister and said, 'Well then, she'll be home any minute, won't she? Go and get dressed, Jean.'

'Oh all right!' she said, and slipped off the bed. I heard her feet padding across the passage and into her room. I stayed sitting on the bed with feelings I could not voice, stealing over me. I remembered glances that had passed between Nathan and my mother, expressions that I did not then recognize. And in my mind's eye I saw my beautiful mother watching the sunrise, not from the stretching sand or even from the top of the cliffs, but from a room in the Hotel de la Mer. I saw her standing at the window, with Nathan Strong at her side, and they were laughing.

'I wonder who stays there?' Jean had asked, many summers ago; and my mother had replied, 'Nobody we know.'

I sat where I was until I heard my mother come home,

and then I got up and went down to breakfast. Jean was already there, hanging on my mother's arm. 'Mummy, I missed you,' she said in her little whining voice.

'Did you, darling? I'm sorry.' My mother was smiling a light, bright smile that flitted across her face like butterflies' wings in the sunshine. She moved as if her limbs weighed nothing at all. I sat in silence at my place at the table. My mother poured herself a cup of coffee and filled a bowl with cornflakes for Jean. She did not look at me. I waited all through that interminable breakfast for her to raise her eyes and look at me.

'Aren't you hungry?' asked Jean, noticing that I touched nothing.

'No!' I snapped. My mother jumped and raised her lashes at last.

'Jean,' she said, in her quiet way. 'Go up to our room, darling, and find all the pieces of that game we were playing yesterday. We must give it back to Mrs Viney.'

Jean pouted but did as she was told. My mother and I faced each other across the breakfast table. I did not want her to speak yet. To me, there was only one possible explanation for what had happened. I had to ask her now.

'Is Nathan Strong my father?'

She looked at me with such anguish that I was embarrassed for her and looked away.

'No,' I heard her whisper. 'He is not your father.'

'Is he Jean's father?' I asked, my mind twisting and turning in blind directions.

'No.'

'Then who is he?' I cried.

I met her eyes. They were questioning and puzzled in the face of my anger. 'No one,' she said at last. 'He's no one. Just a man.'

255

Only when she had spoken did the expression in her eyes change. She had lied. He was not 'just a man'. He was the man she loved. I saw it, even as she turned her lovely head away from me. My mother loved Nathan Strong, and there was no doubt in my mind now that Nathan Strong loved my mother. My anger knew no bounds. They had betrayed me. If Nathan Strong had been my father I could have loved him, but Nathan Strong as my mother's lover was quite another matter.

'How could you?' I screamed. 'How could you? He was my friend.' I hurled myself from the house, sobbing the breathless tears of childhood, my world in pieces.

I did not take the usual route to the beach, past the hotel. I went another way, and wandered aimlessly along the shore until I found myself at the ledge at the foot of the cliffs that Nathan and I had discovered together. It meant nothing to me now, but I stopped there none the less. I sat looking out to sea and hours must have passed by. Then in the distance I heard Nathan calling my name. I did not answer him, or look for him, but still he found me, and sat down beside me on the ledge. I was busy tracing a line in the sand around my feet with a pebble and did not acknowledge him.

'Why are you angry?' he said.

'You lied.'

'In what way did I lie?'

'You made me think that you were my friend, and all the time it was just a way to get to my mother.'

'I am your friend,' said Nathan. 'I was your friend first. Is there any reason why I shouldn't be your mother's friend too?'

'It's different,' I said. 'It's not the same thing at all.'

Nathan did not speak for a while. He sat beside me, thinking. Then he said, 'It's not really so very different, you know. You and I became friends because I think

256

both of us were lonely. You needed male companionship, and so did I. Your mother has been without a
companion for nearly ten years. That's a long time to
be alone.'

'She had us,' I said, concentrating on my feet.

'Yes, she had you.' Again, Nathan paused. 'You
know, there are many different kinds of loneliness. I
was married twenty-two years ago. My wife lived for
six months after our wedding. I loved her very much.
In twenty-two years I have not found another woman
to touch her. No one even came close. Until now. When
you have loved someone like that, and then lost them,
the loneliness can become almost unbearable at times.
I'm not expecting you to understand completely. You're
not old enough. But one day you will. I've missed her
and I have missed the children she and I might have had
together. This summer I met you, and we have done all
the things I imagined doing with my own son, if I had
had one. And then I met your mother. Sometimes, when
you are lonely and you find someone else who understands, other things can grow in a very short time.

'We have been good for each other, all of us, together.
You have no right to be angry.' He stood up after this
long speech, as if he had said more than he meant to.
He stood just in front of me, his hands in his pockets,
looking out to sea. 'Go and find your mother. She's
worried for you.'

The summer my brother was born we did not go to Mrs
Viney's guest house. My mother felt that it was not
really equipped for a tiny baby, and she herself was
not yet up to travelling far. She and Nathan had been
married the previous October, and they had spent their
brief honeymoon at the Hotel de la Mer.

Looking at my tiny brother with his fair hair shot

with red, I could not help feeling a tinge of jealousy. Not only had his parents brought him into being at the Hotel de la Mer, but he would also grow up knowing that Nathan Strong was his father. There had been a moment a year before, when I had believed that for myself, and the loss of it had been acute. Yet I knew that if Nathan had been my natural father, he would not have remained unknown to me for thirteen years. I had found him relatively late in my young life, but I knew now that he would stay. So the jealousy lessened and I was content. Jean was young enough to learn to call him Daddy, but to me he was always Nathan. It seemed the natural name between us. As he became more sure of my trust in him, I noticed that often, particularly in moments of greatest affection, he called me Son. That too seemed to be the natural name between us.

When the old hotel was closed down it was not demolished. It was left to stand empty and forlorn at the edge of the cliffs. Then, some years later, it was bought by a man from London. The swimming pool was refilled, the gardens transformed, and the grand entrance hall restored to its former glory. The rooms were converted into private flats to be sold via the estate agents.

Just before the transformation work was begun, someone reported that the new owner was seen walking slowly around the old hotel, lingering in the large downstairs rooms. He let his fingers rest on the pillars in the dining room and the carved mantelpiece in the lounge and down the curve of the banisters in the entrance hall. He seemed to have a special affection for the place.

'Did you ever stay here?' he was asked.

'No,' he replied. 'I never stayed here. But I came to tea here sometimes, when I was a boy.'

MOIRA FLAHERTY

Juliet McCarthy

Juliet McCarthy was born in San Francisco but has spent most of her life since leaving university moving around the world with her husband and five children. She is presently living in Farnborough, Hampshire. Her abiding interest in people, combined with a love of medieval history, has sustained her ambition to write (more or less) throughout her peripatetic existence.

MOIRA FLAHERTY

Birthdays were never celebrated in my family. There were only the two of us, my mother and I, and she looked upon the traditional milestones which other people celebrated in their lives with scepticism.

'Ah, sure they're only a year closer to the grave. What's there to be so happy about?'

But I remember the summer I turned fifteen with special clarity. It was the summer I met Moira Flaherty, a young woman from Tullamore in Tipperary. She was a girl really, hardly much older than I and she was on her honeymoon.

I always loved the name Moira. I wished my parents had given me an Irish name instead of Teresa. Moira sounded wild and provocative, a little like the girl that lurked beneath my colourless exterior. I was named after the Little Flower, Saint Teresa, who got to be a saint by being obedient and kind and doing ordinary chores without complaint. I was afraid that by being christened Teresa I was in some way predestined to be humble and self-effacing, qualities I noticed were not particularly admired, not even by the nuns at school who favoured the girls who were saucy and bright.

In my adolescent ardour I preferred saints like Joan of Arc who led armies and died at the stake or the beautiful virgin martyrs who were blinded or beheaded for their faith. I would die for my religion but even then I did not know whether or not I would have the courage

261

to live day in and day out like the patient Saint Teresa.

Of course, I've since learned that it's often easier to die for one's beliefs than to have to live up to them and that perhaps Saint Teresa was more heroic than all the virgin martyrs put together. But that was before I met Moira Flaherty, Mrs Flaherty. I never exactly met her. We were never formally introduced and she only stayed at the hotel for three days, but I have never forgotten her.

My mother and I were on holiday in Dublin, an unprecedented thing really, for a family of our means from the country, but Mother read a great deal and had aspirations for her only child. She was a widow, a housekeeper for an English doctor and his family, and despite the fact that she despised them and ridiculed their airs, she often imitated them and had definitely acquired their taste for the finer things in life.

In addition to seeing the tourist attractions in Dublin, we spent hours on Grafton Street browsing in expensive department stores and admiring the fine linen and crystal.

The hotel where we were staying was not unlike a dozen others in the neighbourhood. It had once been a private home. It stood in a row of identical Georgian houses overlooking a park. Neither time nor diminished circumstances had altered the elegance of the simple brick façade with its delicate wrought-iron railings and graceful fanlight that beckoned over the front door. It was owned by an enterprising Dubliner named Julia Dowd. Guests could get room and board for a reasonable fare if they did not mind doing without a private bath or toilet. In those days one did not run into many foreigners staying in the small, private establishments. The Americans preferred hotels like the Shelborne and the Gresham, close to the shops and the theatre. Mrs

Dowd's guests were mostly Irish or English or an occasional German who complained about the lack of heat and the general inattention to housekeeping.

I thought the Vicenza, as it was grandiloquently named, was lovely. I never tired of admiring the imitation Turkey carpets or the sombre collection of portraits that adorned the parlour walls. I especially looked forward to meals, when all the guests crowded into the dining room to sit at their appointed tables and be served by three sullen-looking girls who also did the washing up, as well as making the beds and doing the linens. Conversation was at a minimum. The people were no less formal or friendly because they were few in numbers or shared the same bathtub.

The maids were pleasant to me, I suppose because they seldom saw anyone very young. Mrs Dowd catered to the middle-aged. She did not want any high spirits to disturb her guests or ruin her reputation.

It was the maids who had alerted me to Moira Flaherty's impending arrival and provided me with the titillating information that she was on her honeymoon. They were much more knowledgeable about such things than I but the four of us were beside ourselves with excitement over the prospect of having a new bride under the same roof. Would she be pretty? Shy? Nervous? What of the groom? I spent the entire day wondering about them and anticipating their arrival.

My mother and I were in the parlour when the taxi finally deposited the celebrated couple on the doorstep. Lucy opened the door for them and saw to their baggage while Mrs Dowd steered them into the parlour for a glass of sherry to revive their spirits after the long train ride.

I could hardly take my eyes off the new Mrs Flaherty. Her navy-blue suit was inexpensive and ill-fitting and she tottered clumsily on brand-new, white heels. But to me, unsophisticated and impressionable, she looked radiant. Her skin was fair, not sallow like mine. No one would have asked her if she felt unwell. In fact, we both had blue eyes and red hair, only the colour of her eyes was like the sky on a brilliant June day and mine looked like its reflection in a cloudy pool. Her hair was long and curly, not limp, well-behaved curls, but a lively, confused mass of ringlets that seemed to have a life of their own and refused to be tamed by the silver barrettes that held them off her face. She looked like a schoolgirl sitting there with her knees together and her hands folded in her lap, not like a bride. The only concession to the occasion was a spray of white roses pinned to the lapel of her suit.

I tried to catch her eye, to smile at her. I wanted to let her know that she was among friends but she didn't look at anyone in the room. She kept her eyes fastened on a portrait of a woman that hung over the mantel. Years of having pride of place above the grate had left a grey film of soot and grime over the painting so that the colour and details were no longer distinct, although one could still perceive the haughty expression on the woman's face. She looked as if she could not abide hanging on the wall in the cluttered parlour. A sneer of distaste grazed her thin, pale lips.

Mrs Dowd hovered solicitously over the newlyweds. She spoke in a low, ingratiating manner, exchanging trivial confidences with Mr Flaherty about a mutual acquaintance in Kilkenny, the gentleman who had recommended Mrs Dowd's establishment to the groom. They both ignored Moira.

What, I thought, had that beautiful girl seen in Mr Flaherty? He was at least twice her age, a respectable farmer no doubt, from the looks of him, but dour. When he wasn't talking his mouth turned down at the corners and there was a perpetual frown on his forehead. His hair was thinning and even though he had tried to comb it artfully to disguise the fact, one could see his scalp, pink and tender as a baby's where it was protected from the sun under his hat. His face and hands were deeply lined.

I loathed him. I was physically revolted by his appearance which I examined with the cruel, critical eye of a child, noting the fierce eyebrows and coarse, grey hairs curling out of his ears. The handsome young man I had envisioned sweeping his bride up the staircase had turned out to be old and ugly. I did not have the heart to finish my hot chocolate.

Reluctantly Mrs Dowd arose and suggested the couple retire. As if on cue Mr Flaherty stood up and beckoned his wife. She thanked Mrs Dowd for the sherry which she had barely touched and followed him out into the hall. He mounted the steps slowly and solemnly as if he did not want to appear too eager to be closeted away with his bride, for despite his nonchalance, he could not have been indifferent to the bemused and curious onlookers who watched them ascend the stairs.

I wondered if anyone had remembered to put a few shillings in the meter to take the chill off the room, but then Moira Flaherty was undoubtedly used to undressing in bleak rooms and sliding between sheets that stung with the cold. Perhaps Lucy had drawn a bath for her so she could undress in private away from the scrutiny of that dreadful man. I hoped so. I couldn't bear the thought of him watching her while she went through the ritual of undressing, unfastening her skirt and letting it slide down over her hips, peeling off her stockings and stuffing them into the toes of her shoes, unbuttoning her blouse and exposing her breasts in the flimsy little bra.

The parlour, which was always decidedly chilly, suddenly felt warm and oppressive and I started to perspire. The woollen vest my mother made me wear to protect my chest from the dampness started to itch under my jumper and I could feel my cheeks burning.

Mother and I were about to retire when Mrs Dowd returned. 'I gave them my best suite,' she said. 'I picked some flowers from the garden and put them in a vase on the nightstand. Made it a little special.' She leaned over in what she thought must have been out of my earshot and said: 'It's not often I have honeymooners staying here.' She rolled her eyes as if to emphasize the excitement and delicacy of the situation. Mother nodded.

'Most young people want someplace a little fancier or else they can't afford to go away at all. But Mr Flaherty is the sensible kind.' She smiled. 'He's very comfortable. Owns a dairy in Tullamore. If you ask me that girl has done very well for herself, a young snip of a thing from the looks of her.'

My mother did not look up but I could tell from the tone of her voice that she was annoyed with Mrs Dowd.

'He looked a bit old for her,' she said. I couldn't believe it. My mother, who disdained idle gossip, discussing two strangers with that nosy old busy-body. My mouth must have opened in disbelief for she shot me a withering glance.

'Why, he's a widower,' Mrs Dowd said by way of explanation. 'His wife died last year of a tumour. He's three children older than the bride.' That seemed to tickle her. 'Didn't waste time finding another, did he? If he's not careful he'll have a whole new litter. Now just tell me why a fine man like Mr Flaherty would want a silly shopgirl for a wife,' she said indignantly, but she didn't sound very convincing. She sounded as if she knew the answer.

Mother must have cast one of her deadly glances in the direction of Mrs Dowd for she looked taken aback and apologized for forgetting there was a child present.

'Well, and I'm sure they'll be quite happy all the same,' she said sweetly. She patted my cheek. 'Wasn't Mrs Flaherty lovely now? What a complexion. Only Ireland has girls that look like that.'

Why, oh, why, wasn't I one of those raving Irish beauties, I thought sadly. I wouldn't waste myself on a balding middle-aged farmer.

Mother gathered up her things. 'Come along, Teresa,' she said. 'It's getting late and we have a big day ahead of us.' We went up the stairs, down the narrow hall, past the room where Moira Flaherty was confined with her bridegroom. There was a sliver of light shining under the door.

In the morning at breakfast the maids were unusually cheerful. They kept nudging one another and blushing and when they disappeared behind the swinging door into the pantry one could hear them giggling and whispering. The other guests did not seem to notice, but I knew the object of their mirth was the empty table in the corner reserved for Mr and Mrs Flaherty.

Breakfast was served from seven-thirty until nine. Promptly at nine the breakfast dishes were cleared away and the table set for tea. Lucy was preparing to dismantle the table when the couple walked into the dining room. They made their way between the tables and sat down facing one another. I was relieved to have an unobstructed view of husband and wife.

Mr Flaherty was wearing his Sunday suit and white

starched shirt with a stiff, detachable collar that pressed on the folds of his neck. It looked like he was being garrotted, the knot from his tie squeezing the air out of his pipes and turning the fleshy furrows of skin purple. He had cut himself while shaving and there was a gathering clot of blood on his chin which he kept blotting with his handkerchief. His expression was unchanged from the previous evening, the deep line between his brows, the mouth that turned down at the corners. He propped *The Times* on the table in front of him while his bride poured the tea.

I had expected, what? To see some sort of transformation, at least in the girl. But there she sat in the same navy suit with the identical, enigmatic expression on her face. What secrets did she know? How had she changed? How could she face a room full of strangers with such indifference?

When we returned from Mass Lucy took me aside in the upstairs hall and good-naturedly confirmed my worst suspicions.

'How do you know?' I asked incredulously. She laughed.

'The sheets. You can always tell by the sheets.' I was confused, but I did not doubt that Lucy knew what she was talking about. She seemed to be an authority on those unfathomable rites.

Mr and Mrs Flaherty appeared regularly at all the meals. They never conversed. He sat staring at his plate or the newspaper and she picked at her food or, when he signalled, poured the tea. She was careful to fill the cup exactly half full with hot milk and add two heaping teaspoons of sugar.

I saw her one morning when she was coming from the bath. She had a raincoat on over her nightgown. She seemed startled to meet me in the hall and brushed by without a word. I watched her open the door and go into her room, hoping to catch a glimpse of, I know not what, but I was disappointed. The only thing I saw before she closed the door was the vase full of wilted flowers on the nightstand.

The last time I saw Moira Flaherty was the day she was leaving to go home. I found her on the landing, leaning on the window-sill gazing out over the rooftops. It was a warm day, the window was open and she had discarded her jacket. When she saw me she turned and smiled.

'It's a grand day, isn't it?'

'Oh, yes,' I said, startled by her attention.

'You're not from around here, are you?' she asked. I shook my head. 'I could never live in the city,' she said, which surprised me because I thought all young people longed for the excitement and gaiety of Dublin. My friends and I talked constantly of the time when we would move to the city and put our country ways behind us. I leaned on the window-sill and tried to imitate the wistful, faraway look in her eyes. We were the same height.

'I'm going home today,' she said. She had kicked off her shoes and was standing barefoot on the faded carpet. Her feet were surprisingly small and dainty and her toenails were painted bright red. I wondered if the first Mrs Flaherty, the one who had died of a tumour, ever painted her toenails red. I doubted it; she probably would have disapproved of nail polish.

'And have you enjoyed your stay in Dublin?' I asked boldly. Her face became fixed. The dreamy look left her eyes. I had broken the spell.

'The food does not suit Mr Flaherty,' she said solemnly. She leaned down, retrieved her shoes and retreated up the stairs.

When I went into our room my mother was lying on the bed with the curtains drawn and a wet cloth on her forehead. She was suffering from a migraine.

I sat in a rocking chair in the corner and watched the almost imperceptible rise and fall of her bosom. She was not very old at the time, in her early forties, but her hair was almost white. Her mouth hung open in the abandonment of sleep and she was snoring. She always slept with her mouth open but when I accused her of snoring she denied it – presumably on the grounds that ladies did not make undignified noises or, worse yet, acknowledge them. I continued my critical scrutiny with a growing unease. Mother looked old and very fragile lying there and I was suddenly frightened. It occurred to me, for perhaps the first time, how hard she worked to keep us intact, to afford the school I attended and provide the little extras she considered essential for a young lady. Hard physical labour, scrubbing floors, washing, work that was rarely appreciated and more often criticized. I never heard her complain about the work although she bitterly resented the doctor and his wife for their arrogance.

She went to Mass every morning and we said the rosary every night before we went to bed, but her religion was not an escape, it was a bulwark, private, unsentimental.

I thought how little I really knew about my mother, about her girlhood, her marriage. She seldom spoke of anything personal. When I asked about my father she said he was a decent man, which wasn't very enlightening. My only recollection of him came from his photograph on the mantel which was taken while he was still in school. He was slender and delicate looking. People often remarked on our resemblance but of course, he was such a remote figure in our lives it was

270

difficult for me to imagine any connection with that serious young man.

Mother met him several years after he had been immortalized in that photo. He was a bookkeeper for some company in Cork and her aunt introduced them. She told me once he was very fastidious, but I didn't understand what she meant by that. My friends' fathers were often boisterous or rude. Even the priests I knew liked their drink and tobacco. Fastidious?

At any rate, he died unexpectedly of a haemorrhage in his brain. One minute he was talking to the man next to him and next he was slumped over his desk. It was a blessing he went so quickly, my mother always said. The doctors told her he would have been paralysed and dumb and I think she was relieved that she had been spared looking after him.

'A blessing,' she'd say. It was the only time I ever heard her refer to my father with any tenderness. It was as if she regarded his death as a personal favour.

My mother sat up in bed and squinted over at me. Her face looked pinched and white.

'How do you feel?' I asked.

'Oh.' She shrugged and sank back on the pillows. 'Good for nothing.' She tried to smile. 'I've spoiled our day. It never fails.'

'They went home today,' I interrupted.

'Home? Who?' She didn't sound very interested.

'The Flahertys.'

'Ah, yes.'

The room was almost completely dark. The sun had gone down and the city was bathed in that long, pale twilight of summer. Slivers of grey light were barely visible where the shade did not quite meet the casement.

'Why did she marry him?' I asked, more to myself

271

because it was not in my mother's nature to discuss other people's affairs. 'He's so old.'

I heard her sigh and I could tell that my question had provoked her. I thought if she hadn't had a headache I would be in for a lecture on not judging other people or gossiping like the contemptible Mrs Dowd, but she surprised me by saying: 'I'm sure she had her reasons. I just hope for her sake she doesn't regret it. And for his sake too, poor devil. He had no right to marry that child.'

I was startled, as much by the passion with which she spoke as by what she said. She was obviously agitated. She sat up in bed and was massaging her temples.

'Pride,' she said aloud. And then under her breath, 'And lust.'

Pride? Lust? What did my mother know about such things? I could not believe anyone with her thin shoulders and primly pursed lips could know anything about lust. She always wore the brown scapular pinned to her nightgown and kept the rosary beads under her pillow.

'It's a disgrace,' she said bitterly. And she stood up and began to pace back and forth in front of the window.

'I don't understand,' I ventured. 'It isn't as if she had to marry him.' I hesitated. I knew sometimes couples did have to get married because the girl was in the family way. It was always common knowledge in town, which bride walked up the aisle sweet and unsullied and which ones were in trouble. But somehow I did not think Mr Flaherty had compromised his pretty wife and anyway, I had it on Lucy's authority that Moira had sacrificed her virginity three nights ago and left some mystifying sign on those sheets. But I could never tell my mother I was privy to such squalid information. She would never

272

have forgiven me. So I blurted out: 'Well, no one can force someone to marry against her will.'

'Oh, Teresa,' she said. I did not recall her ever addressing me so tenderly. 'People do foolish, reckless things out of fear, pity, loneliness.' Her voice trailed. She raised the shade and stared out over the rooftops, the dark, uneven shapes barely discernible in the waning light. She had that same look in her eyes that I had seen in Moira Flaherty's eyes that afternoon, as if she were puzzled, trying to understand some great mystery that kept eluding her.

Finally she said: 'That old fool downstairs thinks she married him for his money. Well –' she shrugged as if defeated – 'perhaps, she did. They said that about me when I married your father. If he had any I never saw it. We lived in a flat he shared with his sister. She treated me like an intruder. She raised him, you know.' I didn't. Him. He had a name, Michael, but I'd never heard her refer to him by it.

'She doted on him. Cooked all his meals, washed and ironed his shirts, pressed his trousers. My handiwork never suited her.'

I didn't want to hear any more. I wished we had never come to Dublin, never set eyes on Moira Flaherty. I knew my mother would never have revealed these secrets to me if we were at home. She leaned her head against the transom and closed her eyes.

'I don't know why I married him. I had nowhere to go when my aunt died and I was afraid to live alone.' She started to laugh. 'I was lonely. I wanted . . .' She turned and looked at me as if waiting for an explanation.

'Your father was kind to me,' she said.

Did she marry him because he was kind? She never mentioned love but then I could not imagine my mother

273

young and impulsive, her flesh pricked with desires which for me were still unfocused and confused.

The shade, caught in a sudden draught, tapped against the window-pane like someone knocking softly and insistently to be let in.

'Last night I dreamed about him.' She sounded surprised and annoyed that after so many years he would have the nerve to intrude into her dreams. 'We were in the parlour downstairs. You were there.' She smiled at the absurdity of that and then went on. 'Mrs Dowd was playing the piano. She was very jolly. He was sitting next to me. He wanted to hold my hand. He didn't say anything, he wasn't even looking at me. He was watching Mrs Dowd and smiling, but all the while he kept moving his hand closer to mine. His hands were covered with brown freckles. I didn't know what to do. I didn't want him to touch me.'

She pulled her wrap around her and refastened the sash as if the familiar ritual might exorcize the ghost of my father from her memory.

'Is that all?' I asked.

'I think so.' She hesitated. 'I don't remember.' She went across the room and switched on the lamp beside the bed.

The light, which added little cheer to the dreary room, seemed to bring her back to her senses. She smiled bravely while she rummaged through her handbag for her tablets.

'They're too strong,' she said. 'I woke up and I didn't even know where I was. And all those dreams,' she added. 'Such nonsense. I never dream.'

She shook two pills out of the bottle into her hand, regarding them as if they were responsible for her aberrant behaviour. But they were the only thing that gave her any relief and I knew she was weighing the alternative of spending the night vomiting in the draughty toilet down the hall or having her sleep haunted by memories.

'Well, I'll just take them tonight,' she said finally. 'If I don't get rid of this headache I'll be in no condition to travel tomorrow.'

If my mother had any more dreams she didn't tell me about them.

In the morning we dressed, packed our suitcase and went down to breakfast. It was raining. The empty table that the Flahertys had occupied was framed by the window overlooking the garden. We ate in silence, absorbed by the storm that raged outside while we sat safe and dry, nibbling our toast. The excitement that the Flahertys' presence had generated in the quiet little hotel had vanished. Lucy lurked in the corner with her tray under her arm, scowling at the guests for eating so slowly. She drummed her fingers impatiently in time to the pattern of rain beating on the flagstones.

'We must be on our way, Teresa,' Mother said as if my lingering had caused us to be late. 'I'll settle with Mrs Dowd. Go along and get the suitcase and go to the toilet,' she added. Lucy smirked and the man at the table next to us glanced with distaste in our direction.

At the top of the stairs the door to the Flahertys' room stood open. It had been dusted and swept, the linens changed. As it was the dearest room in the hotel it was seldom occupied but Mrs Dowd kept the door open so that all the guests could at least glimpse the modest luxuries she provided as they traipsed down the hall to their meaner rooms in the back of the house.

I hesitated in front of the door, torn by a desire to explore the deserted room and my mother's injunction to hurry.

The bed stood against the far wall. It was old-fashioned with an imposing mahogany headboard. A

275

peach-coloured satin bedspread, frayed along the hem, was aligned carefully on the bed and a row of small, crocheted lace pillows were placed in precision against the headboard. I ran my hand over the material and marvelled at the smoothness and sheen of the satin, but the rest of the room was disappointing. There was a large wardrobe opposite the bed, a chair and a wash basin in the corner, the greedy electric meter that measured out the heat, and a dressing-table in front of the windows.

I tried to picture Moira Flaherty sitting in front of the mirror combing her hair but I couldn't conjure up the image. It was as if she had vanished and left me with a vague feeling of sadness and loss which I did not understand.

I turned to go when a streamer of silver ribbon lying in the bottom of the wastebin caught my eye. It was a wedding corsage. I stared at it lying abandoned among the rubbish. The petals of the roses were brown and curled around the edges, the spray of fern brittle and dry. Wedding flowers should be pressed between the pages of a heavy book, a token of cherished memories.

I looked up, half expecting to see Moira Flaherty standing beside me struggling to unfasten the corsage, but it was my own reflection I saw in the mirror. I had changed, not to outward appearances of course. I was still a thin, ungainly fifteen-year-old girl. But now I was privy to a terrible knowledge. I felt infinitely sad, wise beyond my years, and afraid.

There was still so much I had to learn. But I was sure I would not be waylaid by foolish dreams. They lay abandoned with the wedding flowers in that dreary hotel in Dublin. And if sometimes I was wont to forget the lesson I learned that summer, I recalled the sad and haunting look in Moira Flaherty's eyes.

RICHARD
REMEMBERED

Leonard Tyler

Leonard Tyler was born in Southend and educated at Southend High School and Jesus College, Oxford. He has lived in Malaysia, Hong Kong and Sudan, but at present works for the British Council in London as an Information Technology specialist. He is based in Islington, where he lives in a Gothic square together with his wife and two children.

Richard Remembered is his first short story to be published. He is currently working on what he hopes will prove to be his first published novel.

RICHARD REMEMBERED

I'm having my tomb built now, just to be on the safe side. At my age you can't take too many chances. I want to be around to see it all done right and proper.

So, it's being made of Purbeck marble with my effigy on top, dressed in full armour, legs crossed at the knees to show that I was a crusader, and my faithful dog (looks more like a faithful cat actually, but never mind) at my feet. Even then you can't trust people nowadays, not the way that you used to be able to in King Richard's time. Take this morning, for example. I was having a sneaky look at the effigy while the mason's back was turned and I noticed these knobbly bits on my knees. (The effigy's knees, I mean, of course; nothing wrong with my knees.) So I called the mason over and I said to him: 'What are these supposed to be, eh?'

'Those, Messire Thomas,' he said politely enough (me being a knight and all that), 'those are your poleyns.'

'Poleyns?' I said.

'Poleyns,' he replied.

'Poleyns?' I said, raising an eyebrow.

'Poleyns,' he said condescendingly, as if he thought he could teach me something, 'are metal plates attached to the knees to afford greater protection than mail leggings alone. You see . . .'

'I know what poleyns are, you brainless worm,' I said. 'The idea that I am trying to get across to you is: what are they doing on my effigy? That's supposed to be me, isn't it?'

'Most certainly, Messire Thomas. And an excellent likeness too. Flattering, one might say. I have the mouth still to finish, but I shall give you a look of grim determination. You will look the very model of the puissant knight – as indeed you do in life.'

'I do, do I?'

'Assuredly.'

'Well, you can give me the look of grim determination in that case, but I never wore poleyns, so hack them off.'

'Oh,' he said, the light beginning to dawn. 'But poleyns are most fashionable these days. I include them now on all my effigies. For example, I recently put them on the tomb of Messire Roger Clifford, a gentleman quite possibly even older than yourself. His family agreed that they were very becoming. They made him look years younger, they said: absolutely bang up to date.'

'We never wore them in King Richard's time,' I said. 'For two years I followed King Richard in the Holy Land and I can tell you that in those days we never wore them. Mail leggings, mail hauberk and coif, helmet: that's what we wore. No poleyns.'

He didn't like it much, I could tell that. He was dead set on poleyns. 'Well,' he said huffily, 'I'd rather have followed King Richard than have had him behind me.' He gave me a knowing look and put his hand on his hip.

'Meaning what?' I asked.

'Well,' he said archly, but with slightly less confidence, 'he had a certain reputation, if you know what I mean.'

'Did he?' I said, pretty cool. 'How would you know?'

He was starting to look nervous now. I might be twice

his age, but I was armed and he wasn't. And nobody was likely to trouble me if I did decide to disembowel the occasional itinerant mason within the bounds of my own manor.

'No offence, Messire Thomas,' he said, swallowing hard. 'No offence meant, and none taken, I hope.'

'You hope wrong then,' I said. Then suddenly I added, 'Why don't you just go for a walk?'

'A walk?'

'You heard.'

'But, the effigy . . .'

'I'm paying you by the day, aren't I? Go for a walk.'

'Anywhere in particular?' he asked, attempting sarcasm, but not quite achieving it.

'By the river. In the river, for all I care.'

He paused for a moment to see if I was serious, and then, snatching up his cloak, flounced out of the church without another word. The door thudded behind him, echoing round the simple stone building. A few stray motes of stone dust still hung in the shaft of late autumn sunshine that fell from the lancet window by the tomb. My tomb.

For a moment I thought of calling him back; after all, what had he done? Nothing really; but I had suddenly felt the years gathering heavy on my shoulders and I wanted to think for a moment, without some fool prattling away in my ear. So I stood waiting until the last faint sound of his footsteps had died away, and then I sat down on one of the wooden stools at the back of the church and just let the memories flood back over me.

He was right about Richard, of course; bent as a five-groat piece, bless him. Not that it bothered any of us who served with him – that was his own business. Richard never did do things the way that other people did them. Nor would we have wanted him to; that was what made him what he was. And what was he? He was the finest soldier that I'll ever hope to see, that's what he was.

It's strange though. In spite of the fact that he towered like some great cathedral spire over the first half of my life, I came face to face with him – I mean to really talk to him – only on a handful of occasions: three in fact, now I come to think of it.

The first occasion would have been more than enough for most people. I must have been fifteen at the time. I was on my way to Woodstock to become squire to Messire Hugh de Merville, who was at that time a member of the military part of the royal household – the *mesnie*, as it was known. I was feeling pretty pleased with myself that afternoon, because I was riding my new palfrey, a parting gift from my father. My father, convinced (rightly as I have since learned) that all young men under twenty were irresponsible fools, had warned me to look after the horse as if my life depended on it. He was particularly concerned that the animal would end up as my ransom if I were captured at some tournament, or that I'd let horse thieves wander off with him. I, convinced in my turn that anyone over the age of thirty was a doddering old simpleton, gave him the usual bland assurances that children give their parents and thought nothing more of the matter. Nothing, that is, until, riding along the sun-lit path through the forest, I saw a lithe shadow dart from the trees and suddenly there was a figure standing in my path, sword drawn.

Now, under circumstances like that, the man straight ahead is the least of your problems; you can always ride down a single man on foot. The difficulty is usually his friends still lurking in the undergrowth, perhaps ahead of you, perhaps behind, particularly if they have long-bows and a clear shot at you or your horse.

So, I checked my pace at once and looked about me. In the forest on either side nothing stirred. All I could see was the man ahead, if indeed he could be described as a man, because, now that I had the chance to look at him properly, I realized that he couldn't be much older than twelve or thirteen. He was reassuringly well dressed too – not a bit like an outlaw or common rob-ber. You might have taken him for the son of a baron, perhaps, or of some other member of the court. His fair hair hung in ringlets to his shoulders and on his upper lip was the merest hint of the beginnings of a moustache. I breathed a sigh of relief (which shows how wrong you can be) and greeted him.

'Good day, young man,' I called to him. 'How far is it to Woodstock?'

Perhaps he didn't hear me, or more likely didn't want to listen, because the boy immediately started on a speech that he must have rehearsed a few times before.

'Know thou, sir knight, that this is a passage of arms,' he began. 'If thou wouldst pass to yonder fair castle, then thou must try thy strength here against me, arm against arm, sword against sword, before thou passeth this broad river.' He pointed to the muddy stream that crossed the track a few yards away.

'Who taught you to speak like that?' I laughed.

'It's the way that knights speak,' the boy said huffily.

'The way they speak in stories perhaps. You've been listening to too many troubadours.'

'How do knights speak then?'

'Well, like me, I suppose.'

'You're not a knight,' the boy sneered. He'd got me marked down as a yokel, which probably wasn't that far from the truth. We FitzAlwynes have as much Saxon as Norman blood in our veins. I wasn't going to let some kid cheek me, though, for all that.

'I'm a squire anyway, or I will be when I get to Woodstock,' I said. 'So I'll have a bit more respect from you, my lad.'

'I'll be a knight before you,' said the boy.

'You could be right,' I said, feeling that we'd explored the subject well enough and that it would take some time to teach him all of the manners that he was lacking. 'Now if you will tell me how far it is to Woodstock, I'll be on my way.'

The boy's grip on his sword tightened. 'If you try to ride past me, I'll turn that horse of yours into a gelding,' he said. 'I said that you were going to fight me and fight me you will.'

An unpleasant child, I thought. A spoilt court brat without doubt – in which case, though, there was no sense in offending him unnecessarily.

So I gave the boy a smile, in spite of my growing irritation. 'I would fain fight with you,' I said in what I hoped was acceptable knight-speak, 'but the day draws on and I must press ahead to King Henry's palace at Woodstock. Perhaps we may test our skill against each other there?' (On some suitably distant occasion, I thought.)

'Nothing doing,' said the boy.

'Very well,' I said, aware that the sun was sinking uncomfortably low in the sky, 'I concede now and without a fight that you are the better swordsman.'

'I'll beat you then, won't I?' said the boy. 'Now get down off that heap of dog's meat that you seem to imagine is a horse and fight me.'

'Dog's meat!' I exploded. He could insult me all he wished, and most of my immediate family, but you have to draw the line somewhere.

284

'You heard,' said the boy.

'You've asked for this,' I said, dismounting. 'When you are lying dead on the ground, just remember that you asked for this.'

I had, of course, not the slightest intention of hurting him, but a few blows with the flat of my sword across the kid's backside would not, I felt, come amiss. I left my shield and mail leggings strapped to the horse. The mail shirt that I wore, which perhaps he had not noticed beneath my tabard, might have been considered an unfair advantage, since he wore no armour at all; but I reckoned that in a fight like this, where we would not be trying to hurt each other, its weight more than made up for any protection it might afford. It wasn't going to be a fair fight anyway, because I had no doubt that I was much the better swordsman – but it would be as fair as he deserved.

'Very well, sir knight,' I said with a grin, 'let us see which of us will prevail on this grim field of battle.'

Or that was what I intended to say. I had got as far as 'which of us' when I had to duck a blow that was clearly intended to take my head off at the shoulders. For the next minute it was all I could do to fend off a whole storm of strokes that descended in quick and murderous succession, driving me slowly and rather inconveniently back towards the muddy stream. Then, thank God, the boy stumbled on a tree root and I was able to get in three or four sharp thrusts that rocked him on his heels. We both paused, panting, and the same idea clearly dawned on us at the same moment: this was not going to be as easy as either of us had thought. But whereas my face, I am sure, fell as the realization crept over me, the boy's blue eyes lit up and with a yell of glee he launched himself again at my unprotected head. How long we fought, I never could quite work out. At

285

the time I could only think of how to ward off the next thrust or cut of my opponent's sword. Difficult though it was to take the time to admire what the boy was doing, however, I was aware that I was fighting against no mere village lad, such as I had fought at home. It was not the force of each stroke that impressed me – I had the advantage of both age and strength – but as the blows fell, it was clear that each one had been thought out as part of a sequence to draw me on or push me back or force me into some error that would leave me open to a final deadly thrust. There was a . . . how can I put it? . . . a grace in the handling of the sword that I had never seen before. If the boy had been a year or two older he would have been unbeatable, but as the fight progressed, I felt that my opponent's strokes were falling less heavily and a little more slowly. The boy was tiring. Perhaps he too realized it, for at this point he made an uncharacteristically rash cut with his sword, bringing it down in a broad silver arc from left to right and leaving himself for a moment unbalanced and with his sword arm outstretched. It was not much of an error, but it was enough. I aimed a short hard cut close to the handle of the boy's sword and knocked the weapon from his hand.

The boy stood open-mouthed, staring in amazement at his now empty glove. He took a step or two backwards out of the range of my sword, glancing desperately right and left. I merely smiled: enough was enough. 'Well, sir knight, I think that you are fairly beaten and I will now go on my . . .' It was another one of those sentences that I somehow never got to finish.

The boy had lowered his head and with a bellow of rage had charged me and butted me in the chest. I was knocked back a few paces and winded, but the boy fell to the ground at my feet.

'Lesson number one,' I thought, 'never head-butt a man wearing chain mail.'

The boy sat up uncertainly. I planted the point of my sword in the soft black mould of the forest floor, where it stood quivering like some gaunt steel sapling. I offered my right hand to help the lad up. Then I was aware of a number of sensations in quick succession.

First, I noticed that the grip on my wrist was rather stronger than might have been expected for a supposedly stunned opponent. Then I felt myself moving rapidly through the air. Finally the ground came up and hit me with unreasonable force, filling my mouth with most of last year's leaves. When I was able to roll over and look up, the boy was standing above me, one sword in each hand. I groaned; not in pain, but in anticipation of the appalling speech that I knew was to come. He did not disappoint me.

'Yield, thou varlet, or feel the point of my sword upon thy unwashed flesh.'

'I yield,' I mumbled, spitting out a few leaves, 'I yield.'

I struggled to my feet, and took the proffered hilt of my sword as the boy returned it to me. You may take it for granted that I was not best pleased by the turn of events. I had, just in case you failed to notice, been defeated by a child. Even as I sheathed my sword I was running through possible excuses for use at court. None of them was remotely convincing. All in all it was turning out to be a pretty rotten day.

'You fought well,' I conceded, with as much grace as I could muster, which probably wasn't much.

The boy nodded as at an unanswerable truth.

'Well, if you will now tell me which way it is to Woodstock, I shall resume my journey,' I said.

'Not so fast,' said the boy. 'We have still to discuss your ransom.'

'Ransom?'

'Of course.'

I laughed. 'You may have problems there. I have nothing at all except my horse . . .'

Well, we all say stupid things from time to time, don't we?

The boy turned to where my palfrey was nibbling at a tuft of spring grass. 'That's settled then,' he said.

'But . . .' I said.

The boy walked over and rubbed the horse's ears. The horse gave a slight toss of the head and turned from the grass to nuzzle the boy's hand.

'What do you call him?' the boy asked.

'Robin,' I said numbly.

'What a stupid name for a horse. I shall call him Gringolet.'

'Look here,' I said as it became clear that he was in deadly earnest. 'I don't know who you think you are, but you are not taking my horse.' But the boy had launched into another prepared speech that finally stopped me in my tracks.

'Know, sir knight, that thou hast been beaten by no ordinary opponent. I am . . .'

But of course, you know who it was. It couldn't have been anyone else really, could it?

'I am,' said the boy, 'Richard Plantagenet, Count of Poitou, son of Eleanor Duchess of Aquitaine and of Henry FitzEmpress, King of England.'

Well, I thought, things might have been worse: I might have killed him. Not much worse though.

'I am Thomas FitzAlwyne,' I said. 'Squire to Hugh de Merville. At least I will be if I can get to Woodstock.'

Count Richard stepped back as if to admire the palfrey. 'Somebody's left their dirty luggage on my horse,' he said with surprise. 'Is this your dirty luggage?'

I looked. It was my dirty luggage all right.

'You'd better get it off my horse then,' said Count Richard.

I unfastened the cloth bag containing my mail leggings and then the leather one with my few possessions in it. I also took down my shield. The boy vaulted into the saddle with a lightness that I could, even then, only admire, and took the reins in his hand as though he intended to ride off without further formality.

'Wait!' I called. 'How far is Woodstock?'

Count Richard paused. 'Are you planning to walk?' he asked.

'I thought that I might,' I said.

'Not really advisable, if you don't mind me saying so. I doubt that you'll make it before nightfall – not with all that luggage anyway.'

'I suppose that you couldn't take some of this for me?'

Count Richard shook his head apologetically. 'I'd love to, but it simply isn't possible. I need to see how fast my new horse will go. You know how it is.'

'Yes,' I said. I knew how it was.

'Well, I'll be off then. These forests can be dangerous places after dark, even if you have a horse – which you don't, of course.'

The Count gave the merest flick of the reins and Gringolet, traitor that he was, started off at an eager trot. Without so much as a backward glance at his former owner my horse disappeared round a bend in the track and was gone. I looked up at the sky. The sun was already low, and I was still unsure how far I had to go. Wearily I picked up the two bags and the shield. The cloth bag in particular felt heavy.

'I've lost my horse,' I said to myself in astonishment. What would I tell Hugh de Merville? But, and this above

289

all, what would I tell my father? What *would* I tell my father?

Taking a firmer grip of my bags I crossed the stream and started trudging along the path in what I hoped was the direction of Woodstock.

It was the following morning when I eventually found my destination, having spent an uncomfortable night in the forest. Old Hugh de Merville was at a total loss to know what to do with a horseless squire and it looked for a while as though I would be sent straight back home. Then, that afternoon, Richard noticed me in the crowd and dragged me out in front of his father. To the whole court he announced that here was the brave knight with whom he had battled all day at the passage of arms in Wychwood Forest. We had, he said, exchanged blows for hours on end, broken swords, shivered lances, dented helmets and generally acted like a couple of Arthur's knights; and at the end of it all he, Richard, had overcome me fair and square on account of being stronger, braver, cleverer and so on and so on. I must admit that I didn't recollect things quite as he did, but princes, as I have since discovered, have very selective memories and I was lucky to come out of it with as much credit as he gave me. Even better was to come, however. To show his recognition of my valour, he said in conclusion, he would now bestow upon me his fine palfrey, Gringolet. There were general gasps of amazement at this generous act and one or two of the ladies sighed. Hugh de Merville breathed a loud sigh of relief, and an hour later I was reunited with my horse. I had to call him Gringolet, though; you didn't argue with Richard about something as important as what you named your horse.

Sitting in the church, I could remember it all as if it was yesterday – better than if it was yesterday, to tell you the truth. I could see it all so clearly that I could almost feel the taste of those leaves in my mouth again . . . then the church door opened and a cold draught blew across my face. The mason poked his ugly head round a pillar. 'I've been for a walk,' he said. 'What shall I do now?'

'Go for another walk,' I said.

He looked at me as though I was not quite right in the head, but pretty cautiously for all that.

'I need to start work on the tomb again, Messire Thomas,' he said.

'Don't worry,' I said, 'I'm not planning to use it today. It will wait.'

'You'll have to pay me for my time, whether I'm working or not,' he said.

'I will,' I said.

'As long as you know,' he said.

'I do,' I said.

'I'll go then,' he said.

''Bye,' I said.

The door closed, and a blessed silence fell again. I closed my eyes. Where had I got to? Oh yes, Woodstock. Richard.

The funny thing is that it was twenty years before I saw him again. The next day Queen Eleanor swept from the court taking her four sons with her. She and King Henry had not been on good terms for some time, and they say . . . well, you know what they say, I have no doubt. Eleanor was not getting any younger and there were always plenty of attractive ladies in waiting around the court. If it hadn't been Rosamonde Clifford it would have been somebody else, and it was none of my business either way.

What it meant, though, was that Richard stayed in the south, in Aquitaine, while my duties at the court and elsewhere kept me in England and Normandy. We heard plenty about the young Count of Poitou, of course: his taking of the supposedly impregnable fortress of Taillebourg after a ten-day siege and his short sharp campaign against the rebel barons. He was set fair to be one of the great military leaders of the age – if he didn't get himself killed first, of course, which on the whole seemed the more likely outcome.

The Plantagenets were always fighting in those days; sometimes against the French king, sometimes against the rebels in the south, but more often against each other. One day it would be Count Richard and the old King Henry against Geoffrey and the young Henry; the next it might be all three brothers (plus John, when he was old enough to join in) against their father. King Henry had a mural painted of four eaglets ripping out the guts of an old eagle, and we all knew what it was supposed to represent. (Kids! Why do we bother, eh?)

At the back of the minds of all of us in those days was, however, the idea that all this warfare was in preparation for the one really worthwhile fight – the defence of Jerusalem against the Saracens. It was a bit of a shock, then, when the Saracens just walked into Jerusalem (and most of the other Christian strongholds of Outremer) while we were all still at each other's throats in France.

Anyway, we all immediately pledged ourselves to another crusade, pinned crosses to our tabards and swore that we would abstain from this, that or the other until Jerusalem was retaken. Some of us actually went to Palestine.

Those, like me, who went early found ourselves stuck in the mud in front of the strong and well-provisioned walls of Acre. Sitting there, you wondered why, when we had given it up so easily, it was now so difficult to get back. The priests who were with us had a theory that God had deemed us unworthy on account of the number of local women who had flocked to the crusader camp. I would have put it slightly differently: we were a disorganized rabble.

The Germans had set out early but, blundering from one ambush to another in the valleys of the Taurus, had mislaid four-fifths of their army on the march. The French had come by sea, and their casualties on the way had been lighter, but they had no desire to share the glory with the rest of us, which made joint operations a somewhat haphazard business. The Pisans were only in it for the money, and the Genoans were only in it to make sure that the Pisans did not get more than their fair share. Like I say, we were a rabble.

Then Saladin showed up with reinforcements for the garrison, and suddenly we were trapped between the walls of Acre and this fresh army. Food ran out; a silver penny would buy you thirteen beans or one egg. When your money was finished, you ate grass. Most of us, frankly, wished that we were somewhere else.

Which, of course, Richard was. He'd set out for Palestine all right, but he'd stopped off in Messina to reclaim the dowry of his sister, Joanna, widowed Queen of Sicily. (By dying, the King of Sicily had clearly reneged on the marriage contract and Richard wanted his money back.) He wintered very comfortably on the proceeds in Messina, then made another detour to conquer Cyprus on his own account. It was in June 1191 that he finally sailed into the harbour, breaking the Saracen blockade. Of course everyone expected Acre to fall straight away, Richard's reputation being what it was. Actually it took him two more months, but that wasn't bad going. Suddenly things were looking up again.

That summer, Richard was in his prime. First he smashed the Saracens at Arsuf. Then Jaffa fell to us without a fight. Richard seemed to be everywhere, leading, encouraging, cajoling. No problem was too big or too small for him. Even the local barons, a pack of ruffians if ever I saw one, were eating out of his hand. The road to Jerusalem lay wide open.

But we didn't take it. You see, things were fine as long as we stuck close to the sea and our galleys, but we couldn't protect our supply line well enough to make the push inland for Jerusalem itself. The men grew restless; what we had all come for was no more than a few days' march away, but we sat tight where we were. At this point Richard opened negotiations with Saladin to see whether he could not talk his way to Jerusalem.

I had seen Richard a lot that summer – from a distance I mean. I was with him in the camp in front of Acre. I was there at Arsuf with the English contingent. I marched after him to Jaffa. But I doubt that he noticed me; I was just another knight in rusting chain mail and he . . . well, he was Richard Coeur de Lion.

Then in September, I think, a messenger was needed to take some news from Acre to Richard in Jaffa. I leapt at the chance to meet him again and, after a dusty ride, was duly ushered into his presence. He was discussing some business with a group of the local barons and merely glanced in my direction as I entered the room. He had changed a lot since the fight at Wychwood. The downy moustache had become a luxuriant golden beard, and the wiry arms were now powerful and muscular. The twinkle in his eyes was, however, just the same, as was the air of total self-assurance. He listened to the trivial message that I had to deliver, nodded curtly and was about to dismiss me when he looked at me again in a puzzled way and finally smiled.

'How's Gringolet?' he asked.

'Long dead, my lord,' I replied.

'The finest palfrey I ever owned,' he announced. 'But it was to a brave and worthy knight that I gave him.'

That was Richard all over; he had the knack (call it a trick if you like – I wish I had it) of being able to give you the impression that, while he was speaking to you, you were the most important person in the world. Not only that, he could convince you, often despite very considerable evidence to the contrary, that you had been constantly in his thoughts since you last met.

'I remember that day well,' he began. 'I must have been thirteen or so at the time. I had walked out from Woodstock armed only with my sword.'

Now, whether the story he was about to tell would have resembled the one he told at Woodstock, or even what had actually happened, was something that I never found out because an unusual thing happened. Richard was interrupted.

'You bastard!' a woman screamed at him. 'You filthy lying bastard!'

He turned to welcome the new arrival. 'Joanna,' he said. 'How lovely to see you.'

'You rat,' she continued, now getting fully into her stride. 'You miserable, contemptible worm. You heap of excrement.'

We all knew that Richard was negotiating with Saladin, and most of us knew that Richard's sister formed some part of the deal. Clearly she had just discovered this as well.

'Pig, snake, louse,' she said, working her way meticulously down through the animal kingdom until she found a satisfactory parallel to her brother. 'I will not marry an infidel. Is that clear?'

Richard considered this remark for a moment.

'But Saphedin is a charming man,' he said. 'Under the

agreement, he will be ruler of Palestine and you will, in consequence, be Queen. Your capital would be Jerusalem itself . . . unless you preferred Acre or Ascalon, say, in which case I could throw in one or the other. Or both. The throne would in due course pass to your children, that is to say to my nephews. It all seems eminently satisfactory.'

'Except,' said Joanna, 'that I will not marry Saladin's brother. Marry him yourself if you like, but leave me out of it.'

'Saphedin would make an excellent husband. Arab men are notably good lovers,' said Richard with a sly wink.

'You'd know all about that,' snapped his sister.

'I cannot, of course, vouch for Saphedin personally,' said Richard.

'This man,' Joanna announced to us all, 'would marry his own sister to the devil if it suited him.'

'Scarcely the devil,' said Richard, soothingly. 'You should take time to consider the matter further. Once you are more used to the idea . . .'

'I will see you in hell first,' screamed Joanna at what we all certainly hoped was the top of her voice. She looked for a moment as though she would slap Richard's face. (She was perhaps the one person in the world who could have got away with it.) Instead she uttered a series of curses that, while common enough amongst the troops, were quite remarkable coming from a lady of the court and showed a surprising degree of anatomical knowledge. Then she turned on her heel and swept from the room as fast as she had entered it.

A stunned silence hung over us. During the tirade most of the party would rather have liked to have crawled under a table or otherwise made ourselves scarce. Only Richard was totally unabashed.

'Good,' he said cheerfully. 'I think that she took that rather well, don't you?'

He beamed at us. We stared back open-mouthed.

'Now, I need somebody to take a message to Saladin,' said Richard, looking round the room. We all hoped that he would pick somebody else, but knowing my luck it did not surprise me to hear him say, 'Ah yes. Messire Thomas. Just the man for the job.'

'Er . . .' I may have said – or something of the sort.

'You shall tell him,' said Richard, 'that my sister would be honoured to marry his brother. She has expressed her desire that the wedding should take place at the earliest possible opportunity.' He paused and then frowned as if he had just seen a problem that the rest of us had missed. 'You should add, however, that it is just possible that the Pope may object to a crowned, and therefore consecrated, member of a royal family marrying an unbeliever. Under those circumstances, Saphedin can have my niece Eleanor of Brittany who, being about twelve now, I would think, is both marriageable and completely at my disposal.'

That was Richard in a nutshell: complete and unreasonable confidence that things would go his way, tempered with just enough realism to save himself from total disaster.

I duly delivered the message to Saladin, who treated me with greater courtesy than any prince that I have met before or since. He seemed to read neatly between the lines of the message and simply sent back a reply that he would consider the offer when it was clear which, if either, of the ladies was actually available.

On my return to Jaffa, Richard announced that he would like me to join his own *mesnie*. Once we were back in England, he said, he would bestow a suitable manor on his old adversary of Wychwood, unless of course I would prefer a fief in Palestine – Ascalon perhaps, if Joanna didn't want it. What, if anything, might have come of this I was never able to find out. Two days later I was taken prisoner while out scouting. This time I was treated with rather less courtesy and did not return to Acre until a general exchange of prisoners took place some months later. By that time Richard had already sailed for home.

He didn't make it, of course. Shipwrecked and captured, he languished in various prisons until the proper ransom could be raised. He then made one of his rare and brief visits to England to be recrowned, before taking ship once again for his lands to the south of the Channel. It was there that I caught up with him for the third and last time.

For once it was not by accident; I was now over forty, and still landless and as penniless as I had been at twenty. I had heard that King Richard was planning to return to the Holy Land, and wanted to take up that offer of a place in his *mesnie*.

So, my horse and I splashed our way through the mud and mire of northern France in the early spring of the year 1199. As we progressed south, the weather grew warmer and the fields greener, until late one afternoon I found myself outside the small town of Chalus, in front of which Richard was encamped. How he'd got there was a long story, but briefly the reason is as follows: a peasant unsuspectingly ploughing his fields near by had unearthed some treasure – to wit, a number of gold figures of a Roman emperor and his court. The lord of Chalus came to the conclusion that his right was greater than the peasant's, on the basis that a lord's right always is. This was probably doing the peasant a favour, because Richard, hearing that substantial loot had been found within his dominions, decided that he had the best claim of all, and that he was prepared to enforce it by any means at his disposal. He was short of funds for the new crusade and, frankly, every little helped. By the time I reached him he had been besieging the castle for two or three days, and was already getting impatient.

As in Jaffa, he blinked a couple of times when I strode into his tent, before recalling who I was. He had been in discussion with Mercadier, a vicious brute of a mercenary on whom Richard relied heavily for doing his dirty work. Smiling, he broke off business to welcome me.

'How's Gringolet?' he asked.

'Still dead, my lord,' I replied.

He fortunately found this remark amusing and, slapping me on the shoulder, suggested that the three of us should take a closer look at the castle. So we walked out into the gathering dusk to view the castle's defences. The walk from the camp to the castle walls also gave me a chance to review Richard. Captivity had not suited him. They had fed him well enough but kept him inactive – a fatal combination for a well-built man like Richard. In Jaffa he had looked muscular; now he looked fat and he puffed slightly as we climbed the gentle hill leading to the fortress. His hair too had started to thin. Only the glorious golden beard was completely unchanged: that and the twinkle in his eye.

The pace that Mercadier had set, though slow enough, seemed a little too fast for Richard because, when he called a halt about halfway up the hill, he was clearly panting for breath.

Together we looked up at the castle walls. It was small enough for us to take in the whole defences at a single glance. Nor was there much evidence of a garrison; only a single figure could be seen on the battlements, a man with a crossbow and, somewhat incongruously, a frying

299

pan for a shield. The lone defender looked down on us from a distance that was certainly within crossbow range. Since no shot had been fired, however, it was a fairly safe guess that they were short of arrows, amongst other things, and that they would save what they had for our assault.

Richard, typically, suggested an immediate attack with scaling ladders. Mercadier stroked his neat black beard (which I noticed contrasted strangely with his scarred and weatherbeaten face) and proposed an alternative: he would get half a dozen of his men to dig a sap beneath part of the wall. It would take a day or so, but once the wall was breached an attack would be easier and safer. Richard nodded dubiously and turned to me. My view was that there was no point in attacking the castle at all. If we sat it out for a week or two they would run out of food and be quite willing to surrender the treasure if their lives were spared. This advice was quickly dismissed. Mercadier had promised the garrison that if they did not surrender immediately (and they hadn't) then he would hang every one of them; he had no intention of going back on his word. Richard was simply unwilling to waste two weeks on a castle which, in the Holy Land, he would merely have bypassed and left to its own devices. In any case, keeping an army in the field cost money, and the profit in this venture was slowly draining away as we stood there.

'Good,' Richard announced suddenly. 'So, it's agreed that we bring up the ladders and assault it straight away.'

Mercadier, who was unaware that he had agreed to anything, turned to Richard as if to remonstrate with him. I however had my eye on the man with the frying pan. He was sighting along his bow, as if trying to decide whether we were in range or not. I was pleased under the circumstances that I had decided to wear my armour, as I usually did when travelling. Richard and Mercadier on the other hand were dressed in light taffeta tunics, with cloaks slung over them against the evening chill. Even as this comforting (from my point of view) thought entered my head, I saw the crossbow release its bolt in our direction. It seemed to waver in its flight, as if caught by the wind, and it landed with a thud a few yards away from us.

Richard looked up with a smile.

'Not bad,' he said. 'But he will need to do better before the day is out.'

He did do better. He must have reloaded quickly because a second bolt was speeding from the battlements towards us almost at once. This time it did not veer from its course, and from the moment it left the bow I was sure that it was coming straight for me. Armour or no armour I flung myself to one side. Mercadier did the same. Richard, either misjudging the bolt's course in the fading light, or perhaps because he was no longer able to move fast enough, just stood there watching the arrow come. Whichever it was, I am certain that it never occurred to him for a moment that, of the three of us, he was the one that the arrow might hit.

'Bravo!' he shouted to the bowman. 'That's more like it!'

I was face down on the grass when I heard the bolt strike home. I rolled over to see the feathered shaft sticking from Richard's shoulder. He was looking at it himself with a puzzled expression on his face, as if he could not quite believe that God had allowed this to happen. It suddenly struck me that he had had the same expression on his face after he had tried to head-butt my mailed chest in Wychwood.

'I've been hit,' he said in a conversational manner,

although whether to me or Mercadier or himself I never quite knew.

Mercadier was on his feet before me and gave the wound a rapid examination. 'My surgeon will remove that straight away,' he said. 'I will help you back to your tent.'

Richard shook his head impatiently. 'Later,' he said. I think that he was trying to pretend that it hadn't happened. It was almost as if he thought that he could will away the shaft and the blood that was beginning to slowly seep through his shirt.

'The sooner that is attended to . . .' Mercadier began to say, but Richard, perhaps made irritable by the pain, shook his head fiercely.

'You will gather a party of men together,' he said through gritted teeth, 'and you will storm the castle at first light. Is that understood?'

'Absolutely, my lord,' said Mercadier. 'I will lead the party myself. I hope that Messire Thomas will do me the honour of joining me in the first group.'

I wondered at the time whether Mercadier really thought that he was doing me an honour; he probably did. He would never have dreamt of being anywhere other than in the thick of the fighting.

We took Richard back to his tent, but he refused to have the bolt removed that night. He must have been weakened, however, because he agreed that Mercadier might try sapping the wall first. When we did eventually make our attack, resistance crumbled at once. I'm not sure why they offered to surrender seeing that Mercadier had made it clear that they would all swing. Perhaps they thought that there was a chance that he would change his mind. (They were wrong, of course. Mercadier never changed his mind.)

Richard refused to have the wound treated for days.

By that time the flesh had swollen, and the shoulder was plump enough to begin with. The arrow was in firmly and deep. Mercadier's surgeon turned out to be as much of a butcher as his master, and he made a real mess of the extraction. I wouldn't have had him operate on me.

Richard lived for another week or so after that, but it was clear that the wound was getting more infected, and he was getting weaker by the day. On the fifth day, I think it was, he sent for his mother, who was a couple of days' ride away at Fontevrault. He never sent for his wife.

Just before he died he fell into a feverish sort of sleep, from which he woke about midnight. I was waiting by his bed, though we all knew that there was little enough any of us could do, and he no longer seemed to notice what was happening. When he awoke, however, he looked about him as though he recognized where he was. He called out as though alarmed. I wondered if he was remembering his own father's death at Chinon, deserted by everyone, as his retainers slipped quietly away to do homage to their new king, Richard.

'Is anyone there?'

'I'm here, my lord,' I said, bringing the candle closer to him.

'Messire Thomas . . .' he said.

'Yes, my lord.'

'How's Gringolet?' he asked. He chuckled to himself, as if he knew the answer. 'You did well today at the castle, you and Mercadier.'

'The storming of the castle was a week ago, my lord.'

'Was it? But you did well. If I live, you will have the manor of Stanton in Essex,' he said.

'Thank you, my lord,' I said, thinking that eventuality unlikely.

Then suddenly he looked troubled. 'Messire Thomas?'

'Yes, my lord. What can I do?'

'Messire Thomas, God will know who I am, won't he?'

'No doubt about that, my lord,' I said.

He looked relieved. 'Yes, I thought so,' he said. 'I thought that he would.'

'Shall I call for a priest?' I asked.

He shook his head. 'Plenty of time for that. They'll only ask me if I repent my sins and I'm not really sure that I do. Not all of them, anyway. Some were actually rather fun.'

He sank back on to his pillow with a quiet smile on his face. A moment or two later I saw that he was sleeping and tiptoed back to my seat, taking the candle with me. He never woke up again.

I was just remembering all this when the church door opened again. It was the mason.

'I've come to collect my tools,' he said.

'Take them then,' I said. My voice was thick, and only then did I realize that I must have been crying. I was grateful for the fact that the light in the church was fading and so he would not be able to see my face. 'Take the tools and go.'

He picked up his dusty bag and slung it over his shoulder, then turned to me.

'I had a chat with your daughter,' he said.

'Oh yes?' I said.

'She agrees with me completely,' he said. 'She feels that the artist should be allowed some licence in these matters. She felt that aesthetic considerations took precedence over mere historic portrayal.'

'No poleyns,' I said.

'If you sleep on it,' he said, 'I think you will find that

304

you agree with your daughter and me on this subject. Your daughter said that she would speak to you tonight.'

I bet she will, I thought. But I said nothing.

'I'll bid you goodnight then, Messire Thomas.'

'Goodnight,' I said.

The door closed for what I hoped was the last time. The west window of the church now blazed orange and red. Outside another autumn day was drawing to its close – perhaps the last autumn that I will live to see. The men who work my lands would be making their way back through the fields, their boots crunching on the dry leaves, blowing from time to time on cold fingers and looking up at the sky to divine what weather the following day might bring. It's been a good autumn – a fine grain crop, plenty of fruit on the trees and the cattle good and fat. Nobody will go hungry this winter, thank God.

But where was I? Ah yes, Chalus.

There's not much more to tell really. We had taken the castle, as I say. Mercadier was as good as his word; he hanged the whole garrison – except for the man with the frying pan, and he had him flayed alive, for the sake of variety I suppose. We carried Richard's body north to be buried at Fontevrault next to his father. Then we all went our respective ways: me to England, Mercadier to sell his services to the highest bidder.

Richard was forty-two when he died. He's been dead for over thirty years now, even though, sometimes, it does all seem like yesterday. It was his brother, King John, who finally confirmed the gift of land that Richard had twice promised me. It was one of John's barons, William Marshall, who saw me right after John's death, when King Henry succeeded him. But my tomb will just record that I followed my lord, Richard Plantagenet (King of England, Duke of Normandy and Aquitaine, Count of Poitou, etc.) and that I saw service under him in Palestine and France. It's not ingratitude to the others. It's just, you see, that there never was anyone like Richard.

The light has almost gone now. I can only just see the outline of my tomb in the corner of the church. The fiery glow on the window has dulled to a purply red. It's time I was going too. My daughter is planning to have a chat with me about the plate armour, is she? (Kids! Why do we bother, eh?) Ah well, tomorrow is another day. Tomorrow is another day.

*

The motorist who, in travelling between London and East Anglia, can spare the time to turn off the main road and drive a mile or so along the narrow lanes to the village of Stanton Fitzalwyne, will be rewarded with the sight of a compact and remarkably unspoilt village, consisting of a group of houses clustered round the village green and the remains of a twelfth-century fortified manor house. The parish church, described by Pevsner as one of the most attractive small village churches in the Home Counties, is built in a variety of styles; indeed each succeeding generation could claim to have left its mark on it. The original Norman nave can, however, be clearly made out, and in one corner of it lies the tomb of Sir Thomas Fitzalwyne, dating from the first half of the thirteenth century. The base of the tomb has been well used as a seat over the years, and the inscription can no longer be made out in full, but the Purbeck marble effigy on top is a fine example of early medieval craftsmanship. It is notable for two things.

The first is that Sir Thomas's face, unlike most of the

grim-visaged portrayals of the period, wears the wry smile of one who is not altogether displeased with the way that things have gone. One corner of the mouth is curled up in a grin that the mason concerned may well have intended to portray smug satisfaction on the part of his subject. But if the smile is indeed there by design rather than by accident, it is unlikely now that we shall ever discover the reason for it.

The second thing is that, although the effigy is of a date when the use of plate armour was becoming relatively common, the figure is shown in chain mail alone. The superbly carved mail stretches unbroken from his head to his feet, without so much as the trace of a single poleyn.

SOMEONE TO SEE YOU

Isa Moynihan

Isa Moynihan escaped from an academic ivory tower four years ago to write fulltime. She lives in Christchurch, New Zealand, and so far has had eight short stories accepted for publication in anthologies and literary magazines. Two novels are being considered by publishers. Any day now she hopes to be rich and famous for at least a week.

SOMEONE TO SEE YOU

It's Friday morning in the waiting room. There's a leg in a cast, a bronchial cough, a pregnant woman with a toddler, a young man with no apparent medical condition, and Shona. Phones ring; receptionists bustle; a talkback raves quietly in the background. Shona stares blankly in front of her. In a doctor's waiting room you never look directly at anyone else. It might seem like prying: *What have you got, then – cancer, heart, AIDS?*

'Mrs McKenzie?' The pretty nurse-receptionist is beckoning with Shona's file cards. 'Doctor will see you now.'

God will see you now, Shona thinks, following the brisk white bottom along the corridor. Doctors deified by upper-case.

Nurse hands Patient's file cards to Doctor and bustles out. Not looking up, God waves Shona to a chair. He hums through the cards, occasionally rising to a high note of surprise. Shona waits for the game to begin.

'Well now, and how have we been, Mrs ... ahm ... ?'

'McKenzie. Not very well, actually. I've noticed recently –'

'Ah – when were you here last?' He scans the dates on the dog-eared cards. 'You've been coming here for some time, haven't you?'

'I know ...' She has let him down by not getting better. 'It's been two years, and –'

'And you've had a lot of tests . . .' He deals the cards. 'X-rays, blood-count, body-scan, mammogram. Mammogram? Now why did we do a mammogram?' he asks himself.

Shona wishes he would look at her occasionally. She plays the Joker: 'You must know me really well by now.' No response. *Why do you treat me like a child? I have a husband, two children, a degree in literature. I understand quite long words.*

'What about that last test?' She points at the card. 'The electro-encephalogram?'

Doctor plays the raised eyebrow. 'Yes, indeed.' He studies it. 'Mm . . . mm. It shows some unusual brain . . . ah . . . waves.' He plays the last trump. 'Yes, indeed. I think we'll have to go in there and have a look round.'

When he looks at her his eyes are a wintry grey, the brows overhanging, beetling. She stands with blinded Gloucester on the cliff-edge.

> *. . . here's the place. Stand still. How fearful*
> *And dizzy 'tis to cast one's eyes so low!*

There is a glass of water at her lips. The nurse's voice: 'You were growing faint.'

'Like the Cheshire Cat?'

'Mmm?' Doctor is writing busily. 'How would next Friday suit you?'

'For . . . ?'

'Just an exploratory. No point in delaying. It will put your mind at rest.'

My mind at rest . . . rest in peace . . . the rest is silence . . .

Outside, the pavements are hot and dusty. Shona walks, balancing her head carefully. Inside, it is an empty, echoing chamber. Something hides and scuttles in the shadows.

Next Friday. An exploratory. Seek and ye shall find . . . No! Please, no. I'm too young to die. Isn't everybody? A week today. Today . . . must get something for tea. Now.

In the delicatessen they're pressed two-deep at the counters. Light bounces off the white-tiled walls. Ham curls off the bone like sliced flesh. Dead fish gaze from silver eyes. The assistant wears pale make-up with scarlet lips. Blonde hair spikes, red nails dart and flash.

'Yes?' Her pale-blue eyes are ringed with black. They pass unseeing over Shona.

'Five hundred grams of liverwurst,' says a male voice behind her.

'Excuse me,' says Shona, 'but I think I was here first.'

'Sorry,' says Medusa. 'Didn't see you.'

That evening at home in her clean, bright kitchen Shona makes a salad.

Donald crashes in through the back door and heads for the fridge. 'What's for tea, Mum? I'm starving!'

Donald is eleven. He perceives Mum as a pair of hands and a voice which doesn't have to be heeded. He does not yet have an image of himself.

'Cold meat and salad. Wipe your feet. And call your sister, please.'

'Hey, Fiona! Tea's ready!'

'When I said "call" I didn't mean yell, Donald.'

'Sorry, Mum.' Donald quite likes his mum. And his dad, of course.

Fiona slouches in and slumps in a chair. She's fourteen.

'Not cold meat and salad! I *hate* cold meat and salad.'

'Sit up straight, Fiona – and don't chew your hair.'

313

'Where's Dad? Why don't we wait for him?'

'Why should we wait? It's only cold meat.'

'Been kept late at the office, has he?' asks Fiona, who reads the agony columns. She loves her dad, reggae and fried chicken. She hates vegetables, cold meat and, frequently, her mum. She sees herself as unattractive and misunderstood, except by her father. Her friends think he's really neat.

'Hello, everyone! Sorry I'm a bit late.' Bruce, the husband-father, is thirty-eight and not unattractive. He plays tennis and squash to keep fit, wears well-cut suits to the office and designer jeans to barbecues. He sees himself as upwardly mobile and a good provider, his wife as a good processor of what's provided.

'What kept you, Dad?' asks Fiona.

'Mmm? Oh, I had to finish up a couple of things at the office – before the weekend. What's for tea?'

Shona fetches some more cold meat. Watching her, Fiona wishes her mother would make more of an effort. Have her hair done properly. Buy some new clothes. Lose weight. No wonder Dad never really looks at her.

Donald finishes off the fruit salad and pushes back from the table.

''Bye, see ya later!' He crashes out through the back door on his way to meet his mates.

'Aren't you going out, Fiona?' her mother asks. Fiona looks wounded. Is her mother implying she's too unattractive to have a date?

'Want to get rid of me, eh?' Fiona casts a knowing look from Mum to Dad. She slouches off to her room.

Shona waits till the door slams.

'Bruce?'

'Mmm?' He's reading the paper.

'I saw the doctor today.'

'Oh . . . yeah.' He flips down the top half of the paper

so that she can see him listening. 'What did he say?'

Break it gently. 'It's probably a false alarm, but I may have a brain tumour . . .' How will he look at me? With fear? Repugnance?

'The usual: "Everything seems to be all right. Nothing to worry about."'

'That's good.' He flips the paper back up.

'But he thinks they should go in and have a look round,' Shona tells the kitchen sink.

'Mmm? Did you say something?'

'Just talking to the dishes.'

'You want a hand?'

'No. Thanks.' Shona is always appreciative of help offered or, more rarely, given.

Later she joins Bruce in the lounge. 'Anything on TV tonight?'

'Not much.' Bruce has finished with the evening paper. He drops it on the floor and stretches, yawning. 'Think I'll take a shower. I might go out for a while, later.'

'Why?'

Bruce is surprised. 'Well, why not? A drink with the guys . . . relax after the week.'

'Can't you relax here?'

'C'mon, love, don't be like that. I'll be back by ten — eleven at the latest.'

'I'd like to talk to you.'

'What about?' Bruce is wary.

Oh, you know, about life, death, the meaning of the universe. About next Friday.

'Not *about* anything. Just talk.'

Bruce is relieved. 'Tell you what — I'll take you out tomorrow, just the two of us. For a meal. OK?'

'But not tonight.'

'Well, OK. Tonight. If you want to.' He looks at his watch. 'So . . . why don't you go and make yourself

315

presentable, and I'll see if I can get us in anywhere. A film?'

'Thank you. That would be nice. I'll see what I can do about the presentable bit.'

Bruce slaps her affectionately on the bottom as she passes him. She's never liked that particular gesture of affection, but it's better than none, right?

Upstairs, Shona opens the door to their bedroom and closes it loudly. She remains outside, listening. Bruce is dialling. A pause, and then she hears his voice, low and intimate.

'Hello. Michelle? Look, I won't be able to see you tonight ... I know ... No, Saturday's no good ... What about Sunday?'

On Saturday, Bruce plays tennis as usual, and Fiona and Donald disappear for the day. Carefully balancing her head Shona goes about her duties, from kitchen to lounge to bathroom to bedrooms. In the late afternoon she sits in the garden, closing her eyes against the setting sun. *Are you in there, little parasite? Riding my brain waves ... hiding from the light ... 'Come out, come out, wherever you are ...'*

Sunday is family day. They usually drive somewhere, and get takeaways on the way home. In the car Fiona says to her mum, 'Why don't you have your hair done properly, Mum? A body wave maybe?' Shona has straight fine dark hair cut in a fringe above brown eyes and heavy eyebrows. She's always worn it like that – so easy to manage. She says she'll see.

About seven o'clock on this Sunday, Bruce suddenly remembers something that has to be done in the office before tomorrow morning.

*

316

On Monday, at the hairdresser's, Shona sits before a mirror, shrouded in black, waiting. Her eyes look back at her, curious: *Do I know you?* Muzak tells her that all she needs is love.

'Are you the body wave, dear?'

'Yes.' *I am a body wave. I am brain waves. I am a pair of hands. A home body. Now I waive my body rights. Which are Michelle's. Now I lay me down to sleep. But not with Bruce.* 'Death is but a sleep and a forgetting' . . . *But life is a sleepy sickness . . .* encephalitis lethargica, *which is caused by a parasite . . .*

On Tuesday the boutique-owner is svelte and smart. Her ash-blonde hair is smooth and silky. In the mirror her eyes are calculating.

'Not quite you, dear, is it?'

It's certainly not quite the woman in the mirror, whoever she is: dumpy, frumpy, forgettable. With a body wave.

'Is that me?'

The other woman smiles professionally. 'What about the hound's-tooth? That was much smarter.'

Smarter. Sharper. 'How much sharper than a serpent's tooth . . .' *But that was an injured father, not a savaged wife . . .*

Wednesday is shopping-for-food day. It may be her last full day as a home body. Must make sure there's enough food for the weekend. Stuff that's ready-to-eat, easy-to-cook. Expensive, though. She watches the figures flashing away her week's budget.

'Is that all, dear?' The check-out woman's eyes are on the displayed total, her finger poised above the final key.

'I'm sorry. I haven't got enough cash. Sorry.' She takes

317

out her cheque book. Behind her the queue stirs restively.

What am I sorry for? It's not my fault. None of this is my fault. I've done nothing wrong. You sound like a child. I do, don't I? And not telling them about the operation – that was childish too: 'They'll be sorry when I'm dead.' Oh, shut up!

Shona hands over the cheque.

'Have you got ID?'

She rummages for her bank card.

You must've had an idea . . . All the cliché symptoms were there: working late, abstracted, no lovemaking . . . I could kill her. Or him. And him. Both of them. I'd get away with temporary insanity. Take a pair of sparkling eyes, take a hank of silken hair, take a body that's slim and taut, and take them away away away . . .

It's Thursday. It's time for tea. Donald crashes through the back door in muddy football boots.

'Hi, Mum! What's for tea?' He tracks mud across to the fridge. Something is missing. 'Mum?' She does not seem to be in the kitchen.

'Hey, Fiona! Where's Mum?'

Faintly above the reggae rap he hears: 'Dunno!'

The fridge is full of shrink-wrapped trays of ready-to-eat food; there is no sign of any cooking being done.

A car comes up the driveway.

'Hey, Dad! Is Mum with you?'

'No. Isn't she here? Have you looked?'

'Well, I called her. Fiona doesn't know where she is.'

'Fiona! Come down at once!'

'Hi, Dad. What's the fuss about?'

'Did your mother say where she was going?'

'I haven't seen her. She wasn't here when I got home.'

318

'She probably got held up at the shops. Let's get tea ready and surprise her.'

Donald wanders over to the cutlery drawer.

'Donald! Take those boots off! And clean that mud off the floor.'

'Aw, Dad!' He goes outside.

'Dad, do you think she's left us?' Fiona asks.

'Don't be silly! Why should she do that?' Bruce takes some eggs from the fridge.

Fiona watches him. 'If she thought you were going with another woman?'

An egg splatters on the floor. Bruce swears. 'Well, I'm not.'

'Yes, well. If she *thought* you were. She might do something drastic.' She's warning him: we cannot do without Mum.

They are eating when the phone rings. Everyone jumps. Bruce grabs it from the wall. 'Yes? Speaking.' He listens.

Fiona and Donald watch their father's face. Fiona is chewing her hair. Donald has stopped eating.

'I see ... Yes ... Yes, of course ... Tomorrow? ... Thank you ... Goodbye.' Carefully he replaces the receiver.

'Dad?'

Bruce falls into a chair; his face is pale; he looks incredulous. 'Your mother ...' It comes out as a whisper from a dry throat. He swallows. 'Your mother has had herself admitted to hospital. They're going to operate tomorrow morning.'

'Operate? What for? What's wrong with her?' Fiona starts to cry. Donald is stunned.

Their father tries to reassure them: 'She'll be fine. It's just an exploratory, they said. To see if ... To make sure nothing's wrong.'

319

'But why didn't she tell us? Why didn't she tell *you*?' They look at him accusingly.

It's Friday. Late afternoon. Shona was wheeled back from Recovery just after lunch. She drifts blissfully from sleep to half-awake. There is no pain. Just people looking after her. Soft voices saying, 'It's all over, Mrs McKenzie. You've had your surgery. Everything's fine.'

Last night she met her fellow patients. Opposite is a hysterectomy; on her left a mastectomy; on her right a benign tumour that she'd gone to school with. Elizabeth. Lucky Elizabeth. Now running her own travel agency. Went home this morning. They'd whispered for hours last night. Just like boarding school. 'An operation like this – makes you think about what's important, doesn't it?' Elizabeth had said. Shona agreed. 'Yes. Concentrates the mind wonderfully.' And makes you grow up, she realized just before falling asleep.

At visiting time that evening she sees Bruce, Fiona and Donald standing in the doorway. Their eyes pass over her, unrecognizing.

Must be this great bandage. She waves. 'Hey, you guys! It's me! I'm here!'

They're looking down at her: Bruce relieved; Fiona tearful; Donald apprehensive.

'Shona!' Bruce takes her hand; looks reproachful. 'You gave us such a fright – why didn't you tell us?'

Because I was afraid to face the truth. Now I'm not.

'What if you'd died! Imagine how I ... how we would've felt.'

'You, I imagine, would've felt relieved. Free to marry Michelle with a clear conscience. Unless she's already married?'

Bruce is appalled. Bringing this up in front of the children! How could she – and at a time like this.

320

Fiona is glaring at him: *You lied!*

Donald looks up from the magazines they brought. 'Who's Michelle?'

Shona holds Bruce's gaze. 'Well, I didn't die, but I did wake up. So, if you want Michelle you'll have to find somewhere else to live.' Turning to Fiona and Donald, 'And you two will have to pull your weight around the place. Once I've got over this,' touching the bandage, 'I'm going to work. Fulltime.'

Three faces: shocked, worried, uncertain. *Is she serious?* One face breaks into a broad grin.

'Good on you, Mum!' Fiona is applauding.

Shona grins back. 'Yay,' she says faintly. 'Way to go.'

NORTHERN LIGHT, SOUTHERN COMFORT

Sheila Kelley

During the past twenty years, Sheila Kelley has worked as an actress and, occasionally, as a playwright. She is currently working with David Jason in a new series of *Touch of Frost* to be screened later this year. The last play she wrote, *Christina*, was commissioned by the Shetland Arts Trust and represented Shetland at the Glasgow Festival which resulted in her winning the 1990 Shetland Literary Prize. She moved out of London ten years ago to live in Leamington Spa with her husband, playwright Stephen Bill, and their two children. This move brought about new experiences: writing fiction, fiddle-playing and relentless gardening.

NORTHERN LIGHT,
SOUTHERN COMFORT

At the edge of the voe in a small makeshift barn Eunice mixed the feed for her sheep. With a shovel she turned the mixture over again and again then rationed it out into a line of plastic buckets. Loose sheets of corrugated iron rattled on the roof. The door, hanging by only one hinge, banged open then shut. Outside a dog barked.

'Be still, Wag!' she yelled. 'Thelma will be here in a wee while. Go and look for her van.'

Into a special bag she poured a thick yellow poison, then sealed it and hung it from her neck by a rope handle. The weight pressed against her breast, the rope reddened her neck.

The dog barked, challenging the swinging door, then jumped at it pinning it open with muddy paws. The hairs on its back stood on end as the wind forced its way through. The dog, the faithful, playful old dog, looked suddenly wild.

Eunice felt in her pockets for a scarf. She wound it tight around her head then around her neck, securing it with a large knot at the back. Climbing over the buckets she stepped outside, her eyes streaming for protection as she walked down to the water's edge. A white salt collar broke against the land cleansing the granite rock. The dog was at her side not knowing what to do with his freedom. He pounced on a wave then, running from the next, he jumped up at Eunice thrilled by the knowledge of what was to come.

'No, Wag! Get away, boy!' she shouted. 'Go and look for Thelma. Where's the van? Where is it?'

He barked out a reply, then pounded towards the road.

Eunice held the special bag to her body and stooping down put one hand into the water then the other, into ice-cold foam. It took the fish powder from her fingers that had clung like chalk, then she dried them on the inside of her pockets and warmed them in thick woollen gloves.

Hurrying back to the shed she pulled at her scarf to shield her eyes from the wind and looked towards the road.

Eunice hated waiting.

Helen licked the tip of her finger in order to pick up the last flakes of croissant from her plate. She always had breakfast alone and always after ten. Brian had been at his work for nearly two hours before she'd taken the first sip of coffee. He had put in his order for lunch before she'd decided on what to wear.

She sat beside the window, her coffee cup poised on her lip, and stared out. The sun shone. The red brick of the flats opposite absorbed its warmth. Clusters of yellowing chimney pots stretched their necks towards a blue sky. The street looked unusually clean this morning. She opened the window and felt the heat on her hands. The blossom on the cherry tree was just beginning to open and its bark sweated out a resin that shone golden. A new energy was rising from under the tarmac, from under the paving stones and it managed to touch even Helen. I must get dressed, she thought, I must do something today.

She had lain in bed too long this morning thinking about getting up, thinking about what to do, what to wear. She filled her lungs with the warm air then blew it away through puffed-out cheeks. If only she had a garden. There was a square of concrete just below the window but it was used for parking the car, and anyway, it really belonged to the ground-floor flat. So the best she could do on a day such as this was to lift the sash window as wide as it would go and sit close enough to feel a breeze and the sun.

Opening her filofax she ran her little finger down a list of names. She searched for a friend, someone who would perhaps give her lunch, perhaps in their garden. But even before reaching the bottom of the page she had decided that this was not a day to go travelling under ground, to be charged at then squashed into a filthy corner of a tube train, and anyway, she still hadn't made up her mind what to wear.

Thelma drove the loaded van along the voe until they reached Trondra. Sheep ran towards them from all directions and jostled for position at the back of the van.

'How will we do this, Thelma?' Eunice asked.

'We'll have to get what bits of wood we can and make ourselves a pen,' Thelma replied.

As she pressed on the handle to open the door two panting dogs jumped the front seat.

'Get back, Lass! *Back!*' Thelma ordered her bitch, but canine emotions were running high this morning and Thelma was forced to duck as the dogs used her shoulders as a diving board into a sea of wool. Pale eyes rolled in bony heads. Fear scattered the flock but hunger brought them back.

'Will I ever get that dog trained!' Thelma cried.

She pulled on a length of nylon rope that was trapped under the weight of the buckets.

'There's some broken fences yonder, let's try and tie them together with this.'

The sheep followed the women across the hillside but all eyes were turned towards the dogs who raced down to the water then circled back to the top of the hill.

The fence was broken because the wood was rotten. It splintered and crumbled in their hands as they lifted it on end and strapped it into the shape of a pen.

'There's no good stuff here, Thelma. It'll not be big enough.'

'We'll manage,' Thelma replied, confidently. 'If they have room to run about they'll take the legs from under you.'

Curious, innocent eyes watched the pen being built. The sheep sniffed at frozen fingers as the rope was tied but then backed away alarmed when the women kicked out to test its strength.

'Did you know that Mary Leask had a bairn last night?' Thelma shouted over her shoulder.

'Mary Leask? The lass from the Scalloway shop? I didn't know she was pregnant,' Eunice called back.

'She didn't know herself by all accounts. She was at one of her prayer meetings at the time and after that she'd arranged to play a game o' badminton.'

'I don't believe it! How could she not know?'

Thelma strained on the rope then took a punch at the makeshift gate.

'Ten of them got down on their knees to pray but eleven of them got back up.'

'My God, how could it happen just like that?'

'That's exactly what Mary Leask said. Jimmy Donaldson passed out by all accounts, he thought he'd witnessed the second coming.'

The women's laughter rang across the voe. Its suddenness scattered the timid onlookers and drew the attention of the dogs.

'Here, Lass! Come on, girl! Your turn to do some work now!' Thelma had a different voice for the dogs. It was a harsh voice that carried effortlessly across the hill, that married with the land. For miles she could be heard and yet it didn't sound like shouting. It was a pitch learnt by instinct, used for generations.

'Down, Lass! Stay down! Wait! *Wait!*'

'Who is the father of Mary Leask's bairn?' Eunice called after her.

'I don't know his name but it's thought that he's an oily man from the terminal at Sullom Voe.'

Eunice turned and took a kick at the gate. The sound of cracking wood filled the air. Taking a firm hold she dragged it open but as she did so she felt a pain that sprang a flood of tears to her eyes. She had impaled her hand on a nail and pulling it away was as painful as the pushing in.

'Stand back from the gate,' she heard Thelma call. 'Get behind them, Eunice. With a bit of luck the dogs might drive them in.'

Eunice did as she was instructed but lifting her hand she looked down on a pool of blood that gradually filled her palm.

Helen unscrewed the top from a bottle of clear varnish that promised to give maximum growth to splits and cracks. She spread her fingers flat on the white cloth and bending over them gave each brush stroke her full concentration.

She had always longed for beautiful hands, red-painted nails shaped like almonds. But some disaster would always occur at the moment of perfection that

329

would take a snag or a crack instinctively towards her mouth and in a second weeks of perseverance would be destroyed between clenched teeth.

Her hands were showing signs of age. Noticeable lines ridged the once-smooth surface of each nail. Her skin had become thin and dry.

'That's what I'll do,' she said out loud. 'Shopping list.'

She removed a page from the filofax with fingers spread like birds' wings to prevent smudging, then wrote, 'Hand and nail cream, Marks and Sparks'. Then in larger letters she wrote, 'FOOD'. This done, her concentration failed her. She drew a wavy pattern around the word, transformed the O's into eyes, added eyebrows and glasses, experimented with a nose and a moustache until 'FOOD' stared back at her in the form of a grotesque mask.

She ripped the whole lot from the top and began again with the hand cream then, placing the paper between her teeth, carried the breakfast things to the kitchen and loaded them into the dishwasher.

A new word had recently entered Helen's vocabulary. Organic. No longer did she call a carrot just a carrot, it had become an organic carrot as had potatoes, onions, cabbages, cucumbers, etc. Vegetables that had been in contact with chemicals were strictly forbidden in Helen's kitchen. Meat had ceased to be a problem since she and Brian had taken to vegetarianism. The only worry in her life now was the invention of meals that could be wholeheartedly enjoyed and not thought of as self-denial. The execution of these unpredictable culinary experiences obsessed her like a new hobby. She read everything, especially the small print on cans, packets and boxes. A trip to the supermarket had become such a serious event that it could last anything from three hours to practically the best part of a day.

Opening the dispenser in the door of the dishwasher she poured in the environmentally friendly powder.

'Coconut, chamomile and citric acid,' she read out loud. 'Envo products are made from natural raw materials and are not tested on animals. Very good,' she said as if congratulating herself. Then, closing the lid, she noticed 'Use Sparingly' written across the corner.

Taking out again the bio-degradable scoop she struggled to retrieve a few spoonfuls of the powder; however, the round spoon would not fit into the square hole. She tried jiggling the door a little to enable it to fall out naturally but catching it as it slid down the smooth surface proved to be impossible. The powder spilt everywhere. The scoop had flicked it around the floor but most of it was lying in the bottom of the machine. What waste! She closed the dispenser and made a mental note not to overfill it next time.

The sheep moved uneasily towards the pen as if they knew their fate.

'Come away, Lass! Stay down! Down, I say!'

The dogs were eager, too eager. They didn't want to lie still. They pursued in full cry when told to walk forward and crawled along on their bellies when given the command to stay still. Several times the sheep turned from the pen and scattered. Thelma's patience gave out. She knew that they themselves had to take up the work of the dogs, and quickly. Waving their arms in the air and giving tongue to sing-song hoots they finally had the flock trapped inside the feeble enclosure. The women followed them in and secured the rope on the gate. Neither animal nor human could barely move in the restricted space.

'Oh God! I haven't got the marker, have you got one, Thelma?' Eunice yelled.

As if performing a magic trick, Thelma produced the thick blue stick from her pocket and, smiling, held it shoulder high as if it was a knife.

'Ready when you are,' she cried.

Straddled across the first of the flock, Eunice immobilized the sheep with the strength of her knees. She held its head to her body while Thelma drew a blue stripe down the bone forehead. With speed Eunice forced a metal gun into the side of its mouth and injected the first of the thirty with the thick yellow poison that killed the liver fluke.

Panic spread through the enclosure. The sheep leapt on to each other's backs, they pushed against the splintering fence but relentlessly the women dragged them by their precious wool and pinned them down in the human vice.

Eunice began to taste sweat. She rubbed a sleeve across her face and buried her mouth in her scarf. There was no time to rest, there was no knowing if the pen would hold.

Eventually, breathing hard, the women stood upright to check every small head looking for that forgotten one that didn't show the blue mark. It was only then that Eunice saw the other stains. The dark-red fingers of blood on white throats.

Thelma untied the rope which caused a rush at the gate. Eunice held on tight to the fence as stampeding bodies pushed against her legs, and as her hand gripped the wood she was aware of the pain again. She could see now it was a deep wound but she said nothing as she hid it clutching the inside lining of her pocket.

Thelma held the van door open for the dogs who pounced on the buckets of feed, spraying the sides of the van with pellets.

'Lie still, you terrible dogs!' she yelled then, turning

to Eunice, 'We'll dose the sheep at the croft then, to give it a chance to get into their stomachs, I think we could have ourselves a drink o' tea.'

Forcing a bright smile Eunice agreed but on the journey home the hand in the pocket throbbed.

Helen's organic régime had begun with a simple diet. It wasn't that she was fat. Good God, nobody could ever call her fat, just slightly . . . well-upholstered. That was Brian's pet phrase for it and although she knew he meant it kindly it always reminded her of an old horse-hair sofa that in poorer days, unhappier days, she'd laboured on for weeks endeavouring to transform it into a thing of beauty.

She had asked Brian once or twice not to use that expression but never too strongly, he might have wanted to know why. And the real reason was not just because of the image of that awful sofa bursting with bristly fibres that pricked into the backs of her legs but with it came a vivid picture of a man sprawled across it. A husband she'd grown to hate, a man she'd hoped to forget. And he was almost forgotten except for those moments when Brian used that phrase that he thought would make her laugh.

So a diet became the answer and whatever she ate Brian ate. She thought that only fair. No red meat, no fried food so no sausages or bacon, but instead plenty of fresh vegetables. They both thrived on it. They felt healthier, they looked healthier. Their hair shone and their skin had a pink glow again; and anyway, when confronted with dinner parties how much easier it was to say, 'I'm a vegetarian,' rather than, 'I'm on a diet to lose all this awful weight.' But the announcement always precipitated lengthy discussions about the dreadful things that we poisoned ourselves with. And so began

Helen's education in organics and the discovery changed her life. She no longer threw away leaflets from Friends of the Earth, she read them. She now considered her twice-weekly shopping sprees to the supermarket as a giant step in saving the environment. By ignoring the polystyrene trays of whiter-than-white leeks and instead choosing the already-nibbled-at dirtier varieties, bugs and all, she felt she was making a protest and it made her feel good. Of course, to grow your own would be the supreme achievement but what chance of that in a London flat? Even the idea of a window-box she'd dismissed. Breathing lead was regrettably unavoidable but eating it was a matter of choice. Not that they could be found guilty of pollution, it had pleased Helen enormously when she discovered that Brian was already unleaded.

However, she wasn't going to be cooped up in her little flat much longer. In a matter of months they would be leaving the city and all its problems and that thought made her rush to the bedroom to get dressed, go shopping, do something.

Since being . . . a vegetarian, she had worn mainly black. It was not a colour that Helen enjoyed but it did help to slim her down, or rather give that impression. 'Clothes maketh the man', so her mother had always said and Helen was in desperate need of new ones. Her wardrobe was practically empty. She slid scores of unused hangers along the rail as she searched for something black but lightweight. Everything had gone to Oxfam or Poland or Romania or Heaven knows where, but she was happy in the knowledge that she was helping to save the world. She had clothed the poor farmers, the growers of vegetables in good St Michael's attire. But what was she to do about the fur coat? In a moment of strength she had hurried it down to the Oxfam shop but they'd refused to take it. So, returned to its place, it hung lifeless from the hook, occasionally receiving a loving touch. She would never wear it again. What waste, she thought.

After dosing the sheep on the croft Thelma loaded the van with bales of straw. Eunice, stooping down, plunged her hand into icy water. The coldness acted as an anaesthetic, the salt, she thought, would cleanse the wound. The first wave licked away her blood but swiftly came back for more. Her hand, numbed, felt no more pain.

'What you doing?' Thelma stood behind her bent double against the wind.

'It's nothing. Just a scratch,' Eunice replied.

'Let me see.' Thelma lifted the swelling hand and rested it gently on the back of her own. It didn't look so bad now that it all had been reddened with the cold.

'A nail caught me when we made that pen. It's nothing. I'll live I'm sure.' Eunice laughed.

'You should have told me. I would have held the sheep. You shouldn't have handled that greasy wool, all manner o' shit could have got into it.'

Thelma helped Eunice to her feet, walked her to the tap and hosed down her muddy boots.

'We can't have you out of action for the lambing. We need every hand we've got.'

Eunice made tea in her usual way, two large spoonfuls from the caddy followed by a handful of cloves. As she poured in the boiling water the steam carried up the sweet clove smell scenting every room in the house.

'So what's all this about Mary Leask? What is this bairn of hers?' Eunice opened a coronation biscuit tin that contained potions and remedies to soothe and heal.

'It was a wee boy she had, according to Dora. She

took her home and called out Dr Goudie. Put your hand on the table and let me tie up the bandage.'

A red ring inflamed the gaping hole and as Eunice opened her hand and laid it flat blood rushed in to fill the gap. It was Thelma that winced as she placed the bandage across her friend's palm and Eunice smiled to prevent showing the pain.

'Tell me if I'm doing this too tight.'

'No, no, it's just fine, Thelma. This oil man from Sullom Voe, he'd not be a Shetlander, I suppose?'

'Oh no, he's an Englishman, by all accounts.'

'With a wife and family on the mainland, no doubt!'

For the father to be an Englishman was bad enough but to be an oil man was, for Eunice, a bigger sin.

The oil men had never been encouraged to mix with the Shetlanders. Before the terminal could even be built two large camps were set up on the remote northern hills to keep them separate, to keep them happy. Their food was imported. T-bone steaks, avocado pears, exotic fruits all flown in from the mainland. They were kept fit in vast gymnasiums, kept relaxed in leisure centres and cinemas the like of which had never been seen on the islands before. The men endured the climate and the isolation in exchange for fat wage packets. The smell of oil soon became a stink in the Shetlanders' nostrils. And still they were coming. Pollution experts, marine biologists, inspection engineers, chemical engineers, men from the cities with skills that the Shetlanders lacked. They came like an invading army and as such were feared, accursed, peeped at, wooed and loved. Their segregation was the lure, curiosity the sin.

Eunice sat silent, her cup of clove tea poised on her lip. She stared out of the window, her gaze fixed on the offshore island of Papa and she grieved for Mary Leask's baby.

Should she pray as she'd prayed for others? Did her prayers make any difference at all?

Suddenly she was aware of a silence. She turned to look at Thelma who was grinning at something she'd just said. Eunice smiled as if she'd heard then got up from the kitchen table and took two lamb chops from the fridge.

'Magnus will be wanting his dinner,' she said, smothering them with lard and banging them in the oven.

'So, as I say, if you have any old clothes of Peter's or James's,' Thelma said, 'or any spare sheets she could cut up until she gets herself sorted out, then I'll take them across to her tomorrow night.'

'I'll see what I have but I'm sure I have nothing small enough for a bairn.'

'Never mind about that. She'll be grateful for anything right now, poor lass.'

'Ay, poor lass,' Eunice replied, wearily. 'Shall we get going again and give those hungry animals their breakfast?'

Helen had been forced to get a taxi to take herself and her shopping home. Sweat had trickled down the inside of her arms as she'd stood on the kerb squinting along the high street. Her shoulders had ached even as she'd raised an arm to hail a passing black cab.

'Lindfield Grove!' The driver spat out the words as if she'd requested the impossible. 'You must be joking, lady, it wouldn't be worth my while switching on the meter. It's only up the road. Look!' He turned irritably in his seat and stretched out a sunburnt arm. 'I can see it from here!'

As he pointed so she turned, stupidly, she thought afterwards, and shielding her eyes from the sun's glare looked towards home. She knew well enough where she lived, it was help she needed to get there. As she turned back, prepared to plead for his assistance, he had already pulled away.

It seemed hours before another came by. Her shopping bags were continually kicked, people allowed their dogs to sniff at them and one little rat even dared to raise its leg before being throttled by a quick jerk on the lead. But the worst humiliation came when a group of hysterical schoolgirls actually knocked her into the gutter. Helen had been so angered by this degradation that out poured a wealth of vocabulary from her cherry-red lips that she wasn't even aware that she knew. But they didn't hear her, they walked on without even noticing what they'd done.

As she hailed the second taxi she made a quick grab for the handle and had herself settled on the back seat before aggressively stating her destination. This time she received only a look from the driver but it conveyed everything that his colleague had said earlier.

Within seconds she was off-loading her various bags in Lindfield Grove but she tipped him, quite generously she thought, yet without so much as a thank you he banged shut his window and drove away shaking his head.

Indoors, being part of a large Victorian house, it was mercifully cool, but nevertheless she opened the window and sat down at the table surrounded by all her plastic bags. The two containing the food she slid to one side with her foot and then for the first time that day she smiled as she began the most satisfying of tasks – that of unpacking and examining all the bargains she had so skilfully spotted.

First out were the silk scarves. What a good idea it was to buy both. What agony she'd put herself through standing in the street with the assistant holding up one and then the other to compare the different shades of blue. To choose between them had been impossible. Nothing was more infuriating than to get home and long for the one that had been rejected. So both it had to be.

Then came the six packets of tights in her favoured black and, just for a change, dove-grey. Then the hand and nail cream which she applied instantly while reading the list of contents on the label of a packet of pot-pourri. Then from the bottom of the Marks and Sparks bag she pushed aside two hand towels and held up a woollen jumper, beautifully patterned in undyed Shetland wool. This was her present to Brian. She laid it across her lap and stroked it. It was so wonderfully soft that she buried her face in the sleeve. It was going to be just the thing for when they moved. For walks in the countryside, to put on in the evening after the sun had gone down on a summer's day.

Still holding the sleeve to her face she breathed in deeply. What bliss, she thought, the sweet natural smell of pure wool, exactly as nature intended it to be. Lovingly crossing the arms she folded it and slipped it back into the bag. She was not going to find it easy to save it until June, to hide it away and keep it a secret until their first wedding anniversary. That was also the day they would leave London and the two coming together marked, for Helen, the real beginning of a new life. She became energized every time she thought of it so, rummaging through the food bags for the organic unwaxed lemon, she skipped out to the kitchen to make herself a cup of tea.

There was one parcel that she'd deliberately left until last; it contained, so the label said, a 'Ladies Weekender'. Helen slipped the strap over her shoulder and traced the outline of tapestry roses with the tips of her fingers. This was to hold everything that she might need on the plane; her portable compact disc player and of course compact discs, her make-up, perfume, brushes and combs, perhaps a thin paperback and, not to be forgotten, the new silk scarves. These she must pack on the top because hadn't Brian mentioned something about occasional strong winds?

Sitting at the table by the window she pushed her lemon tea to one side to accommodate the *Great World Atlas*. She flicked passed Canada, Mexico and South America until she found a double page of the British Isles. She turned the book sideways and stretching her neck looked northwards.

She ran a finger from the Butt of Lewis, past Harris and Benbecula right the way down to Barra Head but she didn't find what she was looking for. She wriggled to the edge of her seat and leaning closer passed from Skye to Canna, Muck and Tiree. She went to fetch her glasses from the bedroom. She looked up the name in the index and, yes, she was definitely on the right page. So where had it gone? Trust Brian to buy the only atlas with a misprint, she thought.

She went to the kitchen to unpack the bag of food but she found herself going back for another look, then another until she picked up the phone and dialled the number that would put her out of her misery.

'Good afternoon, BP Petroleum.'

'Oh hello, could I speak to Brian Pagget, please.'

'Which department do you want?'

'Chemical Engineering, please.'

'Will you hold?'

But before Helen had a chance to reply a loud click was followed by a deadness. Then came a series of loud clicks that made Helen wince, then a burst of office noise, then the deadness again. She sighed heavily into the receiver hoping that the pert voice might be listening.

'Hi, what's up?' At last it was Brian.

'Who's that on the switchboard today? I've been kept hanging on for ages.'

'How on earth should I know? I never see the switchboard.'

'Where's your secretary?'

'Ill. Look, you've caught me at a critical moment actually, is everything OK?'

'No, not really. Where's Shetland?'

'What do you mean where is it?'

'Just explain to me again where it is, will you?'

'Darling, can't this wait until tonight? Try looking it up on the map.'

'I have but it's not there.'

'Of course it's there,' he shouted.

'Where then? I'm looking at it now but I just can't see it.' She sounded almost tearful.

'All right, all right,' he said, calming himself down as much as her. 'Can you see Orkney?'

'No.'

'Can you see the North Sea?'

'No.'

'Oh Jesus, Helen, what can you see?'

'That Atlantic Ocean and please don't shout at me, Brian.'

'OK, you're looking on the wrong side, that's the Hebrides. Move across to the right. You'll see the top of Scotland and if you trace a finger over to Norway you'll have to pass it. OK?' Now Brian sighed heavily into the phone but he endeavoured to do it as silently as possible.

'Oh hang on, I think I've found it but it wasn't my fault, they've put it in a little box in the corner.'

'They put it in a box because it's actually off the map.

341

Now I've really got to dash so I'll see you tonight.'

'Yes, it says Shetland down the side, thanks, darling. Perhaps you could bring one of your big maps from . . .' She noticed she was speaking into that deadness again so she replaced the receiver and went back to the map.

She'd imagined Shetland as one island but now she could see it was made up of hundreds all slotting together like a jigsaw puzzle. She looked for Sullom Voe but that definitely wasn't marked. Perhaps the oil terminal hadn't been built when the map was printed, she concluded, calmly.

In her mind's eye, as she stared down at the specks of bright green surrounded by a border of blue, she imagined a house situated amongst lush countryside. A garden full of flowers stretching down to the shore. Barbecues on a patio, home-grown vegetables and lots of new friends. This last thought was the only one that made her nervous. She had voiced her misgivings to Brian once or twice but he'd assured her that he had every confidence in her.

'And after all, women are women the world over,' he had said and she was sure he was right. Why should the Shetlanders be different?

'And anyway, our house will be pretty remote,' he'd said. 'You don't have to make friends if you don't want to.'

But Helen did want to, and in her mind's eye she saw herself in a cosy living room being the perfect host to many a coffee morning.

A gale blew across East Voe and the massing clouds brought a darkness over the hills.

The two women kicked over the wooden troughs to empty them of rainwater then they filled them up with feed. The straw blew from their hands as they pulled it

342

along the mangers. Their work was done in silence as the strengthening wind made it impossible to be heard.

Every day, from January to May, the sheep had to be fed for nothing grew on the hills until June. And even then, whatever had managed to survive was dwarfed by the action of the winds or bleached back to a barrenness by the sea's salt vapour.

There were times when even Eunice and Thelma found it a struggle to go on, day after day, week after week, while the battling elements claimed precedence over all. But their effort was not thought of in terms of hours of employment but as preparation and enrichment extending over months and years. Every member of a family was duty-bound to some work on the croft, every croft in a township dependent on each other. Neighbourly help was an age-old obligation. Friends were a necessity, not a matter of choice.

'I'll be here same time tomorrow then, Eunice.'

'Ay, I'll be ready,' Eunice replied.